PRAISE FOR THE NOVELS OF

FRAGILE

"An exciting character-driven romantic suspense thriller."
—*Midwest Book Review*

"*Fragile* is about the delicate balance of vulnerability and strength that can be brought on by trauma. It's about love in the face of insurmountable odds. And it's about suspense, mystery, and terror . . . All in all, this is an excellently crafted mystery and romance!"
—*Errant Dreams Reviews*

"The suspense sneaks up on you like a good thriller should . . . One of the best contemporary romances I have read in an age."
—*A Romance Review*

"A complex and intense story that addresses some very dark and disturbing issues . . . One of the most satisfying reads I've had in a while."
—*CK2S Kwips and Kritiques*

"A fast-paced book that sizzles with suspense and sexual tension equally."
—*Night Owl Romance*

"Walker is a master storyteller, and this book has everything you could possibly want in a suspenseful romance. I hope she writes more like this!"
—*Manic Readers*

"This book offers suspense, romance, and an ending that I can't say anything about—because that would be a spoiler, yes? I recommend reading this one."
—*The Best Reviews*

continued . . .

THE MISSING

"A page-turner from the very start. Intense and fast-paced, the action is gritty, the emotion heart-wrenching, and the characters lively. Sexy and romantic, this tale has plenty of action—of the erotic kind—and is loaded with suspense. No wonder Ms. Walker is loved by fans everywhere. This is a winner."
—*Fresh Fiction*

"[A] romantic spine tingler . . . A sweet love story alternates with an exciting manhunt."
—*Publishers Weekly*

"This is a great romantic suspense that grips the audience . . . Action packed."
—*Midwest Book Review*

"Walker certainly has a future in paranormal and/or romantic suspense."
—*The Romance Reader*

THROUGH THE VEIL

"[A] hold-on-to-your-seat tale of demons, hunky warriors, and witches served with a mix of love and betrayal. Fun! If you enjoy otherworldly, action-packed adventures with a hot and steamy romance, this is for you."
—*Fresh Fiction*

"A good read . . . Walker obviously has an unmatched imagination."
—*Romance Reader at Heart*

"Action, adventure, and romance abound . . . An engaging tale."
—*Romance Reviews Today*

"A fabulous, action-packed romantic fantasy . . . Fans will believe that the world on the other side of the veil exists, which is key to this fine tale."
—*Midwest Book Review*

HUNTER'S SALVATION

"One of the best tales in a series that always achieves high marks . . .
An excellent thriller."   —*Midwest Book Review*

HUNTERS: HEART AND SOUL

"Some of the best erotic romantic fantasies on the market. Walker's
world is vibrantly alive with this pair."   —*The Best Reviews*

HUNTING THE HUNTER

"Action, sex, savvy writing, and characters with larger-than-life per-
sonalities that you will not soon forget are where Ms. Walker's talents
lie, and she delivered all that and more . . . This is a flawless five-rose
paranormal novel, and one that every lover of things that go bump
in the night will be howling about after they read it . . . Do not walk!
Run to get your copy today!"   —*A Romance Review*

"An exhilarating romantic fantasy filled with suspense and . . . star-
crossed love . . . Action packed."   —*Midwest Book Review*

"Fast paced and very readable . . . Titillating."
                                                 —*The Romance Reader*

"Action-packed, with intriguing characters and a very erotic punch,
Hunting the Hunter had me from page one. Thoroughly enjoyable
with a great hero and a story line you can sink your teeth into, this
book is a winner. A very good read!"   —*Fresh Fiction*

BROKEN

Shiloh Walker

BERKLEY SENSATION, NEW YORK

THE BERKLEY PUBLISHING GROUP
Published by the Penguin Group
Penguin Group (USA) Inc.
375 Hudson Street, New York, New York 10014, USA
Penguin Group (Canada), 90 Eglinton Avenue East, Suite 700, Toronto, Ontario M4P 2Y3, Canada
(a division of Pearson Penguin Canada Inc.)
Penguin Books Ltd., 80 Strand, London WC2R 0RL, England
Penguin Group Ireland, 25 St. Stephen's Green, Dublin 2, Ireland (a division of Penguin Books Ltd.)
Penguin Group (Australia), 250 Camberwell Road, Camberwell, Victoria 3124, Australia
(a division of Pearson Australia Group Pty. Ltd.)
Penguin Books India Pvt. Ltd., 11 Community Centre, Panchsheel Park, New Delhi—110 017, India
Penguin Group (NZ), 67 Apollo Drive, Rosedale, North Shore 0632, New Zealand
(a division of Pearson New Zealand Ltd.)
Penguin Books (South Africa) (Pty.) Ltd., 24 Sturdee Avenue, Rosebank, Johannesburg 2196,
South Africa

Penguin Books Ltd., Registered Offices: 80 Strand, London WC2R 0RL, England

This book is an original publication of The Berkley Publishing Group.

This is a work of fiction. Names, characters, places, and incidents either are the product of the author's imagination or are used fictitiously, and any resemblance to actual persons, living or dead, business establishments, events, or locales is entirely coincidental. The publisher does not have any control over and does not assume any responsibility for author or third-party websites or their content.

Copyright © 2010 by Shiloh Walker, Inc.
Cover illustration by Tony Mauro.
Cover design by Rita Frangie.
Interior text design by Tiffany Estreicher.

PRINTING HISTORY
Berkley Sensation trade paperback edition / March 2010

Library of Congress Cataloging-in-Publication Data

Walker, Shiloh.
  Broken/Shiloh Walker.
    p. cm.
  ISBN 978-0-425-23241-5
  1. Bounty hunters—Fiction.   2. Neighbors—Fiction.   I. Title.
  PS3623.A35958B76 2010
  813'.6—dc22

                                        2009044142

PRINTED IN THE UNITED STATES OF AMERICA

10 9 8 7 6 5 4 3 2 1

*For Lora Leigh, who told me to get
Quinn's story done before I even knew
he had one. You were right—the book
had been out no more than a week
when I started getting e-mails asking for
Quinn's story.*

*For Renee, answering the million and
one questions about St. Louis.*

*For Traci Sexton, answering the million
and one questions about bailbond
enforcements and bounty hunting.*

*For Lauren Dane, for the chat sessions
when I was trying to plot this story out.*

*For my friend Susan . . . may brighter
days await you.*

*And for my kids and my husband. I love
you all so much. I thank God for you,
every day of my life.*

ONE

*M*AD.

Quinn could hear it in her voice: the old lady was mad. Hell, screw mad. She was fucking pissed. Quinn swallowed the bitter taste bubbling up in his throat. It wasn't a new thing, her being mad. She spent most of her life that way, or at least it sure seemed like that to him. At eleven years old, he couldn't really think of a time when she *hadn't* been mad over something.

Mad because she didn't have the money to score some drugs.

Mad because she didn't have the money to buy more booze.

Mad because the landlord wouldn't take a blowjob in exchange for rent.

Mad because of Quinn—just because he existed.

Always mad about something.

Still, going by that shrill tone in her voice, he had a feeling it was worse than usual this time. He glanced around the dirty little apartment where they lived, calculating the distance to the door, wondering if he could get a window open without her hearing him.

Looking for escape, even though there wasn't one.

It had all of three rooms, a main room where his mother slept on the couch, a kitchen that hadn't ever been used, and a bathroom with a toilet that was permanently stained with urine and shit. He didn't eat in that kitchen, and the only time he used the bathroom was when he had to piss or take a shower under the stingy showerhead.

When he could, he avoided even that. He'd rather sneak into a youth center and get a shower there. Sometimes he even pretended that he might stay, pretended that he could trust the adults there enough to think about staying.

He had found another nice youth center—he'd been going there for a while. It was clean, warm . . . safe. Not the nicest, but still. It was warm there. Warm, cleaner than anyplace he'd ever lived, the people who ran the joint didn't yell at him . . . and they had books.

Quinn didn't own a single book, but he loved to read.

He'd given up trying to keep any books for himself after what had happened the last time his mother had found his stash. She'd beaten him, but that hadn't been the worst. She'd burned every book, right in front of him, tossing them into the sink and using her lighter to set the pages on fire.

All but one. *The Lion, the Witch and the Wardrobe*. That book, she hadn't burned. It had been a gift from a lady that worked at the Calumet Youth Center, a teen shelter run out of a church back in Indianapolis. It still had a card in it—Quinn had been using the card as a bookmark, unwilling to bend the pages of the book given to him by one of the ladies at the shelter.

Because he hadn't thrown that card away, his mom had found out about the shelter where he went almost every day. Because he hadn't thrown that card out, a nice lady had gotten the shit beat out of her by his psycho mother. While he watched, scared, mad, and confused.

It had been two years since that happened, and it left a mark on him, one that wouldn't ever fade. Sometimes he wished he hadn't ever stumbled past the threshold of Calumet Christian Church, and at the same time, he wished he hadn't taken off the few times the people there had tried to help him. If he'd let them help, if he hadn't run when he'd suspected they were calling Social Services on him, he might have gotten away from his mother. Then again if he hadn't ever gone there, a nice lady wouldn't have gotten beaten just for trying to help him.

God, his mother had been mad that day.

About as mad as she sounded now, he thought. He swallowed and wished there was another way out of here. The only way, though, was through the front door. Even as he eyed the windows, he knew he wouldn't get them open without her hearing. He was pretty fast, but still . . . he wasn't going to risk trying to climb out on the fire escape when she was that mad. She just might try to push him.

He was going to have to risk the door. He could hear the sounds of breaking glass, her voice rising as she ranted and cussed.

Slipping out of the bathroom, he kept his back pressed to the wall and inched down the short hallway. She was in the kitchen. If he was quiet enough . . .

"Where the fuck do you think you're going?"

Quinn froze. He swallowed the bile boiling up his throat and made himself look at his mother. "Nowhere."

"Fucking liar. Worthless fucking liar." She sneered at him, curling her lip and revealing teeth that were past the yellow stage and edging toward gray. Some were already close to black. "You taking off to that damned library again? Or are you sneaking off to one of those stupid shelters?"

He didn't respond.

"You ain't nothing but trash. They don't want your kind there," she muttered, shaking her head. Then she frowned and turned back to the mostly empty cabinets, looking at them as though she couldn't quite understand how they'd come to be empty. "What did you do with my drinks?"

"Nothing." He jammed his hands into the grubby pockets of his jeans and stared at the floor. He watched her from under his lashes, though. Watched. Waited.

Part of him wanted to tell her that she'd finished up the rest of her tequila the night before and she'd run out of whiskey a few days earlier. But he wasn't going to do that. He liked keeping his teeth in his mouth, and the last time he'd reminded her she'd finished all of her booze, she'd tried to knock a few out. Or least it had felt that way.

"Bullshit. Somebody had to go and drink it."

Somebody did—you. Still, as much as he wanted to say that, Quinn kept quiet.

She glared at him. Even though he wasn't looking at her, he could feel that angry gaze, all but burning through him. "Fucking useless brat," she muttered. "So worthless. Why in the hell did I ever have you?"

He kept an eye on her as she lit a cigarette, watched the way her hands were shaking. Fuck. That was bad. When she got the shakes, it was always bad.

His mind raced furiously. He needed to get out of there. He could almost hear her ticking, a time bomb ready to go off. He swallowed the bile that burned in his throat and looked up, shoving his long hair back from his face. "I thought maybe you had stashed something under the sink in the bathroom the last time that Sam guy was here."

She had . . . but then she'd drunk it the next day. But she never remembered drinking the booze.

Just like he'd hoped, she took off down the narrow hallway, making a beeline for the bathroom. The second her back was turned, he headed for the door, pausing only long enough to grab the backpack he always kept tucked behind the ragged couch. She yelled from the bathroom, but he didn't wait.

No way. No how.

* * *

His belly was full, pleasantly so, and he was wearing some clothes that were the closest to new that he'd had in a good long while. The youth center had sponsored a clothing drive, and one of the ladies had pushed some clothes into his hands when he showed up at the shelter two days earlier.

Although they'd offered him a bed, Quinn hadn't slept there. He'd gone back each day for a meal and a shower before walking to school. He didn't always like going to school, but that was mostly because of the idiots there, not because of school itself.

If it wasn't for the idiots, he'd actually like school a lot—learning shit was definitely better than hanging around anywhere close to his mother. There were times when he found himself staring at some of the kids, enviously listening to them talk about their parents, seeing a movie on the weekend, taking vacations.

Normal stuff.

Or at least he guessed it was normal. For Quinn, normal was sleeping with one eye open. Wearing clothes he'd either stolen from someplace or hand-me-down stuff he picked up at shelters. Going to bed hungry and waking up cold because she didn't think about food or heating bills, not when she could use the money on booze or drugs.

For Quinn, normal sucked.

Standing in front of the door to their apartment, he listened to the noises coming through and wished he had headed back to the shelter instead of coming here. But he'd already spent too much time at that one—the past two days, and then a few weeks earlier, he'd been there another couple of days. If he hung around any one place too long, somebody almost always made a call to Social Services, and he wasn't doing that shit again.

It was almost worst than home.

Besides, it was the middle of the month and that meant at some point, his mom's caseworker would be by. Quinn needed to make sure the rattrap was as clean as he could make it, and do what he could with the drugs and stuff that she might have picked up over the past few days—and figure out how to remind her about what time of month it was without her belting him.

As much as he hated being here, going back into the system was one thing he had no desire to do.

He swallowed against the knot in his throat and rested a hand on the doorknob. She was in there screwing somebody. Quinn could hear them, grunting and groaning, sounding more like a couple of animals than two people.

He didn't want to go in there. He shot a nervous look up and down the hall and then retreated back against the wall and slid down, settling there with his legs drawn up and his arms wrapped around them.

The food in his belly suddenly felt like a lead weight, and blood stained his cheeks red as the noises from the room got louder and louder.

God, get me away from here. Please.

* * *

HE'D read a book once where one of the characters said, *"Be careful what you wish for."*

Quinn now understood that statement.

He sat in the middle of the police station, a young woman with an overly bright smile on her plump face at his side, chattering away animatedly, despite the fact that he was ignoring her.

His mother was dead.

Sometime after he'd slipped inside that night and hidden himself away in the closet where he slept, she'd overdosed. They hadn't told him that, but he'd seen her body—he knew what dead was. Since he'd seen the drugs and the booze last night, it wasn't a hard leap to make.

"Ms. Groman, I'd like to speak with you for a minute."

Quinn watched from under the fringe of his hair, eying the tired-looking cop standing in the doorway. He had a cigarette hanging out of his mouth and big eyes that drooped at the corners. Those sad eyes flicked Quinn's way and then back to study the social worker.

He barely registered her reply, just the fact that she was moving away from him, following the cop into an office. Quinn's heart beat a little faster and he clutched the strap of his backpack with sweaty hands.

As the door shut, he sprang up and took off running.

He never even made it halfway. A burly bastard caught him, moving a lot quicker than Quinn would have guessed.

"Come on, kid . . . just relax. Nothing bad is going to happen to you here," the cop said, his voice soft and gentle. His big dark eyes said, *Trust me.*

But Quinn knew better.

Trusting people was dangerous.

* * *

TWINS.

Quinn stared at the face of the boy in front of him and had to fight the urge to rub his eyes. It had been two days since he'd first met Luke, and he was still pretty sure he was hallucinating. But on the off chance that he wasn't, he couldn't let them know he was surprised. Or even interested.

Part of him wanted to think it was all real.

The boy had Quinn's face, although his hair was cut neat and short, and clean. Clean, just like the clothes he wore. A dark blue sweater, a pair of jeans, and a pair of shoes that Quinn knew cost close to a hundred dollars—he knew because he'd stolen a couple and sold them for thirty bucks a pair.

His name was Luke Rafferty.

And according to the man who'd shown up in Dayton a few days ago, Luke Rafferty was his twin brother.

Twins . . . Quinn had a twin. Apparently, right after they were born, his mother had disappeared with Quinn, taken him right out of the hospital, leaving Luke behind. Quinn had no idea why—it wasn't like she'd wanted him. She hated him. Maybe she'd done it because of this man, this quiet, soft-spoken man who claimed to be his father.

He'd said his name was Patrick, and he'd also told Quinn, "You can call me Patrick if you want—or Pat. I realize this seems strange to you, so you don't have to call me Dad if you don't want to."

But there was a wistful look in his gray eyes—gray . . . just like Quinn's—that made Quinn think the old man *wanted* Quinn to call him Dad.

Quinn wouldn't ever admit that some part of him wanted the same thing. Earlier that day, right after they'd gotten home from the airport, Patrick had laid a hand on Luke's shoulder, and the kid had looked up at his dad and smiled, said something that made the older guy laugh.

Patrick had hugged Luke. Hugged him and then tugged on his hair.

Quinn couldn't remember a time when his mother had hugged him.

Not once.

Something knotted up in his throat. He blinked his eyes and tried to figure out why in the hell he felt like crying.

"I'll be driving you into town tomorrow so you can get some clothes, some shoes. Maybe get a haircut," Patrick said.

Quinn shoved his hair out of his eyes and sneered at Patrick. "I don't want a haircut."

"Fine," Patrick said, giving him a conciliatory smile. "We'll just stick with getting you some clothes and shoes."

There was a hole in the bottom of Quinn's left shoe that was bigger than his thumb and he'd been covering it with duct tape. Still, he didn't let that keep him from glaring at Patrick and snapping, "I don't want no damn clothes, no damn shoes, either."

Patrick sighed and rubbed a hand over the back of his neck.

Quinn's belly knotted as a look crossed over the man's face. Jerking his attention away from Patrick, he sought out the face of his brother.

Luke. His twin. Luke was staring at Quinn like he had two heads. Curling a lip at him, Quinn sneered, "What the fuck are you looking at?"

The weirdest damn thing happened.

Quinn felt a jolt of surprise shoot through him. But it wasn't coming from *him*. As sure as he stood there, he knew he wasn't feeling *his* surprise. He was feeling something from Luke.

Luke's eyes widened and he shot a look at Patrick.

Patrick sighed and lowered the hand he'd been using to rub his neck. "Quinn, I'm getting tired of telling you that I don't allow that sort of talk from a child of mine."

The words were spoken in a flat, level voice, a quiet voice, even. But still, Quinn flinched, bracing himself unconsciously for a strike.

He'd been pushing the guy for the past two days. Sooner or later, he was going to show his true colors. But the waiting part was hell—Quinn wished Patrick would just get it over with. He smirked and said, "Yeah, and I don't give a fuck."

Then he raised his chin. If Patrick Rafferty was going to whale on Quinn, he just wanted it to happen. He wanted it done and over with. He wanted the man to stop pretending to be nice, to stop acting like he cared.

"Boy, you are going to learn some respect," Patrick said, narrowing his eyes.

Quinn laughed. It was ragged and hoarse and it hurt to do it.

"How you going to make me do that, old man? Beat it into me?" Quinn shrugged. "Won't be the first time."

He waited for the blow.

But it didn't come.

Luke moved forward, frowning at Quinn. "Dad doesn't hit people."

"Yeah, right. Why don't you mind your own fucking business?"

Luke blushed, blood rushing to stain his cheeks red.

Off to the side, Patrick said quietly, "Luke, why don't you go out to the stables, see if you can help the boys for a while?"

Quinn laughed and thought, *Yeah, get him out of here so he doesn't see what you really want to do.* "Yeah, you don't want him to see you hit me."

"Luke, get out to the stables. Now."

"My dad doesn't hit," Luke snapped as he shoved his hands in his pockets and glared at Quinn.

"Shit." Quinn shoved a hand through his hair. Luke's eyes dropped and Quinn remembered too late the bruise on his arm. It was a couple of weeks old, yellow and sickly green. In a few more days, it would be gone altogether.

Quinn flushed, but he didn't try to hide the bruise. He just glared at his brother and demanded, "What the fuck is your problem?"

"What's *yours*?" Luke replied.

Man, Quinn couldn't even begin to list his problems. Setting his jaw, he pushed past the boy who shared his face and the man who shared his eyes. He didn't want to be here.

Really. He didn't.

Never mind that it was clean.

Never mind that it was warm.

Never mind that he hadn't heard hardly anybody yelling.

He didn't want to be here. And as soon as he could, he was going to get the hell out of there.

Get very far away. But for now, he'd settle for out of the house.

* * *

EVEN before he heard the sound of footsteps, Quinn knew his brother was coming.

"She hit you, didn't she?" Luke said as he dropped down on the grass.

Quinn tensed. He didn't really want to talk to this kid. His brother . . . his *twin* brother.

Brother or not, twin or not, he didn't want to talk to Luke and he definitely didn't want to talk about his mother.

Our mother—not just mine. She's his mother, too. Thinking that, though, made him feel even madder, more ashamed. Luke seemed to be one of those *nice* people . . . the kind of people who did nice things, who thought nice things, who didn't have bad stuff happening, who didn't realize all the crap that did happen.

Having *her* for a mom ruined some of that nice. Quinn couldn't understand why, but that realization really pissed him off.

Luke continued to stare at him, waiting. He'd keep on waiting, too, until he got an answer.

"What the hell does it matter?" Quinn mumbled, shrugging.

"Because it ain't right."

"You really think I'm gonna believe that your old man never hits you?" Quinn demanded with a smirk.

"He's *your* old man, too, Quinn. I'm not going to lie and say he's never spanked me. But the last time he did was a couple years ago when he caught me getting into the gun cabinet."

Gun cabinet? Wow. Cool. His eyes widened and for a second, he was overcome with curiosity, so much of it that he almost asked to see it.

"Gun cabinet?"

"Yeah, a gun cabinet. This is a ranch, not the city." A big grin appeared on his face as he stared at Quinn.

"What were you . . . ?" Quinn snapped his jaw shut and looked away. *What did it matter what the Boy Scout was doing?*

"I wasn't really doing anything. I just . . . Dad had been showing me how to hold the shotgun, how to clean it and stuff and I wanted to see if I could do it without his help."

"And when he caught you, he beat the shit out of you," Quinn said, feeling oddly disappointed. He really didn't want to believe that Patrick was anything like his mother had been.

"No. He turned me over his knee and spanked my butt a few times. Sent me to my room. Came upstairs later and gave me one of his 'talking-tos.'"

Quinn blinked. Swatted his butt? A 'talking-to'? His mother had never messed with swatting his butt—she much preferred to smack him or punch him.

"Decent people don't beat their kids, Quinn." Luke said it quietly, his voice full of certainty. He looked at Quinn like he wanted to urge Quinn to believe him.

To trust him.

But Quinn knew better than to trust people.

Period.

Twenty Years Later

ALONE in a night-dark forest, Quinn Rafferty shoveled dirt into the hole. He tried hard not to think about what he was doing. Why.

He tried hard not to think about the still body that lay in the shallow grave at his feet. If he thought about it too much, he was going to lose his mind. He had a fragile hold on sanity and he knew it wouldn't take much to snap.

But he couldn't *not* think. Couldn't *not* remember.

Elena was dead.

"*Trust me*," she had whispered to him. She had given him that serene, enigmatic smile and kissed him, stroked a hand down his chest and murmured, "*Trust me, Quinn. I will do this—one more time. One last time. I have to.*"

She'd been right—she'd done it one last time . . . and it had gotten her killed. Now her last words haunted him. Even as he'd left her alone in the hellhole dive where they'd met to exchange information, he'd wanted to go back to her. Go back, demand that she stop. Demand that she come with him.

Quinn had no idea how he'd possibly have gotten Elena out of Colombia, but he would have worked something out. Broken whatever laws necessary, kept her with him.

But she'd told him to trust her.

"*You look at me like you want to be with me, but you do not trust me. How can I be with a man who cannot trust me?*"

It was something she'd asked him months ago—yet more words to haunt him.

It was quiet in the forest, the air hot and heavy. He worked in the dark, because he couldn't risk somebody discovering him. Not that he feared they would—he almost hoped that would happen soon. But not until he'd taken care of Elena first. Then his team. Had to make sure the team was safe.

Fuck, by rights, he should be doing that *now*. A Ranger didn't leave his team hanging.

But a man couldn't leave the woman he lo—

"Shit." He drove his stolen shovel into the ground and covered his face with grimy, bloodstained hands. He wasn't going there—too fucking late now. Too fucking late. Too late for him, and too fucking late for Elena.

Her body lay wrapped in a blanket that was soaked through with blood. Broken . . . broken, and battered.

Trust me . . .

How can I be with a man who cannot trust me?

He couldn't ask it of her—he never had, and he never would have. But she'd looked at him and known that he felt something. She probably understood how he'd felt better than he did. Quinn sucked at feelings. But he'd wanted her. For always. Elena had known and she'd wanted to give it to him.

But he had to trust her.

Trust me . . .

So he had made himself trust her. And by doing it, he'd let her die.

Tears burned his eyes, but he wouldn't let them fall. He couldn't cry. Not right now. He had to take care of Elena. If he managed that without getting caught, then he would get back to his team.

No time to fall apart, not now.

God, the team. Man, he needed to get back to them. He'd already sent a message back—the mission had been ready to blow up in their faces and he needed to get back to them—*now.*

But he couldn't leave Elena . . .

Trust me . . .

He should have known better. Trust was dangerous, and this time, it had gotten a woman killed.

TWO

"*B*ut *I still can't leave.*"

"*Why?*"

"*Because of you.*"

Sometimes, when she lay there on the thin, uncomfortable mattress, she wondered if the guilt could get any worse. There were days it didn't bother her so bad. But then there were days—or nights—when it hung in the back of her throat, cloying and cold, an ugly knot that made breathing difficult.

Tonight was one of those nights.

"*He wants you dead . . .*"

"*You don't know him. You don't know what he's capable of.*"

The guilt was bad.

Sara Davis squeezed her eyes closed and rolled onto her belly. She pulled her pillow on top of her head and used it to muffle the noises coming from the other apartments around hers.

Off to her left, she could hear the wannabe playboy grunting and groaning while he did the nasty with whatever girl had been stupid enough to fall for his lines. Sometimes, listening to him was amusing—he thought he understood dirty talk, thought he was a real slick piece of work. Tonight, though, listening to them through the thin walls was anything but entertaining. It was close to nauseating, but Sara would have given her right arm to be able to play voyeur just then.

Anything was better than her memories.

"He wants you dead . . ."

To her right, she could hear a baby crying. She couldn't remember the couple's name, but the baby had been crying at night on a regular basis since they brought the little boy home from the hospital.

In the apartment below hers, they were fighting. Nothing new there.

In the apartment above hers, the TV was playing way too loud.

She was wrapped in a cocoon of noise, but the loudest voices came from her memories.

"I can't leave . . ."

* * *

"You can't leave!"

Quinn Rafferty shot a look over his shoulder. He was an attractive man, but something about his face, the way he carried himself, the way he looked at people, made others keep their distance.

His eyes were wide-set and gray—when he was angry, the gray of his eyes could flash hot or freeze over like winter ice. More often than not, though, they were blank. Carefully blank, a mask that revealed very little about whatever thoughts might run through his head.

He didn't smile much and when he did, it was one of those faint smiles, the sort of smile that made others suspect he either didn't *want* to smile, or he wasn't used to doing it.

He spoke only when he absolutely had to, and unless it was something he had to hear, he didn't bother listening to what others said. Talking struck him as an incredible waste of time.

So he didn't bother wasting any words as he waited for Juanita, one of the receptionists at the Gearing Agency, as she came scurrying out from behind her desk. She had little pink slips of paper in her hand—messages. Three of them. The sight of them had him ready to swear, but he managed to keep it behind his teeth.

For now.

The last time he'd growled at her, she'd gotten all teary-eyed and started stammering. If it had been an act, he could have ignored her, but Juanita was a lousy actress.

"Sure I can leave," he drawled, grabbing the doorknob and twisting it. "I open the door. I step out." He demonstrated.

"But Martin wants you to wait! He has a job for you."

Quinn cocked a brow and held up the check in his hand. "Just finished one."

She frowned at the check she'd issued him five minutes earlier. "He has another one for you." She gave him a perplexed look, as though she couldn't comprehend that he really didn't care that she had a job for him.

Jobs meant money. In his line of work, sometimes that money could be very, very lucrative. But he wasn't in the mood.

"Not interested."

She shoved a picture in front of him.

Juanita might be a lousy actress, but she definitely knew what made people tick. The picture she held had him stopping dead in his tracks. As he stared at the battered face of a young woman, rage and hatred curled through his gut.

Hell, she barely looked old enough to be out of high school.

"How old is she?" he asked, his voice rough.

"Nineteen, I think."

"Who's the skip? Her boyfriend?"

Juanita rolled her eyes. "No. He's her husband, if you can believe that. She married him a few months ago. I read the report while I was waiting for you—there were a couple of domestic disturbance calls made to the local police, but this last time was the first time he'd actually been arrested. His mom ended up paying the bail and then he up and disappeared."

"Shit." He shoved a hand through his hair. The long, wheat blond strands fell right back into his face. He stared at the picture for another ten seconds, a muscle jerking in his jaw. "Shit. Fine. Give me the damn file."

* * *

"Not how I wanted to spend the day," he muttered to himself.

His skip had proved to be pretty good at keeping a low profile, not hanging out at home, or with the few friends Quinn had managed to track down.

So he hadn't been able to finish the job yesterday, which meant he had to get it done today. Had to, because he didn't want to waste any more time than necessary on a fucking wife beater.

Of course, the wife wasn't all that interested in helping Quinn find her bastard husband, as evidenced by the fact that he was leaving her apartment with nothing new.

Irritated, he shut the door behind him and made his way down the busted sidewalk to his car. It was one of those crossover SUVs, a Taurus X, black with tinted windows, equipped with GPS, and it was roomy enough to haul in the people he picked up for skipping out on bail.

He'd spent most of yesterday talking to people who knew his current skip, Louis Blanford. That had been a waste of time and today he'd gone by to talk to the wife.

She hadn't wanted to meet his eyes, wouldn't even really look at him, as she spoke in a hesitant, whisper-soft voice. And of course, she didn't know where her husband was, hadn't seen him, blah, blah, blah . . . After spending half an hour trying to get her to talk to him, he gave up and left.

"Hey, wait up."

Quinn glanced back over his shoulder as a young woman came

rushing out of the apartment. She was probably a few years older than her sister and her pleasant, round face might have looked sweet and innocent to some. The look in her eyes, though, was anything but.

Quinn looked into those eyes and saw fury. Hatred. Disgust.

Directed at her brother-in-law, he decided as she came to a stop a few feet away and said, "I can tell you where you might be able to find him."

"Where?" He cocked his head, studying her.

"That dickhead hangs around some bar in East St. Louis." Her blue eyes flashed from behind a thick pair of glasses. "I think it's called *Babes* or *Bitches*—can't remember."

She smirked and added, "It's Wednesday so it's possible you might see him there tonight—Kari used to complain that she never saw him during the week because of her schedule. She had Wednesdays off, but he was always at that dumb bar because they have some sort of special on the wings."

Quinn nodded. Something moved just out of the corner of his eye and he glanced up, saw Kari there. She wouldn't meet his eyes, but she glared at her sister like she wanted to smack her.

"She knows you're out here talking to me," he said, angling his head toward the sister.

The girl set her jaw. "I don't *care*. He won't stop until somebody makes him and Kari won't." Then she sighed and brushed her hair back from her face. "I don't know. Maybe she can't."

Quinn wished he could tell her that he'd make the bastard stop, but unless he put the man in the ground, it wasn't likely.

* * *

OF course, putting him in the ground was an appealing option.

Hours later, as he dealt with the skinny, smelly son of a bitch, he decided the option was growing more appealing by the second. Then the fucker spit at him.

"Do that again and I'm going to knock your teeth down your

throat." Quinn reached into his pocket and pulled out a blue bandanna, used it to wipe the spit off his face. Then he threw the bandanna in the face of the wife beater he'd just hauled in off the streets.

The bastard's bounty wasn't all that much, but for guys who knocked women around, Quinn would do the job for free. If he didn't need to pay for nice little things like food, rent, and gas for his bike.

Lewis Blanford swallowed and stared at Quinn, some attempt at bravado trying to make an appearance. "You can't do that, fuckface. It's illegal and I'll sue your ass."

Quinn lifted a brow. "You'd be amazed at what I can get away with, Blanford." Then he smiled.

It wasn't a nice smile. It was a smile that had made more than one man feel like pissing in his pants.

"You want to see just how much I can get away with? Try it again." Quinn leaned in and lowered his voice as he made the threat.

Blanford went white. He swallowed, a muscle jerking in his jaw. He curled his lip in a sneer, but didn't quite manage to meet Quinn's gaze.

"You just wait until you get a bitch screwing you over and see how you handle it," he muttered.

Quinn didn't bother replying. He'd been screwed over by bitches before, he'd been screwed over by friends, and he'd been screwed over by total strangers. Hell, he'd been screwed over by his mother every day of his life, right up until the day she died.

The day he reacted to any damn thing by beating up a woman was the day he'd sprout wings and fly.

He stepped to the side and gestured to the Taurus. "You going to get in on your own or do I need to help you?"

The last time he'd been forced to "help," it had ended with a trip to the emergency room after he'd broken a man's arm. He really hoped that wasn't going to be how things went this time, but he never really knew how things would play out when he located his skips.

He needed the job, he liked the money, but he was getting damned tired of some of the shit.

Blanford was apparently smarter than he looked. Of course, lice were probably smarter than Blanford looked. The jeans he wore were slung so low, they'd fallen down when he tried to run from Quinn. He'd tripped and ended up landing facedown in the dirt with his skinny, naked ass hanging out. The sweatshirt he wore was so grimy and stained with sweat, no amount of Clorox was going to clean it. He stank to high heaven, and Quinn wondered if the man had any idea soap and deodorant existed.

As Blanford climbed into the back of the car, Quinn decided he was damn glad he hadn't ever gotten around to getting his own car to use for work. He'd just keep using company cars—there was no way in hell he'd let something that dirty in a car he owned. And even though he could do pretty much whatever was needed to bring in the people who went and skipped bail, he figured tying somebody to the top of a car to transport him might just be pushing it.

Bail-jumping. Bounty hunting.

How in the hell had he gotten into this?

"Because you're good at finding scum," he muttered.

Not a rancher like his dad. Not the doctor-type like his twin brother. Hunting down trash seemed to be his calling.

Probably because that's where you came from . . .

You ain't nothing but trash.

It was a sly, insidious whisper, the echo of his dead mother's voice. Long dead—more than twenty years had passed since she'd overdosed.

If it hadn't been for the guy who'd been shooting up with his mom, Quinn didn't know where he'd be right now. It turned out the police were looking for the man, though, and very enthusiasti-cally. They'd busted the door down early that morning, discov-ered their suspect, lying on the floor in a drugged daze next to a corpse . . . and Quinn, in the closet.

If the police hadn't found him that morning, if Quinn had woken up and found his mother dead, he would have hit the streets and never looked back. Which meant he wouldn't have landed with his dad and Luke on the ranch in Wyoming. That one little twist of fate had probably saved his life. If it hadn't been for Dad and Luke, he might have ended up a bottom-feeder like Blanford.

"Now that's a depressing thought," he muttered, slanting a look at Blanford. He rolled his shoulders and shoved a hand through his hair. Then, blowing out a sigh, he climbed into the car.

It already reeked, a sickening mixture of body odor and fried food. As he started the car, he hit the button for the window. A blast of hot air came through, and in the back, Blanford swore.

"Shit, man. It's hot out. Ain't this thing got AC?"

Quinn ignored him.

* * *

"LITTLE cunt."

Ugly words, spoken in an ugly tone, with ugly anger flashing through a pair of pale blue eyes.

"Little cunt, one of these days, I'm going to teach you a lesson."

* * *

A new voice . . . soft, shaking, unsteady.

"He wants you dead."

Sara Davis came awake with that voice echoing in her ears. After two years, she still heard that voice, all too often. She still had the dreams, all too often. And she was still on the run. As soon as she felt like she might actually remember what it was like *not* to run, she would have to pack up and start all over again.

She took a deep breath—through her mouth. In the little apartment where she lived, it wasn't ever safe to breathe too deeply through one's nose. Not when the aromas consisted of a nasty mix of stale food, marijuana, various bodily wastes when the plumbing screwed up, and sweat.

Holding her breath, she counted to ten and then let it back out. Sitting up, she kicked her legs over the side of the plain twin mattress. She hadn't spent money getting a frame for it—the moment she'd looked inside this place, she'd known she'd stay only as long as it took to find someplace else.

That had been six weeks ago, and it was taking a lot longer to find a decent place than she'd hoped. Of course, *decent* was relative. She'd be happy with someplace where she could breathe normally without worrying about the hazard it might pose to her health. Someplace where she wasn't constantly hearing the conversations from her neighbors, someplace where she didn't have to share a bathroom with three other tenants would be a godsend.

But there were a number of things that kept the nicer places out of her reach, and finding a tolerable one was getting harder and harder.

From the apartment below hers, she heard a crash, followed by raised, angry voices. Tuning them out, she covered her face with her hands and thought longingly of the time when she'd woken up in a nice comfy bed. Back then, she'd always slept naked, loving the way her black silk sheets felt as she snuggled into them.

The feel of silk was nothing but a memory now.

Sleeping naked was just plain stupid—you didn't want to be naked when the only locks on the door could be broken by a persistent two-year-old or a clumsy drunk. She slept in cotton jersey pants and a T-shirt, with her hand wrapped around a canister of Mace.

Once upon a time, she'd had a cute little cottage, and her

bedroom had taken up most of the second floor. The walls had been painted a dark, vivid shade of purple, and framed prints of fairies had danced upon them. Her bedroom used to smell like vanilla, lavender, and spice, courtesy of her love for potpourri and candles.

Now she had the lovely odor of unwashed bodies, faulty plumbing, mold, mildew, and fried food lingering in the air. She'd given up potpourri and candles long ago, which was a good thing, because it would have been money down the drain in this dump. No amount of Glade, no amount of Febreze, no amount of potpourri would do anything to improve the atmosphere here.

Candles might—if she lit a few dozen and then the room accidentally caught on fire. If the place burned to the ground, that would be a huge improvement.

The alarm clock on her cell phone chirped and she sighed, pushed a hand through her hair. It was a drab shade, caught somewhere between brown and blonde and cut to chin length. She never let it grow much longer, although she took care of cutting it herself these days.

Questions warred in her mind as she reached for her phone, staring at the time. She had someplace she was supposed to be, but right now, she wasn't entirely sure she should go.

She knew she *wanted* to, but that was a far cry from knowing if she *should*.

The voices downstairs rose once more, and as if on cue, voices from the apartment overhead joined in. Surrounded by angry, raised shouts on what felt like all sides, Sara dropped back on the mattress and reached out, blindly feeling around the little plastic crate that served as a table.

Her fingers brushed up against the napkin and she lifted it, read the address.

Hell. What could it hurt?

* * *

You can know who a person is simply by staring into their eyes.

Somebody had said that to her once, and they were words she lived by.

Sara kept sunglasses on whenever possible. She avoided looking people in the eyes at all costs. If she'd kept to that rule a little more firmly, she might not be standing on a nice tree-lined street in St. Louis's West End. Which would mean she might not have this odd, itchy sensation that something big was going to happen.

Some sort of change. Sara wasn't exactly *opposed* to change, provided she got to do it on her terms and had some control over things. But this wouldn't be one of those changes. She knew it in her bones.

Slipping her sunglasses up, she eyed the old house in front of her. It had been done up into apartments, and she could already see that somebody put a lot of time and love into it.

Gnawing on her lower lip, she shifted from one foot to the other. She didn't need to be here. She should have just thrown the address away the second she had a chance. But she hadn't. She was here, and now she was debating about whether she should just hightail it back to the bus stop and disappear.

Only one thing kept her from doing just that—the kindness she'd seen in Theresa Kingston's gaze the day before. If you could truly know a person just by staring into their eyes, then Sara knew that Theresa was one of the kindest women on earth.

Sara wanted to trust that instinct, but when it came to kindness, she had a hard time. The biggest part of her said she could trust Theresa. But there was a voice, doubtful, reminding her, always, of what could happen if she trusted the wrong person.

She closed her eyes and played the scene through in her head again, tried to figure out what her instincts were telling her.

"*I heard you were looking for a place to stay.*"

"*Hmmm. Maybe.*" Which translated to YES! DESPERATELY.

"*Well, if you're interested, I've got a vacant apartment in my house. It's nothing fancy, just a studio apartment with a little kitchenette.*"

"*Sounds nice, but I'm pretty tight on money right now.*" Tight didn't quite describe it—she saved every last penny she could, and since she didn't make a lot of pennies, she didn't have many left over to add to her savings.

Theresa leaned back against the padded back of the booth where she liked to sit. Every other day, the older woman was there, right at 11:00. Come rain or shine, or at least it had been that way for the past six weeks. "*Ahhh, but I haven't told you how much it costs,*" Theresa said, smiling.

More than I make here, Sara thought glumly. But she pasted a smile on her face and said, "*Sorry . . . I'm just so used to everything being out of my range around here.*" And the stuff that wasn't out of her range, she couldn't risk taking.

Most landlords didn't want to rent out apartments without doing a credit check, a background check . . . driver's license. Sara couldn't chance any of those.

Somebody called Sara's name and she glanced over her shoulder, saw one of her co-workers loading plates onto a tray. "*Be right there.*"

She turned back to Theresa and opened her mouth, but the older woman cut her off.

"*Here.*" She pressed a napkin into Sara's hand, a napkin and five dollars. A five-dollar tip, for a cup of coffee. "*Just come by and check it out, Sara. Really, I think you'd love it.*"

Her instincts told her that Theresa wasn't any sort of threat to her. Still, in hindsight, Sara should have just thrown the napkin away, finished up her day at the café, and then quietly disappeared. She didn't need people noticing her. Being nice to her. Being friendly.

When people started being friendly, it meant only one thing. *Time to go.*

She no longer trusted her instincts—she couldn't afford to. The girl she'd once been would have looked at the elderly woman and fallen in love. Theresa looked like Mrs. Claus, complete with a tidy white bun in her hair and rosy cheeks, and was always ready with a kind word or a joke to share.

Sara desperately wanted to accept that kindness.

Setting her jaw, she shoved the napkin in her pocket and hitched her backpack a little higher up on her shoulder. She was going to go back to the roach motel that masqueraded as an apartment. She was going to pack her stuff. And she was going to leave.

In another month or two, it would start getting cooler. Then winter would settle in. Maybe she'd head farther south this time. Someplace warm. Maybe she could get lucky and even find a place halfway . . . well, like home.

"Sara, is that you I hear out there?"

She just barely managed to keep from flinching when she heard Theresa's voice calling her name. Steeling herself, she pasted a smile on her face and waited as the older woman bustled around the corner of the house, carrying a tray of flowers and beaming.

Huh. People really do beam when they smile that big . . .

Theresa set down the tray of flowers and rushed up the brick walkway to greet Sara.

"Oh, I'm so glad you decided to check out the apartment."

"Actually, I . . ."

But Theresa was a petite, friendly steamroller. She rolled right over her attempts to speak and linked arms. Sara obediently fell in step with the older woman. *Just get it over with.*

This place wouldn't be some dive where she turned over cash in exchange for problems with the plumbing, busted-up plaster, and paper-thin walls.

A place like this would come with a renter's agreement. Credit checks. First and last month's security deposit. Identification.

Even if those things weren't an issue, the price definitely would be. Places in St. Louis's Central West End weren't exactly what she could call *affordable*, not on her income. She could do the walk-through and then when Theresa named her price, she'd have an honest reason to refuse.

But Sara hadn't counted on how much she missed being in a *home*. Even though the apartment wasn't *her* home, it felt . . . well, welcoming. Warm.

There were knickknacks scattered about. A futon that would double as a bed. Another window along the front wall, with a big, overstuffed chair sitting in front of it. In the little kitchenette area, there was a small table set under a window that faced out over the backyard, giving Sara a view of the flowerbeds. Theresa must have been working on them when Sara showed up—vivid bursts of color, vines, plants, and little yard statues.

Staring down at the flowers, Sara lifted a hand and rested it on the pale yellow wall. She wasn't much for yellows—hated pastels with a passion, but this . . . this was nice. Maybe it was because it seemed so sunny and cheerful, and she'd spent far too much time in dank, depressing places where it seemed the sun never quite penetrated inside the room.

"It's lovely," she murmured, her voice husky. With the knot in her throat, it was amazing she was able to speak at all. "I didn't realize it was furnished."

"I'm sorry . . . I thought I'd mentioned it." She stared owlishly at Sara. "Are the furnishings a problem?"

"No. Of course not." Sara turned and smiled at Theresa. "I don't really have all that much stuff anyway."

And that doesn't matter—even if you could afford it, and you can't, you wouldn't be able to move in here.

Taking one more lingering glance around the pretty space, she asked, "So how much is it?"

"Three-fifty a month."

Sara's jaw dropped. "What?"

Theresa's brow puckered and she said, "I'm sorry . . . if that's too high, maybe we could work something out . . ."

"It's not too high. Theresa, you could charge double that. A furnished apartment this close to downtown?" Hell, Sara was paying three hundred a month in cash for that fricking roach motel.

"Really?" Theresa cocked her head and pursed her lips. Then she shrugged and gave Sara a sweet smile. "But I don't need double that. I own the home, you know. It belonged to my husband's parents and they left it to us. He and I, we spent years fixing it up after the kids left home. Now that he's gone, they've all married and moved away . . . well, I'd just go crazy in this big old place all by myself."

Sara took one last look around the apartment. *Want!*

She wanted to sit at that little table and drink coffee in the morning, looking at the lovely flowers. She wanted to curl up on the chair close to the front door and read a book with light streaming in over her shoulder from the window. Hell, she even wanted to wake up and stare at the cheerfully yellow walls.

She wanted to come to a place that could actually feel like *home*.

"It really is lovely, but I'm afraid I can't afford it." It wasn't a lie—she *could* just barely manage the monthly payments, and she wouldn't even have to dip into her precious stash of cash. But she couldn't afford the other things that would come with taking the apartment.

"Perhaps if we made it three hundred . . . and you could help me in the gardens from time to time."

Sara shook her head. "No, I'm sorry." She started for the door.

She had her hand on the doorknob when Theresa spoke again. "You'd be safe here."

Sara froze. Every muscle in her back tensed up and she took a deep breath, consciously made herself relax and give Theresa a puzzled smile. "I'm sorry?"

"You heard me, darling." Theresa sighed and the happy, contented mask on her face fell away, revealing a woman who looked as if she understood worry . . . fear. "You'd be safe. You can pay me in cash and I don't need to run a credit check, I won't ask for identification. There is no security deposit—the only thing I ask is that you not steal anything from me when it's time for you to go."

Her breath was trapped in her lungs. She didn't even realize she'd stopped breathing until her chest started to ache. Releasing a pent-up breath, she collapsed back against the door and stared at Theresa. "What are you talking about?"

God, does she know? Did I give myself away . . . how?

As though she knew every thought running through Sara's mind, Theresa shook her head. "Don't worry, Sara. I don't know who you are and I don't know why you're running or what you're running from. But you *are* running. Aren't you?"

"If you think I'm running from something, the last thing you should do is offer me a place to stay."

"Oh, sweetheart . . . not everybody runs away because they've done something wrong. A lot of people run away because they have no choice." Theresa settled on the futon, crossed her feet at the ankles, and rested her hands in her lap.

People run away because they have no choice—nobody knew that better than Sara.

Staring into Theresa's kind eyes, her heart ached. Those faded blue eyes seemed to hold a thousand secrets and there was a knowledge in her face that made her seem ancient, older than time.

Still, Sara wasn't going to believe in that gentle look. Wasn't going to let herself fall into the trap of trusting somebody. All it would take was trusting the wrong person and life could get shot straight to hell.

"Look, Theresa, I realize you think I'm in some sort of trouble or something, but I'm not. I'm just a waitress, looking for a place to stay." Although the lie left a bad taste in her mouth, she knew she said it convincingly. She'd stood in front of her mirror, practicing each and every lie she'd have to tell, until she could do it without blushing, without blinking, until the lies rolled off her lips with an easy smile.

"Bullshit." Theresa returned Sara's smile with a cool one of her own. "If you don't want the apartment, that's fine. If you don't want to tell me what's going on, that's fine. I don't expect you to, I don't need you to, and truthfully, I don't want you to. But please, Sara, don't lie to me. Not when I'm only trying to help."

Those simple words drove a shard into Sara's heart, and she closed her eyes, dropped her head back against the door. Keeping her eyes closed, she said quietly, "I appreciate that, Theresa. I really do."

"Then let me help. Trust me . . . just a little."

Opening her eyes, Sara stared at Theresa. "How did you know?"

"Instinct, I suppose." Theresa's eyes, kind and gentle, so full of understanding, stared back, held Sara's gaze for a brief moment, and then she looked away, smoothed a hand down her skirt.

"I had three children. My boys are grown—one lives in Minneapolis, married to a wonderful woman. My other son is a bachelor and seems quite happy that way. My daughter . . ." Her voice wobbled and she stopped, pressed her lips together. When she spoke again, her voice was level and steady. "My daughter is dead—the man she was engaged to marry killed her when she tried to break the engagement."

"My God, Theresa, I'm so sorry."

Theresa nodded. "Thank you. It's been more than twenty years, but it's a pain that never truly goes away, you know?" She looked back at Sara, intensity glowing in her eyes. "A few years ago, a friend of mine that lives across the street had her little girl come to her in the middle of the night. Crying, bruised, her mouth busted open. Her husband had hit her—he'd been doing it for a long time, but this time was different. He'd hit their little boy as well. That was the final straw—it pushed her over the edge and while he was sleeping, she left him. But he came looking for her there. Where else would she go? And that's where he found her. The police were called. My friend didn't know what to do. Her daughter didn't know what to do."

"You offered to let them stay here," Sara said when Theresa's voice trailed off.

"Yes." She smiled, staring off into the distance. "I did. And it felt *right*. Ever since my daughter died, nothing has felt *right*. So I started helping. As often as I can. When I can."

Rising off the bench, Theresa came to stand in front of Sara. With her hands folded at her waist, she studied Sara's face. "So will you let me help you? I promise you—you *will* be safe here."

Questions and doubts raged inside her.

You need to leave, Sara. And you need to do it now.

It made sense. Perfect sense.

She took another look around the small, cozy apartment.

Want.

THREE

A FTER swapping out the car for his bike, Quinn made a quick stop by the bank and deposited the check he'd received for bringing in Blanford. Now the punk could spend the rest of the time until his trial in jail, where he belonged. Quinn was realistic, though. It was entirely possible the man wouldn't get much of a sentence, even if his wife did testify against him.

The legal system at its finest.

He hit the expressway early enough to beat most of the afternoon rush. Martin Gearing, the owner of the private detective agency that Quinn sort of worked for, hadn't been in the office— again. That wasn't a surprise, although Quinn really did want to tell the bastard not to ambush him like that again.

Not that it would do any good.

Gearing knew his business well, and he knew his employees well. Even his "sort of" employees, like Quinn.

He defined his job status with Gearing as "sort of" because he didn't want the entanglements that could come with a full-time job, namely, the responsibility of having somebody counting on him.

So he refused offers of full-time employment, kept his freelance status . . . which gave him the freedom to walk out of there after collecting his money from Juanita.

She was busy on the phone, but he ignored her *wait a minute* signals. She wasn't going to trip him up again. After being spit on and dealing with Blanford's stink for half of the afternoon, he wasn't in any hurry to do another job today. No, what he wanted to do was go to the little basement apartment where he'd been living for the past six months, climb into the shower, and scrub the grime from his body.

Then he just might see if his landlady had any plans on cooking tonight. Theresa invited him for dinner nearly every night, and nearly every night he refused. He didn't like getting close to people, but the nice lady made it hard to avoid her, to shut her out.

His stomach was grumbling by the time he pulled his bike into the small space Theresa had cleared for him. He hadn't gotten around to eating lunch and he never messed with breakfast—come to think of it, he'd probably skipped dinner the night before, too.

Days had a habit of running together on him. It was better than it had been, though. For a while, right after he'd left the army, days had passed by in an endless mess with nothing to separate one from the other. Unless he'd drunk himself into a stupor and spent the next day dealing with a hangover as well as guilt and grief.

Grief and guilt, over the death of a woman he hadn't been able to save—Elena. It wasn't until after she'd been lost to him that he realized how much she had meant. It was a serious bitch, realizing too late that he'd finally fallen in love. It wasn't until after she'd died that he'd figured it out, not until after she'd been kidnapped, raped, tortured, and murdered for daring to fight against the drug-dealing bastards who'd torn her country apart.

Don't, man . . . He stopped in the middle of the brick-paved walkway and closed his eyes. *Don't*. He still dealt with the grief, and the guilt still crept up on him, but for the most part, he maintained fairly well.

But today he was pissed off, tired, and in one fucking lousy mood, which meant it wouldn't take as much to push him over the edge. He didn't want those brutal emotions sinking their claws into him again.

It had been one hell of a battle breaking free the last time he'd sunk too low, and it had almost come with a price that he couldn't have lived with. For months after he'd gotten out of the army, he'd lived as hard and fast as he could. He'd skipped things like food and sleep, much preferring to drink himself under the table on a regular basis. He'd picked fights in the hopes that sooner or later, somebody else would win.

It had taken seeing his twin flirting with death for Quinn to realize he didn't like the place he'd been in. He had been flirting with death himself, but he hadn't been doing it for altruistic reasons.

Luke had risked death to save his lady—Quinn had been chasing death because he'd thought it was better than the alternative.

Then he'd seen a man holding a gun on his brother. A man the twins had known, had trusted. Tony Malone had been in the army with them, had fought with them, bled with them . . . lost friends right along with them. But the losses had proved too much for Tony, and the man had gone off the deep end. As unstable as Quinn had been, Tony had been much, much worse.

Tony had let the losses, the grief, the guilt fester inside him and it had driven him crazy.

That wasn't going to happen to Quinn. He wouldn't let it. He wasn't going to get lost in bitterness. He wasn't going to choke on the guilt. He'd done better, too, and not just because he'd promised his brother, Luke, he'd take better care of himself.

Still, it was easy to forget about things like food, decent sleep.

Sex. All too often, he had to remind himself to eat, will himself to sleep. Sex was a nonissue, because he just wasn't interested.

The truth of it was that up until the past few months, he had had a hard time working up interest in much of anything. That was why he had to make himself think about eating. Make himself go to sleep. Force himself to leave the apartment and face the world. Face life.

Life as he knew it had sucked for so damn long, doing anything to try improving it seemed like a waste of energy.

Things had gotten better, though. The fact that he was actually hungry, that he was kind of looking forward to sitting down and talking with a friend—or at least listening to a friend talk—was a step forward.

With his belly rumbling a reminder at him, he sauntered down the walkway and followed it around the house. His nostrils flared and he caught the scent of something absolutely divine—spaghetti. The lady was making spaghetti and when she made spaghetti, she also had homemade garlic bread.

Suddenly, Quinn was damn glad he hadn't hung around after he'd turned over Blanford. If he'd been given another job, he would have missed out on what was rapidly becoming his favorite meal, with a woman who was rapidly becoming one of his favorite people—and that was no small feat. Quinn could count the people he really liked on one hand. Until Theresa had smilingly bowled him over, he would have had a finger left over after he counted up his friends.

He opened the door—

And stopped dead in his tracks as somebody all but fell into his arms. Somebody . . . a woman. And *not* Theresa.

He caught her just above her elbows, automatically steadying her.

"I'm sorry," she said, her voice soft and low.

Then she lifted her face, and Quinn found himself gazing into the biggest, brownest eyes he'd ever seen in his life. Feeling a little dazed, he studied her face while she stammered out another apology.

Quinn barely heard it.

He was too busy staring at her mouth. A very pretty mouth, a cupid's bow slicked with deep, vibrant red. Under his hands, he could feel silken smooth skin and, unable to resist, he stroked a thumb along her inner arm.

Her skin was soft, soft and warm—the creamiest, most flawless skin imaginable. Her shoulder-length hair was a shade caught between blonde and brown, nondescript, but for some reason, he found himself thinking about tangling his fingers in that hair and holding her head still while he kissed that red-slicked mouth.

Well, hello . . . he could all but feel his libido kicking up as he stared at that mouth. Every last one of his senses tuned in on her—

The way she looked . . . sex and sin.

The way she smelled . . . sex and sin.

The way she sounded . . . sex and sin.

The way she felt . . . the way she might taste. He knew it without a doubt. She'd taste like sex and sin.

His mouth was all but watering.

"Ahhh . . . excuse me," she said, tugging against his light hold.

"Uh . . . yeah." He uncurled his fingers and let go, although he hated every second of it.

She immediately backed away, putting a good five feet between them and eying him nervously. In that moment, he was acutely aware of the fact that he hadn't bothered shaving that morning, or the morning before. He was also acutely aware of the wrinkled state of his gray T-shirt and the jeans he wore. He'd finally gotten into the habit of wearing the unofficial uniform—a black shirt with *Bond Enforcement* printed on the front and back, and either jeans or black fatigues—worn by most of the guys who worked for Gearing. He wore the *Bond* shirts for work, but usually changed

before leaving. Wearing those particular shirts outside of work
had ended up causing him a headache or two.

She continued to stare at him, her face expressionless and
her eyes measuring. She might have just continued to stare at
him indefinitely if Theresa hadn't come bustling down the hall.
"Quinn?"

Tearing his eyes away from the unknown woman, he smiled at
his landlady. It no longer seemed so weird to smile at somebody—as
in he didn't worry his face might crack if he wasn't careful. Still,
the smile on his face did feel odd. "Hey, Theresa. I didn't know you
had company."

She beamed at him. "This isn't company. This is your new
neighbor. She just moved in to the upstairs apartment. Sara . . . I'd
like you to meet Quinn Rafferty. Quinn, this is Sara Davis."

Sara.

Neighbor.

Staring into Sara's dark brown eyes, his heart sank just a little.
Great.

Some people collected books.

Collected knickknacks, or coins.

Theresa collected lost souls, as evidenced by the fact that he
was living in her basement after she'd charmed him into changing
her tire outside Dierburg's a few months earlier.

The last person to stay in that apartment had been a battered
woman hiding out from her ex. Before that, it had been a girl
who'd been all of nineteen, with two kids and a third on the way.
When that one left, she'd stolen from Theresa and skipped out on
the piddling amount of rent.

If Sara Davis was living in Theresa's upstairs apartment, that
made her pretty much off-limits. It didn't matter that his dormant
sex drive was all of a sudden flaring up on him.

The last thing Quinn needed to be around was another lost
soul, not when he still struggled to find his own.

Setting his jaw, he met Sara Davis's dark, velvety brown eyes and gave a single nod in greeting. Then he glanced at Theresa and said, "I'll see you later."

"Wouldn't you like to join us for dinner?" Theresa asked, smiling at him. It was that smile that had suckered him in months earlier—it all but said, *Come now, you wouldn't want to hurt an old woman's feelings, would you?*

Not that he figured Theresa saw herself as old. She was just sharp and she'd use whatever cards she had on hand.

"Nah. I'm not hungry." He just hoped his belly wouldn't start growling and betray him.

"Are you sure, Quinn? You never eat right."

Feeling Sara's eyes lingering on him, he shrugged and said, "I'm fine. Lousy day, and I just want to crash—wanted to see if I could swipe a beer from the fridge."

"Of course. I'll grab it for you. The kitchen is a disaster right now." Theresa bustled back into the kitchen.

Leaving him alone with Sara Davis. Feeling her eyes on him, he glanced at her.

She gave him a smile. "I hope I'm not the reason you're passing up a meal."

Fuck, that voice . . . He could imagine that voice, whispering in his ear as he crouched over her body, driving deep, deep inside . . .

Mouth dry, he swallowed and made himself shrug. "Like I said, I'm not hungry."

"I don't know how anybody could smell that spaghetti and *not* be hungry." Another smile, a wide, friendly one.

It was the kind of smile that made others want to smile back. Quinn just shrugged.

Silence stretched out between them. Normally, Quinn didn't mind silence. Even strained silences were better than most of the bullshit that passed for "polite" conversation. But as the seconds ticked into a minute, and then two, he became more and more uncomfortable.

He was actually searching his mind for a way to break the silence when Theresa came back into the room, a basket in hand.

He couldn't help but grin as she pushed it into his hands. It held two bottles of Bud Light *and* a container full of spaghetti, as well as what he suspected was some of her bread, wrapped up in a paper towel.

"Humor me," she said, returning his smile. "I'll feel better knowing you have something besides TV dinners or peanut butter on hand. And sometime soon, you have to have dinner with me. It's just not the same cooking for one."

"You're not cooking for one," he pointed out with a glance at Sara.

She waved that away and then said, "I've got to finish things up in here. Sara, why don't you help me put together a salad?"

Quinn lingered long enough to watch Sara fall in line next to Theresa—and long enough to admire her very nice ass.

* * *

"THAT'S your other tenant?" Sara asked, listening as the door closed quietly behind Quinn Rafferty.

"Yes, that's him." Theresa smiled over her shoulder at Sara as she opened the refrigerator door. "Don't let him bother you—he's the quiet sort. A little gruff, a little blunt, but he's got a good heart inside him. He's a dear."

Sara blinked. *Dear* wasn't exactly the sort of term that came to her mind.

Wounded warrior.

That was what she'd first thought when she stared at him, into gray eyes that gave absolutely nothing away. Then she laughed at herself. *Warrior* might fit him well enough, but she couldn't figure out where she got the *wounded* from.

There were no scars marring that very perfect body, at least not that she'd seen, and she'd definitely looked while he'd been talking to Theresa.

She couldn't *not* look. Very easy on the eyes was Mr. Quinn Rafferty.

He had blond hair, long enough that he could wear it in a short ponytail if he wanted. The blond wasn't just a uniform color, either. It was shot through with strands that ranged from almost white to nearly brown—the kind of highlighting job women would pay serious money for. But she had no doubt he didn't pay a red cent for his hair to look like that.

His eyes were gray, fringed with long sooty lashes. The power of his gaze was palpable. When he looked at her, the power lingered, an unseen touch against her flesh.

His body was long and lean, his shoulders straining against the seams of a worn, wrinkled T-shirt. The short sleeves of the shirt had revealed hard, corded muscles, but not that overdone, muscle-bound weight-lifter look. She hadn't seen any sign of spare flesh anywhere on him and she'd bet that under that shirt, he had a six-pack. His jeans were almost as worn as the T-shirt, and they molded to his legs in the most delicious way imaginable.

Oh, yeah. Very easy on the eyes.

But still, she couldn't quite define him as a *dear*.

Theresa turned away from the refrigerator and pushed lettuce, tomatoes, and carrots into Sara's hands. Automatically, Sara took them.

"Why don't you wash those up and then make us a salad? I just need a few more minutes to get out some plates . . . and a bottle of wine." Theresa paused and cocked her head, studying Sara. "You don't mind if I have a glass, do you?"

"It's your home, Theresa."

"Oh, I know. I just . . . well, some people are uncomfortable around alcohol."

There were unspoken questions in Theresa's voice, in her eyes. *Fishing*, Sara decided. Very subtle, but still, fishing none the less. "Don't worry about that with me. I wouldn't mind a glass of wine myself."

Over dinner, Sara realized that fishing was something that Theresa excelled at. Despite her earlier claim of not wanting to know any information about Sara, she managed to sneak in very clever little probes. If Sara hadn't become very paranoid over the past few years, she just might have let herself get tripped up.

After deflecting yet another question, Sara took a sip from her wine and gave Theresa a friendly smile. "So, how long have you had your other tenant?"

It worked—Theresa leaned back in her chair, a thoughtful look on her face. "Hmmmm. I guess close to six months."

"What does he do for a living?"

There was a cagey look in Theresa's eyes, one that Sara recognized. She wasn't the least bit surprised that her new landlady was a matchmaker.

"Oh, Quinn does a little bit of everything, I think."

"That's vague." Sara tore off a chunk of bread and popped it in her mouth.

"It's the truth. He knows his way around cars, has helped me some around this old house. Even knows his way around horses, from what I can gather . . . not that he'd need it much around here. His dad has a ranch somewhere, in Montana, I think. Or maybe Wyoming. Just a handy sort, in a lot of ways." Theresa paused and eyed her clean plate for a second. "I really shouldn't but I think I'm going to have some more. Would you like another helping?"

"No. I'm stuffed." She really should head out. She'd already spent far too much time talking to her new landlady.

But even as she thought about getting up, Theresa started talking again.

"I'd seen Quinn around at Dierburg's a few times. A man who

looks like that . . . well, I may be old, but I'm not dead. He's not easily forgotten."

"I've got to agree with you there." Quinn Rafferty did *not* blend.

"He actually helped me out once before I even knew his name. This girl and her boyfriend were bothering me in the parking lot—claimed they had car trouble and desperately needed a ride—supposedly they'd left their baby alone with a teenage neighbor just to run to the store for a few minutes, then the car wouldn't start."

Theresa frowned and gave Sara a narrow look. "Regardless of what some people think, I'm neither naive nor soft in the head. They were up to no good. When I told them I was pressed for time, they pushed the issue. I was actually getting a bit scared and then Quinn comes up—seemed like out of nowhere. Gives the two this look and threw a couple of quarters at them—told them to call a tow truck and leave me the hell alone. They took off like he'd pulled a gun . . . or a badge. I tried to tell him thank you, but he acted like I hadn't said a word and just headed on up to the store—although he didn't go in until I'd gotten into my car and pulled out of the parking space."

Theresa paused and took a drink of her wine. "A few weeks later, as it happened, I was at Dierburg's again and I had some car trouble—I picked up a nail and when I came out of the store, my tire was flat as a pancake. Quinn was leaving the store about the same time and before I had a chance to call AAA, he told me he could change it if I had a spare."

"So how did he end up in one of your apartments? Did you come right out and offer it to him like you did with me?" Sara asked, keeping her tone light.

"No . . . of course not," Theresa laughed. "Although I didn't just come right out and offer it to you. I was being nosy and overheard you talking to Lori when you asked if she knew of anybody that might have a room to rent out."

She blushed and gave Sara a wry grin. "And I must admit, I was being a nosy busybody with Quinn, too. He set his bags down to change the tire and while he was working on it, I glanced inside, saw one of those magazines with apartment listings. Figured it couldn't hurt to offer the basement apartment to him. It was empty at the time. A man who would take the time to change my tire, and help me out when those two were bothering me, can't be a bad guy to have around."

Depends on what you consider bad, Sara thought.

"And I was right. I had some problems with the plumbing a few weeks back, and he took care of it, quick as could be. Wouldn't even let me pay him for it and when I told him not to give as much for rent, he just ignored me. He's fixed up some things around here as well, and he won't take a red cent for it. The girl that lives across the street is constantly leaving her headlights on and needs a jump every now and then, and Quinn helps her out. He has a motorcycle, but I don't mind if he uses my car to give her a jump."

Then she laughed. "But I'm starting to think Trilby is leaving her lights on just to drain the battery so she can come over here and flirt with Quinn. Of course, it's a wasted effort on her part— she's far too young for Quinn."

"Some men like them young."

"Young as in still a teenager . . . and decent adult men don't go after teenage girls, even when it's being offered," Theresa said. There was an edge in her voice, a hard light in her eyes.

"Your daughter?" Sara asked, unable to hold the question back.

"Yes." Theresa toyed with the stem of her wineglass, staring at the table. Grief made her voice rough.

"I'm sorry."

Theresa forced herself to smile. "So am I." Then she took a sip of wine and looked back at Sara. "Trilby, my neighbor, is seventeen. She was a bit of a 'late bloomer,' or at least it seems late nowadays. Up until last summer, she still looked more like a skinny boy than anything else. Then, practically overnight, that changed and she's turned into a bit of a flirt. Practicing on Quinn is safer than trying it on the boys in school."

"Safer?"

Nothing about Quinn looked too safe to Sara.

"Definitely safer. He's not going to take her up on anything and he also won't hurt her feelings, even if she can be a bit annoying."

"Other than fixing cars and water pipes and making teenage hearts flutter, what does he do?"

"Like I said, a little bit of this . . . a little bit of that."

Sara wasn't going to get anything more than that unless she came right out and said, "Hey, is he somebody who could cause me trouble?" And she wasn't going to do that. It lacked subtlety.

For reasons that had little to do with handyman and knight-in-shining-armor tendencies, he made her nervous. Made her wish she'd passed on Theresa's offer, even if it did mean staying in that nasty one-room apartment where she had to sleep with one eye open.

But it was too late now. She'd already moved her stuff, what little she owned, into the apartment upstairs and she wasn't going back to the other place.

Sara would just have to wait and see, and be ready.

* * *

"STUPID cunt. You didn't actually think I'd let you get away, did you?"

"Please, James . . ."

Sara came awake and for two seconds, panic tried to take over. But she didn't give in.

"Just a dream," she told herself, her throat tight. She swallowed, but it didn't do a damn thing to ease the tightness. There was a lump lodged halfway down and it wasn't going to go away anytime soon. Not after that. "Not real."

She lay still and quiet, let her heart settle as she took in what she could see without moving anything more than her eyes.

White ceiling, sloped and pristine—not stained and cracked. Sunlight filtering in through curtains. There hadn't been a window in the last place she'd stayed.

Angling her head to the left, she stared at the table sitting neatly under the window, eyed the yellow walls.

Yellow . . . ?

Then her memory kicked in.

Theresa.

The apartment.

Closing her eyes, Sara blew out a sigh and wondered if it would ever be over. If she'd ever have a chance at anything resembling a normal life again. Then she sat up and stretched her arms over her head, wincing at her stiff back and neck.

The apartment was a godsend, but that futon was a torture device straight out of hell. With a grimace, she rolled off it and settled on the floor next to it. Grimly, she did a series of crunches, hating every second. She gritted her teeth through the push-ups that followed. Those were followed by the other exercises that she'd started doing over the last two years.

Leg extensions, lunges, squats.

With focused determination, she went through them all. Sweat was gleaming on her body by the time she started walking herself through the different self-defense techniques.

Martial arts was the one form of exercise she didn't loathe and despise, although it might be because she didn't let herself *think* of martial arts as exercise. At first, it had been harder to practice without a partner, but she'd gotten used to it.

In a little while, she'd dig out some tennis shoes and take a run around the neighborhood—that particular bit served a number of purposes. She could scout out the area, figure out some escape routes.

And it kept her strong, kept her ready.

Being out of shape just wasn't acceptable.

Thirty minutes later, she was done with everything but the run. She went into the bathroom and paused in the doorway, unable to keep from smiling as she studied the cheery blue and white interior. A far cry from the cracked, urine-stained toilet and soap-scum-lined shower she'd shared with three other people over the last couple of months.

She caught sight of her face in the mirror and paused. She almost looked . . . content. Really content, not just the "everything is fine" mask she wore for the world.

"Don't get used to it," she muttered.

Getting used to something meant falling into a routine.

Falling into a routine meant she got sloppy.

With that sobering thought, her half smile faded and she once more found herself staring at a grim-faced stranger. Nothing like the woman who'd stared back at her reflection just over two years ago.

Everything looked different. Her hair was short, the color drab. Her face was thinner, her mouth unsmiling. The worst change, though, came from inside. Anger—carry it on the inside for too long and it started to show on the outside.

Nobody, not even her own mother, would recognize her.

* * *

QUINN lay on the weight bench, ignoring the nagging ring of his phone. It was somebody from the Gearing Agency. Quinn used specific ringtones for the few that had his number—that way he could decide if it was a call that he could put off indefinitely or if he needed to answer it just to get some peace.

When certain people called, namely, his dad or his twin brother, Luke, Quinn usually answered. Calls from Jeb Gray, a friend from his army days, were a little more iffy. Sometimes Quinn felt like talking to Jeb. Other times, he didn't.

Then there had been a few calls from Theresa, and although it surprised the hell out of him, Quinn answered each and every one of those calls. Hell, he answered those calls more often than he answered calls from Luke and his dad.

The rest of the calls, though, more often than not, came from somebody at Gearing, and Quinn rarely answered those. He often wondered why they even bothered calling. They had better luck getting in touch with him via e-mail.

Most likely they were calling about another job. If that was the case, they could e-mail Quinn the details. So it rang and rang, and stopped, then started all over again. He tuned it out. After about five minutes, the ringing stopped.

Staring at the ceiling, he slowly lifted the bar up, lowered it back down. Again, and again, going through his workout on autopilot.

But his mind wasn't on reps.

It wasn't on building muscle mass.

It wasn't on maintaining his physical strength.

It wasn't on work.

No, he was actually reliving a very, very vivid dream. A dream that had had him waking up with a raging hard-on, a dream that still danced through his mind hours later.

A dream that had starred none other than the very sexy lady who had taken up residence a few floors above him.

A dream about having a taste of that mouth of hers, seeing if she was as soft as she looked, seeing if she tasted as sweet as he thought she'd taste.

As he finished the last rep, he heard footsteps going by the window. He glanced up but couldn't see much more than a pair of tennis-shoe-clad feet and shapely calves. He hadn't managed to get a glimpse of those calves yesterday—he'd been too busy focusing on her mouth, then on her ass, but he knew it was her.

Sara.

She was pacing back and forth.

Back and forth.

On her third pass by his windows, he grabbed a bottle of water and headed for the door. He climbed the stairs that led to his private outside entrance and leaned against the railing as he eyed his new neighbor.

She had her hair scooped up into a stubby ponytail and was staring at her feet as she paced. Halfway down the brick sidewalk, she stopped and turned, staring at the gardens. Judging by the grim look on her face, he had a feeling she wasn't admiring Theresa's pride and joy.

"Everything okay?"

She flinched and went dead white. Her eyes cut to him and he watched a series of emotions flit across her face. Nerves. Something too close to fear for his liking. Determination. Then, finally, recognition.

She was good. He had to give her that.

In the span of maybe three seconds, she went from ready to fight or flee, to giving him a rueful grin. Quinn suspected there were quite a few people that wouldn't have picked up on that quickly hidden fear, even though it caught his attention.

"Pep talk."

"Pep talk." He cocked a brow. "Looks more like pacing."

"Mental pep talk combined with pacing." She rolled her eyes and sauntered his way.

It took a focused effort to watch her face and not the sway of her hips as she drew nearer. Nice hips . . . way nice, sweetly curved, the kind of curves that would cradle a man just right. She had on a pair of black running shorts and a fitted tank top that molded to a set of world-class breasts, big and round, the kind that would fill a man's hands perfectly.

Quinn's hands itched to peel the cloth away from her body. He wanted to see what color her nipples were, wanted to cup her hips and hold her steady as he rocked his cock against her.

"I need to go for a run and I know I need to go for a run but I hate running, so I'm mentally going over all the reasons I need to just do it anyway." Her voice was full of a self-deprecating humor.

He braced an elbow on the railing and shrugged. "If you don't like running, don't do it. Seems pointless to torture yourself if you don't need to."

"Doctors everywhere would hate you for that statement," Sara drawled. "It doesn't matter if people hate to exercise or not . . . they need to do it, right?"

"If you're just looking for exercise, find one you don't hate so much. Find one you like, you wouldn't have to pace and give mental pep talks—you'd enjoy it. If you like it, you're more likely to stick to it." Quinn recognized the sound of his voice, but didn't quite believe the words coming out of his mouth.

Small talk. He was making small talk with his gorgeous neighbor. He was actually engaging in a fucking conversation.

Shit, he was either hornier than he thought or he was still asleep. Quinn didn't do small talk. Quinn *hated* small talk.

"The problem is that I don't like *any* exercise, and trust me, I've tried quite a few. I'm just naturally lazy." She shrugged her shoulders and said, "I'm also a born procrastinator, so I need to just shut up and get this over with."

As she headed down the walk at a slow jog, Quinn remained where he was, admiring the view until she turned and disappeared out of sight.

FOUR

THE offices of the Renaissance Group took up an entire floor. The head of the company sat in his office, staring out the window at Lake Michigan. A thin, nervous man waited in front of his desk.

"Have you found my wife yet?"

"No, James. But I believe we're getting closer," Don Hessig said, shifting from one foot to the other.

Don had worked for James for ten years and in those ten years, he had done a myriad of tasks that hadn't been listed in the job description. Locating James's missing wife had kept him occupied for much of the past two years.

Actually, he spent more time laying a false but convincing trail to keep his boss satisfied.

It wasn't working anymore. For the most part, James had allowed Don to handle things, because he didn't want any undue attention focused on him. For whatever reasons, that was no longer the case.

Spinning around in a custom-crafted leather chair, James faced Don. He lifted his hands, pressing the fingertips of one against the other. In a mild voice, he pointed out, "That is what you told me two months ago. Supposedly you had information that she'd been seen in Billings, Montana. Whatever came of that?"

"It wasn't her. Poor information."

James's face didn't change. He didn't say anything. Didn't even move.

But there was a look in his eyes that had Don wishing he was anywhere but where he was.

"I suggest you be more cautious about how you gather your information, then," James said, his voice silky. "I suggest you verify it before bringing it to me."

"I certainly will." His mind was blank—he was a problem solver by nature, but the sort of problems he was used to solving were the kind written in black and white, or the sort that were aired in a boardroom. Numbers. Give him numbers, figures, facts, and tables any day of the week. "I'm going to talk to my contacts again, run another credit check—"

"She hasn't put anything on credit or even attempted to purchase anything under her name in more than two years. I don't believe she's going to start doing it now." James stared at him, his icy blue eyes devoid of emotion. "I want my wife found, Don. This has been going on for far too long. I've had some matters come up that need my attention, and there are loose ends that must be dealt with before I can deal with them.

"I want my wife found. Now." He paused and then gently asked, "Am I clear?"

Don nodded. "Of course." Without waiting another second, he turned and left the office. He paused at the receptionist's desk, a polite smile on his face. As was customary, he let her know that he would be away from his desk for some time.

As he walked away, his mind was racing.

Other matters—James might have been intentionally vague, but Don knew what those *other matters* were. Or rather, who.

Alison Mather—the governor's daughter. James had set his

eyes on the woman after they met during the summer, but it would be hard for the man to really pursue a relationship when he was still legally married.

It had been long enough that James had legal options open to him, but he hadn't once tried to take advantage of them. Letting his wife slip away just wasn't tolerable. She couldn't *slip* away. James had to *throw* her away.

That was the reason for the renewed interest in his wife. His pride might have allowed James to push her to the back of his mind for a time, but it wouldn't happen again. Pride and the fact that James understood the need to be discreet—while it was acceptable that he desired to find his wife, there were other circumstances surrounding her disappearance that were less than acceptable.

James did not want any attention being focused on those other circumstances.

Or at least he hadn't. But things had changed.

Don didn't know how much time he might have, but he did know he couldn't keep this charade up for much longer.

Locking himself away in the smaller conference room, he settled down at the long, empty desk and took out his laptop. Although he had a computer at his desk, he preferred to handle this matter as privately as possible. He could work undisturbed in the conference room and James wouldn't think anything about it.

James appreciated discretion.

Don appreciated the fact that when he was behind closed doors he didn't have to maintain such a rigid mask. He allowed himself to relax minutely, although like most of the other rooms in the office, the conference room was equipped with video capabilities. He wouldn't put it past James to spy on him as he worked.

With that thought in mind, he brought up his e-mail and settled down to work. But only half of his mind was on his current task. In the back of his mind, he was thinking about plans and options. He worried. He brooded. In the back of his mind, he remembered.

Bruises on pale flesh.

Tears gleaming in dark eyes.

"What happened?"

A low, husky voice shaking with fear . . . possibly anger. Possibly both.

"Nothing." A forced smile, a stilted laugh. *"Just my own clumsiness."*

He also remembered the money. He also remembered the threat.

"One way or another, I want her out of the picture. Permanently. Now . . . you can either take care of the matter, or I will take care of you."

* * *

JAMES Morgan sat alone in his office. Don, the pathetic weasel, had left looking scared enough to piss his pants. Of course, Don was too efficient to do that—it would require a change of clothing and time away from the job, and Don was nothing if not efficient.

It was one reason James hadn't fired him.

The man knew too much, far too much, and he began to present a liability. That was another reason.

That he appreciated Don's usefulness put him in a bit of a quandary. He didn't like the liability, but as far as he was concerned, it was outweighed by Don's pathetic weakness. He'd played into that weakness several years before, and now he was as much a liability to Don as Don was to him.

That pleased him, because he didn't want to have to replace Don.

Good help was hard to come by. Although Don had yet to produce results in this particular area, he was excellent in others. Quick, efficient, discreet, respectful. He understood the value of following orders. He didn't forget the little details. Even fear, like James had just glimpsed in his eyes, wasn't a bad thing. It kept Don on edge.

As far as James was concerned, those qualities were nearly irreplaceable in an assistant.

Much as in a wife.

Some of those qualities had been why he'd married the woman who'd been missing for close to two years. She'd been discreetly beautiful, a very able hostess for the many business functions that went hand in hand with his job. She had an eye for detail, never forgot a face or a name, and when she chose to, she could charm a snake.

Sadly, she too often forgot her place, and that hadn't been acceptable.

A muscle jerked in his jaw as he lowered his gaze to study the picture of her that sat on his desk. It was from their wedding day—she'd looked lovely, her dark brown eyes sparkling with happiness, a shy, sweet smile on her lips as she rested her head against his chest.

His hand closed into a fist. He refrained from hurling the picture out the window, just as he had so often in the past two years. The time to put it away was coming. He hadn't been making idle threats when he told Don that his patience was coming to an end.

It was time that he moved on with his life, and he couldn't do that until he'd dealt with his wife.

He would have done so long before now except it had proven harder to find her than he had originally anticipated.

Much harder.

If Don didn't find her soon, then James would take matters into his own hands.

* * *

It was hotter than hell outside, but Quinn was cold.

Almost shaking with it, he was so cold.

Too close.

Way too close.

His hands had a fine tremor to them as he climbed off his bike. He stood there, staring at them. They were clean, but he could still see blood.

Still smell it.

"God, please, mister . . . don't hurt him. He didn't mean noth-ing by it."

The girl's words had been hard to understand, because her lower lip was bruised and swollen. As was her left eye. She had bruises ringing her arms and wrists.

Quinn had been sitting in the agency car, waiting outside for one Marc D'Angelo to leave his latest girlfriend's apartment. D'Angelo had a nice little rap sheet, ranging from petty theft to assault. He was all of twenty-three and so far, it looked like he had the makings of a career criminal.

By all rights, Quinn could have just taken the door down. A reliable witness had seen D'Angelo entering the house. But Quinn hated doing it that way. He had seen a few little toys littering the cracked sidewalk in front of the apartment. As he had parked his car, he'd heard a baby crying from inside.

So he'd waited.

But then he'd heard a sound that turned his blood cold—a child's cry, followed by a woman's desperate scream, *"Marc, don't, please!"*

That scream was one he already knew was going to haunt his dreams. One more guilty weight he'd have to bear. He should have gone in. Because he hadn't wanted to take down some thug in front of kids, those kids had seen that thug pounding on their mom.

God.

He'd gone through the door and found a child huddling by the couch, holding a crying baby in his arms and sniffling, while across the room, his mother lay on the floor, huddled in a ball.

Something had snapped. Even now, he couldn't quite remember what he'd done. A blur—grabbing D'Angelo. Taking him down. The satisfaction of flesh striking flesh.

Then a hand on his arm—*"Oh, God. Please. You're gonna kill him . . . he didn't mean nothing by it."*

"Does she really believe that?" he muttered to himself. Three hours later and he could still see the tears in her dark eyes as she begged him not to hurt her boyfriend. Begging him not to hurt the bastard who had hurt her.

He pressed the heels of his palms to his eyes, trying to drive the memory out, but another one replaced it. A memory even darker, even uglier than seeing a man beat on a woman.

Elena. Lying on the ground while her blood mixed with the dirt.

Bruises covered her body. Blood. Semen.

In death, her face had been a terrified mask, so severely beaten, he barely recognized her.

A laugh shattered the spell, and Quinn flinched, spinning around. But there was nobody there. The laugh came again and recognition hit. Nausea pooled inside him as he recognized it as Sara's. Distantly, he could hear her voice, and Theresa's.

"Shit." He scrubbed his hands over his face and then jammed them deep in his pockets. He didn't want to see them right now— didn't want to see anybody, talk to anybody, not until he got his head together.

Then you need to move to Antarctica, man. You aren't ever going to get your head together.

He slid through the door, keeping his gaze on the ground. He heard Theresa call out his name, but he ignored her. He needed to get inside. Needed to be alone. Needed to climb into a scalding hot shower and scrub the blood away. Scrub away the blood, and then maybe drink away the memory.

"No. Can't do that." He rubbed the back of his hand over his dry mouth. Couldn't drink the memory away—that was how he'd started that slide down the last time, using alcohol to numb the pain. He'd just have to take it.

Have to live with it.

As he jogged down the stairs, the phone on his belt started to ring and vibrate. He grabbed it, just barely resisted the urge to crush it into the ground under his heel.

It was Luke. He didn't bother answering. He didn't want to talk to *anybody*, including his twin. Not right now.

As he pushed his key into the lock, he used his other hand to flip the phone open and turn it off.

There. Now nobody could call. Alone. He could be alone.

His hand shook as he tried to unlock the door. Shaking too bad. Gut felt like ice. Acid burned its way up his throat. Shaking. Cold. Fuck. *Inside. Get inside.*

"Quinn?"

He froze as Sara said his name.

Squeezing his eyes closed, he gave the key one last desperate twist and, thank God, it unlocked. Without glancing up the steps, without even answering, he pushed the door open.

Blood roared in his ears as he started inside.

A hand touched his shoulder.

He reacted blindly and until he had her body trapped between his and the brick wall of the stairwell, he hadn't even realized he'd moved. Now he found himself staring at Sara Davis, her dark brown eyes wide and locked on his. She gasped, a soft, pained sound, and Quinn jerked back from her, letting her go so suddenly, she stumbled.

"What the hell is the matter with . . ." she started to demand, cradling her wrist to her chest. Then her words trailed off and she stared at him. "Quinn?"

Quinn wasn't looking at her face. He was staring at her wrist. It was red, vibrant, angry, and red already; it looked like a bruise was forming.

A bruise . . . he'd put a bruise on her. He'd hurt her—

The shaking got worse. His vision tunneled down until the only thing he could see was that mark, so ugly against her soft white skin. A harsh, rasping sound hit his ears, and he realized he was gasping for breath, all but sobbing.

Tearing his eyes away from the mark he'd put on her, he looked into her eyes and snarled, "Get the fuck away from me."

* * *

THE door slammed shut in her face.

Part of her wanted to be pissed off.

Part of her was scared, even though she didn't want to be.

But there was an even larger part of her that wanted to cry.

God, his eyes . . . The look in his eyes wasn't one she ever would have expected to see from him. Desperation. Fear. Pain. Fury. Shock. His pupils had been mere pinpricks, and the hand gripping her wrist had been cold, clammy with sweat. And shaking . . . he'd been shaking.

Compassion, concern rose within her. She wanted to knock, wanted to follow him inside and learn what had put him in that state. Soothe it. Fix it.

But even though she usually sucked at doing the wise thing, self-preservation wouldn't let her do what she wanted to. She'd just looked into the eyes of a man on the edge, and she wasn't going to push him over.

She scrubbed her hands over her face and sagged back against the door. "I should have moved. The minute I looked at him, I should have just disappeared."

It had been two weeks since she'd moved into the little apartment on the third floor of Theresa's house. Two weeks of peace and quiet, the nights uninterrupted by shouts or sirens. Two weeks in which she'd only caught the occasional glimpse of her sexy neighbor.

Wounded warrior. She remembered thinking that the very first time she'd seen him, thinking it, then dismissing it because it didn't go with the man. Except she'd been wrong.

He was a wounded warrior and that blunt, gruff exterior, those blank expressions, were nothing but a mask. Something had shattered that mask today and when she looked into his gray eyes, she saw a deep, screaming hell.

Pain. A pain so deep and cold, it left her heart aching. With that mask shattered, when Sara looked into his eyes, she saw a million wounds, the slow-bleeding kind that led to festering and death.

Something hot touched her cheek and she reached up, startled to realize she was crying. Taking a deep breath, she wiped the tears away and then looked at her wrist. It was already bruising. He hadn't been trying to hurt her—she knew that as well as she knew that if he *had* been trying to hurt her, she wouldn't have been able to stop him.

There had been too much strength, too much speed, too much power in him. She'd touched his shoulder and in the blink of an eye, he had her pinned against the wall. It left her shaken how quickly he'd moved, how quickly he had trapped her.

She'd worked too damn hard to let somebody take her off guard like that. To let somebody get in close enough to hurt her, and she hadn't so much as tried to strike back. Of course, she suspected fighting back would have been an exercise in futility.

Once more, she found herself wondering what in the hell it was he did. He didn't set her cop radar off, but he sure as hell wasn't the handyman type that Theresa had made him out to be.

You just need to stay the hell away from him. Stay away . . . and probably move. No. Not probably. Definitely.

Good advice. Shoving off the door, she started forward. Her bare foot brushed up against something and she glanced down, saw the large white envelope with the big UPS symbol emblazoned across it.

Scowling, she stooped and picked it up. That envelope was why she'd followed Quinn down to his apartment when he hadn't heard Theresa calling him. She'd offered to run it down to him. With a sigh, she trudged back up the stairs.

She'd let Theresa handle the surly bastard.
But even as she thought it, she kicked herself.
He wasn't a surly bastard.
He was . . .
It doesn't matter if he's a bastard or not. Stay away from him.
Good advice.

* * *

ONCE upon a time, Sara had been very good at giving advice. She didn't do it much now. The life she now led wasn't the sort of life that put her in contact with many who would listen, even if quite a few of them could use it.

Still, she knew good advice when she heard it. Too damn bad she wasn't very good at *following* good advice.

She'd told herself to avoid Quinn Rafferty. She'd told herself she just needed to move. But she hadn't moved, she didn't plan on doing so just yet, and now she was sitting in the backyard, watching one Quinn Rafferty and wondering about him. She was doing the exact opposite of avoiding him.

Brooding, she sat in the shadows on the deck, watching the man as he paced the backyard. She'd been sitting out there, just enjoying the cool night, staring up at the sky while the full moon played peekaboo behind a bank of clouds.

Then he was there. She hadn't heard him leave his apartment, hadn't heard the door shut. He moved too damn quietly. She pegged his height at a little over six feet, and that body of his was hard, solid muscle—he shouldn't be able to move quiet as a cat, but he did. Restless as a cat, too, it seemed. He had been pacing and prowling the backyard for a good ten minutes.

She sighed and pushed up off the lounge chair. As she moved to the railing, he stopped his pacing and stared at her. She'd been wondering if he knew she was out there, but as their eyes met, she knew the answer without even asking.

He'd known she was there. Known she was there and had been ignoring her. Somehow, she had a feeling this guy was aware of just about everything that happened around or near him.

It was a thought that bothered her.

A lot. Sara had gotten by thus far because most people only looked at the surface, but that wasn't Quinn. He looked below the surface and somehow, she suspected that the lies that fooled so many would be wasted on him.

Silence hung between them as they stared at each other. He started toward her, and Sara had to squash the urge to back away, dart inside the house, and run up to her apartment, lock herself inside. Maybe shove a chair in front of the door for good measure.

Five feet away, he stopped. "I'm sorry," he said, his words flat and hard.

Remembering the pain she'd seen in his eyes, she had to steel herself not to reach out to him. Whatever had been going through his head earlier, whatever ugly secrets his past held, she suspected he needed compassion and understanding and kindness. Things that he'd probably see as pity.

"You should be," she said with a sniff. She was tempted to poke her lip out for good measure, but restrained herself.

He didn't react. Just watched her. Then he nodded and went to turn away.

Sara did the same, brushing her hair back from her face with a sigh.

Halfway to the door, he said her name.

Sara stopped and turned back around, waiting as he mounted the steps. A faded blue T-shirt stretched across his chest and shoulders, clinging to his muscled form. His blond hair fell into his face and her fingers itched to brush it back.

As he moved into the pool of light cast by the porch light, she tucked her hands into her back pockets. He stopped in front of her, closer this time. Too close. No more than two feet away.

Without saying a word, he held out his hand.

Sara frowned at him.

"Let me see your wrist," he said.

There was an odd strain to his voice, and he was so tense, the air around him all but vibrated.

"It's fine," she said huskily.

"Let me see."

He'd stand there all night if that was what it took. Rolling her eyes, Sara pulled her hand out of her pocket and held her arm out in front of her. There was a ring of dark mottled bruises around her wrist.

His breath hissed out between his teeth. "Fuck."

"It looks worse than it feels." She started to let her hand drop back to her side, but he caught it in his hand, gently lifting it up so he could see it better.

A perfectly innocent touch, but for some reason, her heart started to race. She shot him a look from under her lashes. That brooding look on his face was entirely too appealing. Sexy brooders were dangerous.

Mouth suddenly dry, she tugged against his hold and said, "Look, I bruise easy. I always have."

He didn't say anything, and he didn't release her wrist, either. He turned it this way and that, like he was memorizing every last detail of the bruise. His thumb stroked over the flesh and he asked, "Does it hurt?"

"Some, but don't worry about it." Awkwardly, she shrugged. *Geez, get your hormones under control.* Why in the world had her libido just now decided to wake up? She shot him another nervous glance and this time, he looked away from her wrist at the same time.

Their gazes locked. Her heart skipped another beat and she tugged once more on her wrist. He finally let go and she immediately stepped back. It didn't help, putting that distance between them. Hell, it didn't even help that he'd let go of her wrist. She could still feel his hand, warm, his palm calloused, the slow glide of his thumb stroking over her flesh.

Forcing a smile, she said, "I'll just have to make sure I remember not to come up behind you anymore."

"Trust me, you're better off just staying the hell away from me period." Something flashed across his face.

For a brief second, she caught another glimpse at what lay behind that mask he wore, but then it was gone. Quietly, she said, "You didn't mean to do it, Quinn."

"Tell me something, Sara," he said, a cold, ugly smile curling his lips. "Do those words just come naturally to females?"

"What do you mean?"

A weird light glinted in his eyes as he stared down at her. "*'You didn't mean to do it,'*" he quoted back, his voice thick with mockery. "You've got a bruise on you that I bet hurts like hell no matter what you say and how do you respond? '*You didn't mean to do it.*' It's got to be second nature or something. I've heard that line one too many times—a woman gets banged up by a man and she just excuses it away."

That hit a little too close to home. She buried her instinctive response down deep and calmly said, "I've got a bruise on my wrist, sugar. It's just a bruise and I can guarantee you I've done worse to myself just putting away groceries. It's a pretty far sight from you belting me."

He flinched. Like she'd belted *him*. His mouth spasmed and he turned on his heel.

Unable to stop herself, she reached up, touched his shoulder.

He froze.

Moving to stand in front of him, she tipped her head back and studied him. That beautiful face of his, all hollows and angles, was cast into shadow.

"It was an accident—you didn't know I was there and I caught you off guard. You can't really stand there and tell me that you *meant* to put a bruise on me."

"Doesn't matter if I *meant* it or not, *sugar*," he said sarcastically. "I did put a bruise on you."

"Yeah. You did. And you're beating yourself up over it enough. I don't really see any reason to add to it." Planting her hands on her hips, she glared at him. "If it would make you feel better, I suppose I could wail a few times, squeeze out a few tears, or slap you."

He blinked, looking a little startled. Then he smiled—at least she *thought* it was a smile, a faint twist of his lips, there and then gone almost as quick as it had happened.

"No, you couldn't."

"Wanna bet? You know what, come to think of it, it might be therapeutic for both of us if I slapped you once."

"Oh, I bet you could slap me . . . although I got a feeling you'd be more likely to punch than slap." He averted his gaze, staring off behind her. Big shoulders rose and fell as he took a deep breath. When he looked back at her, he had that blank, composed mask settled firmly back in place. "But I was talking about wailing or squeezing out a few tears. I don't see you doing them on command."

"Good point. But if I get mad enough, I tend to cry sometimes. And when I'm pissed off, I can wail like a banshee."

That faint grin twisted his lips again.

It made her heart skip a beat or three. Man, she wondered. Did he ever smile? *Really* smile? She was probably better off not knowing, though. She didn't know if her heart could handle it.

"Is that your subtle way of telling me that I'm pissing you off?" he asked.

"I'm not much for subtle. If you piss me off, I'll let you know." She rolled her eyes and said, "Stop beating yourself up already. It *was* an accident—we both know that. If you'd intended to hurt me, if you didn't care that you had, you wouldn't be beating your-self up over it and you wouldn't be warning me to stay away."

In the faint silvery light cast by the moon, she could just barely make out his face, his eyes dark and unreadable, his mouth unsmil-ing. A muscle jerked in his jaw and he said harshly, "You don't know me."

"No . . . I don't. But I know the kind of men who get off on hurting others, and I know the kind of women who'll just excuse it away. You're not that kind of man. I'm not that kind of woman."

"You've talked to me all of three times and you think you know enough to say that?" he demanded.

Sara shrugged. "Well, you know me well enough to know that I'd probably punch a guy before I'd slap him. And you know me well enough to know I'm not an on-demand crier."

Seconds ticked away as he stared at her. His nostrils flared as he dragged in a breath, his shoulders rising and falling. His lids drooped over his eyes and he tore his gaze away from her.

"You don't know what kind of man I am," he said.

"No, I don't . . . but I think I know what kind of man you aren't. You aren't the kind of man who'd intentionally harm a woman, Quinn. So stop acting like you put me in the hospital or something."

She leaned in, acutely aware of the fact that he had tensed up. The heat of his body warmed her through her clothes, and the scent of him, warm and male, flooded her head. Brushing her lips against his cheek, she settled back on her heels. "I'm going to head in . . . stay out here and beat yourself up if it will make you feel any better. But it's not necessary."

Turning on her heel, she hurried inside before she could talk herself into staying.

He was bad, very bad, for her state of mind.

FIVE

SARA was in one lousy ass mood.

Somebody had seen the bruise on her wrist, despite the fact that she'd made the attempt to hide it under a collection of colorful bangle bracelets, a couple of chain bracelets, and a cuff of hammered silver. It had resulted in Annette, one of the café owners, cornering her in the bathroom and offering to listen if Sara needed an ear.

No. What Sara needed was peace and quiet and the ability to block out unwanted thoughts.

Because Annette's offer had brought back memories, and those memories were never very far from her mind.

"You don't know what kind of man I am."

"No, I don't . . . but I think I know what kind of man you aren't. You aren't the kind of man who'd intentionally harm a woman."

That sort of man was one Sara was all too familiar with. She'd seen that kind of man up close and personal, and Quinn definitely wasn't one of them.

Stalking down the sidewalk, her hand resting on her purse, she tried to blank her mind, but she just couldn't.

Another voice kept playing in her memories. Over and over. This one low, husky, rough with tears.

"You . . . you don't realize what kind of man he is."

The next voice was cynical and flat, but nothing could hide the rage that lurked just below the surface. *"Don't I? He's the kind of man who'd beat a woman. That's not exactly a ringing endorsement of his character."*

"I can't leave him. I can't."

Can't.

No matter what happened.

"He wants you dead . . . You don't know him. You don't know what he's capable of."

Guilt wrapped a fist around her heart, and when she hit Theresa's street, she was all but running. Too bad she couldn't leave the memories behind as easily as that. She'd become a world-class marathon runner if she could outrun the memories. Outrun the past.

She bolted up the stairs of the private exterior entrance and as soon as she was inside started stripping out of her clothes, belt, shoes, jeans, T-shirt. They smelled like food and coffee, desperately in need of a washing. Tossing her belt and phone onto the futon, she left the clothes lying in a puddle on the floor as she made for the bathroom.

A shower. Long and hot. She let the water pour down on her muscles, let it soak her hair, pound against her tense spine. It wasn't until the water started to chill that she climbed out.

But still the memories lingered.

Brooding, she muttered, "It's his damn fault."

His . . . Quinn's. Because she couldn't stop thinking about him, no matter how much she told herself she needed to. There was a mile-long list of reasons she needed to avoid him and all those reasons were tied to her past.

The more she tried not to think about *him*, the more she found herself reliving that past.

* * *

SHE liked being outside.

It was something Quinn had noticed about her over the past few days. Sara liked to sit outside in the evening and stare up at the sky. No matter how late she got off of work, she always came out to the deck and sat there for nearly half an hour.

On Monday, he'd gotten in around midnight and been heading out of the garage when he caught sight of her on the deck, gazing up at the sky. And now here she was again. It wasn't so late tonight, not quite ten thirty. Her hair was wet, so he figured she'd worked and then come home, taken a shower.

He'd been out in the backyard, telling himself that he was just enjoying the cool night after how hot the day had been, but he wasn't quite buying it. He was out here to see her. Lurking in the shadows . . .

"Man, you need to get a grip," he muttered.

No, what he really needed was to get laid. Maybe if he could relieve some of the frustration trapped inside, he could stop mooning over his sexy neighbor. Problem, though. He wanted *her*.

He rubbed a hand down his jaw. Stubble scratched under his hand and he grimaced, raked the thick growth, and tried to remember when he'd shaved. Yesterday. He thought.

He was about to go back inside when she yawned, stretching her arms over her head. Then she shifted on the padded bench and sighed. For reasons he didn't understand, the sound of that sigh, soft and sad, wrenched at his heart.

His feet had already taken him halfway across the yard before he realized he was moving. Moving toward her—when what he needed to be doing was moving in the opposite direction.

She jerked a little as he mounted the steps, her eyes widening, then narrowing as recognition settled in. "You need to wear a bell or something," she told him, a scowl wrinkling her forehead. "People aren't supposed to be that quiet."

Bracing his hips against the railing, he shrugged. "Sorry." He'd learned early on how to be quiet. When his mother had been sleeping off a drunk, the last thing he wanted to do was make too much noise and wake her up.

"How's your wrist?" he asked, forcing the question out before it lodged in his throat.

"It's fine," she told him. She lifted her hand and waggled her fingers at him. She pursed her lips and studied him with narrowed eyes. "Are you done kicking yourself over it yet?"

No. But he didn't say that. He just shrugged.

"I'll take that as a '*no.*'" Sara brushed her bangs from her face and leaned her head back, focusing her attention once more on the sky. "Somehow I get the feeling you spend a lot of time kicking yourself over things."

He stiffened and had to will himself to relax as her brown eyes cut back to his. Studying. Weighing. Measuring. Quinn had done it to others often enough to know when somebody was evaluating him and trying to pick apart the pieces that made him who he was.

He didn't much like it. Shoving off the railing, he crossed the deck and settled down next to her, sprawling his legs out in front of him.

"I'm not much for armchair psychologists," he drawled. "If I spend a lot of time kicking myself, that's my business. Same way it's your business if you want to make yourself go for a two-mile run every day, even though you hate it."

A smile flirted with the corners of her mouth and she cocked a brow. "Point made."

They lapsed into silence and Quinn leaned his head against the railing, staring up at the sky. The stars were barely visible. It had been a while since he'd spent much time back on his dad's ranch in Wyoming, but there, the stars were bright, diamond-bright against the velvet darkness of the sky.

"Can't see much of the stars here," he murmured.

"You can never see the stars very well in a city." She sighed, and there it was again, that quiet sadness.

"I used to live in Wyoming. You could see stars there."

"I've never been there." Then she pushed up off the bench and paced away from him, tucking her hands into her back pockets. "But I'm not really into stargazing. Just trying to relax a little before I go to bed."

He echoed her movements, rising off the bench.

She turned to face him, her eyes unreadable.

"I'm not really into stargazing, either. I came out here because I knew you'd be here."

The only reaction was a faint flicker of her lashes. She didn't smile. She didn't blush. She didn't look away. "Was there something you wanted?"

"Other than to see you?" He closed the distance between them, stopping when he was close enough that he could see the faint flutter of the pulse in her neck, beating wildly against her skin.

"No."

"See me?" Sara cocked a brow at him. "Didn't you tell me a few days ago I'd be better off keeping my distance from you?"

"Yeah, I told you that."

"Hard to do if you come looking for me."

Quinn shrugged. "I don't see you walking away."

"I was here first," she said pointedly.

"So does that mean you want me to leave?"

She scowled at him, her brows drawing together over her eyes, her mouth flattening into a thin line. "I didn't say that. You're the one who told me I should stay away, but here you are making small talk about stars and Wyoming."

"You don't like small talk?"

She shrugged restlessly. "Seems like a waste of time."

"Yeah. It does. So maybe I should stop wasting it." Then he kissed her.

Caught off guard, Sara gasped as his mouth covered hers. Moaned low in her throat as he cupped the back of her neck. Shivered as he rested his other hand on her hip.

His tongue stroked over her lower lip, then pushed inside. A groan rumbled out of his chest and the hand on her hip tightened. Through the thin cotton of her pants, she could feel the heat of his hand, the strength. Leaning into his body, she rose on her toes.

Damn. The feel of all the soft, sweet curves pressed against his body was a sensation so pleasurable, so damned erotic, he almost hurt from it. Somewhere in the back of his head, a voice demanded, *What in the hell are you doing?*

He was doing exactly what he'd wanted to do from the first time he'd laid eyes on her. Kissing her. Feeling that soft, sleek body against his. All those amazing curves lay just inches away and it took everything he had not to let his hands stroke all over her. Everything he had to keep from stripping away her pants, her panties, unzipping his jeans, and then lifting her up, fucking her right there, right on the porch where anybody could see.

She moaned into his mouth and the sound of it, soft and hungry female, went straight to his head. His heartbeat kicked up a few notches. *More . . . damn it, give me more . . .* He slid his hand into her hair and fisted it in the soft, silken strands. Tugging her head back, he kissed her deeper, harder, driving his tongue into her mouth the same way he wanted to drive his aching dick into her body.

In his arms, Sara shivered. She caught his tongue between her teeth and bit him lightly, then sucked on him.

Mindless, he slid his other hand under her shirt. He caught the full, soft weight of her breast in his hand. Through the thin, silky material of her bra, he circled his thumb around her nipple. She arched into his hand, whimpering in her throat.

Tearing his mouth away from hers, he grabbed the hem of her shirt and shoved it upward, baring her breasts. They strained against the silk and lace of her bra, rising and falling rapidly as she gasped for air. He wrapped an arm around her waist and lifted her. Sara cried out, braced her hands on his shoulders. Her knees came up, hugging his hips.

They both groaned as that action had the ridge of his cock nestling snug against the wet heat gathering between her thighs. He dipped his head and buried his face between the full mounds of her breasts, breathing in the soft, sweet scent of her body. "Fuck, Sara . . ."

He'd wanted to do this from the first time he'd laid eyes on her and damn it, he was tired of not taking what he wanted . . .

"Ahem." Somehow, that soft, gentle sound managed to convey a world of amusement.

They both froze. Sara jerked her head up, staring over his shoulder. The porch light was bright enough that he could see her blush. Hell, was it a pretty sight, too. It started at the mounds of her breasts, the blush climbing higher and higher until her cheeks were pink with it. She wiggled around and caught her shirt, lowered it over her breasts. Still, her voice was pretty level as she said, "Hi, Theresa."

He lowered her to the ground, gritting his teeth as her body rubbed against his, a teasing, erotic sensation. Inside the tight confines of his jeans, his cock ached, throbbed. As Sara's feet touched the ground, she backed away and Quinn had to fight to keep from reaching for her again.

Behind them, Theresa murmured, "Hi, yourself. Lovely night out, isn't it?"

Her mild tone didn't do a damn thing to hide her amusement. Sara was still blushing, her ivory cheeks gone pink. Her eyes darted his way and then she smiled back at Theresa. "Very nice night. A little hot, though."

Hot. Yeah, hot *seems to be the right word.* Amused, not entirely sure why, he grinned down at Sara and then glanced at Theresa over his shoulder. "I don't much mind the heat."

"No, I bet you don't." Theresa lifted a brow at him and then gave an utterly fake, utterly unconvincing yawn. "You know, I'd planned on sitting on the deck awhile, but all of a sudden, I'm exhausted."

She disappeared without another word.

Left alone with Sara once more, he studied her face.

She dragged her tongue across her lips and Quinn could have gone to his knees. She started to talk and he had to focus just to understand her words.

"I think I'm going to head on inside."

"Why?" he asked. He slid his hands into his pockets and rocked back on his heels, watching her.

"Because it's hot," she said lamely.

Quinn shrugged. "Wasn't bothering you that much a few minutes ago."

"Maybe the heat got to me." Her gaze dropped to his lips, lingered for a moment, and then she took a deep breath. "I'm thinking a little more clearly now. I really don't need anything complicating my life."

"Complications are a pain in the ass." Something twisted inside him. He didn't fully comprehend it. Frustration. Need. Longing . . . *loneliness.* Smiling bitterly, he said, "You're a smart lady for recognizing that."

He circled around her, careful not to let their bodies touch. Fuck, he hurt, and it wasn't just his damned dick, either.

"Quinn," she called out from behind him, her voice soft and husky.

He stopped at the steps but didn't turn around to look at her.

"Look, it's not you—"

Now he did turn. With a bark of laughter, he turned and looked at her. Hooking his thumbs in his pockets, he said, "Please spare me that trite bullshit. *It's not you, it's me.* It's not like we've got any kind of relationship going and you're trying to give me a nice brush-off. You don't want anything to do with me. I get it. Just leave it at that."

"It doesn't have a damn thing to do with *you*," she snapped, glaring at him. She shoved her hair back from her face and then folded her arms across her chest. "My life is enough of a mess as it is—I don't need to make it worse by getting involved with somebody. It's a complication I can't handle right now."

"Can't? Or don't want to?" Even as he asked, he wondered why he was doing it. She'd made herself clear—he just needed to walk away. He couldn't. He just couldn't. Not without understanding why.

A sad smile curled her lips. "Oh, I want to. Like you wouldn't believe. But I can't *afford* it." She didn't say anything else, just stared at him for a long moment, the air between them hot, heavy, and tense. Then, wordlessly, she slipped inside the house and shut the door behind her.

SIX

"*I can't run away. If I run away, he's going to hunt me down and find me. He'll kill me then.*"

"*And if you stay, he'll kill you anyway.*"

Staying hadn't been an option.

Running was proving to be a lousy one.

"*You don't know what he's capable of.*"

"*He wants you dead.*"

Sara sat at the small table, hunched over a cup of the strongest coffee she could manage. She hadn't slept worth shit the night before. It wasn't unusual for dreams to disturb her sleep, but last night, the dreams had been intense.

Jumping back and forth between dreams of the hot and sweaty variety, featuring none other than the very kissable Quinn Rafferty, to the same nightmares that had plagued her for more than two years.

Troubled, she studied the fading bruise on her wrist. It was still a little sore, and it had that mottled blue and purple rainbow thing going on. Staring at it, she knew she shouldn't find it so hard to make herself stay away from Quinn.

Sexy brooders . . . they were dangerous. She knew that, and Quinn was redefining *sexy brooder.*

She barely knew him, yet she found herself dreaming about him. Thinking about him. Wondering what it was that had caused the pain and sadness she so often saw inside him.

He was good-looking, but she'd known plenty of good-looking men. They had spoken a few times and none of the conversations had lasted more than a few minutes.

So why couldn't she get him out of her mind?

Those erotic, hot dreams from the previous night shouldn't have her so unsettled.

He shouldn't have her so unsettled.

"Can't? Or don't want to?" Quinn had asked.

Man, if that guy had any idea just how much she'd love to have the complication of him in her life . . . Even if it was just a quick, torrid affair. Hell, a fricking one-night stand, even. She'd been living without the things she wanted, the things she needed for so long, she yearned for the chance to reach out and take, gobble up any and every indulgence she could have.

Spending a night under Quinn Rafferty would be one hell of an indulgence, she already knew.

Too dangerous, though. He was too dangerous. She'd recognized that almost from the beginning. If she'd been smart, if she wasn't so damned tired of running, she would have already left St. Louis.

Left Quinn behind before he could become a threat.

"Too late," she muttered morosely. He was already a threat, just not the kind of threat that she was used to avoiding. He was a threat to her sanity, to her heart. He'd gotten to her. The first time she'd looked at him, she'd thought *wounded warrior* and she'd been right. He had scars on his soul. Wounds that still struggled to heal.

She wanted to help.

Wanted to stroke, comfort, soothe . . . and then she wanted to strip that long, rangy body naked and ride him until neither of them could take any more.

She suspected she could get lost in him.

It was a luxury she didn't have and some of the darker dreams from last night had driven that fact home hard. Very hard. She squeezed her eyes closed as one of the more vicious scenes from the nightmares danced through her head. Fists clenched. Bruises, blood, and screams. The echo of a low, ugly voice that promised more pain the next time.

Then the knife. She hadn't even realized she was holding it . . .

"What are you going to do with that knife?"

"Use it on you, if you come even a step closer."

"You don't have the guts." He smiled as he said it.

"Take another step and we'll see if I've got the guts or not."

Her cell phone chirped out a little tune and she was strung so tight, she flinched at the sound. She reached across the table for it and flipped it open, called up the message. It was a phone number. Nothing else. No name.

"Four weeks already?" she muttered, glancing at the date on the phone display. Mentally she tallied the days in her head. *Yep. Four weeks.* Sighing, she repeated the number to herself, over and over, until she knew she had it memorized. Her memory was nearly photographic and even jumbled in with all the other phone numbers she'd memorized over the past two years, she knew she wouldn't have any trouble committing this one to memory.

After she'd memorized it, she called the number and listened as a familiar voice came on the line.

"I'm fine."

"Good. Lose the phone soon." Then, just like that, the phone went dead. Lowering it, Sara sighed and once more huddled over her coffee.

There was another call she needed to make. Reluctantly, she grabbed her phone and dialed.

"It's me."

The other voice on the phone was caustic. "I've got caller ID. I know it's you."

Sara rolled her eyes. "Don't be an ass. Anything going on?"

"Hmmm. I don't know. It's possible. But don't get your hopes up."

Sara knew better than that. Sighing, she pinched the bridge of her nose and said, "Be careful."

"Always."

The call ended and Sara was left in silence, sitting in a sun-drenched kitchen and fighting the urge to cry.

She needed to get up and go through her routine. Make herself go running.

But . . . not yet.

Not just yet.

* * *

THE second he saw her standing in the yard, doing the same thing she did every morning, Quinn knew what he was going to do.

Hell, he'd been thinking about it all night. He hadn't slept a whole lot, which was nothing new. But it hadn't been bloody, vicious dreams keeping him awake.

"Oh, I want to. Like you wouldn't believe. But I can't afford it."

Her words rang in his head and common sense told him he needed to leave her alone. Stay away.

He'd listened to his common sense once before. He'd been listening to common sense when he'd walked away from Elena that last day—common sense, duty, whatever the hell he wanted to call the voice that kept whispering to him that Elena knew what she was doing, that they both had a job to do. He'd listened to common sense, and not his heart, and they'd both paid the price.

He doubted whatever was complicating Sara's life was anything so extreme, although he had every intention of finding out. But he wasn't keeping his distance from a woman he wanted, from a woman who wanted him, over a bunch of bullshit "complications."

Quinn was damn sick and tired of never going after the things he really wanted. He was tired of not listening to his heart. He was tired of being alone. He was tired of living without the things he craved . . . the things he needed. People he needed . . .

If she really didn't want him, fine, so be it. He'd leave her the hell alone. Then at least he wouldn't have another reason to keep asking himself, *What if . . . maybe* and *what might have happened.*

She'd turned to fire when he'd touched her. She wanted him. Which meant what he needed to do was wear her down.

Quinn had dodged bullets, jumped out of airplanes, lived through knife fights, and helped take down some of the most notorious criminals in the world. He'd had people spit at him, shoot at him, threaten to rip his eyes out, cut his dick off.

He knew how to handle tense situations.

He could handle Sara.

He hoped. He tried not to think too hard about it as he dug out a shirt to throw over the cotton gym shorts he'd pulled on earlier.

His cell phone started ringing just as he headed out the door. It was a familiar ring, and one he'd ignored too much the day before. Guilt had him pausing long enough to grab it and flip it open.

"Call back later."

"Nice to talk to you, too, brother. Yeah, I miss hearing your voice," Luke said.

With a snort, he said, "If you want to hear my voice, talk to yourself. We sound the same."

"Well, at least you're talking today."

Quinn angled his head around to look out the window. Yep,

Sara was still doing her mental pep talk and pacing deal. "Haven't much wanted to talk the past few days."

"Usually, when you're *not* in the mood to talk is when you need to be doing it. Something sure as hell has had you worked up and when I try to call? You ignore me."

Identical twins, the two of them had one of those inexplicable bonds, each instinctively knowing when the other one needed him. For a lot of years, Quinn had kept himself closed off from his brother. It was something he'd decided he needed to stop and had been working on it the past year.

But he didn't have time for this right now.

"Save the armchair psychology for somebody else, Luke. I'm fine—had a bad day. I'm good now."

Luke said something else, but the words fell on mostly deaf ears. Quinn was too busy staring out the window, watching Sara's tennis shoes make another lap down the sidewalk. If he had it timed right, she was going to make two more, and then she'd start her run. A thirty-minute run, then she'd return, that excellent body of hers covered with a fine sheen of sweat and a grumpy look on her face.

"Devon and I were wondering if you wanted to come out for a visit."

"Huh?" Quinn tore his gaze away from Sara's legs and focused on the phone. "Come out there? To Kentucky?"

"No, genius. Mars. We moved there earlier in the summer." Luke paused and said, "Yeah, Kentucky . . . as in where I live. You come for a visit. That's what I've been talking about. Are you in outer space or something?"

"Or something," he muttered, rubbing the back of his neck. "Look, I'll think about it. Job keeps me pretty busy."

Luke started to say something else as Sara's pacing stopped. *Shit.* Interrupting his brother, Quinn said, "I gotta get, man. I'll call you later."

It wasn't until he was jogging up the steps that he realized something—he'd just lied to his brother. Well, not exactly lied. Not outright at least. One of those lies of omission. The freelancing he did managed to keep him pretty busy, but he had enough money saved up from the last few jobs that he could take a few weeks off, probably longer, and be just fine for it.

It wasn't the job that kept him from going.

It was Sara.

* * *

I hate this.

I hate this.

I hate this.

It was the same mantra she did every time she ran, the same mantra she'd still be saying if she was doing this shit in five years. Hate was heat. Hate was anger. Anger was good, because it helped dull the fear. Helped her forget about the worries, the regrets about the life she'd lost. She channeled it, fed it into someplace deep inside her soul that she kept hidden away, and she hoped that one day soon, she'd be able to vent all that pent-up rage.

Feet pounding on the pavement, she had settled into a steady pace by the time she hit the end of the street. She wasn't ever going to win any marathons, but she could run a few miles without collapsing, which was a far cry from the girl she'd been a few years ago. She might huff and puff and wheeze like she was dying, but she could make the run.

Somebody drew alongside her and she automatically edged over to let him pass. When he didn't, she glanced over.

It was Quinn.

"Mind if I join you?"

If she said anything, she was likely to start babbling. Assuming she had the breath to run and talk at the same time. It wasn't anything she'd ever tested before. She always ran alone.

I always do everything alone . . .

Jerking her thoughts away from that depressing fact, she shrugged in response.

"Is that a yes or a no?"

"It's an *I don't care but I can't talk and run very well at the same time* shrug," she said, gasping every other word.

Quinn grinned at her. "You know, you really could find some way to stay fit that you didn't hate."

Sara stubbornly shook her head. The point of her staying fit wasn't to *enjoy* it. She didn't *want* to enjoy it. It was just another change that she'd been forced to make to her life, and she kept track of all those little changes. Because at night, she sometimes lay awake listing them and thinking of ways to make the bastard responsible pay—

"What about swimming?"

She scowled at him.

"Sorry. The talking and running thing?"

"Yep."

They fell into silence, a surprisingly easy silence. Although she hadn't noticed him running before, he had no trouble keeping pace—hell, he wasn't even breathing hard. Barely sweating.

One of those evil people who made it look easy.

She focused on the sidewalk in front of her instead of him, tried to find that semi-aware state she fell into when she worked out. But it didn't come that easy and she kept falling out of tune with her silent mantra. Every time she'd finish the line, she'd find herself glancing over at Quinn.

Or his arm would brush against hers.

Or she'd feel him looking at her.

And it seemed like he looked at her a *lot*—even more than he looked where he was going. Man, if she tried to do that? Look in any other direction but the one in front of her? She'd probably trip over her feet and fall flat on her face. Athletic grace wasn't one of her strong suits.

Seemed to be one of his, though. He ran easily, his muscles shifting and flexing smoothly. By the time they reached her destination, a small neighborhood park about a mile and a half from the apartment, she was slick with sweat, her breaths coming in harsh, ragged pants. He hadn't really even broken a sweat and his breathing was about as level as hers was when she walked across the room.

Slowing to a walk, she shot him a dark glare.

"What?"

"I hate athletic people."

"This exercise thing you've got is confusing," he said. He was smiling as he said it, that faint little half smile, the one that sat on his face like he really wasn't used to smiling a lot.

She was trying not to think about that smile, though. Or how his mouth had felt against hers . . . *Good job not thinking about it, Sara.* Bracing her hands on her hips, she sucked in another deep breath and tried to calm her breathing a bit more before responding. "What's so confusing about it? I hate exercising and I hate athletic people who make it look so easy."

Quinn shrugged. "Still confusing. If you hate it so much, why do you run every day?"

"Because I don't want to be out of shape," she said, shrugging.

His eyes dropped, lingered on her chest, and then made a slow, leisurely journey over the rest of her body. Then that smoky gaze returned to hers and he murmured, "Oh, trust me. Your shape is just fine."

She blushed.

Unsure what to say, she tore her eyes away from his. "I have to head on back—have to shower before I go into work."

"You never leave until two. You've got time," he said, as he fell into step along with her.

"How do you know when I leave?"

"Because I've seen you doing it."

Frowning, she slowed her pace and looked over at him.

He cocked a brow. "What?"

"You frequently pay attention to when I head out for work?"

He reached up and touched a finger to her lower lip. "I frequently pay attention to you."

Her mouth went dry.

"I pay attention to you period. Haven't you noticed that yet?" Moving in closer, he stared into her eyes and murmured, "Whether you're leaving for work, or whether you're out in the yard pacing and doing your mental pep talk before you go running. Even though I tried to tell myself not to, I keep doing it. Can't help it. If I'm not out working, then it seems like I'm looking for you. It's getting to be a habit and trust me, that's really weird for me."

"Then why are you doing it?"

"Because I can't help it," he muttered. He started to lower his head and then stopped, swore. "Shit. When I kiss you again, I'd rather not do it in public."

Those words rang in her head the entire way back. *When I kiss you again.*

When.

Not *if.*

Her heart raced within her chest. The sensation wasn't an unpleasant one, although it had been years since she'd felt this kind of anticipation. While it wasn't unpleasant, it was troublesome. Worrisome.

Careful.

She had to be careful.

* * *

THAT caution of hers was back in full force. Quinn ran along next to her, watching the way she tried not to watch him. In his mind, he ran through a dozen scenarios that might explain just why she was so determined to keep her distance.

Most of them he trashed before they even fully formed.

He didn't see her as a woman struggling to get over a broken heart—just didn't feel right to him. He damn well *hoped* that wasn't the case, because he really hated to think he was chasing after a woman who was on the rebound.

It definitely wasn't because she wasn't interested. Quinn had his share of arrogance, but still, he was too honest with himself for self-delusions. He knew when a woman wanted him. Sara definitely wanted him.

Maybe she was married, separated from her husband . . . even as that idea had him wanting to break something, he pushed it aside. Again, it didn't feel right.

Quinn was too often quick to judge people, but he had reasons—he was good at reading people. If Sara was involved with somebody, she'd make sure he knew. That was just the sort of person she was.

As they drew close to home, an idea danced briefly through his mind.

He *could* find out what her story was. Put together the pieces so he could figure out how to handle this. How to handle her.

She was guarded, something he'd picked up on right away, and he suspected she wouldn't want to tell him what her story was. That didn't mean he couldn't find out.

One thing stopped him, though.

He had secrets of his own, and if somebody went behind his back to find out those secrets, it would piss him off something awful. And . . . well, if it was somebody he knew, somebody he wanted to trust, it would hurt.

He wanted her to trust him, know him.

He couldn't stand the thought of hurting her.

So he'd wait. See if he could get her to trust him enough to tell him.

Trust . . . Man. He wanted her to trust him. He wanted to trust her. Bizarre. Other than his dad, his brother . . . and maybe Elena, he couldn't think of people that he'd actively *wanted* to trust.

As they came to a stop in front of Theresa's big old house, Quinn kept his hands to himself as Sara bent over and braced hers on her knees. Her shoulders rose and fell as she dragged in harsh, ragged pants of breath.

"Easier to catch your breath if you stand up straight," he said, wiping the sweat off his brow with his forearm.

Sara shot him a dirty look and stayed exactly where she was, her breaths coming in harsh, high-pitched gasps. He frowned, listening closer and wondering what it sounded like when people wheezed. Amused and concerned at the same time, he muttered, "You're awful damned stubborn."

"Thank you." Her breaths came a little easier. After another fifteen seconds, she straightened up and met his gaze.

He decided he rather liked that—she met his gaze easily. Quinn wasn't exactly an easy person, and he knew it. A lot of people didn't like looking him in the eye, but Sara didn't seem to have much trouble doing it. She met his gaze levelly and stared right back at him without blinking.

Silence stretched out between them. She didn't seem in any hurry to break it, although for some reason, he did. He wanted to talk to her. *He* wanted to talk to her. Quinn never wanted to talk. But as he stared back at her, he realized he had to fight to keep quiet.

Questions burned inside him. He wanted to ask her if she'd mind if he went with her tomorrow when she did her run. He wanted to ask her where she worked. How old she was. What she liked to do. It was unfamiliar, this desire to talk, to get to know her . . . to get close.

Quinn avoided getting close to people like the plague—those he *was* close to ended up like that despite his efforts otherwise. Luke, their dad, Theresa . . . even Elena. *Elena*—

It hit him, out of the blue. Guilt, followed closely by grief. *You stupid fuck, you can't be doing this.* He couldn't stand here staring at Sara, wanting Sara, while memories of the one woman he'd loved danced through his mind. Did he even have the right to want Sara? Did he deserve to?

More questions, questions he had no idea how to answer.

Even as he struggled to handle everything rushing through his mind, the door opened and Theresa called out. "Quinn, Martin keeps trying to call you. Said if you don't call him back this time, he'd come out here and talk to you."

Fuck. He'd been ignoring the calls from the agency for a few days now. He knew Martin well enough by now to know that if the guy was that serious, he probably needed to see what was going on.

"Who's Martin?" Sara asked, lifting a brow.

"Sort of my boss," Quinn said, sighing. He shoved his damp hair back. "I better go, see what he wants."

"Probably for you to work—that's usually what bosses want." A smile flirted with the corner of her lips.

Quinn found himself wanting to bend over her and press his mouth right there, right where that faint smile formed.

So what if she'd decided he'd just complicate her life? He could complicate it in all the right ways if she'd just give him half a chance.

At least for a while.

A while . . . like you did with Elena. Yeah, you complicated her life, all right. The voice jeered inside his head and a wave of nausea rose up to slam him straight in the gut.

A muscle jerked in his jaw and he swallowed against the knot in his throat. Voice gritty, he muttered, "I've got to go."

A frown darkened her face as he turned away.

Sara scowled at Quinn's retreating back and muttered, "The man has a hot/cold switch I can't quite figure out."

One minute he was teasing her, smiling . . . she thought he had even been thinking about kissing her, despite what she'd told him about not being able to afford him in her life.

She had certainly been thinking about him kissing her. Thinking about how it would feel, how he would taste . . . whether or not he'd try. If he had tried, she would have let him. She would have enjoyed it. Then later, she probably would have kicked herself.

But it would have been good while it lasted.

Then he went and pulled some iceman act, pulling back and away while something cold and ugly moved through his eyes. For a brief moment, he'd stared at her almost like he didn't quite recognize her, and then when he did, he'd flinched.

Sighing, she rubbed a hand over her chest and took another deep, slow breath. "You need to just stay the hell away from him," she muttered. "Just like you'd already decided."

Yes. She definitely needed to stay away.

It wasn't going to be all that easy, if he kept looking at her like he wanted to kiss her. But if he could just keep that iceman act handy, she could probably manage it.

* * *

"I've grown tired of your incompetence."

Don flinched at the sound of the scathing voice on the other end of the line. "James, truly, I'm doing everything I can think of, considering the restraints I have to work with, the obstacles that keep popping up."

Restraints like keeping you from finding out what I'm really doing.

Obstacles like lies and subterfuge to keep you from finding her.

Don knew that if James had been any less arrogant, he would have already given up on having Don find her. Then he would have taken care of it himself. But James's arrogance blinded him—he couldn't imagine one of his employees betraying him. Especially considering the leverage he had over Don.

He clenched a fist, forced it to open. He could handle this. James would never suspect him of anything.

"Clever men know how to handle restraints. They expect obstacles and deal with them accordingly. Since you're obviously incapable, we're taking a different approach."

"A different approach . . ." Okay, James would never suspect him, but he had obviously run out of patience. *Careful, Donnie. You gotta be careful here.* "James, you realize we would need to proceed with caution. Your wife isn't going to be as easily satisfied as the police. Don't forget there are other issues."

The moment he said it he knew he'd made a mistake. James's angry voice came back over the line, icy and cold. "Do you think I'm a fool? You think I've forgotten anything?"

"Of course I don't think you're a fool. I know you fully understand those other issues. There is a lot at stake here for you and I'm just trying to protect your best interests. That's what I do." He kept his voice meek and consoling, using that wheedling tone he hated so much. It was effective, as he had expected it to be.

"Of course. Yes. I understand the need to be cautious, but caution is one thing. Cowardice is another." There was a moment of silence and then the sound of paper rustling. "You realize that this is trying my patience, don't you, Don? Two years. This has gone on for two years."

"I know, James. You've been very patient." James had been patient, but Don wasn't fool enough to think it was anything magnanimous on his part. He hadn't wanted the extra attention, hadn't wanted anybody to know that his wife had up and disappeared.

Disappeared and stayed gone for two full years.

Two years—a hell of a long time to keep this charade up. Although after the first few months, it hadn't been that bad. Not until now. Not until the past few weeks. Early on, Don had been forced to keep up this tap-dancing routine, lying to the man who signed his checks, playing a risky game and knowing it wouldn't go well for him if he screwed up. Risky games, he amended silently. Too many—he was juggling too many chain saws in this game and if he got through without dropping one, it would be nothing less than a miracle.

He'd managed it, though, and had started to breathe easier. James's interest seemed to focus elsewhere, and he'd been satisfied with the half-assed reports that Don had passed off to him semi-regularly.

Then things changed. Suddenly, drastically, things changed, and once more, Don had to figure out the best way to get through this mess without having it blow up in his face. There were certain things he had no control over—certain things on a specific time-table. So very little that left him maneuvering room. So very little.

Sweat beaded on Don's upper lip as James said, "Just be aware—my patience is rapidly coming to an end."

The call disconnected and Don lowered the phone, staring at it nervously. Damn it, he didn't know what to do. This wasn't the sort of mess he had signed on to handle.

But how could he walk away? Anytime he tried to even consider it, he remembered the bruises. The blood. Soft white skin swollen and discolored.

Don didn't see himself as a particularly strong man, and definitely not a brave one. He was a numbers man, a facts man. A knight in shining armor, he was not.

Truly, there was only so much he could do. Only so much that he could be expected to do. Only so much he knew how to do.

* * *

JAMES Morgan disconnected and tossed the phone to the desktop, eying the neatly typed list that rested on the blotter. He'd been debating this next step over and over for quite some time.

It was completely unacceptable for his wife to remain hidden for as long as she had, but up until the past few months, he'd forced himself to wait. To bide his time.

He drummed his fingers on the arm of his chair, staring out his window at the glass-and-concrete canyons of Los Angeles. It had been two years. Legally, he could've started divorce proceedings after one year. It would be a time-consuming process of forcing a spouse who had abandoned him. So many things he'd have to do that would require he share his private business with others. He would much rather find his wife and deal with her his way.

Quietly, of course. He sneered, remembering Don's comments about proceeding with caution. Foolish little weasel. Nobody understood the need for caution more than James. He had to handle this quietly, but he would handle it.

It was hard enough to deal with the cops under good circumstances. Harder still under bad circumstances. A rich man like him, and his wife disappeared. The police would automatically assume he had something to do with it. He'd already dealt with that once, and he had no desire to catch their interest again.

So he had kept calm, remained quiet, and trusted Don to do his job. Sooner or later, she'd mess up. Sooner or later, he'd find her. Then he would deal with her.

Deal with the humiliation of having her leave him. She'd pay for that. She'd pay for all the inconveniences he'd suffered. And it would be sweet—now that the heat of his rage had passed, once he did find her, he would be able to thoroughly enjoy her punishment.

Vengeance, after all, was a dish best served cold.

Don, as James had expected, still had no news. If by some slim chance there *had* been news, James would have been rather surprised. Very little surprised him, because he knew people. He understood their motivations, how they thought, how they reacted, what drove them to succeed or fail.

It had taken some time, though, to realize why Don had failed, time and again. Don wasn't finding James's wife because he didn't truly *want* to. It was a sobering realization and one that had him picturing using Don's skinny, ratlike face as a target for his many frustrations.

"James? Am I interrupting?"

He glanced up and realized he wasn't alone. Pushing back from the desk, he made himself smile. "Not at all, Alison. You're never an interruption."

SEVEN

"*You have to leave. Take as much money as you can, don't use your credit cards. Don't get a P.O. box. You need a job where they pay you cash, because if you pay taxes, he can find you like that. You can't use a regular cell phone—get one of those pay-as-you-go.*"

"*How do we stay in contact?*"

"*I'll have a phone, too. We'll stay in contact.*"

"*How long? How long do we have to do this?*"

Blister packs were a creation of the devil, Sara thought as she used a knife to slice open the prepaid cell phone's package. She barely missed nicking her finger and ending up dropping the knife.

It was the one day a week she had off. After her new cell phone charged for a while, she was taking the old one to Best Buy and tossing it in the recycle bin. She'd already wiped every last call from it, then took the added precaution of wiping it down so that none of her fingerprints would be found on it.

Using gloves, she'd opened a new box of sandwich bags, put the cell phone and cord inside one bag, and then tucked that bag into another. She'd used the outer bag as a "glove" of sorts when

she dumped it, keeping her prints off the phone and the bag that
held it.

Even if somebody was so inclined to go through the damned
recycle bin, there was no way to link it back to her. Paranoia,
it was a lovely way to live. She knew all of her precautions were
probably overkill, but she felt better doing them.

Once she managed to get the fricking blister pack open and the
phone out, she plugged it in to charge. Then she settled down with
a map she'd bought a few days earlier.

Plotting out her next route, figuring out her next move. It
wasn't something she really wanted to do, but she didn't have
much choice.

She'd been in St. Louis for close to three months now. It was
time to move on. It was harder to think about than she'd anticipated, which meant she'd already waited too long.

Too long, and a huge part of the reason started with the letter Q.
Although how in the hell that had happened, she didn't know. They
hadn't so much as had a date. Other than that one very excellent
kiss, they'd never even touched. Of course, during that very excellent kiss, they'd managed some very excellent touching as well.

It's not the quantity of the time . . . it's the quality.

Morosely, she muttered, "Why couldn't he have been a lousy
kisser?"

If he had been awful at kissing, no matter how hot he looked,
she wouldn't still be having all the hot and sweaty dreams she'd
been having. But he was a very excellent kisser.

Still, kisses shouldn't be enough to slow her down, make her
change her routine—she couldn't let them be.

Leaving shouldn't feel so wrong.

Leaving *him* shouldn't feel so wrong.

How had he become such a dominating presence in her life?
She just didn't get it. No dates. They never called each other. They
knew next to nothing about each other.

Well, not entirely nothing. He knew she hated exercising and made herself do it anyway, and she knew that fact amused the hell out of him. He had gone running with her two more times in the past week, appearing silently out of his apartment in the basement while she stood out in the side yard. He ran alongside her and when she grumbled under her breath about how much she hated running, he teased her.

She knew he had a protective streak in him that probably should have her backing off, yet it was oddly appealing. Maybe it was because it seemed like some old-world chivalry more than anything else—something that should have seemed out of place with him, but instead, it fit.

She'd seen him come up out of his apartment to help Theresa carry in groceries. There had been a few nights when she'd gotten off the bus to find him waiting there—it might have freaked her out to some extent, except she had a feeling he was . . . well, watching out for her, in the protective kind of way, not in some uber-creepy stalker sort of way.

It had been a damn long time since she'd felt protected, and if it was anybody other than Quinn, it probably *would* have freaked her out. She didn't want people watching out for her, didn't want people noticing when she did things. Hell, she didn't really even want people to notice her, and for the most part, they didn't. After spending more than half of her life being the center of attention in some way, shape, or form, she had perfected the art of blending into the background.

It was wasted on Quinn. He noticed everything, it seemed . . . from what time she got off the bus, to what time she'd start her workout. She was getting too damned predictable—he had her timed down to practically the minute.

She hated that she'd become so predictable. She liked change, but she wanted it on her conditions. Changing just because she had no other choice only served to piss her off.

Lately, she longed for some kind of consistency, some kind of normalcy. And she longed for the chance to spend time with him, even though she knew that wasn't smart.

"Girl, you have got to stop thinking about him," she muttered, pinching the bridge of her nose. She shot a look at the clock and swore, realizing she'd spent the past half hour daydreaming about Quinn instead of taking care of priorities.

Pushing him out of her mind took a concentrated effort, but she finally managed to plot out several potential moves, memorizing each one, making mental notes after consulting assorted bus and train schedules.

It was nearly five by the time the phone had taken a sufficient charge, and she took a few more minutes to activate it, yet another tedious task that she'd gotten used to. Just like moving every few months. Just like memorizing bus and train schedules. Just like adapting to a new city and the minute she was used to things, changing them all over again. Just like sending out a text message that held nothing more than her new phone number. Just like making those rare calls where she hoped for good news, even as she knew it wasn't going to happen.

Tucking the new phone into the clip on her belt, she took the plastic-bagged old one and dumped it into the small purse she carried. A glance at the clock assured her she'd have time to catch the Metrolink if she hurried.

She was jogging down the front steps when Quinn pulled up in front of the house. His motorcycle was a shiny, slick piece of work, all black paint and silver chrome.

Geez, he was the living embodiment of a girl's bad-boy fantasy—worn jeans that clung to long, lean legs, his wheat blond hair just a little too long, a heavy growth of stubble darkening his face. Straddling that bike, he made a picture that was almost too perfect to be real.

Oh. Oh, man, girl, you gotta be careful here . . .

Her heart skipped a beat as she eyed him on the bike, then it jumped into her throat as he turned his head and met her gaze.

A slow smile curled his lips, but that wasn't what had her heart lodged just above her trachea.

It was the very vivid, very ugly black eye.

Screw being careful. She strode over to him and caught his face in her hands, turning it to the side to better study the bruise. It spread out over his cheek and there was swelling as well as discoloration.

"What happened?" she asked, unaware that her voice had gone flat; unaware that she was gingerly probing the bone just under his eye with gentle fingers.

The only thought in her mind was that somebody had hurt him.

"Got hit," Quinn said easily. He'd been checked over for injuries often enough to recognize when it was being done by a professional. The calm, practical tone of her voice, the steady and skilled way she examined his bruise, they both said, loud and clear, that she had training, although he wasn't exactly sure what kind. Something medical.

He could have told her that he'd already been subjected to a quick examination by a paramedic earlier, but that might make her stop touching him. So he sat there and enjoyed the feel of her fingers, cool and competent, on his face.

"Yes, Quinn. I can see that you got hit," she said, tongue in cheek. "What I'm wondering is why . . . ?"

"Got in somebody's way and the guy wasn't too happy about it."

The guy had been built like a fucking Mack truck, too. Quinn's face hurt like a son of a bitch. Up until he'd seen Sara heading out, the only thought in his mind had been taking some Motrin, putting a bag of ice on his face, and collapsing into bed.

It was amazing what just the sight of her did to him. How in the hell could a woman manage to both soothe and excite at the same time? Sara managed it, though. His blood heated and his heartbeat sped up and at the same time, the ache in his head started to recede. By the time Sara finished looking him over, he was no longer in the mood to fall into bed, unless she took the fall with him.

"You done playing doctor?" he asked, keeping his tone light.

That blank mask appeared on her face and the smile she gave him was the same empty, polite one she'd give a stranger. He hated that smile. He wanted the real one, the one that made her eyes light up.

"I need to make my diagnosis first—I say you'll have one hell of a headache later on," she said, keeping her tone light.

"Already do. Or did. It's not so bad now . . . but if you want to kiss me, that might help." He reached out and toyed with the top button on her shirt.

"If it's not too bad, then you don't really need me to kiss you, do you?" She sidestepped neatly, taking herself and her buttons out of his reach.

"I think I heard somewhere about how it's always a good idea to kiss a pretty lady." He glanced at her purse, a small affair that settled neatly on her hip. The strap cut diagonally across her breasts and she kept her hand on it, a light, easy touch, but one that made him think she'd either had a purse stolen before or she was just used to the threat. "You heading out?"

"Yeah. Thought I might go down to Crestwood Center. It's my day off, thought I'd pick up a book or two, get some pizza." Absently, she reached up and started toying with the button the same way Quinn had been doing.

He stared at her hand and when she saw where he was looking, she blushed and lowered it to her side. Quinn felt a grin tugging on his lips. Man, what he wouldn't give to see her slip that button free. Then the next. Then the next . . . revealing more and more of that soft, ivory skin.

"Want a ride?" he asked, forcing his mind away from her buttons and her soft ivory skin.

She blinked. Glanced down at the bike and then up at him. That careful, blank mask look fell away from her eyes and she gazed at him with blatant wariness written all over her face. "Ahh . . . I was going to catch the Metrolink."

"Why?" He flicked a look at his watch and then smiled at her. "You'll have to run to make it, and you hate exercising."

"Oh, now that's clever, Quinn."

*   *   *

AM *I on a date*? Sara wondered.

She stood in the women's restroom, staring at her reflection and trying to figure out the answer to that question. It shouldn't be such a tricky one, but it was.

Granted, it had been a long time since she'd done the dating bit. Even then, she'd been more on the fringe of the dating scene. And nobody had ever grabbed her attention the way Quinn did. Her attention, her libido . . . more.

A group of girls came in, giggling, chattering, and blushing.

One of them was looking over her shoulder as she did. "Man, did you *see* him? He's just so *hawt*."

"I wonder how he got that black eye."

Sara smiled at her reflection as the girls broke up into groups, some lingering by the mirror to fluff hair and fuss with makeup. A few drifted toward the stalls.

"You think he's got a girlfriend?"

One of them rolled her eyes and said, "Stacy, he's *old*."

Stacy, a willowy blonde, gave a sigh. "He's not *old*. I bet he's only maybe ten years older than we are. Fifteen, tops."

If they were talking about Quinn, and she was pretty sure they were, then Sara suspected they were looking at a bigger age gap than that. These kids wouldn't care—Sara remembered being that age, remembered being utterly convinced of her own maturity.

Sighing, she brushed her hair back from her face and then set her shoulders. Coming in here to hide from Quinn and try to settle herself was only going to work if he didn't realize she was hiding. If she lingered too much longer, he would figure her out. She circled around the girls and slipped out of the bathroom.

Quinn was waiting on the opposite wall just down the corridor, his eyes on hers. She paused by the water fountain to get a drink and as she straightened, a tired-looking young woman intercepted her. "Excuse me, miss . . ."

Sara politely listened to the girl's hard-luck story, all the while eying the worn clothes, the lines of strain fanning out from her eyes. Before the woman had finished, Sara dipped a hand into her pocket. She pressed a ten into the woman's hands. Tears welled in the woman's eyes.

Uncomfortable, Sara moved to go around her.

Quinn watched her with a cocked brow before glancing over her shoulder to look at the other woman. From the corner of her eye, Sara could see the woman duck her head and shuffle around them, moving away at a fast clip.

"You realize that plenty of people will hand you those stories just to get you to shell out the cash—feeding you whatever lie they think will tug your heartstrings," Quinn said.

As they started down the corridor, Sara shrugged. "I know. But if she's just bullshitting me, that's on her. I tried to help—best anybody can do."

"And if you see her walking into a liquor store a half hour from now?"

"Same response . . . I realize she could be lying. But her actions have no effect on mine." She shrugged again.

"So if you see her walking into a liquor store, you're not going to get pissed, not going to feel a little manipulated?"

She pursed her lips, thinking about it. "I think I'd probably feel sorry for her. If that's her idea of really living, then she definitely deserves some pity."

Behind them, she heard some giggles and glanced back. The group of girls from the bathroom trailed along after them. The blonde Stacy looked Sara over from head to toe. One of her friends elbowed her. "I think I broke somebody's heart just now," she said, glancing up at Quinn. "There were some girls in the restroom sighing over some *hawt* guy in the hall, wondering how he got his black eye. One of them was curious about whether or not you had a girlfriend."

His expression didn't change, but there was a gleam in his eye. "Some *hawt* guy? What makes you think it was me?"

"I didn't notice anybody else that fit the description of *hawt* and had a black eye." Sara was pretty sure that Quinn fit the definition of *hawt* down to a *T*. Hell, the guy could have written the definition.

He snorted, still staring straight ahead.

Sara wasn't sure, but she thought he just might be blushing a little. There was the faintest red tinge along his high cheekbones.

Unable to resist, she hooked an arm through his and grinned up at him. "I heard rumors that you have a knack for making teenage hearts flutter."

"What?" He scowled down at her.

"The girl across the street . . . Trilby, I think. Theresa says the girl's got a thing for you."

The red became more pronounced—oh, yeah. He was definitely blushing. "Trilby's a kid."

"Doesn't mean you can't make her heart go pitter-pat."

Quinn stopped in his tracks. Since she still had her arm hooked through his, she had to stop, too. Tipping her head back, she smiled up at him, watching as his brows drew together, as the blush spread across his tanned face.

"Pitter-pat?" he echoed.

"Yeah . . . you know, gets a little uneven, does a little racing, makes the blood rush . . . pitter-pat."

She was messing with him, Quinn realized. It was written all over her expression—the gleam in her eyes, the wide grin on her face. Hell. He thought his heart was about to start doing some of that pitter-pat shit. He wasn't used to people teasing him—other than Luke, and maybe Jeb on occasion, it wasn't something people did. Not with him.

Reaching up, he caught Sara's chin. Pressing his thumb against her lower lip, he said gruffly, "I'd be a lot more interested if it was *your* heart that was doing the pitter-pat thing." Then he replaced his thumb with his mouth, kissing her quick and light.

Pulling away after two seconds took a hell of a lot of control. But he did it. As they started walking down the mall corridor, Sara sighed. He slid his hand down and caught hers. She twined their fingers and then glanced up at him. "Don't worry, Quinn. You make my heart do that pitter-pat thing quite a bit."

* * *

ONE of these days, he just might figure out the puzzle of Sara Davis, Quinn told himself.

One of these days.

She talked like she wanted him to keep his distance, then she flirted with him in the middle of the damn mall. Teasing him. Smiling at him. Making *him* smile.

She moved with the streetwise confidence of somebody who'd had her fair share of rough times, but then she gave money to a woman after a ten-second sob story. Quinn had no idea if the girl had truly needed the money or not. He had a pretty good bullshit radar, thanks to his mother—that woman had conned hundreds of people out of money.

But he'd been too focused on Sara's response and hadn't spent more than five seconds looking at the other woman.

She seemed determined to keep her distance from people, but right now, she was standing close to the checkout counter in the bookstore, talking with another woman about books. The other woman had picked up three books on Sara's recommendation— Quinn could understand that. Sara had gotten very animated when she started discussing books, grinning, her eyes glowing.

How stupid was it to feel a little jealous of the fact that books made her smile like that?

He wanted to be responsible for putting a smile like that on her face.

Wanted to flirt with her, like she'd been flirting with him, but he was clueless about how to do it. Flirting too often struck him the same as small talk—a waste of time. Something two people used when they were trying to figure out if they wanted to roll around on the sheets together or not.

Quinn never saw the point of wasting the time—if he was attracted to a woman, he might want to sleep with her. Five minutes of conversation tended to answer that for him—if she talked so much it put him into a boredom-induced coma, or if the shit she talked about revolved around her hair, her clothes, her shoes, her makeup . . . well, he'd move on. He didn't need to waste time flirting to figure it out.

But if he could figure out how to handle it, it wouldn't feel like a waste with Sara. Not if he could make her smile. Not if he could get that soft look to come back into her eyes.

Hell. How fucking hard could it be? He doubted he'd be able to slip her a bunch of smooth lines . . . they'd twist and tangle on his tongue and he'd end up looking like an awkward loser. But there were other ways to flirt, right?

Idly, he glanced around the bookstore and wondered if they had something along the lines of *Flirting for Dummies* or *The Complete Idiot's Guide to Flirting with the Opposite Sex.*

A man who knew how to disable bombs, build bombs, hotwire

damn near any vehicle known to man could figure out how to flirt. He thought.

Of course, the tricky part was figuring out just how to do it.

He already knew he could make her laugh. Maybe he could just try to build on that. And of course while it became glaringly obvious to him that he was failing at the flirting, maybe it wouldn't be too obvious to her.

* * *

HE made her laugh.

For some reason, Sara hadn't expected that. Even though she'd spent enough time with him over the past week or so that she'd already glimpsed some of that dry, biting humor, it still managed to catch her by surprise.

Chuckling over the comment he'd made about a couple of kids walking by their booth, she leaned against the padded pseudo-leather back and smiled. The vivid color of his black eye had intensified, and she couldn't imagine that it didn't hurt, but he acted like he wasn't even aware of it.

"So how exactly did that black eye happen?" she asked. The question slipped out before she could stop it. Damn it—getting curious wasn't smart. She couldn't afford to be curious.

"Told you . . . I got in somebody's way." He jerked a shoulder in a restless shrug. "The man wasn't happy with me."

"You got in somebody's way." She should have just let it go at that, but now she was even more curious. The faint smirk on his lips only added to her curiosity, too. It was like he was amused by the fact that he'd gotten hit over being in somebody's way.

"Yeah." The smirk widened a little and a wicked light started to gleam in his eyes.

"Come on, Quinn." Sara rolled her eyes. "There's more to it than that. I don't see you as the kind of guy somebody would hit because you got in their way."

"Maybe he didn't like my attitude, or what I told him he could do with his complaints. Which was basically to fu—uh . . . shove it."

Sara snickered. "I've heard the word before, Quinn." The restaurant was fairly quiet, but she kept her voice low.

"My dad heard me talking that way around a lady, I'd never hear the end of it," he said with another one of those restless shrugs.

"Your dad, but not your mom?"

His lip curled in a sneer. Something cold and flat flashed through his eyes. But his voice was level as he said, "No. Not my mom. She's dead."

"Oh . . . I'm sorry." Looking down, she studied the scarred wooden surface of the table. "My mom died a few years ago. I still miss her."

"I don't miss my mother, Sara. We didn't have a good relationship."

The words were so flatly stated, so cold, so unemotional. And his eyes, they were like winter ice.

"I'm sorry," she said again. What else could she say? She hurt for him, though. There was a story there, and it wasn't a happy one.

Quinn sighed. It was a heavy sound, and when she looked back up, those wounds she'd glimpsed in his eyes were there again—naked misery, pain, loneliness. He scrubbed his hands over his face and then swore, wincing as he gingerly touched his bruised cheekbone. "Shit, I forgot about that."

"I don't see how."

"I've been hit a time or two. Guess you get used to it after a while."

Sara had her doubts about that—she wasn't sure anybody could ever get used to having a mark put on them.

"I don't talk about my mother. I don't like thinking about

her . . . and I don't want you apologizing over any of it," he said, his voice flat and hard.

The ache in her heart grew. Although he wouldn't share any more than that, Sara sensed a world of pain hidden behind those emotionless words. But she knew how miserable it was to talk about painful subjects, especially when you wanted nothing more than to forget. Forcing a smile, she reached across the table and brushed her fingers over the back of his hand. "Then we won't talk about her."

The ice in his gaze melted away, replaced by an intensity that had her heart skipping a few beats. Eyes hooded, he studied her. He turned his hand over and caught hers, twined their fingers together. From under his lashes, he studied her and the look in his eyes was hot. Hot enough to sear, scorch, burn . . . He lifted her hand and pressed his lips to the back of it.

"What would you like to talk about?" he whispered, his voice low and rough.

Part of her wanted to say *You*. If he didn't want to talk about his mother, that was fine. She wanted to know more about *him*. But there were problems with that. That kind of conversation tended to be two-way. He'd expect her to talk about herself. She couldn't do that.

Even though she had an entire story memorized, nice, simple, and pat, she didn't want to give it to him. She didn't want to lie to him.

"Who says we have to talk about anything?"

His lips trailed over her skin, left a sizzling, hot trail in their wake. "Always thought talking was overrated myself."

Hell. He wasn't kidding. Licking her lips, Sara tried not to whimper as he turned her wrist over and kissed the soft, sensitive flesh on the inside.

Shooting her a look, Quinn opened his lips and touched his tongue to her skin. She stared at him, her eyes half-closed, the warm velvety brown hot and sweet. Looking into her eyes made him think of melted chocolate, sweet and rich.

Up until recently, he hadn't ever had much of a sweet tooth, but damn if he didn't want a better taste of her. Raking his teeth over the soft skin of her wrist, he said gruffly, "You really shouldn't look at me like that in a public place, Sara."

"Look at you how?" she asked, her voice almost as hoarse as his own. She blinked at him, looking a little dazed.

Before he could answer, they heard a crash off in the distance, followed by the sound of breaking glass. As a few of the customers in the restaurant started to applaud, Quinn leaned back against the seat and slouched down.

"Like that," he muttered. He shifted a little on the seat, uncomfortable. But there wasn't a whole lot he could do about it, not sitting in a public place, wearing a pair of jeans and sporting an erection so hard it hurt. "The way you're looking at me now. It could get us both in all kinds of trouble."

"What kind of trouble?" Then she blushed, almost like she wished she hadn't asked.

Quinn smiled. Glancing around, he slid out of the booth and settled down next to her, crowding her until she slid over a little. They were tucked away in the back corner of the restaurant, and since the group of teens had left a few minutes earlier, they were alone in the section. Keeping an ear out for their waiter, he bent over her and nuzzled her neck.

"You really want to know what kind of trouble?" he asked. Half of him prayed she'd spare him the strain on his sanity and tell him no. The other half was all but ready to beg her to say yes.

She slid him a look from the corner of her eye. "Something tells me I ought to say no. I already know you're more trouble than I need right now."

"You've said something like that before." He laid a hand on her thigh, feeling the warmth of her skin through the jeans she wore. "If I went by what you say, I'd just have to keep my distance. But then you look at me like that's the last thing you want."

Therein lay the problem—him keeping his distance wasn't at all what she wanted. She should just tell him, loud and clear, that she wasn't going to sleep with him. That she really did need him to keep his distance. Then, once they got back to Theresa's place, she needed to pack up her stuff and get the hell out of town. She'd already been here too long anyway.

Not to mention the fact that she was giving him all sorts of mixed signals. Telling him she needed to keep her distance from him, but then when he showed up again, did she do anything to dissuade him? Hell, no. It was like she wasn't even capable of it.

Or rather, she didn't *want* to be capable. She didn't want him keeping his distance, she didn't want him pulling back, and she didn't want to ignore him, avoid him. And no way in hell did she want to leave.

Keeping her distance wasn't working, even though she knew better than to get close. Getting close was dangerous, and the fact that something about him called to her shouldn't matter. Couldn't get close, couldn't get involved, and couldn't get attached.

It was too late.

She was already attached, and sometime soon she knew she was going to get a hell of a lot closer. She shivered as he stroked his thumb across her thigh. His lips feathered over her cheek as he waited for her answer. Tipping her head back, she stared at him.

"So which is it, Sara?" he asked, his gaze lingering on her mouth. "Do you want to know what kind of trouble you're asking for?"

Sara was so tired of doing what her brain said was the *right* thing. The *safe* thing. The *smart* thing.

She wanted to listen to her body. Listen to her heart. So for the first time in ages, she let her heart, her body dictate her mouth. Smiling up at him, she whispered, "Why don't you tell me what kind of trouble it is . . . then I'll make up my mind."

One of these days, my mouth is going to get me into trouble . . . too much of it. It just might be today, but she was going to enjoy every last second of it.

He hissed out a breath and then reached up, cupped her cheek. Stroking his thumb over her lower lip, he murmured, "Are you sure about that?"

Staring up into his eyes, she caught her lip between her teeth. Was she sure? No. She wasn't. But she desperately, desperately needed to feel his hands on her. Feel that mouth on hers. Feel his body moving against hers.

She took a deep breath and then reached down, covered his hand with hers. His mouth twisted and he started to shift away, tried to tug his hand away. She wouldn't let him. Pressing her hand down against his, she whispered, "I have no idea what I'm getting into, Quinn . . . but I'm absolutely positive I want to find out."

His lids drooped low over his eyes and he sucked in a breath. That long, lean body tensed. When he lowered his head to kiss her, she tried to brace herself . . . it just wasn't possible.

It wasn't the sort of kiss a woman *could* brace herself for.

The sort of kiss that a man should give a woman in a public place.

The sort of kiss that should happen anywhere outside of a bedroom.

Because it left her wanting to strip out of her clothes, tear his away, and then climb on and ride him, ride him until that long, powerful body shuddered and quivered under hers.

His tongue rubbed against hers, teased and stroked. He nibbled at her lower lip, then sucked her tongue into his mouth and bit down. Sara groaned in her throat and arched closer. Much, much closer. Fisting a hand in the worn cotton of his T-shirt, she held on tight.

He crowded her against the padded back of the booth. The hand lying on her thigh slid higher, higher . . . Instinctively, she clenched her knees together, trapping his hand. He didn't let that keep him from rubbing his fingers against her covered sex.

Her breath locked in her lungs. Painful need cramped her belly. She whimpered into his mouth.

He lifted his head and she gasped for air as he glanced around. When he looked back at her, his eyes were glittering, hot. Damn . . . who knew the color gray could smoke and burn like that?

"Spread your thighs for me," he muttered, pressing his lips to her shoulder.

She blushed. She could feel the blood, hot and sudden, rising to her cheeks. "We're in the middle of a restaurant," she whispered.

"No . . . we're tucked away in the corner in the back of a restaurant, and nobody is paying us any attention. The stupid waiter is more interested in talking on his cell phone, and nobody else is back here. I'll hear anybody coming . . . now spread your thighs."

There was no way in hell she was going to do that . . . except even as she thought it, she was shifting on the seat and easing her legs apart.

"Good girl." He skimmed his lips along her shoulder, nuzzled her neck.

As good as his mouth felt, though, everything in her body was focused on his warm, hard hand. Resting on her thigh. Not moving. A few inches away from the one place she really wanted him to put that hand. Squirming around, she managed to inch a little closer.

Still, he didn't move. That hand continued to rest just there, while he nuzzled her neck, nipped her earlobe.

"Damn it, Quinn."

He laughed and then lightly, oh, so lightly, brushed the tips of his fingers against the denim covering her sex. So light, tauntingly so. Her breath escaped her in a shudder. Bracing her feet on the floor, she canted her hips higher and rubbed against that teasing hand.

Quinn stilled and once more he lifted his head.

Damn it, what is he doing looking around when I'm sitting there all but dying . . . oh. That was her last coherent thought. He covered her mouth with his, pressed the heel of his hand against her mound, lightly grinding it against her clit.

Deep inside, she was shaking. As he kept up that light, steady pressure, as he kissed her like he was gorging on her taste, the shaking spread outward until she was all but vibrating under his hands and mouth.

Too much.

Entirely too much.

Tearing her mouth away from his, she sucked in a desperate breath and whimpered. There was a scream building inside her— trapped inside her throat and begging for escape.

"Shhhh," Quinn muttered. "Shhhh . . . you don't want somebody to hear you."

Don't want somebody to hear . . . ? The words didn't make sense. Even when she forced heavy-lidded eyes open to stare at him, they didn't make sense. The hand between her thighs, his mouth rubbing against hers, *that* made sense. Her eyes landed on the brightly colored light fixture hanging over the table and logic tried to work its way back in.

But logic had nothing against heat. Nothing against need.

She came, gasping against his mouth and when the scream started to tear free, she bit her lip instead.

"Fuck, Sara . . ." he muttered against her lips.

Oh, would you?

That was the only coherent thought in her mind as she tore her mouth away from his and stared at him. The climax rippled through her, her womb clenching, her body throbbing. Her nipples, hard and tight, stabbed into the cotton and lace of her bra. Her blood roared in her ears, a song of ecstasy that filled her, flooded her, threatened to overwhelm.

But the pleasure faded, all too quickly. Letting her head fall back against the bench, she stared up at him and licked her lips.

She could taste him.

She wanted to taste more.

Wanted more of him period.

"Would you?" she whispered.

He cupped her face in his hand, rubbed his thumb across her lower lip. "Would I what, baby?"

Blood stained her cheeks red. "You just said, '*Fuck, Sara.*' I'm asking if you would."

EIGHT

RIDING a motorcycle with an erection was brutal. It was torture, the way the bike vibrated under him, with Sara sitting behind him, her thighs pressed against his, her hands gripping his hips.

He'd attempted to flirt and he'd ended up two seconds away from trying to strip her naked. He wasn't entirely sure, but he suspected flirtation was supposed to be a little more subtle.

Subtle was one skill he absolutely did not have. However, he couldn't really complain about how things had turned out, either. Even if she ended up walking away once he got her home. He might end up taking a cold shower for the rest of the night, but still, it wasn't something he'd undo, either.

The miles between Crestwood Center and home seemed to take forever, even though most of the traffic had died down as evening bled into night. As the clear, summer blue skies slowly changed to indigo, he tried to figure out just what in the hell he'd been doing.

He knew what had come over him—Sara. She'd hit him in the gut like a sucker punch the second he'd laid eyes on her. But pawing her in a fucking restaurant was a little extreme.

He slowed to a stop as the light ahead went to yellow. Bracing a foot on the ground, he gripped the handlebars and swore silently when Sara rested her cheek against his shoulder. It didn't seem possible, but she somehow managed to snuggle even closer.

He could feel her heat. Feel the soft curves of her breasts pressing into his back. The strong, sleek lines of her legs. It was probably his imagination, but he thought he could even feel the damp heat between her thighs. He wanted to strip her jeans away, her panties, press his mouth to the source of that heat . . . taste her, then ride her, ride her until the burning hunger inside him eased.

Which, for her, might be never.

If she got much closer, she'd have to crawl inside him . . . or him inside her and damn it, that wasn't a picture he needed in his head just then. Especially since he'd spent the better part of twenty minutes convincing himself that he needed to cool his jets, because it was entirely likely Sara would have a change of heart by the time they got to the house.

Just like the night she turned to fire in his arms and then, just as quick as you please, pulled away.

He'd come on way too strong that night, just like he had tonight.

Subtlety. Man, it was definitely something he needed to get a better grasp of. Subtlety . . . so he could seduce her, slow and easy and by the time she *did* have time to slow down and think, pulling back would be the last thing she wanted. The last thing she needed.

Maybe he could make her need him the way he needed her.

She was attracted to him, but that didn't mean she wouldn't appreciate . . . well, something more than getting pawed in a fucking restaurant.

"Would you?"

"Would I what, baby?"

"You just said, 'Fuck, Sara.' I'm asking if you would."

Hell, yeah. He'd just about give his right arm to put his hands on her body, his mouth on hers, and bury his aching dick so deep inside her that he lost himself.

Fucking Sara had become his favorite fantasy. Fuck her, hard and fast, then make love to her, soft and slow. Spend the night holding her in his arms so when she woke up, he could do it all over again. He wouldn't sleep—he couldn't ever sleep with a woman in the bed beside him, but lying there and holding her while she slept would work just fine for him.

Quinn wasn't going to bank on any of that happening, though. Once she started thinking, she might just remember how she'd told him that she didn't need any complications in her life. Even if she did melt in his arms, it might not mean much.

Even if she had looked at him, her pretty face blushing pink as she asked him if he'd fuck her. The heat in her eyes, the way she watched him as though she wanted him the way he wanted her.

Then the way she looked at him when she laughed. The way she smiled. The sadness . . . the grief in her eyes. The anger he glimpsed from time to time before she buried it. The way she'd already managed to wrap a fist around his heart. The way he couldn't go a day without thinking about her. A day. An hour. Even a stretch of minutes seemed to be pushing it anymore.

Fuck, he needed her.

Needed her, but he wasn't so sure he could handle her.

Shit. Maybe *he* couldn't afford the complications that she'd bring. From the minute he'd laid eyes on her, she'd complicated his life, making him think about her at the most inconvenient times. Making him dream about her.

What in the hell are you doing?

As he pulled up into the garage, it was a question he still couldn't answer.

Sara slid off the bike first and he ached at the loss of her warmth. The feel of her. He had to fight the urge to grab her and haul her close. The silence between them was heavy. It wasn't uncomfortable, but then again, Quinn was rarely uncomfortable with silence. Talking was much more likely to bother him. Except with her, it seemed.

He kicked a leg over the bike and took his time as he turned to face her. The single lightbulb hanging down from the ceiling didn't do much to illuminate the dark, cramped space, but he saw her well enough. Thin slivers of moonlight fell through the windows, highlighting her face, turning those warm brown eyes to black.

The feel of her mouth, the taste of it, was burned on his mind. He went to close the distance between them and she glanced away. The rejection, subtle as it was, cut deep, but he didn't let it show. He'd been expecting it—he could handle it.

Instead of reaching for her, he did his best to shove his need aside. "Come on. I'll walk you in."

"Walk me in?" she asked, tipping her head back and studying him.

He frowned at her. "It's dark . . . I'm walking you to the door."

She was the one who closed the distance. Taking one small step, then another, until she stood in front of him. Then she reached up, using the tip of her finger to trace an imaginary pattern on his shirt. Through the worn cloth, he could feel that light touch and it had his heart bumping against his rib cage.

"I thought you were going to tell me more about this trouble I'm asking for," she said, her gaze locked on his chest.

He could just barely make out the faint pink blush creeping up her cheeks. Thick black lashes shielding her eyes—that pissed him off. He wanted to see her eyes. Had to.

Cupping her chin in his hand, he angled her head back and made her look at him. He wanted to ask her if she was sure. He wanted to tell her she was going to drive him nuts if she went and pulled back on him again. There were other things he wanted to tell her, ask her, but he didn't entirely understand them well enough to try.

Talking hadn't ever been his strong suit—even when it didn't strike him as a waste of time, too often the right words just didn't want to come out. So instead of trying to make that happen, he dipped his head, pressed his lips to hers.

He kept the contact light and soft, touching only her face. She might seem sure now, but what if she changed her mind?

What if he moved too quick, did something wrong, freaked her out? What if she suddenly remembered she didn't want anything complicating her life? He'd have to stop. And Quinn suspected that just might do him in.

So he held back, keeping it slow, gentle. Even though what he wanted to do was slide his hands around her waist and haul her up against him. Cover those soft, sexy curves and feel her move against him as he rode her.

Sara sighed against his lips and rose onto her toes, resting her hands on his shoulders. She used her tongue, traced it along his lower lip and then pushed inside. Slow, lazy, but there was nothing hesitant, nothing uncertain, in her kiss. Or in the way she slid her hands down the front of his chest and eased them under the hem of his shirt so that she could touch bare flesh.

Damn, did she touch. She scraped her nails lightly over his back then ran her fingertips along the waistband of his jeans. Her fingers encountered one of his scars. It lay along the left side of his lower back. But she didn't pull away and ask questions—she just explored it, using the pads of her fingers to outline it as though she wanted to learn it through touch. She did the same with another scar he had on his right side, tracing the ridged flesh, stroking it with her thumb.

His hands itched to touch her the way she was touching him, to roam over those sweet, soft curves, cup the weight of her breasts, and slip inside her jeans, inside her panties.

But still, the only place he touched her was on her face, his hand cupping her chin as they kissed. By the time she pulled back and settled flat on her feet in front of him, Quinn was ready to tear off every last thread of clothing and lie at her feet, just to get her to keep touching him.

He wanted to tear off every last thread of her clothing, too, but instead, he lowered his hand to his side and clenched it into a fist.

"You change your mind?" she asked, easing back until a few more inches separated them. Her voice was calm, a little hoarse, but level. If it wasn't for the look in her eyes, naked heat and hunger, he might have even believed she wasn't all that affected.

"No," he murmured. Reaching out, he caught the front of her jeans and slipped his fingers inside, tugged her close. "I just need to be sure you're not going to. Very sure, because I already feel like I'm dying here."

A smile flirted with the corners of her mouth and she leaned forward, pressed her lips against his chest. "I'm not changing my mind," she murmured, her breath a soft caress through his shirt.

"I thought you didn't want anything complicating your life right now." He cradled the back of her head in his hand, tangled his fingers in her hair, and tugged until she looked up at him.

She swallowed. Something flashed in her eyes. Then she smiled again, an easy, confident smile that matched her light and flirtatious voice as she murmured, "Maybe I realized it didn't have to be all that complicated."

"Trust me, Sara . . . if I put my hands on you the way I want to, it's going to get complicated." Hell, it was already complicated—for *him*. Against the back of his fingers, he could feel the soft, warm flesh of her belly and he used his thumb to stroke her skin.

A sigh shuddered out of her body and she closed her eyes. When she looked back at him, a rush of nerves appeared in her eyes. "As complicated as my life already is, maybe I won't notice one more complication."

"Oh, you'll notice this one," he muttered as he covered her mouth with his.

He'd damn well make sure of it.

It had been years since Sara had done anything remotely like this. *Years.* Maybe never. She had an impulsive nature, but when it came to some things, she was . . . well, reserved. Sex was one of those things. She wouldn't have called herself overly cautious, but when it came to men, she tended to take her time. Look before she leaped. Not always, though.

Now her life was in upheaval and wasn't at all conducive to romance. She wasn't made for casual sex and yet the way she lived . . . well, casual was about all she could handle.

So now she was careful. Now she was cautious. Now she was all but celibate.

For two years, she'd lived a lie, letting caution and fear dictate her every step.

Tonight, though, she was going to be impulsive—in ways she hadn't ever been impulsive. Tonight she was going to be reckless—in ways she hadn't ever been reckless.

Tonight she was going to listen to desire, listen to need. A need that burned hotter and hotter with every passing second.

He held her hand—something so seemingly innocuous, but as they walked, he stroked his thumb along her inner wrist. Each light brush set her pulse all a-jitter.

She followed him down the narrow stairwell that led to his apartment, fighting to level out her breathing.

She wanted this.

There was no question about it.

But nerves were dropping down on her like leaded weights, nerves, old fears, and worries that never really wanted to die, no matter how hard she tried to bury them.

You barely know this guy.

You can't afford to get to know this guy.

Why in the hell am I getting ready to have sex with some guy I hardly know?

Why does he want me?

What if I disappoint him?

Damn it, what kind of panties am I wearing? Shit, when did I shave my legs?

She followed him inside and leaned back against the door as he hit a light switch. When he turned to look at her, the voices clamoring for attention inside her head faded away into nothingness and there was only one thing that mattered.

The way he looked at her.

Like he saw only her.

Like nothing else existed.

Like she was every bit as beautiful and perfect to him as she wished she really was.

Flags of color rode high on his cheeks and those gray eyes glittered as he stared down at her. The heat of his body, so close to hers, was like a blanket, and she wanted to press herself against him, wanted to get lost in that heat.

He braced his hands on the door by her head and leaned in, nuzzling her neck.

"You sure about this?" he whispered, raking his teeth over her neck.

Turning her head, she brushed her lips against his cheek and said, "Haven't we already gone over this?"

"Just wanted to make sure." He lifted his head and gave her one of those faint grins. Then he dipped his head, nipped her lower lip, and added, "Trying to be a gentleman here, for a second at least. Don't worry. The second's over."

She didn't even have a chance to catch her breath—his mouth came crushing down on hers while his hands flew over her body. He stopped kissing her only long enough to strip her shirt away and then his mouth was back on hers. She gasped into his kiss as he cupped her breasts in his hands, dragging his thumbs over her cotton-covered nipples.

They throbbed, ached.

"Fuck, I love your body," he muttered as he kissed a blazing line down her neck. At the same time, he jerked open the button of her jeans. The zipper sounded terribly loud as he lowered it. He stripped her jeans off, pausing just long enough to fight with her shoes.

She figured it might have taken him all of forty-five seconds to strip her down to her bra and panties. Maybe. Dazed, she leaned her head back against the door as he went to his knees in front of her and pressed his mouth against the cotton that covered her sex.

"Love the way you smell," he whispered, lifting his head to stare up at her.

Their gazes locked and held as he slid his hands inside the waistband of her plain white cotton bikini panties and stripped them down. Still staring up at her, he leaned in and nuzzled the tight, light brown curls that covered her mound.

Sara's legs wobbled under her and she braced her hands on his shoulders, staring down into his storm-cloud eyes. The vivid blue and black bruise ringing his left eye didn't do a thing to detract from how utterly beautiful he was to look at. If anything, it added to his harsh, uncompromising beauty.

He licked her, using his tongue to open the lips of her pussy and then teasing her clit with the tip of it. He groaned against her. The hungry male sound vibrated through her and she felt it all the way down to the soles of her feet. His hand, callused and rough, but oh so gentle, came up, gripped her calf, and then stroked higher and higher.

Catching her lower lip between her teeth, she just barely managed to keep from crying out when he pushed two fingers inside her and started to pump, in . . . out . . . all the while stroking her clit with his tongue.

"Damn it, Quinn, please . . ." she whimpered, reaching down and fisting her hands in his hair. The overlong, wheat blond strands felt like silk against her hands and she tugged him closer, arched against his mouth as he used his tongue in just the right . . . "There, please . . . just like that . . . oh . . ."

Hot and spicy-sweet. Now that he had the taste of her on his tongue, he wanted more. A lot more. Quinn groaned as he covered her clit with his mouth and sucked on her. She whimpered, panted, and whispered, hot, sexy little demands and pleas that set his already heated blood to boiling.

"Please . . . right . . . oh . . ."

As he worked her closer and closer to orgasm, her words became more and more broken. Right before it would have been too late, he stopped.

Sara snarled at him and reached for him. Laughing, he caught her wrists and stood. Pressing her hands back against the door, he bent and brushed his mouth against hers. "I'm going with you."

Then he stepped back and dealt with his own clothes. He had to leave her standing by the door long enough to dip into the bathroom. When he came out, saw her standing there, still leaning against the door wearing nothing but a lacy white bra, his heart just about stopped.

Fuck—she was perfect. The white bra kept him from seeing her completely, but damn, there was no doubt in his mind, she was perfect. Pale, creamy skin, a narrow waist, and those hips that had been driving him insane for days. Weeks. Pale brown curls covered her mound, and he could see moisture gleaming there. She wasn't very tall, but her legs seemed to go on forever and just like the rest of her, they were perfect. She was soft skin, soft curves, and so fucking female.

A grin curled her lips as she watched him watching her. A faint blush pinked her cheeks, but she didn't look away and she didn't try to hide herself either.

Her eyes lowered to the box of condoms he held in his hand. "If you plan on coming with me, you better hurry."

"Why?" he asked, tearing the box open and pulling out the strip of rubbers. He tore one off and tossed the box onto the table before going back to her. "You going to go without me?"

"I just might." A mischievous grin curled her lips, and she rested a hand on her belly, gliding lower and lower until the tips of her fingers brushed against the curls between her thighs.

Quinn's hands shook as he ripped the foil packet open and pulled out the rubber. Staring at her hand, he muttered, "Let me see."

The blush on her cheeks deepened. Then, her lashes lowered over her eyes and she started to stroke herself, circling her fingers around her clit.

Mesmerized, he watched her hand as he rolled the rubber down over his cock. The rigid flesh jerked under his touch and need screamed inside him.

Her fingers moved, quick and sure, stroking her clit. Her breathing sped up and then a soft, broken whimper fell from her lips and his control broke, falling to shreds around him. One long stride had him close enough to touch. Stooping low, he wrapped an arm around her waist and then straightened his legs. "Hold on," he muttered against her lips.

Her head fell back and she stared at him, her breath coming in harsh, ragged little pants. Her nails dug into his shoulders. Tucking the head of his cock against her entrance, he pressed against her. She closed around him, tight, slick, and hot. Through the thin barrier of the rubber, he could feel her heat, feel how soft she was. How fucking tight . . .

She clenched around him, the silken hot flesh rippling around his cock.

Take—

It was a driving rhythm pulsing through his head, the need to take, take, take, but she was so tight . . . he retreated, then slowly sank back inside her.

Slow. Nice. Easy. Slow . . . he told himself.

Sara arched against him, wrapping her legs around his hips and tightening them, urging him deeper. "Easy, girl," he whispered against her mouth.

"Don't want easy." She caught his lower lip between her teeth and said, "Want you."

Want you—

With a growl, he gripped her waist and held her steady as he drove deep, impaling her on his cock. Sara cried out. He went still.

"Am I hurting you?" he demanded.

"No . . . oh, no . . . again, do it again," she pleaded, sliding a hand into his hair and tugging his head down until she could kiss him. A hot, greedy, hungry kiss.

Greed, hunger—

"Fuck nice and easy," he muttered.

"Fuck nice and easy," she agreed. She bit his lower lip and then added, "Fuck me *hard*."

Hard. He took her hard, took her deep. Harsh ragged breaths filled the air, echoed with the slap of flesh against flesh. He caught her behind the knees with his arms, holding her open. He stared down at where they joined, watched as he drove his sheathed cock into her pussy. The sight of it, watching himself take her as it happened, was enough to kick his hunger into overtime. Growling, he dipped his head and kissed her again.

Starving—fuck, he was starving for the taste of her. For the feel of her. She writhed in his arms, rubbing her breasts against his chest. Naked. Damn it, he needed her completely naked and he'd forgotten about the damn bra. Dragging his mouth away from hers, he rasped, "Your bra's in the way. I want to see you . . . all of you."

She let go of his arms and reached for the cups of the bra, shoving them down until the cotton and lace bunched up under her breasts, lifting them higher. Her nipples were dark pink and tight. She tugged him back to her and rubbed herself against him. The soft mounds pressed flat against his chest. She shivered and sighed.

"Kiss me," she whispered, sliding her hands up over his arms, along his shoulders until she could lace her fingers behind his neck. "I love the way you kiss me."

Quinn rubbed his lips against hers. "How do I kiss you?"

"Like you're starving for me . . . like you don't ever want to stop."

"I am starving for you." He nipped her lower lip and licked her. "I don't ever want to stop. Open for me, pretty girl . . . let me in."

As their mouths met, each seeking the other, he leaned into her, shifting higher until he could stroke his body against her clit every time he sank inside her. She arched against him, crying out into his mouth, while her pussy clenched around his cock.

The muscles in her belly started to spasm—he felt them jumping under her soft skin. Her pussy hugged him, clutching around his dick, gripping him with a milking caress.

"I want you to come for me," he whispered against her mouth. She was close . . . so close to coming. He could feel it, in the way her pussy convulsed around his cock, the way her body tensed and tightened, fighting his possession and at the same time, demanding more.

She was close . . . but she fought it. He could see in her eyes that she was fighting it.

"You coming with me?"

"Fuck, yeah."

As though that was all she'd been waiting for, she started to come. Her pussy rippled around him, tightened and clenched and stroked. As she cried out, he swallowed the soft, whimpering sounds.

His own orgasm bore down on him and he gave himself up to it, lost himself to her. Shuddering, shaking, he collapsed against her as the most powerful climax of his life took hold of him.

NINE

Quinn came awake in the early hours before dawn and lay there, feeling the soft caress of Sara's breaths against his chest. They'd fallen asleep tangled in each other's arms, and that was something of a novelty for him.

He didn't sleep very well around others and he hadn't ever been able to sleep with somebody in the bed next to him. Not once in his entire life.

Maybe he could write that off to being drained from the best sex he'd ever had. Once he'd caught his breath after the first time, he'd carried her to the bed and done it all over again, but slower. Taking his time where earlier he had feasted on her like a starving man.

By the time they were done the second time, every muscle in his body felt like putty and his mind was one sweet, blissful blur. When a man spends close to two hours riding a woman until they both collapse, it would be enough to give even an insomniac like him a little bit of peace.

It went deeper than exhaustion, though. Quinn could deal with exhaustion. It didn't matter how tired he was and it didn't matter that he'd just had the best sex of his life—he'd fallen asleep wrapped around her body, because it was Sara.

Inside, he felt a sense of peace and satisfaction that he hadn't ever felt. Not even with Elena.

The second he thought about her, the ugly swell of guilt tried to rise within him, but he shoved it aside. Elena was gone . . . other than the job, a few quick minutes together, a few stolen hours, and a whole shitload of *what-might-have-beens*, they hadn't had much together. He hadn't once been able to sleep in her arms. Not once, and it wasn't because he hadn't tried.

He had tried, and failed. It hadn't felt right, he hadn't been able to settle his mind or his soul, and in the end, the one whole night he'd had with Elena had been spent with him sitting on the dirt floor of the small shack where they stayed while she slept on a thin, lumpy mattress.

Falling asleep with Sara felt as natural as breathing. More. He'd slept the whole night through and awoken with a smile on his face.

Peace. Contentment. Quinn wasn't entirely sure, but he thought that maybe, just maybe, he might be happy. It wasn't a feeling he'd felt very often in his life, and not at all in recent memory.

Brooding, he stroked a hand up Sara's naked back, enjoying the soft, satiny feel of her skin even as he tried to get a better grasp on what was taking place inside him.

He found himself thinking about his brother, Luke, and his new wife. Back when his twin had first started dating Devon, he'd been nervous as hell with her. Uncertain and hesitant, two things that were very not Luke.

Closing his eyes, he remembered a conversation he'd had with Luke about Devon.

"What's it like?"

"What's it like?" Luke had repeated.

"Yeah. This thing . . . with her. You love her?"

"Not real sure yet. Yeah . . . Yeah, I think I do."

"So what's that like?"

"I don't know that I can explain. I wake up and I want to see her. I go to sleep and I miss her, even if it's only been an hour since I saw her last. I think about her, wondering what she's doing, if she's had a bad day and if there's anything I can do to make it better."

"Sap."

Sap—that was exactly what Luke had sounded like, and now Quinn understood it completely. Over the past few days, he'd found himself thinking about Sara at times that he really needed to be thinking of other things—distracted when the last thing he needed to be was distracted. Hell, half the reason he had one massive black eye was because he'd been thinking a little more about Sara when he should have been focused on the three-hundred-plus-pound moron who'd gotten caught embezzling from some of his clients and then tried to skip town.

Absently, he reached up and touched his fingers to the bruise spreading down over his cheek, checked the swelling. It was puffy, but it didn't hurt too much as he probed the area.

The paramedic had told him he needed to get an X-ray, but that required going to a hospital, or a doctor's office at the very least. Quinn didn't do hospitals unless he had to and he never went to a doctor's office. He'd rather get his eyeteeth ripped out with a pair of pliers than go see a damned doctor.

The last time he'd willingly walked into a hospital had been right after Devon had nearly died—his former commanding officer had drugged her and had been just a whisper away from killing her and Luke. For months, the poor lady had been hassled and stalked, pushed to the very edge of insanity, because of a madman. The madman had been this close to killing her, too. This close . . .

God. Quinn couldn't imagine what it would have done to his twin if Luke had lost Devon. It would have destroyed him. Devon and Luke had become a unit—a matched set—and destroying one would irreparably damage the other.

"You should probably get an X-ray," Sara murmured, her voice drowsy.

Startled, he glanced down at her and realized she was watching him from under her lashes. A grin spread across his face. "Didn't know you were awake. "

"Hmmm. I'm awake. Barely. You need to get that eye X-rayed."

"Don't like doctors." He pushed a hand through her hair, stroking it back from her face.

"A lot of people don't like doctors, but they still go see them when they need to," she said.

"And if I needed to, I might go." *Need as in bleeding from every orifice or dying from a massive infection.* Other than that, he'd rather just suffer. "But it's just a black eye. If anything was broken, it would hurt more."

"You say that as though you have a lot of practice."

He shrugged. "Enough. Don't worry about it." He reached down and caught her hand, guiding it to his cock. "If you feel like worrying about me, maybe you could worry about this."

"This, huh? Does it hurt?" she asked, tilting her face up and giving him a look of wide-eyed innocence.

"Bad. Real bad."

She wrapped her fingers around him and stroked down, then up. As she neared the head, she tightened her grip and twisted her wrist. Quinn's eyes all but crossed at the pleasure of it and he arched his hips up to meet her on the upstroke as she did it a second and third time.

"Real bad, you say. Can you think of anything that might make it feel better?"

"Yeah." Slipping a hand into her hair, he tangled his fingers in the silken strands and said, "I can think of a couple of things. I'll let you make the call, though. You do what you think is best."

Early-morning light filtered in through the small windows set high along the walls of his apartment, splashing across the bed as she sat up and threw a leg over his hips.

"Maybe we could start with this," she teased, settling against him so that his cock was nestled between the slick, wet lips of her sex. Slick. Wet. Hot. It was a teasing, taunting enticement and one that threatened to destroy his already faltering control. Nothing between them . . . fuck. Quinn groaned and closed his hands around her hips, holding her steady as he dragged her back and forth. The sensation was enough to fry every last nerve ending in his body. Hot and slippery. Clinging to his fraying control with desperation, he gritted out, "Grab a fucking rubber."

She reached over, straining to grab one from the bedside table. It brought her breasts right in line with his mouth and he lifted his head, caught one plump nipple between his teeth. Sara's breath hissed out and she braced her hands on the pillow by his head, holding still as he licked the peaked tip and then nipped her gently.

"Put the rubber on me," he muttered, letting her sit back up. "Now."

Her hands shook as she did it. Once she finished, she held him steady with her hand and started to lower herself. Her hair fell down, shielding her face.

Quinn reached up and pushed it back, watching her face as she took him, one slow inch at a time. Her eyes widened, then fluttered closed. Her pretty mouth fell open as she moaned. She caught her lower lip between her teeth and bit down, whimpering when his cock jerked and throbbed inside her.

Watching her face did strange things to him—it twisted his heart even as the erotic beauty grabbed him by the balls and wouldn't let go. He tore his gaze from her face and looked down, watching as she lifted up and then began the slow process over again, slowly, so fucking slowly, inch by inch, sinking down on him.

"Oooohhhh . . ." Sara moaned as she impaled herself

completely, the thick, hot length stretching her. He throbbed inside her, the head of his cock nudging against her in just the right way. As pleasure jolted through her, she shivered and clenched down around him. Her hands flexed, kneading his chest.

Quinn caught her hips and started to move her, guiding her into a slow, easy rhythm. Slow and easy . . . tauntingly slow.

"More," she whimpered, fighting against his hands to move quicker, take him deeper.

"You're bossy," he teased, hooking a hand over her neck and hauling her down to kiss her. He kept up that same, teasingly slow rhythm with his hips, but his kiss was voracious, starving. Rough and demanding, it made her shiver and whimper as he tangled a hand in her hair and tugged lightly.

"No . . . I'm desperate. Please." She raked her nails down his chest and rolled her hips. Desperate . . . dying . . . she was so hot, she felt like she was going to explode. Clenching down around him, she used her inner muscles to milk him. "Please . . . Quinn, please."

He feathered his lips across her cheek. "Shhh."

Gripping her hip, he held her steady and started to move, quick, shallow thrusts that only made her burn hotter. Sobbing his name, she fought against his hold, fought to take more, take all.

Quinn swore and then shifted. In seconds, she was sprawled on her back with him between her thighs. He caught her knees and pushed them high, tucking her rump against him.

His eyes had gone opaque, burning hot and locked on her face. Twin flags of color rode high on his cheeks, and his mouth was twisted in a sexy little snarl. With her knees hooked over his arms, he leaned over her and started to move, driving deep, deeper.

Sara cried out in shock, staring up at him. Hardly able to move, hardly able to breathe, she lay there and stared at him as he rode her. Flesh slapped against flesh. His voice, a low, hoarse growl, echoed in her ears, but she didn't know what he was saying. Couldn't think. Couldn't think—

He twisted his hips and that slight shift was enough that the head of his cock rubbed against the bundle of nerves buried inside her pussy. Closer . . . almost . . . oh, hell, she could feel it—

Then he slowed his pace.

"Don't stop," she demanded.

"Look at me," Quinn growled, dipping his head and nipping her lower lip.

Mindless, she rocked upward, tried to ride the thick stalk of his cock. He pressed down with his hips, pinning her in place. He let go of one leg and cupped her face in his palm, angling her chin higher. "Look at me."

Sucking in a desperate gulp of air, she focused on his face and whimpered. "Quinn, please . . ."

Heat flared in his eyes. A faint smile curled his lips. "Just keep watching me . . . I want to see you . . ."

With their gazes locked, he started to move. Once more, he was riding her deep, riding her hard . . . taking her higher. The climax moved closer and closer and this time, he didn't stop. He moved and rocked and thrust while she whimpered and wiggled and moaned.

It exploded through her, and deep inside, she felt the convulsive jerking of his cock. He came with her and it lasted forever . . . each time she thought it might end, his cock throbbed inside her again and set off another series of aftershocks.

When it finally ended, she was so limp she could barely move.

He collapsed atop her with his head pillowed between her breasts.

"I'll move in a minute," he muttered.

She could feel the ragged rise and fall of his chest as he struggled for air. Looping an arm over his shoulders, she squeezed and whispered, "Don't want you moving."

"Bossy."

She wasn't sure, but she thought he smiled.

TEN

THE ringtone was the last one Don Hessig wanted to hear.
Even with his boss several thousand miles away, he wasn't
getting any peace. Not this time.

"It took you long enough," James bit off. "I don't pay you to
sit around."

"Of course not. I'm sorry, Mr. Morgan, I was dealing with the
matter we discussed a few days ago."

"The matter." James snorted. "About that matter—have you
made any progress?"

Propping the phone against his shoulder, Don automatically
adjusted his tie. Even though James was on the other side of the
country and they were talking via the phone, he checked his tie,
his cuff links and smoothed down his hair as he answered, "I'm
afraid not. I do have a few other options . . ."

Liar.

He didn't have *any* options. He'd been ad-libbing for the past
two years, hoping an answer would appear out of thin air. It had
yet to happen and Don had worn himself out trying to think up
other options, other avenues, other explanations or suggestions
with the hope he could buy a little more time.

Now, all he really needed was a little more time. A few weeks, no more than a few months. But he wasn't going to get it.

"What sort of options?" James asked, his tone bored.

"I've been researching the divorce laws of the state. I know we've discussed this before. But perhaps you've reconsidered the matter. By Illinois law, if one spouse has abandoned the other for a period of a year or more, the remaining spouse can file for divorce. Would you be interested in discussing this further with your legal counsel?"

"No. I do not wish to discuss this with my legal counsel." His voice as cold, sharp as a blade. "Were there any other *options* that you had considered?"

Don stared at the surface of his desk, seeing blood. Seeing tears. And hearing a voice—James's voice.

"One way or another, I want her out of the picture. Permanently. One way or another. Now . . . you can either take care of the matter, or I will take care of you."

His mouth dry, he swallowed. "No, I'm afraid that had been my most realistic option."

"So in other words, you have nothing new for me."

"No sir. I don't."

"Somehow I knew you'd say that." James's voice was gentle, polite. But it didn't mask the anger that throbbed underneath. Or the threat. "You are aware of the fact that I'm disappointed."

Oh, yes. Don was well aware.

"But it doesn't matter. I knew that would be your answer. I knew this was coming and I've decided to take a more hands-on approach." James paused and then continued, "Effective immediately, I'll be the one handling the search for my wife."

"Sir, do you truly have time for that?"

"No, and if I wasn't short on time, I'd fire you and have your replacement take over. But I haven't the time or the patience for that currently. So you'll continue to investigate the matter, but you'll work from my information, rather than trying to gather your own. I also want detailed reports on the steps you've taken to take care of this matter. So be prepared."

Time was up.

Don kept his voice level, made mental notes of each bit of information as it was relayed and answered each question for James quickly, using his iPhone to look up the information as James requested it.

"I'll need to do a bit of research, see if I can find the people who are going to best suit our needs," he said.

"Just be quick about it—I'll be back in the Chicago office on Monday and I expect to have everything I need waiting for me."

"Of course." He could have the information in a matter of hours, but he didn't mention that to James.

Inside, he was sick with fear and nerves. Sick with guilt.

What if this worked . . . ?

What if James found her?

There was a part of him that knew it wasn't a matter of *what if* he found her. But *when*.

He needed to let her know.

* * *

In his Los Angeles offices, James slipped a portfolio inside his briefcase. He used his iPhone to check his calendar and noted that Don had made a few minor adjustments to the schedule, along with notes explaining each change.

A few meetings rescheduled, a phone conference added. Nothing terribly time consuming, which was good. With what he felt was reasonable optimism, he hoped that sometime in the next couple of weeks, he would need to work in time to deal with his wife.

She'd be found.

This time, he was sure of it. Now that he'd made the decision to move the search out of his assistant's hands and into the hands of professionals, she would be found and—he hoped—relatively quickly.

Discreetly.

They had to be discreet.

Making that decision rubbed him absolutely raw. It was the best choice available to him, letting a bunch of unknown individuals know of his personal life, how his wife had run away from him. It had him all but sick with fury and disgust—nearly as furious and disgusted as he'd been when forced to let the police investigate her disappearance two years earlier.

He knew what they'd *believed*—that he'd killed her and disposed of her body, then made up the story about her disappearance and the other tawdry details just to cover it.

They took him for a fool. A man in his position wouldn't kill his wife, because law enforcement always suspected the spouse. He had no reason to kill his wife, no reason to risk the smear such an act would leave on his image.

There were other ways to deal with her, and it was high time he acted on them.

* * *

"He won't quit looking for me. James doesn't let go of things easily, especially not his things. And that's how he sees me."

"Then we'll just have to make it very hard for him to find you."

Very hard.

Sara came awake with memories lingering just beyond the edge of her consciousness. Dreams. Nothing but dreams, the same dreams that awaited her every time she slept.

The same dreams.

The same fears.

But this morning was a far cry from the way she'd gotten used to things. She wasn't alone. She wasn't lying in a solitary bed and wondering if she'd ever have something better to occupy her thoughts in the morning.

She definitely had better things to occupy her thoughts. There had even been a night or two in the past two weeks when memories weren't lying in wait for her when she closed her eyes. A few nights when dreams about Quinn dominated and she didn't have the time to remember the nightmares. Didn't have time to remember the fear.

But today wasn't one of those days. Something dark and oppressive hung in the air. She could feel it, chilling her gut, leaving her palms sweaty and damp. Her spine itched and her head pounded. Unable to linger in the bed and try to sleep, she threw her legs over the side.

"Where you going?" Long, warm fingers loosely shackled her wrist and she looked up, saw that Quinn was lying there watching her. His blond hair was tousled, falling into his eyes. His lips quirked up in that faint smile of his, and he watched her . . . the way he always watched her.

Sara shivered at the sound of his voice, low and rough, sleepy and sexy.

It had been a week since they'd first been together, a week since she'd first woken in his arms. She suspected the sound of his voice would still have the power to make her shiver in a hundred years.

She went to respond, but then their gazes connected and the ability to coherently say anything disappeared.

Staring into those gray eyes, her mouth went dry.

He was smiling, she realized.

His lips were curled up in that happy, content kind of smile people had when all was right with their world. It somehow managed to warm her heart and break it at the same time.

He lifted a brow at her and she realized she'd been staring at him while he waited for her to answer him. Licking her lips, she angled her head toward the bathroom. "I need to use the bathroom . . . get dressed."

He slanted a look at the clock. "You going for a run?"

"Yeah." She rolled her eyes.

Quinn laughed at her. Then he reached up, tangled his fingers in her hair, and tugged. "Mind if I come with you?"

The devil made her do it, she'd swear to it. Turning back to him, she settled on the bed next to his hips and reached down, wrapped her fingers around his cock. "I love it when you come with me."

His grin faded away, replaced by a sensual twist of his lips. He arched into her touch and muttered under his breath. Then he reached down, closed his fingers around her hand, adjusting her grip, guiding her strokes as he thrust his hips up, pushing himself into her touch.

Sara stared, watching the way he moved, reveling in the feel of him, satiny skin and under it, he was so hard. She stroked a thumb over the head of his cock, watched as a bead of clear fluid welled on the crown. Unable to resist, she dipped her head and licked it away.

Quinn swore, his voice low and shaking. Then he slanted a look at her and said, "We keep this up, I'm going to be coming alone."

He tried to tug her wrist away, but Sara resisted until he finally stopped, his hand falling away to his side, clenched into a tight fist. The veins stood in sharp relief and every muscle in his body seemed to tighten.

"Squeeze harder," he rasped and then he reached down again, once more covering her hand with his and tightening her grasp. At the same time, he started to thrust up with his hips—faster, his movements almost desperate as he drove his cock back and forth against the friction created by her hand.

Once more, another drop of clear fluid welled from the head

of his cock and once more, she stroked her thumb over the head of his cock, spread it over the smooth surface. Quinn swore, his other hand fisted in the sheets, twisting and tugging. "Sara . . ."

He came in her hand, groaning and shuddering as hot, pulsating jets of semen spilled out. Sara smiled at him and dipped her head to kiss his lips.

"Hmmm. That was fun . . ." she whispered.

Quinn nipped her lip and reached out, grabbed a fistful of the sheet, used it to wipe the fluid from his belly. Sara lifted a brow at him. "I ought to make you do my laundry."

"Works for me," he said. "You do that anytime you want, and I'll do the laundry for you anytime you want."

She traced the scar on his side with her index finger and chuckled. "You work cheap. You cook, too?" She went to stand and he caught her.

"A lousy cook. Maybe we can try this instead," he muttered. In seconds, she was bent over the bed, her upper body braced on the mattress while Quinn knelt behind her.

"Now I'll come with you," he muttered. She heard foil tear and then he was pressing against her, pushing his way inside.

Sore and swollen, she whimpered. Burying her face against the tangled sheets, she sucked in a deep breath and tried to will herself to relax. Regular sex hadn't ever been *regular* for her, and although they didn't spend every night together, when they did, it seemed as though they couldn't get enough of each other.

Quinn smoothed a hand along her back, then around, working between her lower body and the mattress. He touched her, stroking her entrance with a gentle fingertip. "Are you too sore?"

"Probably . . . but I don't care." She pushed her ass back against him and winced as it took him deeper. A little too deep, she realized, as pain sliced through her.

"Easy," he muttered, using his other hand to hold her still. He

started to stroke her, teasing her clit, petting her until the pain
bled away into a mere ache.

She hummed under her breath and tried to push back but
again, he used his hands to still her body, used his body to control
hers, keeping the pace slow and easy.

"Quinn, please."

"So impatient," he whispered against her ear, nipping her
earlobe.

"Damn straight." She clenched around him and once more
tried to guide him into a quick, deeper rhythm, but he wasn't having any of it. He kept his strokes slow and steady and all the while,
his fingers, wicked and clever, stroked her clit, teasing the peaked
flesh.

"Damn it, Quinn, you're killing me."

"No . . . I'm loving you."

Those words twisted her heart, even though she realized he
hadn't meant it that way. Tears stung her eyes and she blinked
them away before she looked at him over her shoulder. Giving him
a wicked smile, she said, "Do it harder."

"No . . . you're sore."

"I don't *care*."

"I do," he whispered, leaning over her and pressing his mouth
to her neck. His lips brushed against her flesh, down to her shoulder. He raked his teeth along her, bit her lightly. Sara's awareness
centered down on those three things, the feel of his mouth and
teeth on her body, his thick cock lazily thrusting in and out of her
pussy, and his fingers caressing her clit with light, rapid strokes.

The fiery sensations, intense on their own, were too much
to handle all at once, and she started to rock back to meet him,
fighting against the rhythm he'd set. She clenched down on him,
because she knew it drove him crazy. Then she reached down and
back, catching his balls in her hand and squeezing.

"Damn it, Sara," he snarled.

Orgasm was just a wish away. And then the wish was coming true as the hand on her hip tightened and he started to push deeper, harder, faster. The caressing fingers between her thighs became less teasing and gentle, becoming more demanding, rougher. His teeth raked over her skin, leaving a fiery, stinging trail behind as he nipped and kissed his way back up her neck.

"You come with me," he muttered, pinching her clit and tugging on it. He worked his other arm around her waist and held her steady as he shafted her, hard, fast, rough. "Come . . ."

"Quinn . . ." she gasped out, angling her head and seeking his mouth. He was there . . . waiting. She pressed her mouth to his, greedy and desperate. She moaned in her throat, broken and ragged. The need for him swelled around her, grabbed her, pulled her under, and she let it. Lost in him, she climaxed, her body trembling, her heart pounding.

And for some odd reason, tears stung her eyes.

ELEVEN

*D*ON'T *get excited.*
  Sara stared at the message displayed on her phone and told herself again, *Don't get excited.*

Call me. That was all it said. It could be nothing. It could be problems. It could be a warning. No reason to get excited, she knew.

Still, her fingers shook as she made the call. "Yeah?"

"I'm close."

She licked her lips and asked, "Close to what?"

"Not telling you. But I'm close." The call ended.

"Damn it," Sara snarled. She threw the phone down on the counter and turned, staring outside. Close . . . close to what, and how close?

She'd put the maps away, tucked them out of sight so she didn't have to see them, even though she didn't need the glaring reminder. But now she went and pulled one out, staring at it. She hadn't made any notes on the map—never a good idea, but she remembered the routes she'd planned, outlined in her head.

Was it possible that she wouldn't need to leave?

She didn't even want to hope. Part of her, though, couldn't help it.

Maybe, just maybe, she wouldn't have to leave.

Maybe, just maybe, she could keep Quinn. For as long as he wanted her, anyway.

* * *

"DAMN, Sara. I don't know what you're doing lately, but I want some of it."

"Huh?"

Sara looked up from the counter where she was counting out her tips and found Meagan watching her with a wicked grin. "I said I want some of it."

Sara looked at her tips and then at Meagan, scowling. "You've got your own tips."

Meagan laughed. "Not talking about the money . . . I'm talking about whatever has that smile on your face lately."

"A man," Annette said from behind the cash register where she was also counting up money. "Only thing that makes a girl smile like that is a man."

"I dunno . . . good chocolate can make me smile pretty big," Sara hedged while blood rushed up to stain her cheeks red.

"So you were thinking about chocolate?" Meagan snorted. "Honey, chocolate might make you smile, but it won't make you blush. So . . . is it a man?"

"Ahh . . ." Sara didn't know how to answer that. Girl talk was something she'd been lacking in, almost as much as just regular old small talk—except while she abhorred small talk in general, she'd always loved sitting around and talking with friends.

She missed it.

It was dangerous, though. Too dangerous. Even though a sliver of hope had settled inside her heart, she wasn't going to mess up. She had to stay careful. She shot Meagan a small smile and shrugged, keeping her voice level as she said, "There might be a guy."

"Might?"

"Might be. We're mostly just friends, though."

"Man, I need a friend who can make me smile that way." Meagan rolled her eyes and then added, "Well, other than a battery-operated one."

Annette snickered. "Batteries don't operate good enough to bring on that kind of smiling."

They all laughed, and finished counting things up in silence. When it was time to leave, just like he normally did, Annette's husband Arnold walked Meagan and Sara to the bus stop. An ex-Marine, he still had that hard, tough look to him, and the thugs that might have hassled the women that late at night cut a wide berth around him.

"You be careful getting off, honey," he said, smiling kindly at Sara as her bus slowed down.

"I will."

The bus stopped just a block from Theresa's, and while it was late, it wasn't that late. Most of the time, her ride was uneventful, and this one turned out the same way. A lesson in monotony, slow at this stop, drive by that one, slow . . . drive by . . . slow . . . by the time it slowed for her, the rhythm had all but lulled her to sleep and she knuckled her eyes before rising from the seat and making her way up front.

She paused at the door as it opened, pleasantly surprised to see Quinn waiting there for her.

"Everything okay?" the driver asked from behind her.

"Yes." She shot a smile at the lady over her shoulder and then jogged down the stairs. She stopped on the curb and they waited in silence as the bus pulled away. She tucked her hands into her pockets as Quinn pushed off the railing. "Waiting for somebody?" she asked as a foolish smile spread over her face.

In lieu of answering, he reached out and hooked a hand around the back of her neck, tugging her up against him. As his mouth came down on hers, she grinned against his lips and said, "I guess so."

When the kiss ended, she sighed and settled back down on her feet. Grinning up at him, she said, "You're definitely better than chocolate."

Quinn arched a brow at her. "I am?"

"Oh, yeah."

"This something you've thought about a lot?"

Sara shrugged. "Not until a few minutes ago. I was getting off work and apparently I had this grin on my face. Somebody asked about it, and then somebody else said only a man makes a woman grin like that. So I say I've grinned like that about chocolate, but I think I might have lied. You're definitely better than chocolate."

"Glad to hear that." He cupped her face in his hand and stroked his thumb over her lip.

She kissed him there and then pulled back, started down the sidewalk. He fell into step beside her. Glancing at him from the corner of her eye, she said, "This is getting to be a regular thing."

"What?"

"You waiting here when I get off of the bus."

He was quiet for a moment. When he did speak, his voice was neutral, carefully so. "Is that a problem?"

Sara shrugged. It *should* be a problem. She knew that. *He* should be a problem. And in a way, he was, but it was the wrong kind of way. Instead of wanting to keep him at a distance, she wanted him close, all the time close, which really led to more problems.

How was she ever going to manage leaving him?

"Not really a problem . . . just wondering why."

"Maybe because I like seeing you," he said, shrugging. Then he stopped and reached out, catching her hand to bring her to a halt as well. "Screw that. I do like seeing you. Besides, it's not like you're walking home in broad daylight. You never get home before ten and I'd just rather not think about you making the walk at night."

Cocking a brow at him, she pointed out, "I've made the walk a million and one times at night and haven't had any trouble. And this is definitely a better neighborhood than I'm used to—nothing much ever happens around here."

"I know that." He shifted from one foot to the other, shoving a hand through his hair. His eyes stared off into the distance, like he wasn't entirely comfortable meeting her gaze.

Nervous, she realized. He was nervous.

It was a rare thing for him to actually *look* nervous, Sara decided. She'd seen him pissed before, seen him irritated, seen him amused, but *nervous* was new.

"Look, I know you can take care of yourself," he said, jerking a shoulder up. "I just feel better walking with you."

His eyes cut to hers, but whatever he felt besides nervousness, he kept hidden, tucked away behind that blank, gruff exterior. "You want me to stop?"

"Would you?" she asked, tilting her head.

He gave a single, short nod. "If you tell me you want me to stop, yeah, I'll stop. I'll be pissed off, but I'll stop."

Sara took one step forward. That put her close enough so all she had to do to kiss him was rise up on her toes. His mouth lowered to meet hers, but she didn't kiss his lips. She angled her head and brushed her mouth against his cheek, then over to his ear. "You don't have to stop."

"I don't?"

"No." Settling back on her heels, she smiled up at him. "I'm not used to having somebody who wants to watch out for me . . . it's kind of weird, but I like it."

* * *

"No."

Sara wasn't really a light sleeper, but the talking, along with Quinn's restless thrashing, was definitely enough to drag her out of sleep. Confused, she lay in the bed, staring up into darkness while her brain tried to function.

Next to her, Quinn jerked and spoke again. His voice was barely more than a sob this time, so guttural and hoarse, it barely made sense.

It was a name, though. Like a bucket of ice-cold water had been dumped on her, she was suddenly very, very aware. Although as he said the name again, she wished otherwise.

It was a woman's name.

Elena—

Jealousy ate at her even while her heart broke a little at the pure misery in his voice. Uncertain, she lay there. Did she try to wake him up? Did she get pissed off? Storm off? Kick him out of the bed?

Then he whispered, "I'm sorry." His words were so tormented, so full of pain that her heart decided what she should do before her brain could even process it. She snuggled closer, working an arm around his waist and rubbing her cheek back and forth against his sweat-dampened chest. Tears stung her eyes as his chest heaved. A sound suspiciously like a sob ripped from him, harsh and raw.

His name leaped to her lips—she wanted to shake him, urge him out of whatever awful dreams held him captive. But her sense of self-preservation had her holding her tongue. She remembered the last time she'd caught him off guard, and while she definitely wasn't mad about it, she really would rather not catch him off guard again—especially while he was caught in the grip of a nightmare.

So instead, she held him and stroked him, used her body to reassure him as best she could. It finally worked. In his sleep, he turned to her, wrapping his arms around her and holding her close and tight.

"I'm sorry," he muttered again.

Unable to stop herself, she slid a hand down his back and murmured, "Shhhh . . ."

He came awake, his entire body jerking. He rasped out, "Fuck."

She kissed his chest. His heart was racing, pounding against his ribs in a hard, fast rhythm. "You okay?"

"Just dandy," he muttered.

Tipping her head back, she stared at him as he rubbed his eyes. It was too dark to make out his face clearly, but she wasn't certain that was a bad thing—she wasn't certain she could handle seeing his face just now.

"You were having a nightmare."

"Yeah." He sighed and turned his head away. "I have them sometimes. Did I wake you up?"

She shrugged.

"I'm sorry."

Kissing his chest, she shrugged again. "Don't be sorry." She licked her lips and then hesitantly asked, "You want to talk about it?"

He didn't respond right away, and she wasn't sure if she should be glad or not. She wanted to know, but at the same time she didn't. She didn't want to know who Elena was, but she had to know. She didn't need to find out too many details about the guy, but at the same time, she needed to know more.

But then he wrapped his arms around her, once more pulling her close, clutching her against him, like he desperately needed to feel her against him. "You really don't want to know what kind of shit I was dreaming about, darlin'. Trust me."

"I dunno . . . it sounds like maybe you should talk about it. Talk about her." She kept her voice level and flat, keeping her own anguish locked away.

He tensed and she caught her lower lip between her teeth, deciding she was definitely glad she couldn't see his face clearly just then. Because that meant he probably couldn't see hers too well either, which meant he wouldn't see the misery in her eyes.

"Her?" he echoed back, his voice husky.

"The woman you were dreaming about. You said her name a couple of times . . . then you kept saying 'I'm sorry.' Over and over."

"Shit." He jerked away from her and climbed out of the bed, stalking across the room.

Tears burned her eyes. Drawing her knees to her chest, she smoothed the blankets around her and then pressed her brow to her knees.

"I'm sorry," he said.

She shot him a glance. He stood by the window, staring out into the night. Faint light filtered in through the curtains, and she could see his face now. But she still didn't want him seeing her. "Sorry for what?" she asked woodenly.

"I wasn't . . . I . . . she. Fuck." He lifted his hands and covered his eyes. "Help me out here a little bit, Sara. I don't generally spend the night with women, and this is the first time I talked about one woman while in bed, sleeping with another. I'm not real sure how to handle this—how to handle you."

"You don't need to *handle* anything," she snapped, shoving her hair back. "I don't need *handling*. You had a bad dream—they happen, and it sounds like it was a whopper. If you want to talk about it, I'll listen. If you want to talk about her, I'll listen. If not, that's fine. But I don't need *handling*."

He was quiet, too quiet. Restless, she kicked free of the blankets and sheets and stood. Spying his T-shirt at the foot of the bed, she grabbed it and jerked it over her head as she stormed into the kitchen.

She went to open the refrigerator, but stopped cold as he finally spoke.

"She's dead."

Her hand fell away from the handle and she turned back to stare at him. "What?"

He reached out, hitting the light switch.

She flinched against the harsh light, blinked as her eyes worked to adjust. She was still squinting when he started to speak again. "She's dead. She died the year before last—and she died because of mistakes I made."

"What?" She'd heard the words. But they didn't make any sense. They just bumped and banged around inside her head, not connecting and leaving her feeling even more lost and confused.

"Fuck." He turned away and once more stared back outside. His shoulders rose and fell on a sigh. "She's dead because of me, Sara."

Finally, the words started to connect and she could make some sense of them. A woman had died. And Quinn said it was because of him.

"I don't believe that." She shook her head, tried to wrap her mind around that information, but it just wouldn't settle. It didn't fit.

"Yeah, well, believe it." He shot her a look over his shoulder, and that screaming, endless hell she'd glimpsed in his eyes once before was back.

Wounded warrior—so tortured and torn.

Licking her lips, she opened her mouth and tried to figure out what to say. Nothing seemed right. Nothing felt right. In the end, she said nothing—she just crossed the room and wrapped her arms around him, pressing her lips to his shoulder.

His body shuddered and then he turned around and slipped his arms around her waist, pulling her close.

"If you want to tell me about it, I'll listen," she said.

Quinn just shook his head.

She stroked a hand down his back. "Are you sure? Trust me, I'm a pretty good listener."

"Doesn't have anything to do with trust," he said. "I just can't talk about it. I'm sorry, but I can't."

"I'm sorry, too." She kissed his neck and snuggled in close. "For whatever happened, I'm sorry."

* * *

THE dream had been a bad one.

Quinn didn't know where in the hell it had come from, blindsiding him like that. Although why in the hell it had to happen with Sara lying in the bed next to him, he didn't know.

Right now she was asleep, cuddled up against him with her hand resting just above his heart. He reached up and covered her hand with his, stroked his thumb along the inside of her wrist.

He'd hurt her.

He had seen that flash in her eyes before she buried it. He wanted to take it away, but he didn't know how.

And still, as bad as he felt, the pain wasn't like it had once been.

It was a dull ache inside his chest, but the vicious intensity that normally came with one of those dreams wasn't there. The guilt was only an echo of what it usually was.

Part of him said it was just because he was moving on.

The other part of him said it was because of Sara. Because of the woman who now lay in his arms, sighing softly in sleep. The turmoil inside him always seemed less when she was with him. The anger faded. And pain ceased to exist.

Sighing, he eased away, but instead of climbing out of the bed, he pushed up onto his elbow and studied her face. Her lashes lay against her cheeks and her pale skin was softly flushed from sleep. A frown tugged at the corners of her mouth and she reached out, stroking a hand down the sheets like she was looking for him. He leaned in and pressed his lips to her neck then rubbed his cheek against hers.

Sara sighed and the frown faded as she cuddled deeper into the blankets.

His heart twisted a little as he climbed out of the bed. Damn it, she'd gone and gotten to him, hard and fast, turning him into a messy knot of nerves and need. Every day that passed drew that knot tighter and tighter—binding him to her.

It wasn't that long ago when Quinn had wondered if he had anything left of a heart inside him—if he'd ever had one. But the way things were going, he no longer had those questions. One big question lingered, though . . . was he about to put his heart in this woman's hands?

He suspected the answer was yes—and he suspected he had no control over the matter, either. He wasn't entirely sure how he felt about that.

*   *   *

WHEN Sara woke up, she was alone in the bed.

But she hadn't been for long.

Rolling over, she stroked a hand down the sheets, felt the lingering warmth of his body. Sighing, she sat up, and that was when she saw the note on the pillow. She reached for it and settled back against the headboard as she opened it.

Had a job come up—had to leave.

See you later.

Scrawled at the bottom, added in almost like an afterthought, was the word *Thanks*.

"A man of many words," she murmured with a reluctant smile. She folded the note back up. She was sure there were men who'd penned prettier notes to women they'd spent the night with. She was equally sure that quite a few of them would have had a whole slew of words to explain, apologize, or otherwise excuse away what had happened.

Even if he didn't have much control over his dreams.

It wasn't like he'd been having some hot and heavy XXX fantasy of Elena—whoever she was. Sara doubted she would have tolerated that very well. Snuggling back down into the bed, she stroked a hand down the spot where Quinn had been. The warmth was fading away, but she could still smell him. A smile curled her lips, one of those goofy, loopy, giddy grins.

Yeah, there were guys out there who would leave much prettier notes, but she doubted many of them would have left her smiling like this. She was also equally certain that he was probably the only man she *could* smile about, only hours after he'd been whispering another woman's name while sleeping next to her.

Her smile faded quickly, though, as the faceless Elena filled her thoughts. Dead . . . whoever she was, Elena was dead, and according to Quinn, it was his fault.

Sara was well acquainted with guilt, knew how the mind could play tricks on a person, make them think the strangest things. How guilt and grief could twist and skew logic so out of proportion.

She wanted to know what had really happened.

With a sigh, she swung her legs around and sat up on the edge of the bed. Staring down at the note, she read it through once more. No confessions of undying love, no poetic turns of phrase. But just reading it made her heart feel all warm and soft.

She knew better than this.

She knew better than to get attached, to develop any sort of connection.

Part of her wanted to argue, *It's not a connection . . . or it doesn't have to be. You're sleeping together. He left you a note; it wasn't a declaration of love.*

Still, she couldn't make herself crumple the note up and she couldn't wipe the foolish grin from her face, either. Instead, she smoothed the note out and then carefully folded it one more time, tucking it into the little table next to the futon before climbing out of bed.

Every muscle in her back screamed at her and she shot the futon a dirty look. "Man, what I wouldn't give for a real bed again . . ."

Bending over, she touched her toes, trying to ease the tight muscles and knots. A shower would do a better job, but she hated to shower before she worked out.

She was halfway through her workout when the phone rang. Not the little chime that sounded when she had a text message, but a ring. It was the standard loud, blaring ring because she hadn't ever changed it to one of the polyphonic tones that had come with the phone. She didn't see the point, because she only got a few calls a month. Hell, she could count the number of calls she got on one hand and still have fingers left over.

With one leg bent in front of her and the other stretched out behind her, she wobbled, frozen in the middle of a lunge. Staring at the phone like the damn thing had grown teeth.

A second ring.

Her heart slammed away inside her chest, but it didn't have anything to do with the lunges. Straightening up, she started toward the phone as the third ring sounded. She grabbed it from the table with a hand that shook. Relief punched through her as she saw Quinn's name on the display.

Relief . . . and a little bit of anger. Grabbing the phone, she answered the call just before it would have gone into voice mail—or rather attempted to, because she hadn't set up the voice mail, either. "Hello?"

"You in the middle of working out?" he asked.

She huffed out a breath and flicked her sweaty hair back from her face. "What gave you that idea?"

"You're out of breath and you're irritated. You're always irritated when you work out."

Actually, I'm irritated because you got ahold of my number. Because you programmed your number into my phone without asking me. She made a face, tried to decide if that would sound as petty out loud as it did in her mind. "Yes, I'm working out . . . and probably a little irritated." As soon as she said it, she bit her lip.

She didn't sound *irritated*.

She sounded like an outright bitch.

"Somehow I get the feeling you're not irritated because you're working out . . . or at least, not just because of that," Quinn said, his voice slow and measuring.

Shifting from one foot to the other, she debated what to say.

I'm irritated because I never get calls and when the phone started ringing, it scared me to death.

I'm irritated because I didn't give you permission to call me.

Of course, he hadn't asked . . . if he had, what would she have done? Seemed kind of strange that she'd sleep with the guy but not give him her number. Hell, she hadn't been at all irritated when he'd started showing up at the bus stop to walk her home.

Getting pissed over a phone call, but not the bus stop thing, seemed stupid in the extreme.

And of course there was what had happened last night—he'd been mumbling another woman's name while lying in bed next to her and she'd hadn't been irritated like this. Hurt, yeah. Jealous, oh, shit, yeah. But not irritated.

She couldn't help it, though, and she felt more and more stupid with each passing second for even being irritated. All because he had her phone number.

Of course, if her life was anything bearing a similarity to normal, she would have already given him her number . . . assuming he had shown any interest in her to begin with.

Back in her normal life.

"You're mad at me."

Quinn's level voice couldn't quite disguise the hurt she sensed in it. Now she really felt like a bitch.

Grimacing, she once more pushed her fingers through her sweat-dampened hair. Softening her voice, she said, "I'm not mad.

Not exactly. I just . . . I wasn't expecting anybody to call and it kind of startled me to see your name on the display. I don't handle surprises very well, I guess."

He was quiet for a few seconds, and Sara squeezed her eyes closed. *This is why you don't do attachments. This is why you don't get close to people.*

"I guess maybe I should have asked you for your number," he said finally. "I'm sorry. Look, I've got to go . . . I'll talk to you later."

"Wait!" Her eyes flew open and she racked her brain for something to say as he came back on the line. She finally just blurted out, "Why did you call?"

"Because I wanted to hear your voice. I've got to go."

"If you wanted to hear my voice, then why are you so quick to hang up?" she demanded.

"Because I don't see any reason to stay on the phone with you if you don't want to talk to me," he said, his voice thick with cynicism.

"I never said I didn't want to talk to you," she snapped defensively. "I just wasn't expecting anybody to call."

"Usually people have phones because other people call them."

Not me—I keep a phone so I can get a couple of text messages a month, and maybe two fifteen-second phone conversations. She rubbed the back of her neck, wincing as her fingers dug into tense muscles. "Yeah, I've heard that a time or two before. Look, I'm sorry . . . I'm being a little bitchy and I know it. I just . . . well, like I said, the call surprised me and I don't do surprises well."

He was quiet and then finally, he said, "Yeah, I'm not much on surprises, either. And I *am* sorry . . . I shouldn't have messed with your stuff without asking you."

"So next time you'll ask permission before you go programming numbers into my phone?" she asked, forcing a lighthearted note into her tone. Already her brain was churning, though. What was he going to think when she had to change her phone, change her number . . .

You're making the assumption he's going to notice . . . or that you'll still be here. You know you have to leave soon, her common sense whispered.

"Nah . . . next time, I'll make *you* program the numbers into your phone."

In the background, Sara could hear the buzz of voices, the sound of a phone ringing, somebody yelling. "Where are you?"

"Work. Getting ready to head out for a few hours. It might be late before I'm done today."

He worked late sometimes. She'd noticed there'd been a couple of times when he came home even later than she did, and he was often gone before she got up in the morning. Curiosity gnawed at her. She wanted to know where he worked, and exactly what he did that had him working such weird hours. He would be gone for two or three hours one day, twelve or more the next.

She'd noticed that there were days it seemed he didn't work at all. There wasn't any sort of pattern to it, either.

But she didn't ask.

Couldn't ask.

"I guess maybe I'll see you in a day or two?"

He started to answer, then there was a loud noise. A series of crashes sounded through the connection, followed by raised voices. "Yeah, hopefully tomorrow, Sara. I've got to go."

The phone disconnected and she lowered it, staring at it in bemusement.

"You know," she murmured. "I think that's the first real phone conversation I've had in a very long time."

TWELVE

"SOMETIMES *I wonder if maybe I deserve this.*"

"*Deserve it? Damn it, Sar, what kind of thing could you have done to deserve what he does to you?*"

A soft sigh. "I know, I know. I just . . . I can't help it. I keep wondering how this happened. I . . . I don't know. I always thought I'd get married, have a couple of kids, and just live happily ever after. You know . . . the fairy tale."

"*Fairy tales aren't real, but that doesn't mean you don't deserve a happily ever after.*"

Happily ever after.

Sara was living in a fucking fairy tale, if ever there was one. Brooding, she shoved her hands under the running water and scrubbed them clean. One of her customers had managed to leave half of his food behind—*in* the seat—and she'd just spent the past five minutes cleaning up the mess.

Drying her hands off on a towel, she took a moment to take a deep breath, hopefully clear the irritation from her face. Irritated waitresses weren't conducive to good tips. After one more deep breath, she pushed through the swinging door, leaving the kitchen behind.

She'd been in a lousy mood most of the day, and all because she'd woken up in a mood so cheerful, it would have put Little Mary Sunshine to shame. And why had she been cheerful?

The bell over the door chimed and she glanced up, felt her heart skip a beat as the reason for her good mood, and subsequent shitty one, appeared in the doorway.

It was entirely possible to be blissfully happy and heartbroken, all at the same time. That knowledge had been creeping up on Sara over the past week or so, but as she stared at Quinn, she knew she couldn't hide from it anymore.

He made her happy, and at the same time, that made her miserable. It didn't help that she'd gotten that damn message, either— one of those messages that indicated she needed to make a call and there had been yet another insubstantial hint that there might be a change coming. But she couldn't *hope*. Couldn't *plan*. Couldn't do much more than wait.

Quinn saw her but didn't say anything, didn't head her way. As one of the other waitresses showed him to a vacant booth, one of her regulars flagged her down. She stopped to chitchat for a few seconds, but she couldn't have recalled what she said five seconds after she said it.

She was too aware of Quinn. She could feel him watching her. Feel the slow, lazy way his gaze roamed over her body. Under the cotton of her T-shirt, her nipples went tight and hard. Low in her belly, she ached.

That wasn't the worst of it, though.

He smiled at her and that faint grin hit her dead in the heart. She smiled back at him and he arched a brow, nodded at the empty place across from him. She glanced at the clock on the wall and then nodded. She hadn't taken her break yet and they weren't busy. She took a few minutes to turn in the orders she'd just taken, checked with one of the other waitresses to make sure her tables would be covered, then she started back to Quinn.

His eyes were half-closed, that smile tugging at his lips. She felt the warmth of his gaze roaming over her, and it left a heated trail, one that left her skin buzzing and her nipples tingling. She wished she'd taken a few more minutes to go back to the bathroom. Not that she could do much about the way she looked, wearing a T-shirt and jeans, her hair pulled back out of the way. Grimacing, she smoothed the shirt down as she slid into the booth across from him.

Over the past two weeks, the vivid bruising around his eye had gone from blue and black to green and yellow and now there was just the faintest discoloration along his left cheekbone. He smiled and reached across the table, catching her hand and lacing their fingers together.

Her heart melted at the gesture, but she managed a breezy grin as she said, "I dunno, maybe I'm a little forgetful, but when did I tell you where I worked?"

"You didn't." He lifted her hand and nibbled on her knuckles. "The pie did."

"The pie? You mean the pie from last night?" She blinked and frowned. She'd brought home half a pie the night before and they'd ended up eating it on the couch in Quinn's basement while watching *The Green Mile*. "Exactly how did a pie tell you where I worked?"

"I've had Annette's pie before." He glanced up at the older woman who manned the cash register. She waved at him and he nodded back. "Had some work here a few months back and discovered the pie then. Nobody makes chess pie quite the same way she does."

"Good detective skills," she murmured. "Relying on the taste buds. So are you here for more pie?"

"There's still a slice or two left in the fridge."

"Dinner, then?"

He grinned at her, a little-boy grin that brought out a dimple in his right cheek. "Just wanted to see if you were here like I thought."

"You could have asked."

"Yeah. But it didn't occur to me until I was at work today. Got to thinking about you and after I finished up, decided to swing by here." He leaned back in the seat, studying her with narrowed eyes. "I'm not pissing you off again, am I? Showing up here like this?"

"No." She *should* be irritated, but she wasn't. How could she get irritated because he'd wanted to see her? It wasn't like they'd been able to see each other much over the past few days. He'd been working late, and she didn't have a day off this week until Sunday. "Glad you were able to satisfy your curiosity. I haven't had dinner yet . . . you feel like hanging around to eat with me?"

"I was kind of hoping you'd ask." He slumped in the seat and read the menu that was written on a chalkboard along the wall behind the counter. "I'd planned on just getting a sandwich to take home if you weren't here. Eating with you sounds better."

Sara had eaten way too many solitary meals over the past few years. She had no problem sharing a meal—especially not with Quinn.

Meagan came to get their order. As she walked away, they fell into silence, Quinn toying with her fingers. Feeling somebody's eyes on her, she looked up and saw Meagan standing by the window behind the counter. As their gazes locked, Meagan started fanning her hand back and forth in front of her face.

Sara scowled and blushed.

"What's wrong?"

Jerking her attention back to Quinn, she gave him a smile. "Ahh . . . nothing."

He cocked a brow and glanced back over his shoulder. Meagan pretended to be busy. The second Quinn turned back around, the girl laid a hand over her heart and started patting her chest.

Sara decided she just needed to ignore her. Preferably before Quinn noticed.

"You been working here for a while?"

"A couple of months, I guess. This is where I met Theresa." Sara shrugged, hesitant to say much more. Old habits died hard, and she really didn't like talking much about herself, not to anybody, even him. Quinn rarely asked, so even though they'd been spending a decent amount of time together over the past few weeks, they didn't know too many personal details about each other.

Hell, she still didn't even know what kind of work he did and she was leery to ask, just because she hadn't wanted him doing the same. Of course, he'd gone and figured it out all on his own—and all because of a piece of pie.

With everybody else, she kept to herself because it was safer, because it was wiser. With Quinn, it was even more important, because he was so damned good at seeing below the surface—she didn't want him knowing her secrets, and she definitely didn't need to know more about him, because the more she knew, the more she liked.

But she was fooling herself. Not talking about herself didn't keep him from getting to know her, or vice versa. They both loved horror movies, although Quinn didn't get freaked out over some of the blood and gore the way she did. They both read a lot and even had some favorites in common, mostly in the fantasy or science fiction genres.

She'd even gotten him to read a romance—he was halfway through a J. D. Robb, and since she knew he didn't bother finishing a book he wasn't enjoying, she knew he liked it.

Not talking wasn't keeping her from falling for him, in the worst way imaginable.

"Theresa is how I ended up here to begin with," he said, grinning at her. "She also brought home some pie. She mentioned this little place where she liked to eat dinner before she went to play bingo, and after I had some of the pie, I looked this place up when I was in the area working."

"Annette's pie is addictive," Sara said.

Once more, silence fell between them. Those eyes of hers hid so many secrets, secrets that were driving Quinn crazy. As much time as they'd spent together lately, he still didn't know that much about her.

He knew about as much personal stuff about Sara as he knew about the receptionist at Martin's office . . . hell, less. He never would have thought something like that would bother him, but it did.

He wanted to know everything about her.

He wanted to know why she looked so sad sometimes. Why sometimes she looked so angry and frustrated. There were times when he caught a glimpse of the pain she kept hidden so deep, but when he tried to ask her if she was okay, she'd give him a smile, offer some kind of excuse about being tired . . . or she just redirected his attention elsewhere, using her hands and mouth until he couldn't even remember his own name.

He wanted to know why she worked at a place where he knew most of the employees were paid under the table.

He wanted to know why she dyed her hair. He'd suspected it for a while, ever since the night they'd first slept together—the curls between her thighs were lighter than the hair on her head, a little odd, but he hadn't asked.

A few days ago, when he'd left her house, the roots of her hair had been several shades lighter than the rest of it. When he saw her the next morning when they went running, her roots were the same shade of brown as the rest of her hair. He'd bet his bike that her reasons for doing it had nothing to do with vanity or a preference for dark blondish brown hair.

He wanted to know why she never talked about herself. Why she never asked him much of anything personal. He wanted to know everything . . . and too often it seemed he knew less than nothing.

Quinn was falling for her.

He no longer had any questions about whether or not he was about to put his heart in her hands. It was just a matter of time, because he was completely gone over her.

Yet he didn't know much more about her than her name. They talked books. They talked movies. But he didn't even know if she had any family. He didn't know where she'd been born, where she'd gone to school. He didn't know if she'd ever been married.

One thing that was proving to be very frustrating was the fact that he could find out all of those things, and damn easy. He had the tools he'd need right at his disposal and she wouldn't ever have to know. But he wanted her to tell him.

You could try asking.

Yeah. He could. But instinctively, he knew she didn't want to tell him anything about herself. The few awkward attempts he'd made, she'd neatly sidestepped answering much of anything, and she'd done it in a way that made him think she'd been dodging anything personal for quite a while.

She was hiding.

He just wished he could get her to open up and tell him what she was hiding from. He wanted her to trust him enough to tell him. He wanted that trust . . . he wanted it like crazy.

But in addition to wanting that trust, he wanted to help. Whatever or whoever it was she was hiding from, he wanted to help. The bad thing about hiding was that sooner or later, whatever a person was hiding from always caught up. He couldn't do much of anything to help her until he knew what it was.

The last time you tried to help a woman, it didn't really end too well, a sardonic voice drawled inside his head. Quinn tried to block it out—this wasn't the same situation. Elena was a world away from the woman in front of him now.

Different, yeah. But both have secrets, don't they? Or at least Elena did before she got killed. You even knew what most of those secrets were and you still couldn't help her . . .

"Quinn?"

Jerking his mind away from the dark misery of memories, he looked up and found Sara watching him, a concerned look on her face. There was also a plate of food in front of him, and he didn't even remember the waitress bringing it over.

"Sorry . . . just thinking about something."

"Must be a pretty serious something," Sara said softly. "You looked like you were about ready to spit nails."

"Serious enough." He reached for his fork and studied the plate in front of him. It was a steak, cooked medium rare, a huge pile of steak fries on the side. A few minutes ago, he'd been fairly hungry. Now his stomach was a hard, cold knot. He glanced at Sara, wondered if she'd ask him what he'd been thinking about.

Wondered if he could tell her if she did. He *wanted* to tell her, but just because he wanted to didn't mean the words would come.

But she didn't ask.

The silence between them no longer felt as easy as it always did, at least not for him. He ate mechanically because he didn't want her asking him what was wrong. He'd either have to lie or tell her that he was getting pissed off because she wouldn't talk to him, because she wouldn't tell him the things he needed to know.

Needed to know . . . man, was that a fucking switch. He didn't just want to know about her, he needed to. It was becoming an obsession, just like she was quickly becoming the center of his entire world.

Everything he did, it seemed he somehow managed to link it to her. He was finally in the habit of shaving regularly because he didn't want to scrape her soft skin with stubble. He'd gotten in the habit of eating fairly regularly because even though he didn't always feel hungry, he'd realized he was sometimes more surly than normal when he hadn't eaten in a while. He was even answering the stupid phone when the agency called, because he'd rather get done earlier than work late into the night. He'd much rather spend those nights with Sara.

God, was he ever falling for her . . .

"Man, if you looked like you were going to spit nails a few minutes ago, now you look like you've been hit across the head with a two-by-four."

He lifted his eyes away from his plate and found her staring at him, her chin propped on her hand. "Huh?"

A smile curled her lips. "I said you look like you've been hit across the head with a two-by-four. Thinking those same heavy thoughts?"

"Thinking about you." He caught her free hand, rubbed his fingers over the back of it.

She grimaced, her nose crinkling. "Man, I don't know if I like being the source of heavy thoughts, Quinn."

"I kind of like it," he said. He lifted her hand and nibbled on her knuckles. "Beats out a lot of the miserable shit I've had trapped inside my head."

"Wow." She cocked a brow at him. "That's flattering."

Scowling at her, he replayed those words through his head and then winced. "Hell. That does sound a little less than flattering, doesn't it?"

"Hmmm." She continued to gaze at him, but her eyes danced with suppressed laughter.

Fuck. He loved those eyes. Loved seeing the smiles that danced there, hated the sadness that too often broke his heart. He could look into those eyes every day for the rest of his life . . .

Son of a bitch.

Son of a fucking bitch.

Right there, right in the middle of a meal he didn't really want, in the middle of a crowded, mom-and-pop diner, he realized he was in love with her. He'd already gone and put his heart in her hands—and he was terrified.

Floored, his mouth dry and his heart racing, he leaned back against the padded bench and stared at her. Unable to tear his eyes away from her face, unable to speak, even when she started to squirm around under the weight of his stare.

"Ahhh . . . you're doing it again," Sara said, licking her lips. "Doing that drift off into outer space or something."

"No, I'm not," he answered, forcing the words past his dry throat.

He could look into those eyes, every day, for the rest of his life. And do it quite happily. He was in love with her.

And Quinn was abso-fucking-lutely clueless about how to handle it.

*   *   *

"WHY in the hell aren't you answering?" Quinn muttered to himself while he waited for somebody to pick up on the other end.

Quinn had tried calling Luke's cell phone and after it rolled over to voice mail, he'd hung up and tried calling the house. Back in his basement apartment, he paced the floor, listened to the phone ring, and tried to figure out if he'd lost a grip on reality.

Finally, somebody picked up the phone and Quinn didn't even wait for a greeting before he barked out, "Damn it, it's about fucking time."

There was a pause, and then a soft, female voice said, "The voice is pretty familiar, so I'm going to assume this is Quinn. You can't be Luke . . . I just left him out in the backyard. Besides, he knows I'd kick his ass if he came on the phone sounding like that."

Blood rushed to his cheeks and he swore. Immediately, he could have bit his tongue. "Ah . . . sorry, Devon. Uh . . . you said Luke's in the backyard?"

"Yes. I assume you want to talk to him?"

"Yeah . . . uh, yes, please." He pinched the bridge of his nose and tried to figure out why talking to the woman who'd married his brother always made him feel more than a little tongue-tied.

Actually, most women tended to do that to him . . . unless he disliked them. The ones he disliked, he just ignored or avoided. Trying to talk to them wasn't even an issue.

Sara was easy to talk to, though. He could talk to Sara forever . . .

"I'm getting him now. Is everything okay?"

"Yeah."

"That's good. Are you still in St. Louis?"

Quinn grimaced as he paced the floor. "Yeah, I'm still in St. Louis. Probably hanging around here, too."

After all, Sara was here. He wasn't going anywhere unless she went with him.

"That's good to hear . . . do me a favor, though. Call a little more often. Luke worries about you," Devon said quietly.

"He doesn't need to. I'm doing fine. Actually better than I have been in a while." A vague sense of shame rose within him, made him itch, but it wasn't the kind of itch that could be scratched. He didn't call his brother enough—he knew that. It normally didn't bother him. But having Devon point it out definitely did. "Look, I'll try to call more often."

"Good."

He heard the door open and then Devon's voice as she called out to Luke.

A few seconds later, Luke came on the line and his voice was flat and harsh. "What's wrong?"

"Nothing's wrong." Quinn scowled. *Well, other than the fact that I'm in love and I don't know what to do.*

Luke was quiet for about two seconds. "Nothing? You sure?"

"Yeah, I'm sure. I think I'd know if something was wrong," he snapped.

"Don't take this wrong, but if nothing's the matter, why are you calling?"

"You act like I've never called you before," Quinn said.

"Oh, you've called before. But it's almost always when I'm either pissed off, or something else is off with me. But I'm not pissed and there's nothing off. You don't ever really call just to talk." He blew out a breath and added, "So . . . are you calling just to talk?"

Once more, shame curdled inside. "Uh . . . well, not exactly."

"Shit. I knew something was wrong," Luke muttered. "Out with it, man. Just get it over with."

Seconds stretched out as Quinn tried to figure out what to say. What he needed to hear. How to say what he needed to say, and how to ask the questions he needed to ask. But the words were lodged in his throat, and in the end, it was all he could do to manage one single sentence.

"I met somebody."

"Somebody?" Luke parroted back.

Through their vague connection, Quinn could feel Luke's bemusement. He didn't get it—Luke didn't. Quinn had always picked up more from his brother than Luke could pick up from Quinn and right now, Quinn really hated that. He didn't know how to say whatever he needed to say, and if Luke could just pick up on what Quinn was feeling . . .

Then Luke *did* pick up on it. Quinn felt it echo through his twin only a heartbeat before Luke said, "Somebody . . . as in a female somebody, maybe?"

"Yeah." He reached the wall but turned around and instead of continuing on his marathon pacing session, he slumped back and sank to the floor, keeping his back braced against the wall. "A female somebody."

Once more, he picked up on something from Luke—a whole slew of somethings. Delight. Amazement. Disbelief. Curiosity.

"Okay . . . so tell me about this somebody."

"God, where do I even start . . ." Quinn closed his eyes and rested his head against the wall.

"Why not start with her name. What she looks like. Where you met her. Stuff like that, and we can work up from there."

"Her name's Sara . . ." He didn't realize it, but he was smiling. Smiling as he pictured her face, smiling as he told his brother about the woman who was becoming the most important part of his life.

THIRTEEN

Don stared down at the piece of paper in front of him, eyed the image of the smiling woman, and then looked back up at James. He swallowed nervously and said, "Are you sure this is the way you want to handle this?"

For two weeks, he'd wracked his brain, tried to think of another way, another road, another choice. And for two weeks, he'd failed. He'd known time was running out and tried to prepare himself for the possible outcomes, but he hadn't seen this one.

"If I wasn't sure, I don't believe I would have told you to go forward." James looked at his own copy, a frown on his face. "This was a last resort option. It's definitely not the ideal way to proceed. But a man does what he must."

Don swallowed, fear and anger bitter on his tongue.

So many might be fooled into believing that James was a devoted husband, one who was heartsick at the disappearance of his wife.

But Don knew better.

He cleared his throat and pasted a small, professional smile on his face. Despite the fear roiling inside him, despite his own doubts, despite the fact that he was nearly overcome with terror, he met James's stare levelly. His voice didn't shake as he asked, "Did you have any particular starting point in mind?"

Something on the computer screen on his desk caught James's attention. As the other man leaned forward and frowned, Don waited in silence. For a few moments, there was no sound but the hum of electronics while James took a pen from his desk and jotted down a few notes.

Tossing the pen aside, James leaned back in his seat and focused on Don once more. "I've already done most of the hard work. Surely you can figure out how to distribute the information in a suitable manner."

Don nodded and turned to go. As he pushed open the frosted glass door, James called his name. Pausing, he looked back.

"Don, don't mess this up. I will not tolerate further incompetence on your part."

* * *

"Stupid cunt. You didn't actually think I'd let you get away from me, did you?"

It was quiet—the only sounds were the unsteady breaths coming from the woman, and the man's calm, measured ones.

"Please, James . . ."

She fought against the dream, fought to surface. It clung to her, like an anchor, trying to drag her back down.

A warm hand stroked down her side and desperately, she snuggled close to the hard, strong body that lay next to hers. Even in sleep, she recognized him. She breathed in his scent and sighed out his name.

He wrapped an arm around her shoulders and kissed her temple. Comforted, she drifted back down into sleep and this time, if she dreamed at all, it wasn't any sort of dream that she had to hide from.

Hours later, the phone chirped out a familiar tune as she drifted in the twilight place between dreams and waking. Wrapped in Quinn's arms, she felt secure, safe, and loved.

The last thing she expected was to hear that synthesized little melody. It was enough to have her coming completely awake. She jerked up and stared across the room at the phone like it had suddenly turned into a monster.

"You okay?"

Even though her mind was racing, she looked at him and smiled. "Sure. Just wasn't expecting any messages this early."

Quinn glanced at the window. Already, vivid golden sunlight streamed in. It really wasn't all that early, maybe a little before eight, but she couldn't exactly tell him the truth, could she?

He canted a grin at her and caught a lock of her hair, tugging. "It's not really what I'd call early, baby."

"*Early* is a matter of opinion. Anything before ten is like the break of dawn," she said, keeping her tone light. Then she shifted to the edge of the mattress and swung her legs over the side. Her muscles kept trying to knot up on her and she had to make a concentrated effort not to tense up as she reached for the phone.

She called up the lone message and read it.

The message consisted of one single word.

Problems.

Her heart sank to her belly like a stone and her mind started to race.

Sara had all sorts of problems in her life.

She'd been working under the table and not paying any sort of taxes for two years.

She was living under an assumed name.

She couldn't go home.

None of the people she loved in her life knew where she was. She hadn't spoken to them since she'd started running.

She'd left behind unpaid bills. She'd left behind responsibilities.

She'd left behind her entire life—but none of that was what kept her up late at night worrying. None of that had anything to do with the message on her phone.

There was only one problem that would have her getting that message. Her hand wanted to shake. She didn't let it. Quinn lay in the bed watching her, and even though she knew no more than a few seconds had passed, if she didn't head back to the bed soon, as in the next second or two, he was going to ask questions. She didn't want him asking questions.

She didn't want to lie to him.

God, she was so tired of living a lie.

After she deleted the message, she laid the phone back on the table and turned back to him, giving him a look of practiced aggravation. "Text messages annoy the hell out of me—whatever happened to people just calling to talk to you?"

"Everything okay?" he asked.

Apparently her practiced look of aggravation wasn't fooling him. She shrugged and said, "Yeah."

No.

He'd shifted, sitting up in the bed with his back braced against the headboard. His body, long, hard, and scarred, gleamed like gold next to the soft white sheets. He sat with one knee drawn up, an elbow resting on it.

He looked like a dream come to life.

Hell, he *was* a dream come to life. She just wished he could be *her* dream.

But that wasn't going to happen. It couldn't happen and she couldn't pretend otherwise. Not now. Not anymore.

With her gut clenching and knotting, smiling at him was one of the hardest things she'd ever done. She sauntered back to bed, acting like she didn't have a care in the world, and inside, she thought that her heart just might be breaking.

Problems. And just when she'd been ready to let herself start to hope.

There was no reason to figure out what the problems were. There was only one thing she could do.

She had to disappear . . . again.

Leave behind the life she'd started to make here.

Leave behind Quinn.

Sinking down on the bed, she settled next to him, lying with her head on his chest and blinking her eyes against tears that threatened to fall free. She couldn't cry. Couldn't cry. Couldn't let him see . . .

"You sure everything's okay?" Quinn asked, his voice soft and low.

"Ummm. Just tired. Might try to get a little more sleep before I head into work."

He rubbed her neck, his fingers working the knotted muscles until they were soft as putty. "You didn't sleep too well last night. Bad dreams?"

"I dunno. Maybe." She didn't always remember her dreams, but something had disturbed her—she remembered feeling that ugly, snaking fear, hot, vicious rage . . . and then Quinn. Everything else had faded and he was all that existed for her. "I don't always remember when I have nightmares, but I definitely didn't sleep well."

"Then you should sleep some more." He threaded a hand through her hair, stroking it back from her forehead.

"Maybe you could help me get back to sleep." She glanced up at him and gave him a smile she didn't feel. Laying a hand on his belly, she stroked down until she could close her fingers around his cock.

"Maybe." His lids drooped low over his eyes. He rocked his hips upward and covered her hand with his, using his fingers to tighten her grasp. "You could probably talk me into trying, at least. If you ask real nice."

Her heart was breaking.

She smiled at him, despite the ache in her chest, and wiggled down in the bed. She lowered her head, licked the head of his cock. Quinn jerked, his breath hissing out of him.

"How nice should I ask?" she whispered, opening her mouth and taking his penis inside, sucking lightly. She wanted more. Wanted everything. Needed to take it . . . *now.*

Desperation drove her as she shoved her hair back over her shoulder and looked up at Quinn, staring at him as she wrapped a hand around the base of his cock, held him steady. Their gazes locked as she licked him, from root to tip.

"How nice should I ask, Quinn?" she demanded, lifting her head up to stare at him once more.

"I think you're asking just fine," he muttered, sliding his hand into her hair and tugging her head back down.

The head of his cock nudged her lips and she opened her mouth, sucked him inside. Sucked him deep. He bumped into the back of her throat, but she didn't stop until pain and the lack of air made her. Over and over again, until he was growling under his breath and swearing, his voice harsh and ragged.

"Enough, Sara." He jerked on her hair, forced her to still. "Stop, okay?"

Gazing up at him, she whispered, "I don't wanna."

Quinn shifted and sat up, reached between her thighs. Pumped two fingers inside her pussy and twisted his wrist. "Too bad. Ride me."

He tried to tug her on top of him but Sara pulled away. She turned around and smiled at him over her shoulder. "Maybe I want you to ride *me* . . ."

Quinn's mouth went dry as she bent over, the graceful line of her back, the round, firm curve of her ass. He came to his knees and bent over her, pressing his lips to her spine. "I need to get another rubber," he rasped.

"No, you don't. Touch me, Quinn."

His hands shook as he laid them on her hips. "This isn't the best idea, darlin'."

She looked at him over her shoulder, her eyes dark and unreadable. "I don't care. I'm clean. If you weren't, you wouldn't have ever touched me."

"Other issues."

Her lashes lowered over her eyes and then she shook her head. "Not so much an issue . . . bad timing."

Not smart. Not smart at all. But Quinn wasn't overly concerned with being smart. He just wanted to get lost inside her. He used one hand to hold his cock steady as he pressed against her. She was slick, satiny wet, as she closed around him. She rocked back to take more and he had to use both hands to slow her down.

"Easy, darlin'."

He squeezed the soft flesh of her rump, ran his thumb along the crevice between as he began to shaft her, keeping his pace slow and steady. She shivered as he touched her. Watching her with hooded eyes, he used a firmer touch, pressing his thumb against the tight pucker of her ass. Sara whimpered and pushed back. A high, startled cry escaped her lips as he pushed just the tip of his thumb inside the tight passage.

"Please . . ."

Quinn stilled. Then he bent over her and kissed her shoulder. "Please what?"

She pushed back demandingly against him and when he pressed harder against her, forcing just a little deeper inside, she sobbed and demanded, "That . . . please . . ."

He swore and pulled away. "Stay there."

Quinn might not always be prepared for anything, but he was damn good at improvising. Sara kept a bottle of baby oil in her bathroom and he grabbed it, striding back to bed. His cock throbbed and his mouth was all but watering as he climbed back on the bed and knelt behind her.

He squeezed some of the baby oil out, used it to coat his fingers, and then he pressed his index finger against her anus. "Is that what you want, Sara?"

She groaned and rocked back, taking him inside. Gasping for air, she said, "Yes . . . oh, please . . . yes . . ."

"Just this, or more?" He twisted his finger and stroked, working the oil deeper inside, easing past the tight muscles.

"More."

"Tell me what you want," he demanded.

"Fuck me . . . right there. Please, Quinn."

He grabbed the bottle of oil and with shaking hands, slicked it over his length, gritting his teeth against the near-torturous sensation of his hand gliding over his cock as he prepared himself.

"Tell me if I hurt you."

"You won't."

Hell, he hoped not. He was clinging to what little remained of his self-control. Wrapping his hand around his cock, he braced the other low on her spine. Fitting the head to her entrance, he pressed against her. The soft, tight flesh yielded to him, flowering open around him.

She took it with a moan, bearing down on him.

When she started to stiffen, he stopped and pulled back, then once more started the slow, painfully erotic process all over again. Each time she started to tense up, he pulled back, and each time, he worked a little deeper inside her until she had taken all of him. Buried inside her, her ass pressed snug against his pelvis, Quinn squeezed his eyes closed and sucked in harsh, desperate gulps of air.

Sara shifted and then, between his thighs, he felt the light brush of her fingers over his balls. "Don't," he ordered through gritted teeth.

She did it again, wiggling a little more, and then she closed her fingers around his balls, tugging lightly.

"Damn it, Sara, stop." Sweat popped out on his brow and he

squeezed the soft flesh of her ass under his hands, tight, too tight, but damn it, he couldn't think, couldn't breathe . . .

She tugged again and he growled. Using his weight, he bore her flat to the bed and started to shaft her, deep and hard.

Sara cried out, her voice sharp, a keening hungry sound. He gripped one hip in his hand, canted her a little higher. He braced his free hand by her head and she reached up, wrapped her fingers around his wrist, her nails biting deep into his flesh.

"Please . . . harder!"

Flesh slapped against flesh.

Harsh groans and whimpering cries filled the air.

A desperate need filled him, spurred by her hot, wild hunger. His balls burned, ached, chills raced down his spine, and the need to come was almost painful. But not . . . yet. Not yet . . . oh, fuck. Sara clenched around him and shuddered. She started to come and he swore, clenching his teeth as she tightened around him, milking his cock.

Unable to fight it, unable to resist another second, he climaxed, his cock jerking and pulsing as he emptied himself deep inside her ass. It lasted forever . . . every time he thought he was empty, she'd clench down around him again, and it was like it started all over.

Finally, he collapsed atop her, his muscles shaking so bad, he doubted he could even stand up. Wrapping an arm around her waist, he rolled to his side. She whimpered and snuggled back against him. He lay there with his chest against her sweat-slicked back. Both of them were still struggling to breathe. His cock twitched against her rump as she shuddered. Laying a hand on her hip, he kissed her shoulder.

She sighed and angled her head around, pressing her lips to his arm. "Quinn . . ."

"Yeah?"

When she didn't answer, he managed to push up onto his elbow and peer down at her. "What?"

She smiled solemnly and murmured, "Nothing . . . I just like saying your name." She wiggled around until they faced each other. "Lie down and hold me for a while."

Hold me . . .

I just like saying your name.

Man, he could hold her forever. He could lie there and listen to her sighing out his name forever. Wrapping her in his arms, he rested his chin on her head and murmured, "You okay?"

"Ummm. Ask me in a few hours. Might be able to figure out the answer then."

A few hours wouldn't work for him.

A few years wouldn't be enough for him to untangle the knots she had him tied into. Assuming he was even inclined to try . . . which he wasn't.

"Probably won't be here in a few hours," he said, stroking a hand down her back. Although, man, he'd sure as hell love to be. He couldn't think of anything he'd rather do than spend the day in bed with her. But it wasn't an option. "Sooner or later, I've got to get up. I've got to get some work done today . . . boss is bitching. Kinda surprised he hasn't already started calling . . ."

And his cell phone chose that exact moment to ring. He recognized the ringtone and swore. Easing away from Sara, he lay on his back and stared up at the ceiling. After three rings, it stopped, but apparently Martin wasn't in the mood to leave a voice mail because it started ringing again almost right away.

"Speak of the devil," he muttered.

"Sounds like somebody wants to talk to you," Sara said, her voice husky.

"Sounds that way." He rolled into a sitting position, eying the phone where it lay on the table next to Sara's. It was on the third ring again. Silence. Then it started all over again.

Shoving out of the bed, he went to the table. Feeling Sara's eyes on him, he turned to look at her as he answered. "Yeah?"

"Need your ass in here, Rafferty. As in today. Got something major and if you don't get here soon, don't bother coming in again, period," Martin snapped.

"If that's supposed to scare me, it didn't work," Quinn drawled. He doubted Martin was serious, but he did some mental tallying anyway, calculated how much money he had in the bank, and while it wasn't anything to write home about, as long as he was careful, he could go a few months without steady work.

Sooner or later, he'd need a job, and not too many were going to pay Quinn the sort of money he made working for Martin. But he wasn't too inclined to share that bit of information.

"Damn it, are you listening to a thing I'm saying or not?

Scowling, Quinn said, "Sorry. Preoccupied. What are you snarling about?"

"I said, I'm not trying to scare you, man," Martin repeated, his voice edgy. "You're good at this. You're fast, you're smart, you don't complain, and you produce good results. But I need somebody reliable around here, somebody who actually bothers to answer the phone when we call. Somebody with a semi-regular schedule."

"Shit, Martin, I've been answering the damn phone and doing it pretty regularly. I put in three days this week already and four last week. What the hell else do you want?"

"That semi-regular schedule would be nice. The way things are right now, I could really use you full-time, but I damn well need you in here today."

Quinn frowned. "Why?"

Martin started to answer, but then off in the background there were raised voices, loud, and getting louder by the second. Martin had to raise his voice to be heard over the screamers. "Just get in here and I'll explain. Hurry it up, though . . . Juanita called in sick and Carolyn's running late. This place is a zoo."

He disconnected and Quinn lowered the phone with a frown. He glanced back and found Sara watching him with a serious look on her face.

"Everything okay?"

"Yeah." He tossed the phone down and said, "I need to get a shower, though. Head in for a while. Sounds like they've got a mess on their hands." He paused, absently wondered, yet again, if she'd ask him what he did.

But she didn't. She just gazed at him solemnly, lying on her side amid the tangled sheets. "Then I guess you'd better get going."

He went back to the bed and knelt at the side, kissing her cheek gently. "Are you okay? I didn't hurt you . . . ?" Stroking a hand down her side, he rested it on her hip.

"I'm fine." She turned her head and pressed her mouth to his. "Stop worrying."

"I'll try." He forced a smile, kissed her again, and then pulled away before he ended up crawling back into bed with her. He had to shower, and then he had to get going.

But he didn't want to leave. She gazed at him with sleepy eyes, that solemn smile on her lips, and all he wanted to do was climb back into bed with her and wrap his arms around her. Never let go.

Never.

Standing by the bed, he gazed at her and tried to understand why all of a sudden, he couldn't seem to make his feet move, couldn't get his body to cooperate.

"Why don't you come get me when you get home from work?" he said, even though he already knew he'd be outside waiting for her.

"Sure . . . that is if you're not waiting for me." She smiled as she said it and then yawned, stretched. "You better get going. Don't want your sort of boss getting ticked off at you."

* * *

Quinn really wasn't too concerned if his sort of boss got too pissed off at him. No, he didn't really want to end up without a job, but he wasn't too convinced this was how he wanted to spend the rest of his life. He'd already spent more than a decade of his life dealing with scum, first in the Rangers and now here working for Martin.

But he also couldn't think of much else that he'd be good at.

And he wondered what Sara would think about his job. It wasn't the first time he'd thought that, and more than once, he'd almost brought it up, but he hadn't been too sure how to do it. Having any sort of serious relationship with a woman was new territory for him—he hadn't had a serious girlfriend in high school, and his life hadn't been conducive to it when he was in the army. Elena had been the first woman he'd been serious about, and their lives definitely hadn't been conducive to intimate or personal conversations.

What if she didn't like what he did? Quinn frowned and thought that over, decided if she didn't really like it, then he'd find something else. It wasn't like he was seriously attached to the job—she mattered more, so if it bothered her, he figured he could find something else.

He doubted she'd ask him, but the bounty-hunting thing was something he'd stumbled into—he could figure out something else he'd be good at, something that wouldn't drive him crazy doing it. No desk jobs—he could do a lot of things for Sara, but he couldn't see himself doing a desk job for anyone.

There were other jobs, though. Other options. Granted, he might not qualify for a lot now, but that could be rectified. He was reasonably smart, so if he could just figure out something he did want to do, he could get whatever training or education he needed to do it.

Of course, it was entirely possible it wouldn't be necessary. Maybe Sara wouldn't care what he did for a living. It wasn't like he was selling drugs—illegal shit would definitely bother her, but that wasn't an issue.

And it wasn't like he was a Ranger still. His job came with some risks, but as long as he was careful, it wasn't really dangerous.

They needed to talk about it, he decided. They actually needed to talk about a lot of things, and since Sara didn't seem to be in any rush to initiate some kind of relationship talk, Quinn was going to do it.

Granted, the thought of doing so tied his tongue into knots, but he wanted her to know how he felt about her. He wanted to know how she felt about him. He wanted to know more about her, and he wanted her to know more about him—or rather he *needed* her to know about him.

Some of his darker, uglier secrets he didn't want to share, but he needed to—needed her to know him. Completely.

Just like he needed to know her, completely.

He was sick and tired of pretending this was some sort of casual relationship.

So they were going to have to talk.

Now . . . if he could just figure out how to go about it.

FOURTEEN

It was very hard to pack while crying.

The last time it had been this hard to pack up her belongings had been two years ago. Hell, she didn't know if it had been this hard then, even though she'd left a lot more behind.

She'd hated it, but she'd known she had to do it.

Now . . . now she just wasn't sure. Or at least she told herself she wasn't, even though she knew there weren't any other choices. Her hands shook as she folded her few clothes. Tears rolled down her cheeks to plop onto her shirts, and she ended up using one of them to wipe her face dry.

"Stop crying," she told herself. Her voice wobbled. Setting her jaw, she closed her eyes and said, "Stop crying. You knew this was coming."

Yeah, she'd known. But for some reason, she hadn't expected it to hurt like this. She hadn't thought *anything* could hurt like this.

God, she didn't want to leave.

She wanted Quinn. Wanted to call him and tell him to come back, make him come back here so she could tell him everything. It would take hours and by the time it was done, it might even be too late . . . she didn't even know how much time she had. Maybe

if she took enough time, she would not have a chance to leave—
the choice would be taken away from her, and she wouldn't have
to disappear without saying so much as good-bye to Quinn.

She didn't even know why she was running.

"Bullshit," she muttered.

She was running because of one fucking message that said
Problems. There hadn't been any messages since, and no calls,
although she waited on pins and needles. For all she knew, it was
something slight . . .

"And yet more bullshit," she snarled, hurling the clothes she
held onto the futon and storming to the window.

She'd apparently gotten very good at bullshitting herself.

Too good at it.

Leaning her brow against the glass, she stared outside, taking
in the bright splashes of color that painted Theresa's yard. The
flowers were in full bloom, a myriad of pinks, purples, yellows,
and reds. Cheerful oranges mingled with mellow blues. Roses and
morning glories climbed a trellis set near a stone bench along the
back of the property line.

Tears stung her eyes as she stared at the bench. A couple of
days ago, she'd actually made it home before Quinn and she'd
waited on that bench for him to get off of work. They'd made out
on the hard slab of stone like a couple of horny teenagers. It had
been hot, sweet . . . and fun.

There wouldn't be any more nights like that.

All because of a selfish, cruel bastard . . .

Her hands closed into fists, nails biting into her palms. She wel-
comed the rush of anger. She'd take the anger any day over the pain.
She'd take it, store it up . . . and someday, she just hoped she had
a chance to use it. Setting her jaw, she dashed away the tears and
tipped her head back, staring sightlessly at the ceiling. She breathed
the anger in, let it chase away everything else.

Yeah, she'd take the anger any day of the week.

She finished the rest of her packing on autopilot. It didn't take that long. She'd accumulated a little more during her time in St. Louis than she'd planned to, but most of it was clothes or books. Things she'd have to leave behind.

She scrawled a quick note on a piece of paper and left it on the table, along with her rent money.

Theresa, I had to go. Here's the rent for the month. You're welcome to the books or you can give them to Goodwill, if you like. Thank you.

That was it.

She also scrawled a note for Quinn, tucking it inside the book she'd borrowed from him.

I'm sorry to leave like this. Things came up and I can't stay. I'll miss you.

How mundane.

How empty.

She was going to miss him like nothing else.

She'd miss him more than she missed the life she'd left behind when she started running. She wasn't sure if there would be a day when she didn't think about him.

I'll miss you. It didn't even touch on what she wanted to tell him. *I'll miss you. I don't want to leave. I just don't have a choice. I think I'm in love with you and I'd give anything to stay.*

Anything.

But she didn't tell him any of that. He wouldn't understand why she had to go, and she didn't want him trying to figure it out. Part of her questioned the wisdom of the notes—questioned the wisdom of leaving behind anything at all.

She didn't like leaving any piece of herself. And there were pieces . . . and not just the clothes or books she couldn't take. Somewhere along the way, she'd started to settle in here without realizing it, although looking back, she could see it clear as day.

She'd put flowers in a little vase by the window. There was a pretty throw that she'd picked up shopping one day, draped over the back of the futon. A small glazed bowl that she had bought at a shop in the mall. A couple of large mugs that she'd bought for her morning coffee—the ones that Theresa had in the apartment were those dainty, delicate sort of cups that she could empty in three gulps.

This wasn't some nameless flop that would be taken over by another desperate soul in a matter of hours . . . this had been something close to home. She loved the place, even the pastel yellow walls and that miserable excuse of a bed. Well . . . maybe not the bed.

But she loved it here.

She was leaving a home behind. Again.

Only this time it was worse, because she was also leaving Quinn behind. And the part of her she was leaving with him wasn't something that she'd ever be able to replace.

* * *

"It's your lucky day," Martin said as Quinn came in and dropped into the seat across from his desk.

The chair, like the desk, was worn and well used, but comfortable. Quinn slumped low in it and crossed his arms over his chest. "If it was my lucky day, I'd still be in bed."

Wrapped around Sara.

Making love to her again. Then maybe having that talk. Or maybe talking first, then making love to her.

Unaware of Quinn's wandering attention span, Martin laughed.

"Oh, you'll change your mind. It really is your lucky day . . . I'd planned on turning this over to Connie—she's a little more experienced in straight missing persons' cases, but apparently her daughter has gone into early labor and she needed to be with her. She won't be in for a few days and this isn't going to wait."

"I don't do missing persons," Quinn said, frowning.

"You do now. Think of it as a promotion. You're hell on wheels when it comes to bond enforcement, but when I was trying to fig-ure out who to give this job to since Connie is out, my gut said to go with you. So that's what I'm doing." He pushed a manila folder closer to Quinn. "Our client here apparently has a lot of money to spend. He's selected some of the top detective agencies in the country to help locate his missing wife, and my agency is one of the ones selected. He's offered me a very nice chunk of money up front, regardless of whether we find her or not, to cover expenses while we search for her. If we're the ones to locate his wife, we get an even nicer chunk of change."

Lifting a brow, Quinn asked, "How nice?"

"Nice enough to make the money you get for bringing in skips look like chump change."

Since he made pretty decent money bringing the skips in, some-thing that made those jobs look like chump change sounded rather nice. Still, he wasn't much for the missing persons bit.

"Any idea what the wife's story is? Did she leave him?"

Martin shrugged. "No. I didn't ask, and I don't care. My job is finding the wife—that's all I care about. That's all you can care about if you take the job." He paused for a second and then asked, "Do you want the job?"

Still not looking at the file, he tapped it against his knee and studied Gearing. His gut was telling him to pass. Finding skips was one thing—these were people on the run from the law, and regardless of guilt or not, somebody had plunked down a chunk of change to ensure they'd hang around for their hearing. Skipping out on bail, in Quinn's mind, was just plain shitty. It violated a trust, it cost somebody money, and most of the guys he'd brought in had been the kind of scum that really did need to be off the street. He could even view it as a community service.

But missing persons . . . he wasn't entirely comfortable with it.

He thought about his mom, wondered what his life would have

been like if his dad had been able to find him early on—different. Better. But still, not everybody who disappeared was anything like his mother.

Some people disappeared because they had to.

"Martin, I've got to be honest with you. I'm not real comfortable going on the hunt for a woman who may have perfectly good reasons for disappearing. What if I find her and it turns out the husband was beating on her or something?"

"Then she can file for divorce. He's already seen the contracts— he's well aware that he can't use our services if he has any sort of malicious intent." Martin replied.

Quinn snorted. "Words on paper, man. They sound all nice and legal and yeah, it covers your ass should somebody get hurt, but they are still just words and they won't do a damn thing to stop a man who's determined to hurt somebody."

"Rafferty, you never struck me as the Boy Scout type." Martin rolled his eyes. "You also never struck me as the dramatic type. This is a job—all you have to do is find the woman for him and we get paid."

"So just find her and tell him where to find her?"

A cagey smile appeared on Martin's face. "Well, there *is* a bonus for delivering her to him, although the wife isn't on the run from the law, so you can't exactly apprehend her. But a clever man could figure out a way to work things out."

Quinn's gut continued to churn. The file in his hand felt like it weighed a ton, even though it was just a few sheets of paper. Paper . . . words and pictures on paper that would give him the info he'd need if he was going to try locating a woman who probably didn't want to be found. Maybe a woman who shouldn't be found.

He glanced down at it and then back at Martin. Shaking his head, he tossed it onto Martin's desk. "I don't think I want any part of this, Martin."

"Aren't you the least bit curious how much money this could get you?"

Martin leaned back in his seat, smiling.

Rising to his feet, Quinn shook his head. "Money's not everything." Even as he said it, though, he found himself thinking about the discussion he wanted to have with Sara.

What if she really wasn't big on him doing the bond enforcement bit? He didn't see her as the kind of woman who'd expect him to change for her, or a woman who'd even ask, but he wanted her to be happy.

Money's not everything, but if I could get some more money put aside, maybe I could look into going to college or something . . .

It would give him options. A lot of options. Maybe he could even find something a little more normal. Normal—hell, he wasn't certain he even *wanted* normal.

But the lack of choices really ate at him sometimes. He grimaced and shoved a hand through his hair.

Martin, sensing Quinn's sudden wavering, named a figure.

Quinn's eyes widened, then narrowed. "Excuse me?"

"You heard me. One million dollars to the agency that finds her. You'd get 25 percent."

"You're shitting me." *A million dollars?*

"Oh, I'm dead serious. I don't joke about money, my friend. If we find her, you'll get two hundred and fifty grand." Martin grinned and shook his head. "I'm not kidding, Quinn. This isn't the kind of job that comes our way very often, and Connie may well kick my ass for not offering it to her, but I'm not wasting time on this. We've already received the up-front money—one hundred thousand, to be exact—and I'll give you 10 percent if you agree to the job. Hell, I'll have Juanita cut the check for you now—all you have to do is say yes. And if you find her, we get the million. Plus, if you deliver her, the bonus is yours. One hundred percent yours, since you'll be the one doing the work."

Quinn looked back at the file and swallowed. Acid churned in his gut. Indecision, something he was unfamiliar with, weighed on him. He wanted to say no . . . but he wanted that money. Hell, if he had that kind of money, he could take some time, maybe really think about going back to school and figure out what he wanted to do with his life.

"Look, Quinn. I think I understand why you're so leery of saying yes. Let's assume that the woman *is* running away from him because he's dangerous. Sooner or later, he's bound to find her. Since you're already concerned about that, maybe you'd be the better man to find her anyway, because you *are* concerned. You can make sure she knows she has options. I'll even have Juanita do some research, see if we can't figure out some options a battered wife might have."

Quinn knew when he was being conned. Despite how much he could use that money, he still had the inclination to say no. There were two things that kept him from walking out—he did need that money, needed the options it could give him. And, assuming he was the one to find her, he damn well would make sure he wasn't turning a woman over to a man who had hurt her. Options. Yeah, he could make damn sure she knew she had options.

Blowing out a breath, he lifted his gaze and focused on Martin's face. "You're a conniving bastard, you know that?"

"It's what makes me a good businessman." Martin didn't look the least bit offended

"Yeah, well, you can shove your businessman tendencies up your ass. I'll take the job."

Martin grinned, but before he could respond, Quinn held up a hand and said, "*But* I'm doing it on my terms. All the way on my terms."

"Meaning . . . ?"

"Meaning I'm not doing any kind of progress reports with the husband, or with you. Assuming I'm able to find her—and you realize that's one big fucking *if*—I'll talk to her and make my own call on whether or not I need to inform the husband of her whereabouts."

"That's not how this works, Rafferty."

"If you want me to try and find her, and obviously you do, then that's how it is going to have to work," Quinn replied with a shrug. He leaned forward, bracing his elbows on his knees. "Hypothetically, let's say I *do* find her. Let's say I tell the husband where to find her, and let's say he was abusing her and that's why she ran. What's it going to do to you if he kills her? If you put her in his hands, or even if you just give him the means to find her and he kills her?"

A muscle jerked in Martin's cheek and his eyes fell away from Quinn's.

"I don't know about you, man, but I've got enough things keeping me awake at night," he said quietly, shaking his head. "I don't need to add to it. So, again, if I do this, I do it my way."

Martin's cheeks puffed up and then he blew out a hard, heavy sigh. "Fine. But you had better be very, very certain there are legit reasons—it's not just money on the line here. It's my business, my reputation. I won't have you getting suckered by a pair of tits and big brown eyes. You got it?"

Quinn smirked and rolled his eyes. "Yeah, like I'm going to be that easy to get suckered."

He shook his head and then flipped open the file.

For a few seconds, his eyes didn't make sense of what he saw.

They just couldn't.

Martin started to talk and Quinn tore his eyes away from the picture in the file, certain that he'd been imagining things. He listened to Martin ramble, although none of that made much sense either, and then after a few more seconds passed, he rubbed his eyes and looked back down.

This time, it made sense.

Big brown eyes. Pretty breasts, framed enticingly by the lace of her wedding dress. Her hair, swept up and back in some complicated female style.

Sara Davis.

No . . . not Sara Davis.

According to the info listed just above the picture, her name was Sarah Elizabeth Morgan.

She was thirty years old, nice Ivy League college education.

And she was married.

Fucking married.

* * *

"It won't work."

"Yes, it will. You just have to be careful."

Once more, they went over everything. Sitting in a truck stop off I-65, just a little north of Indianapolis, they poked and prodded at each detail, tried to answer every question that might come up once they parted ways.

Occasionally somebody would glance at them, and each look made her skin crawl, although she understood what caught their attention. Even the sunglasses wouldn't hide a black eye that size. No amount of makeup could disguise the swollen mouth or the little cut.

"No P.O. boxes, Sarah. You understand me?"

"Yeah, I understand."

"No library cards."

"I get it!" Her voice was loud, harsh. Then she slumped in the seat and covered her face. "God, what if this is a mistake?"

"It may well be. If you have other suggestions, I'm all ears. Hey . . . I know. We could try going to the police. I mean, I realize it's a radical idea, but why not give it a shot?"

Sarah curled her lip at the idea. She wasn't at all interested in going to the police—she didn't trust them.

Maybe she should have thought a little longer, a little harder, tried to come up with other suggestions. Now it was too fucking late, and on top of everything else, she had to deal with a broken heart that seemed to ache more and more with every beat.

Two years ago, this had seemed like the way to go forward. Not exactly the *ideal* way, but the safer way. Safe—as in it was safer to drive 120 mph down the highway wearing a seat belt as opposed to driving 120 mph down the highway *not* wearing a seat belt. There hadn't been a lot of good options—this had just seemed like the best choice at the time.

Sara stood in the doorway of the little apartment and took one last look around. Now, regrets, guilt, grief, and doubts were tearing into her with razor-sharp claws.

If she gave in to those emotions, though, she was going to collapse and she didn't have time to collapse. The damned phone in her pocket weighed as much as an anchor—one that tied her to her past, one that reminded her of promises that had been made. She wanted to pull it out of her pocket, throw it on the ground, and dance on it until it was nothing but busted plastic and wires.

Instead, she checked her bags, the money she'd hidden away on her body, and the time. With her duffel bag slung over one shoulder and her carry-on-sized suitcase in the other hand, she slipped out of the apartment. As always, she'd packed light. Anything she didn't have to have she left behind.

Normally that just consisted of a few changes of clothes, her money, and a small toiletry kit. One extra thing had ended up in her bag this time, though. One of Quinn's T-shirts. It had been thrown over the foot of her bed and while she was packing, she hadn't been able to resist picking it up, bringing it to her face, breathing it in. Tears had knotted in her throat as she pushed it inside her bag. If she knew herself at all, she suspected she'd be sleeping in that T-shirt until it fell apart on her.

It had taken a lot longer than normal to pack up, but she suspected she was subconsciously delaying herself.

Hoping Quinn might call.

Hoping he might get home early.

Just plain hoping.

Tears blurred her eyes as she locked the door of the private outer entrance. She didn't want to go through the other door and risk seeing Theresa in the house. Risk having to talk, having to evade questions she couldn't answer.

She was so done with telling lies.

She was so tired of running.

"How much longer do I have to keep doing this?" she muttered.

But there was nobody there to answer.

Sighing, she started down the steps. She had a half hour before she could catch a ride downtown on the Metrolink. From there, she'd go to the bus station. Instead of heading south, though, she was going to head west. Get even farther away this time. Sometime soon, she'd have to make a phone call and figure out just what the *problems* were, but she couldn't handle it now.

She rounded the corner of the walk and her heart jumped into her throat.

Theresa was sitting on an iron bench that wrapped around the base of a towering oak—almost like she'd been waiting. The older woman's gaze lingered on Sara's suitcase. Their gazes locked and Theresa smiled a sad, knowing smile.

"Already time, huh?"

"Ahhhh . . ."

Theresa waved a hand. "Oh, don't feel like you need to tell me anything. I'd rather you say nothing than offer me lies, and I realize that it may not be easy for you to tell the truth. Maybe you can't." Leaning her back against the tree trunk, she said, "Tell me something, Sara . . . Do you get tired of running?"

A knot lodged itself in Sara's throat, one she thought was going to choke her. She swallowed while tears started to well up in her eyes. "Do I get tired of running?"

One tear broke free and she dashed it away. Angry and hurting, she glared at Theresa and demanded, "Do you think I *like* running? I hate it and I wish I could stop, but I just can't see too many alternatives."

"I believe you," Theresa said quietly. "I do. I don't know what you're running from, or why. I do know you've been happy here and I hate that you're going to lose that.

"You know you can't run forever." She rose from the iron bench and walked over to Sara. Sara stood frozen as the older woman enfolded her in a hug. She smelled like spices, fresh baked bread, and White Diamonds perfume. "Sometimes when you're lost inside a problem, Sara, it can be very, very hard to see that there are other alternatives, other options. There's almost always a way, darling."

FIFTEEN

*M*ARRIED.

His gut burned, his throat ached, and his chest felt like it was going to explode.

The information from the report was imprinted on his mind. Approximately two years ago, Sarah Elizabeth Morgan had disappeared from the home she shared with her husband. She'd taken with her some clothes, a car that had been a Christmas gift a year earlier, some pretty expensive antiques, and all of her jewelry.

The antiques had been worth somewhere in the neighborhood of a million dollars, easy—and that was at legal auctions. Keeping them out of the public eye, for private bidders, there might be even more money. A few of them had resurfaced in legit markets, but many were still unaccounted for.

It took only two days to locate her car. It had been auctioned off and the check was deposited. Half of the money was withdrawn a week later and that was the last time they could find any record of Sarah Elizabeth Morgan. It was as though she'd just dropped off the face of the earth. She never once tried to access the rest of the money from selling her car. On occasion, some of the jewelry would turn up, either at a pawn shop or in an auction, but none of those had yielded any concrete information about her. The same with the antiques—a few of the stolen items had been recovered over the past two years, but nothing had provided a trail back to Sarah.

There was other information in the file, and he'd skimmed through it before taking the papers out and shoving them into his pocket. There was also a check for ten thousand dollars. All his. It was for "expenses," but hell, what fucking expenses was he going to run into?

There would be another two hundred fifty thousand and all he had to do was make a phone call and tell one James Morgan that his wife was currently residing in St Louis, Missouri. Hell, if he could get her to Chicago, Quinn would net another two fifty.

All he had to do was make the call. But he couldn't do it.

Not yet.

He had to look at Sara—*Sarah*—and know why.

Why she'd lied to him.

Why she had run away from her life.

Why she'd stolen from her husband.

Why she'd changed her name.

Why she'd made a half-assed attempt to change her appearance.

Why she was living off money made under the table.

Why she was hiding out in an apartment in St. Louis, Missouri, instead of living in some slick mansion in Chicago.

Why she'd *lied* . . .

"She didn't really lie," he told himself as he shot off the exit, weaving in and out of traffic.

Horns blared but he ignored them. Lights went from yellow to red and he just blasted through. He needed to get to the house. Needed to look Sarah in the eyes and have her tell him why.

God, he'd trusted her . . .

Fool. Stupid fucking fool.

He knew better than to trust people. He'd assumed she was on the run from something, but he hadn't figured she was *married.*

A married woman.

A thief.

Fuck.

He slowed to take the turn and as he did, he caught sight of a familiar head of hair. Sarah—hotfooting it down the sidewalk, heading away from him, with a bag slung over her back and a bag rolling along behind her. Leaving.

Oh, hell no.

She sure as hell wasn't leaving.

And not because of the fucking money he'd get once he made the call to her husband. *Husband.*

Quinn wanted answers, damn it. He had to have them. A muscle jerked in his jaw and he was having a hard time breathing—felt like he had a chain wrapped around his chest, drawing tighter and tighter, trying to choke the life out of him.

He started to speed up, but then he made himself stop. He needed a few minutes. It was pretty obvious she was leaving, and for good, so he'd just follow her, see where she was planning on going. Give himself a little bit of time to settle.

Get himself under control so when he confronted her, she wouldn't have any clue about the huge, gaping hole she'd just put in his heart.

* * *

You can't run forever.

She hadn't wanted to run forever, but the one chance she had at stopping kept eluding her.

The words chased her as she made her way to the bus station. Chased her, haunted her, mocked her.

Even with those words echoing in her head, even with the memory of Quinn's face with those somber, quiet eyes, she managed to get to the bus station without breaking down.

She got through the ticket line without breaking.

She even managed to hold it together for the first few minutes as she paced in endless circles, watching the clock tick away the minutes. But then, as the hour hand began to creep closer to the *3*, it got harder and harder to hold the tears back.

They burned her eyes, lodged in her throat, threatened to choke her, and finally, she couldn't fight it anymore. Dashing into the bathroom, she locked herself in a stall and broke down. Harsh, ugly sobs tore from her throat.

The tears blinded her. The pain deafened her. Lost in misery, minutes ticked away and by the time the storm of grief began to ease, her throat was sore, her eyes burned, and her head pounded.

She slipped out of the stall and hoped nobody had come in while she was indulging in her breakdown. Her hopes were dashed as a woman slipped out of the stall next to hers.

Studiously ignoring the other woman, Sara made her way to the sink, rolling her little carry-on behind her. The strap of her duffel was cutting into her skin, but she wasn't about to take it off. She'd had one stolen before and if she hadn't already learned the lesson of keeping her cash on her body, she might have been up a creek.

With a flick of her wrists, she turned on the tap and bent over the sink, splashing cold water in her face. A quick glance in the mirror told her that the water hadn't done much to help, but at least there weren't dried tear tracks on her face now.

She braced her hands on the sink and stared at her reflection. Red-rimmed, unhappy eyes stared back at her. Her mouth was unsmiling, her face was paler than normal. Her hair, that nondescript, drab brown, fell into her face and she shoved it back, fighting a wave of helpless anger.

She looked pretty much like shit.

Fitting, since that was precisely how she felt.

You can't run forever.

The phone in her pocket vibrated and she heard the faint chime that signaled a text message. Pulling it out, she read the brief message: *Where are you?*

She keyed in a response. *Bus station.* Then she closed the phone and tucked it away. She'd have to get a new one soon—it was the first thing she should have done, but she hadn't wanted to take the time today.

God only knew what kind of *problems* were behind this latest move and she had already lingered too long.

"God, I don't want to do this," she muttered, her voice raspy.

She wanted another option, wanted another way out, but she just didn't know if there was one. She was so fucking *tired* of running. She just didn't have much choice.

"Sometimes when you're lost inside a problem, Sara, it can be very, very hard to see that there are other alternatives, other options. There's almost always a way, darling."

Theresa's words started to circle around in her mind.

Lost inside a problem. That definitely described Sara's current state. Lost inside a problem with no viable solution in sight.

You can't run forever.

When this whole mess had started, some of the other options hadn't seemed feasible. She'd been running high on worry and adrenaline and hadn't taken the time she needed to slow down and evaluate things as well as she should have.

Now she felt like she'd travelled so far down the road that going back didn't seem possible. If it was just her, it might be different—

The phone in her pocket chimed again, and with a grimace, Sara pulled it out and flipped it open. She read the message with narrowed eyes. *Why haven't you gotten a new phone?*

Been a little bit busy hauling tail to get out of town. Feeling more than a little bitchy, she almost added in something else, but she stopped herself before she could do so. Being a bitch wasn't going to change things. Pining over what she wasn't meant to have wasn't going to change things.

Of course, being stoic and just dealing with things as they came wasn't changing things, either.

"Maybe I need to stop waiting for something to change," she whispered, staring at the phone without really seeing it.

Time wasn't doing the trick.

Running sure as hell wasn't.

She was still lost inside the problem.

* * *

SHE'D been inside the restroom long enough that Quinn was starting to get tense. He checked out the surrounding area—the restrooms weren't placed against an outside wall, so she wouldn't be able to slip through a window or something equally dramatic. That was assuming she'd try, and she really didn't have any reason to go for it.

She hadn't realized he was following her. Quinn would have seen it if she'd made him and if by some slim chance she *had* realized he was following her, she had no way of knowing *why*.

She didn't know that he knew.

Hell, Quinn wished he *didn't* know.

He glanced at his watch. According to the lady he'd spoken with at the window, Sarah was leaving on the 3:20 to Kansas City. She still had an hour before the bus started boarding, so he'd give her a few more minutes. But if she wasn't out soon, he'd be going in after her.

The door opened and he looked up, his eyes locking on the older woman coming out before moving off disinterestedly. Three more times, the door opened, and each time, it was somebody other than Sarah.

Shoving off the wall, he started across the hallway. Patience hadn't ever been his strong suit—he could wait when he had to, but he was done with waiting now. Just before he reached the door, though, it opened, and Sarah stood there.

Her eyes widened.

Her jaw dropped.

"Quinn?" Something flashed through her eyes—there, then gone.

It looked like happiness, but Quinn knew better. Angling his head, he said, "Hello, Sarah."

"What are you doing here?" she asked, shifting from one foot to the other and fighting two very opposing urges. She wanted to hurl herself against him. She also wanted to slip away and get lost in the crowd. There was something about the way he watched her right now that made her very, very uneasy.

People milled around, not paying them any attention as Quinn closed the distance between them, not stopping until his booted feet nudged the toes of her worn tennis shoes.

"I'm kind of wondering the same thing about you," he said. His eyes roamed over her face, as though he was searching for something.

"I guess you got my note."

He lifted a brow.

She blushed and looked away. "Look, I'm sorry I have to leave like this. I wish I could explain . . ."

"You can. Just open your mouth and do it."

She shot him a look from the corner of her eye. His face was cold, his gray eyes flat, his mouth a firm, unsmiling line. A muscle jerked in his cheek as he stared, and the weight of his gaze seemed to bore completely through her. "If it was that easy, I would have already done it, Quinn," she said quietly. "How did you know I was here?"

"Saw you leaving Theresa's."

She blinked and frowned. He must have shown up while she was talking to Theresa, although she didn't know how he could have done that without being noticed. "So you followed me here?"

He jerked a shoulder in a shrug. "Seemed like the right thing to do."

"Following me seemed to be the right thing," she echoed.

Actually, the right thing seemed to be grabbing her and hauling her close, dragging her back to his apartment, and locking the door. Throw away the phones. Trash the computer. Cut off any contact with the outside world—she couldn't run away and nobody would be able to track her down.

That was what his heart was telling him to do.

His head was laughing, though. She'd completely fooled him, and he was still hung up on her. He glanced around them and scowled. Looking back at her, he said, "We need to talk."

Understatement of the century.

She licked her lips and looked away. She was having the hardest time looking at him, he decided. She'd never had that problem until now, and it pissed him off even more.

Still, staring at her made his heart ache. Her dark brown eyes were red-rimmed, her ivory skin paler than normal.

"I've got a bus to catch soon, Quinn. Besides, there's really not much to talk about. I have to leave. That's all there is to say."

He reached out and hooked his fingers in the waistband of her jeans, tugging her close. Giving in to the urge, he dipped his head and skimmed his lips over hers. "Is that really all there is to say?"

Sara shivered as his mouth brushed back and forth over hers. He had one hand on her hip, stroking lightly as the other came around her waist and urged her closer. He didn't seem to care about all the people around them, and after about fifteen seconds of his touch, she didn't care all that much either.

She wanted to press herself against him and cling tight. It had only been a couple of hours since she'd seen him, but they had seemed endless, her heart aching as she acknowledged the fact that she wouldn't see him again.

But here he was. Watching her face with cold eyes . . . then touching her. Kissing her.

Wrenching herself away from him, she backed away. She almost tripped over her carry-on and righted herself just before she would have fallen into a couple of people walking along behind her. Steadying herself, she laid a hand on the duffel resting against her hip. "I have to go, Quinn. I really am sorry."

He held something up.

Sara's eyes widened as she realized it was her money—not all of it, but a decent chunk, the money she'd rolled up and tucked inside her front pocket. She never used a purse when she travelled. They were too easily stolen, too easily misplaced. She kept the money tucked inside various pockets or zipped up inside the special belt she wore around her waist.

Instinctively, she touched a hand to her right front pocket. It was empty. Gaping at him, she stared at the money he held in his hand. He'd fucking taken it out of her pocket while he kissed her! It was five thousand dollars, money she'd need over the next few months.

"You going to leave without this?"

"Give me the money," she said.

"Sure. After we talk." He tucked the money into his pocket, and she suspected she'd have a much harder time getting it away from him.

"You can't just keep that money, Quinn," she gritted out. "It's called theft."

Something flashed in his eyes and a smile tugged at the corners of his mouth. "Yeah. I heard something like that somewhere." Then he shrugged and said, "Call 911. Bus station will probably have some cops close by, plus there's onsite security."

She rolled her eyes. "I'm not going to call 911. You just need to give me my money."

"After we talk."

SIXTEEN

"Has there been any news?"

Don shook his head and swallowed, glad that James seemed preoccupied today. Preoccupied with something other than finding his wife.

It had been two days since the flyers had started going out. Already, James had spent more than a million dollars and they had yet to hear back from several of the agencies they'd contacted. When it was all said and done, the man could very well spend twenty times that in his search for his missing wife.

Of course, he could afford it.

Although Don might blanch at the figures, he knew that James could afford it and if he even missed the money, he'd make it up in little time. If nothing else, James Morgan knew how to make money.

"Well, it's only been a few days. We can't expect this to be a quick process," James murmured, not bothering to look away from the screen. Whatever he was looking at held him suitably entranced.

"Of course not." Don's palms were sweating. He hadn't had a

chance to go through all the data he'd received, but so far, there had been very little that yielded any sort of potential. Very little.

But he couldn't take comfort in that. James was casting his nets far and wide this time. Sooner or later, he'd land some fish.

Part of him insisted it was time he cut his losses and get the hell out of town.

But he couldn't—those issues, again. Issues on a timetable and the clock was ticking.

* * *

WARILY, Sara followed Quinn into the hotel room. He barely looked at her, hadn't spoken more than a few words since she'd left the restroom at the bus station nearly an hour earlier. She'd missed her bus.

She'd pointed that out to him and he'd just shrugged. "Exchange the ticket."

"I wouldn't *have* to exchange the ticket if we could have just talked back at the bus station."

That hadn't had any effect on him. He also hadn't had any trouble using her cash to pay for the room at the Marriot in Union Station. "You know, you've got a perfectly good apartment thirty minutes from here," she told him as she followed him down the ornate hallway. "There was no reason to use my money on a hotel room we don't need."

Quinn patted the pocket that held her remaining cash and shrugged. "It looks like you're not really running low on money. Sure hope you remembered to pay Theresa her rent before you split."

"Of course I paid her. What sort of person do you think I am?" she bit off, narrowing her eyes.

"Haven't quite decided yet." He stopped in front of a door and used the key card. It opened and he stood aside, holding the door open as he waited for her.

She passed close by him, close enough that she felt his body heat, his breath teased her hair, the scent of him flooded her senses. Damn it—her heart skipped a beat and then started to flutter within her chest as heat began to creep through her body.

He closed the door behind him and strode into the room, depositing her carry-on by the wall.

Sara remained by the door. The strap of her duffel was cutting into her skin and she slipped it off, dropping it to the floor. Her shoulder ached from the weight, and she absently reached up, rubbing the tense muscles and watching him.

He stood with his back to her, and although she couldn't see his face, she could read his body language easily enough. He was pissed. Well beyond pissed, she suspected.

Tucking her hands behind her back, she stared and waited until he turned to look at her. "So exactly what is it that we need to talk about?" she asked.

"Why are you leaving?"

Sara lowered her gaze and studied the floor. "Because I have to," she whispered. It was all she could say to him, at least right now. She couldn't look into those cold eyes and explain that she'd left because she got a damned message saying *Problems*.

She could have said it earlier . . . she thought. If he'd shown up while she was packing . . . hell, even now if he wasn't looking at her like he didn't quite recognize her, she thought she could have maybe tried to explain. Maybe if he hadn't made that jibe about Theresa. Maybe . . .

Those eyes of his . . . they were so cold.

"Why?" he asked, and his voice was closer.

Startled, she lifted her head and realized he'd crossed the room and now stood close enough to touch. Her heart slammed against her ribs as he lowered his head and rubbed his lips across hers.

Again, he whispered, "Why?"

"Because I had to," she said lamely, turning her head to the side.

He brought up his hands and rested them on her waist, slid them lower. He gripped her hips and hauled her against him. "I don't like that answer . . . give me another one."

"I don't have another for you."

He slid a hand under her shirt, his palm warm against her side. "Maybe you can start with telling *why* you had to. What are you running from?"

Sara clenched her jaw to keep from blurting it out. She wanted to . . . God, did she want to tell him. Sucking in a deep breath, she lifted her eyes and stared at him. Maybe she could try. Maybe, if she looked into his eyes and didn't see that wall of ice this time . . .

A sob built inside her throat as she met his eyes. His icy, wintry eyes. A cold, guarded stranger—how could she possibly lay herself bare before a cold, guarded stranger?

"No," she whispered, shaking her head.

She couldn't tell him. Somehow, she knew nothing she had to say would penetrate the shroud of ice he'd wrapped himself in. For some reason, he was already willing to believe the worst of her.

He nuzzled her neck, scraped his teeth down the side of it. She shivered and turned her head aside, staring at the wall.

"No?" he echoed. "No, what? No, you aren't going to tell me?"

"No, I'm not going to tell you."

She might not have been looking directly at him, but she saw the fury wash over him pretty damn well. The silence in the room grew brittle, as though one harsh breath would shatter everything— shatter her.

From the corner of her eye, she saw him move. She fought not to flinch as he lifted a hand and trailed his fingers over her mouth, along her jawline, before dipping into her hair. "Are you afraid of me?" he whispered in her ear.

"Right now, I don't know."

He laughed. It was low and ugly, and the sound of it hurt her heart, hurt her soul.

"If you were smart, you would be." He tugged on her hair, his fingers restlessly kneading her scalp. "The night after I put that mark on you, I said you'd be wise to stay the hell away from me. You should have listened. Now it's too late."

A shiver raced down her spine. Reluctantly, she turned her head and stared at him. "Too late for what?"

He watched her from under his lashes, his eyes dark and unreadable. "Too late for both of us," he said gruffly. The hand resting on her waist slid higher, until he could brush the bottom curve of her breast with his thumb.

Sara caught his wrist, stilled his hand. "Stop being so melodramatic, Quinn. You're pissed off at me for leaving, and believe it or not, I can understand that, but drop the drama already."

"Drama." He smirked and tugged his hand free, bracing it on the wall by her head. "You think I'm being melodramatic?"

"Aren't you?" She arched a brow. "You can drop the broody, macho posturing. We both know you're not going to hurt me—you're pissed off, but sooner or later, we'll leave this room and we'll do what we have to do. You can go back to your life, and I'll get on with mine."

"If you're so sure I won't hurt you, then why are you afraid of me?" He curved his hand around her neck, resting his thumb in the hollow at the base of her throat.

Was she afraid of him? Maybe a little. Disturbed by his seriously weird attitude, but she wasn't afraid because she thought he might hurt her. She knew better.

"If you're so certain I should be afraid of you, then why don't you give me a reason to be?" she challenged.

His eyes narrowed. The fingers on her neck tensed. He stroked his thumb over the fragile skin of her neck, up and down . . . up and down. Her pulse leaped under his touch and her breath was lodged somewhere in her chest. Holding her gaze, he pushed off the wall and then hooked his hands in the neckline of her shirt.

He jerked and buttons went flying. He crowded her against the wall, using his body and arms to trap her in place. Her mouth was dry. Her heart was racing.

"Is that supposed to do it?" she asked, reaching for a bored tone and failing. Her voice came out soft and breathy, like some sex-starved little nympho who'd gone too long without a climax. She might not be too far off target.

But at least she didn't sound afraid.

Staring into his eyes, she smirked at him and waited.

His mouth came down on hers, rough, brutal. Sara reached for him. As he kissed a line from her mouth to her ear, she gasped for breath, tried to clear her head. His hands were on her, streaking under her clothes, rubbing against her covered sex. He popped the button of her jeans and dragged the zipper low.

"Tell me to stop, damn it," he growled.

Sara slammed her head back against the door, fought to breathe. Fought to think. Fought to force the words from her throat. "I don't want you to stop."

"*I* want to." He bit her lip, too hard, and she didn't care.

She bit him back and then shoved against his shoulders, forcing enough distance between them so she could look into his eyes. "If you don't want to do this, then why did you start it?"

"Because I had to."

That, she understood. It was inexorable, like fighting the setting of the sun. Just being near him made her want him. Just hearing his voice did. Touching him made her want to wrap herself around him, cling tight, and never let go.

She lifted a hand and laid it against his cheek. Stared into his eyes as she pushed up on her toes to kiss him. He didn't kiss her back. But he didn't pull away.

Confused, she whispered against his mouth, "Are you so mad at me that you don't want me now?"

"I'll always want you." He curled his hands around her waist and brought her body against his. "Even when I shouldn't."

"Why shouldn't you want me?"

His hands cruised up, cupped her breasts. Through her bra, she could feel his heat, feel his strength. Then they fell away. Closed into tight fists that he held at his sides, stiff and still. "Because you can't be mine."

God. Closing her eyes, she buried her face against his chest and tried not to cry. She desperately wished she could be just that—but how could she, when she had to leave? When she didn't know where she was going to land next?

You can't run forever . . .

No.

She sure as hell couldn't. And she was damned tired of trying.

No more. Damn it, I'm done. She deserved some kind of life. She deserved some sort of peace.

And as much as she didn't deserve it, she wanted that life with Quinn. Wanted that peace with him.

Closing her eyes, she kissed him through the cotton of his T-shirt. He held still. When she rested her hands at his waist, he held still. When she slipped his T-shirt up, stretching to strip it away from him, he held still.

Through all of it, as she pulled off his clothes and hers, he didn't move. As she reached down between them and wrapped her fingers around his cock, his head fell back and a harsh sound escaped him. She stroked him, slow and steady, kissing his neck, his shoulders, wherever she could reach without letting go of him.

Finally, he touched her. His hands came up, fisted in her hair. "Sara . . . fuck."

Tipping her head back, she stared at him.

His gray eyes glittered as he stared down at her. A muscle

jerked in his jaw. His eyes closed, and for long, tormenting seconds, she thought he'd pull away. "We shouldn't be doing this," he muttered, opening his eyes once more. "*You* shouldn't be doing this."

"Why?" she demanded. *Why in the hell do you keep saying that?*

He didn't answer. Just watched her, his eyes cold and unreadable.

Chilled, she pulled back, brought up her arms and hugged herself. She felt exposed—too exposed—and it had nothing to do with the fact that she'd just stripped out of her clothes. Bending over, she grabbed her shirt and jerked it on. But when she went to button it, there were no buttons, just loose threads. She stared down at it and caught the sides, drawing them closed over her chest.

He caught her wrists.

She tugged against his hold. "You win, Quinn. We aren't doing this."

"I already lost . . . and yes, we are." He crushed his mouth to hers, wedged a thigh between hers.

She was already wet, already aching. Whimpering, she tore her mouth from his and stared at the wall without seeing it. He skimmed his lips along her neck, set his teeth in the curve where it ran into her shoulder and bit down. Sara shuddered.

Against her belly, his cock throbbed. Wedging her hands between them, she stared up at him, torn between wrapping herself around him and pushing him away. Her mind was a confused mess, and her body, heart, and soul ached for him.

In the end, pushing him away wasn't an option—not for her. From the beginning, she'd had the hardest time resisting him, and that wasn't about to change now. Even when he stared at her with unreadable eyes, even when he looked at her like he barely recognized her. Reaching for him, she pushed up on her toes and pressed her lips to his jaw.

Quinn caught her wrists, pinned them over her head in one hand. His eyes bored into hers as he reached between her thighs and cupped her sex. "You're so fucking wet for me," he muttered. "So fucking wet."

He pushed one finger inside her pussy and they both shuddered. His shoulders rose and fell as harsh, ragged breaths escaped him. "I want you . . . God help me, I want you."

She tugged against his imprisoning hand, wished he'd let her go so she could hold him. "Then have me, Quinn. I'm right here."

"Not enough." He moved between her thighs, reached down, and caught her left knee, pulling it up. The head of his cock nudged against her entrance, throbbed. "It's not enough."

She whimpered as he stroked himself back and forth against her clit. "Quinn, please . . ."

"Not enough," he said again as he pushed inside. His head fell back and a harsh, rasping sound, too close to a sob, escaped him.

He drove deep, deep, deep, burying himself inside her with one hard stroke. Sara cried out and he caught the sound with his mouth, swallowing it.

He wasn't gentle—he took her hard and rough, demanding everything from her, taking everything. She loved it . . . loved him.

The climax hit her hard and fast, stealing her breath away. Dazed and whimpering, she let her head fall back against the wall and still he moved on her. He dragged a second climax from her, a third.

He took her to the floor and sprawled between her thighs, pressing his mouth to her sex. "Not enough," he muttered as he made her come again.

She was so tired, she ached. So empty—she felt hollowed out, as though he drained everything from her. With her heart breaking, his touch now brought as much pain as pleasure.

"Quinn, please . . ." She wasn't even sure what she asked

for. She wanted him to hold her. Wanted him to make love to her. Wanted him to look at her the same way he had just that morning.

"Sara . . ." he rasped, pulling his mouth away as he levered his body up to cover hers. And as he did it, he looked down at her with the cold, flat stare of a stranger.

No—

A wordless denial exploded through her and she put her hands against his chest, shoved. Staring up at him, she had to bite her lip to keep from begging. To keep from pleading.

He cupped her chin in his hand, angled her face up to meet his. His mouth came down on hers, demanding, determined.

He took her to orgasm again, and this time, when she came with a hoarse wail, he went with her. With his face buried in her hair, he let go and when it ended, for a minute, his body relaxed and he cuddled her close.

Once more, he held her close . . . like she mattered.

Like they mattered.

But it didn't last for long.

Only for a minute. The siren call of sleep beckoned her, but as she felt him pulling away, she tried to fight it, tried to reach out to him, grab him, hold him close, never let him go.

But, as ephemeral as a dream, he slipped away and she fell into dreams alone.

SEVENTEEN

"*You can't run forever.*"

She heard Theresa's voice and turned, searching for the woman. The older woman wasn't there, though. She was alone—
"*So what else is new?*"

The dream splintered and fell apart, reformed.

"*Why are you leaving?*"

Quinn's voice—cold and flat. His eyes, cool and distant. And he stared at her like he didn't even know who she was.

Her heart ached. She reached for him. But when she tried to touch him, her fingers passed right through him. Confused, she tried again, and this time, he faded away before her very eyes.

"*Quinn? Damn it, come back!*"

"*I told you that I'd find you.*"

It was a voice that sent shivers down her spine. It made her furious, even as it frightened. Turning, she found James standing behind her, staring at her with a look of naked contempt on his face. "*Stupid cunt. You didn't actually think I'd let you get away, did you?*"

It was quiet—the only sounds were the unsteady breaths coming from the woman, and the man's calm, measured ones.

"*Please, James . . .*"

"Go to hell," she snarled.

"I told you I'd find you," he said again.

"I told you . . ."

"I told you . . ."

"I told you . . ."

Sara came awake with a start—she was alone in the bed.

Some dreams she forgot before she ever woke.

Some dreams lingered with her for days. She wasn't entirely sure which one this was. A jumbled mess of images bounced around in her mind and she slowly forced her body upright. Various aches and pains made themselves known and she grimaced. The muscles in her legs screamed at her and between her thighs, she was swollen and sore.

It was dim in the room, only the faintest light seeping in from under the curtains. There was one wall sconce on, the light so faint it served no purpose other than illuminating the way should somebody need to make a trip to the bathroom in the middle of the night. She squinted at the clock on the bedside table and blanched as she realized it was past ten.

Shit. She should already be on a train, heading to New Mexico by now.

Pushing her hair back from her face, she swung her legs over the edge of the bed. That was when she saw Quinn.

He was standing at the door, his back resting against it.

She swallowed the yelp that tried to come free and made herself smile. "Hey."

He didn't respond.

It was quiet in the room, one of those awful, weighted silences. She hated it. Frowning, she reached out and grabbed the blanket, wrapping it around herself. "The silent treatment is starting to piss me off, Quinn."

He shrugged. "I asked you some questions earlier and you wouldn't answer them."

"I *can't*." Or at least, she wasn't supposed to . . . but she could, and she wanted to, and if he'd just stop acting so fucking weird . . .

"Maybe if I give you an idea on where to start, it might be easier for you to answer those questions."

His voice sounded almost normal. Her heart skipped a beat. Seeking out his face in the dim room, she strained to pick up some kind of clue. Some kind of warmth. *Tell him—*

It was time. That was for damn sure.

She licked her lips and tried to figure out where in the hell to start.

He reached out and hit the light switch. She flinched at the sudden brightness, turning her head away. That was when she saw it. A piece of paper sitting on the little bedside table. It had several creases on it, like it had been folded up for a while.

Dread flooded her. Blood roared in her ears as she stared at the paper. It looked so innocuous—something she could tear to shreds, something she could set a match to and it would be gone in seconds.

A piece of paper and just the sight of it made her gut clench. She recognized the picture immediately. One very similar to it had been carried in her wallet for ages. It had been two years since she'd seen that image the last time.

She skimmed the brief paragraphs on the page, the blood in her veins turning to ice. Her heart went crashing down to her feet and suddenly, Quinn's bizarre behavior didn't seem so bizarre.

Sure hoped you remembered to pay Theresa her rent before you split.

We shouldn't do this.

You *shouldn't do this.*

You can't be mine.

There was a laugh bubbling up in her throat, hysterical laughter, the kind that too easily turned to tears. Closing her eyes, she thought silently, *You fucking moron.*

But she didn't know if it was directed at him . . . or at her.

She was somewhat pleased to see that her hand was steady as she reached out and plucked the page up. She was a shaking, nervous mess on the inside, but none of it would show on the outside. She wouldn't let it.

The information on the piece of paper was damning.

"Interesting reading material," she said, giving him a sardonic smile. She dropped it back down on the table and looked back at him. "You find that at the library?"

"Why did you run away from him?" he asked.

Sara lifted a brow at him. "Does it matter?"

"If it didn't, I wouldn't ask. Why did you run away?"

She didn't respond. She'd be damned if she'd give him those answers now. And to think how damn close she'd been to doing just that. How close she'd been to trusting him—completely. With every dark, closely hidden secret. Close—entirely too close.

Quinn shoved off the wall and stalked her way. "Why did you run?" he asked a third time. He didn't shout. His voice actually dropped, and if he hadn't been standing close enough to touch, she wouldn't have heard a word he said.

She would much rather hear him yell.

He crouched in front of her, resting his hands on the mattress. The veins in his arms stood out in sharp relief as he closed his hands into fists. Sara eyed him warily and fought the urge to pull back. The look in his eyes . . . it was unnerving, to say the least. She knew he wouldn't hurt her—he just wasn't that kind of man— but he was sure as hell making her nervous.

"Did he hit you?" Quinn asked.

Sara bared her teeth at him. "Any man that lays a hand on me in violence will go to sleep and never wake up."

"Then why?"

Turning her head aside, she focused on the abstract art print that hung over the dresser.

"Answer me," he rasped, catching her face in his hand and forcing her to look back at him.

Well, at least his eyes weren't cold. They were hot. Hot with anger, hot with hunger, hot with other emotions she couldn't quite put her finger on. Her heart skipped a beat and her mouth went dry.

"If this is all you wanted to talk about, Quinn, you've wasted your time," she said quietly.

"I want you to fucking answer me," he rasped.

"And I want you to get the hell away from me," she snarled back, shoving her hair back from her face.

"Oh, I will. After I dump you back in your *husband's* lap."

She blinked at him. "Excuse me?"

"You heard me." He shoved upright, glaring down at her. "There's a nice little bonus involved if I actually deliver you to him."

"*Deliver* me? What in the hell am I? A cow?"

Quinn jerked a shoulder in a shrug. "Apparently you're his wife and he's quite anxious to have you back."

"You can't make me go to Chicago."

Something flashed in his eyes. A smile twisted his lips. He knelt back down in front of her and pressed his lips to her ear. "You want to bet on that, darlin'?"

She jerked away, scrambling back on the bed and drawing her knees to her chest. "I don't want to go back to Chicago," she said, trying not to let her voice shake. But even as she said it, somewhere deep inside, she had to wonder. Maybe this was the way to do it . . . maybe this was the way out. Back the way she'd come.

You can't, you're not the only one in danger. You can't take that risk.

No. Theresa had been right. She couldn't run forever . . . and *now* she had some sort of control. Going back because she was forced wasn't the kind of control she'd prefer, but it was control.

It was time. She couldn't put it off any longer. If she could, she'd send out a warning. But she was going back home.

Quinn, unaware of her internal conflict, shrugged. "I don't much care if you want to go or not. I was just going to send word back on where he could find you, but you went and tried to skip town. I'm not about to let you slip away that easily."

"Why?" She blinked away the tears that threatened.

"Because I've got a job to do, and I'm going to do it."

A job—damn it, what the hell kind of work did he do? "Exactly what is this job and how does it involve me?"

"I work for a private detective. Mostly I just bring in those who've skipped out on bail. You just sort of fell into my lap."

His eyes, flat and emotionless, stared into hers.

A private detective agency. Money. He had come after her because of money. Was that why—

Her heart screamed in denial. Unconsciously, she fisted her hands. Her nails tore into her skin, but she never even noticed.

"So how long . . ." The words didn't want to come. She didn't want to ask, she didn't want him to answer. But she forced the question out anyway. "How long have you been looking for me?"

He flicked a glance at his watch. "Less than twenty-four hours. You're the reason my boss called me in yesterday. The information just came into our office early yesterday." Rage, ugly and hot, flashed in his eyes, and his mouth twisted in a cold smile. "Can you imagine what a surprise I got when I opened that file folder and saw your face staring out at me? Your fucking *wedding* portrait."

She glanced at the picture in question. It had probably hit him like a punch in the gut. Part of her even understood how furious he was. The evidence was damning as hell.

But jaded as she'd become over the past few years, she wouldn't have automatically expected the worst—not from somebody she cared about. Not from somebody she loved.

Obviously, she couldn't say the same for him. It was damned

obvious he'd expected the worst. No trust. No understanding. He just made his assumptions and fuck all.

The lack of trust was painful, a twisting, burning grip on her heart that refused to let go. Staring at him, she searched for some sign that he *wanted* to believe—

Believe what? He obviously doesn't believe in me.

Yet still she searched his face. Searched for some sign that she was wrong. That some part of him doubted.

But she saw only ice and fury. If he was hurt, it sure as hell didn't show in his eyes or on his face. She swallowed against the knot in her throat. She managed a derisive tone as she asked, "How much money has that bastard offered up?"

"Enough."

"How much?" Not that *she* really cared, but it could be important. Information—information was key. She needed to know as much as she could.

"Why?" A blond brow cocked up. "You thinking you might beat it? You still have money from the shit you stole lying around somewhere?"

Curling her lip at him, she said, "I'm not about to try and bribe you. If the money is that fucking important to you, you'd just turn around and try to get a sweeter deal from him anyway. I sure as hell can't pay anything close to what *he* can cough up."

Quinn just stared at her.

She was really starting to hate that stare. Cool, blank, hard. Like a fucking mask. She'd rather face almost anything but that emotionless façade. Even his anger.

She bared her teeth at him in a mockery of a smile. "So . . . when do we go?"

"You that ready?" he asked. A muscle jerked in his cheek.

"Well, since it's pretty clear that you're not going to take no for an answer, I might as well accept the inevitable." She glanced at the clock and then back at him. "Are we leaving tonight?"

He jerked a shoulder up. "Don't see why. It's late. We'll leave in the morning." His mouth twisted in a sneer and he added, "Besides, you already paid for the room."

"Well, I'd hate to see that go to waste," she muttered, looking away. Her mind raced. If he wasn't planning on leaving yet, then she had some time. Time to figure out if she was going to try telling him anything. Time to figure out if she was going to just merrily go off with him to Chicago. Time to figure out where she needed to go from here.

Was one night enough to get all those answers?

She used the sheet to drape around her body, feeling his eyes on her as she made her way to her bags. A few feet away, she froze and gaped, staring at her open bags.

The small carry-on suitcase was unzipped, the clothes messed up. Her duffel bag lay next to it, and it was in the same condition. She sure as hell hadn't gone through the bags.

She hadn't—*Quinn* had. Fury bubbled inside her. He'd gone and rummaged through everything. Her pathetically small collection of panties and bras lay in a heap on the floor. Her jeans were haphazardly stacked, her shirts draped over top. The T-shirt of his that she had taken lay discarded on the floor like some piece of trash.

"Was there any reason to go through my belongings?" she demanded, glaring at him over her shoulder.

Quinn didn't answer.

Giving him a withering stare, she grabbed her cosmetic case and the top and lounge pants she used as pajamas. "Am I allowed to shower?" she asked mockingly.

"Sure." He shoved off the wall and sauntered over to the bed, flopping down on it.

On the way into the bathroom, her phone chirped. Frowning, she turned back and saw Quinn holding it in his hand, obviously reading the message. "Do you mind?" She held out her hand.

From the bed, he smirked up at her. "You're not getting the phone back." He turned it around and showed her the message. "Who keeps texting you? This is like the fifth one."

Only five? "It's none of your business."

"Well, I guess they'll just have to keep sending the messages then, because you're not using the phone unless I know who it is."

"Afraid I'll call for the cavalry?"

"Just being cautious."

The door closed behind Sarah, and Quinn closed his eyes as the shower came on, tried not to think about her standing wet and naked under the spray of water. Definitely not the image he needed in his mind right now.

He was having a damned hard time blanking his mind, too. Jackknifing off the bed, he prowled the room. He was restless. He was edgy. He was irritated. And hurt. No matter how deep he tried to bury the hurt, it kept working free, rising to taunt him.

Trust—he knew better.

He'd trusted again and it had come back to bite him, leaving a gaping, open wound square in the middle of his chest.

Married.

He still couldn't wrap his mind around it. In the back of his mind, there was a derisive voice, one that mocked the hopes he'd unconsciously started to build, the plans he'd consciously started to make. Hopes, plans, thinking about something besides getting through the day . . . looking forward to the next day, just because it was one he'd get to spend with Sara.

Having all of that smashed hurt like a son of a bitch.

It hurt almost as much as that look he'd glimpsed in Sarah's eyes once or twice. Something like pain. Like misery. Like shock. She looked at him—like he'd been the one misleading her—and that pain flashed through her eyes. But only for a second, then it was gone, like she'd locked it down, put it away.

Or maybe he was just imagining it. Maybe he wanted so badly

to believe there was a lot more going on than he realized and he was dreaming up things that might make that belief easier.

After all, if she was hurting, too, that must mean she cared a little. Maybe she really hadn't wanted to leave . . .

He stopped his pacing and turned, staring at her open suitcase. She'd had one of his T-shirts in there. Until he'd gone through her clothes, everything in her bags had been neatly, almost ruthlessly organized—except for his T-shirt. It was shoved inside, like she'd done it at the very last minute.

Why did she have one of his shirts?

The whisper of her voice danced through his mind. She'd told him, repeatedly, that she couldn't stay, that she couldn't explain. Maybe . . .

"Fuck." He came to a stop in front of the dresser and scrubbed his hands over his face. He was doing it again, trying to make up excuses, trying to explain away what she'd done, how she hadn't told him the truth, reasons for misleading him. He was so desperate to believe there was something else going on, even though she'd yet to give him a reason to believe otherwise.

He wanted to trust her again—to believe in her. Wanted to pin his hopes on the fact that she had one of his T-shirts stowed in her bag, to believe something other than the obvious, all because he *thought* he saw unhappiness in her eyes.

"Stupid, so fucking stupid," he muttered, shoving a hand through his hair. He never should have trusted her in the first place and here he was, desperate for her to give him a reason to do it again. To trust her. To believe in her.

From the corner of his eye, his reflection caught his attention. Slowly, he turned his head, studied the man he saw in the mirror. He looked much like he always had, lean face, hair that needed cutting, an unsmiling mouth.

Cold eyes.

Angry eyes.

He didn't like the man he saw, he realized abruptly. Not right now.

He didn't like how pissed off he was, how angry, feeling like he shouldn't trust Sarah, that he was right for not doing it. He didn't like any of it. Dragging his eyes away from the mirror, he dropped down in the chair in front of the desk, staring at the gleaming wood surface without seeing it.

He wanted to trust her. Part of him needed to try.

Why was it such a bitch for him? Why now? Why was it so fucking important for him to believe her? She'd already proven to him that he *couldn't* trust her, but here he was miserable because he didn't want to let that go.

Abruptly, he shoved out of the chair and stormed to the door. Out in the hall, he pulled his phone out and dialed up Luke.

"Be home, man," he muttered under his breath. He pinched the bridge of his nose as the phone rang.

And rang.

And rang.

Devon answered on the third ring, and Quinn managed to keep from swearing. Just barely.

"Sorry, Quinn." A yawn interrupted her words and he glanced at his watch, wincing as he realized he'd probably gotten her out of bed. It was close to midnight in Kentucky.

"Luke's working tonight . . . try calling his cell. He's usually got it on, so unless he's in the middle of something, you can probably get through," Devon said.

"No." He shoved off the wall. "I'll just talk to him later."

"Are you okay? You sound kind of . . . well, more pissed off than normal."

Quinn laughed and the sound was so bitter, it all but choked him. "You've got good ears. I *am* more pissed off than normal."

Her voice was hesitant as she asked, "Is there anything I can help with?"

"No." He went to disconnect. Then stopped. Cleared his throat. "I dunno. Maybe."

"What is it?"

He blew out a breath and focused on the door in front of him. He couldn't hear the shower from here, didn't know if she was done—the phone. Fuck . . . "Hold on." He pulled his key card out and swiped it, pushed the door open just enough to glance inside. He could hear the shower. From where he stood, he could see the hotel phone. Careful. Had to be more careful than that.

What if Sarah got ahold of whoever was trying to call her? What if whoever it was tried to help her slip away? Not that Quinn planned on letting her out of his sight—not until he had answers.

Answers—fuck the money, he wanted answers.

"Quinn?"

Devon's voice jerked him out of his thoughts. Leaning against the doorjamb, keeping the door propped open with his foot, he half listened to the sound of water coming from the bathroom.

"Sorry," he said into the phone.

"It's okay. How can I help with . . . well, whatever is going on?"

He felt like a fool, standing there trying to figure out how to ask what he needed to know. But he wasn't sure *what* he needed to know, so how could he ask?

A memory flashed through his mind. Months earlier, after Devon had left the hospital, he'd gone by the house where she lived with Luke. The scars on her arms—her childhood had been even more screwed up than Quinn's had. Not that she'd explained much about it, and Luke hadn't, either. But Quinn knew—somehow, he just knew.

Quinn and Devon, both of them were broken, battered souls. Two of a kind. Or at least Devon *had* been . . . until Luke.

"You have a hard time trusting people, Devon?" he asked.

"Do I have a hard time trusting people?" she echoed. Then she snorted. "In a word, yes. In three words—oh, hell, yes."

"Do you trust Luke?"

"Luke . . . ?" She paused and then asked, "You want to know if I trust Luke?"

He could all but hear the confusion in her voice. Blood rushed to his cheeks. *Hate this*—hated, hated, hated. "Yeah. I want to know if you trust Luke."

"Quinn, if I didn't trust Luke, I wouldn't have married him."

The water in the shower turned off. His heart skipped a beat and he stared at the bathroom door. "How did you know you could trust him? How did you know you *should*?"

"There wasn't ever much of a question. Part of me trusted him pretty much from the beginning. Otherwise . . ." Her voice trailed off and she sighed. "Look, this is complicated, and very personal, but I never consciously made a decision to trust him. I just did. I just knew I could. I knew I should."

"Never had doubts?"

Devon laughed. "Oh, I had plenty of doubts . . . but the voice in my heart managed to be louder than the doubts in the long run."

Seconds ticked away and Devon finally broke the silence. "You still there?"

"Yeah. I'm here."

"Are you okay? Ahhh . . . well, maybe this isn't my business, but Luke mentioned you'd met a lady. Is—well, is this about her?"

"Yeah. No. Shit." Still staring at the bathroom door, he tried to focus on the conversation, tried to think past the blood roaring in his head. "Beats the hell out of me. I don't know what in the fu— hell. I don't know what's going on inside my head."

"I'm going to take that as a yes. Look, I'm a lousy person to offer any kind of advice, but you know people, Quinn. You may not like a lot of them, but you know them. Whatever the problem is now, I'd say just try to stick to what your heart tells you. What your gut says. Instincts are usually pretty reliable."

The door started to open. His hand clenched on the phone.

Reliable—how could the bloody, bruised mess of his heart be anything he could rely on?

"I've got to go," he said, his voice gritty. Without waiting for Devon to say anything else, he hung up.

Putting the phone away, he stared as Sarah opened the door and came out. A rush of steam followed her. He slipped all the way into the room and nudged the door closed with his foot.

Leaning against the wall, he gazed at her, tried to find some sense in the chaos of his mind. She ignored him, moving about the room as though she was the only one in there. She placed her bags on the bed and reorganized them, neatly folding the shirts, the jeans, even her panties.

"I've got your money," he said. He angled his chin toward the belt he'd draped over the back of the desk chair. There was also money on the desk, the five thousand he'd taken from her at the bus station, along with the money he'd found hidden inside her clothes while she slept. Her jeans had inner pockets sewn inside, and there had been another thousand in each of the pockets, as well as tucked inside her shoes. She was a money bag on legs.

Sarah gave him a withering look. "Yes, I figured that much out."

She didn't ask him to return it. Didn't so much as glance at her belt or the cash on the desk. She just kept on folding her clothes until the bags were once more nice and tidy. She'd slipped his shirt in there, too. Nice and subtle, with no change in her expression as she did it.

Why—

The question leaped to his lips but he bit it back. He wasn't going to ask her. Not right now. Not until he figured out if he could trust anything she said. Not until he figured out if he *wanted* to try trusting anything she said.

After she finished with her bags, she zipped them closed. He went to take one from her, but she had both of them in hand before he managed to get within two feet of the bed. Cutting a wide berth around him, she dumped them by the door and then retreated deeper into the room.

She didn't go to the bed, though. She went to the closet and rose on her toes, grabbing one of the pillows and blankets stashed on the top shelf. Without looking at him, she took them to the couch and settled down.

Quinn frowned. "Take the bed. I'm not going to sleep much."

"I'm fine," she said, her voice cool. And she still didn't so much as glance his way.

"Take the bed," he repeated.

Finally, she turned her head. Her brown eyes flashed as she glared at him. "I don't want to take the damn bed." Then she settled down on the couch, turned her back to him, and pulled the blanket up over her shoulders.

Scowling at her, he stormed to the bed and grabbed a blanket and pillow. He was tired as hell, but he doubted he'd sleep. He might have tried lying down on the other side of the king-sized bed after she fell asleep, because if she moved around any, he'd wake up.

What if she tried to slip away . . . ? Something inside him wanted to scream at the thought.

He ignored it. Maybe if he tried hard enough, he could ignore that screaming, and the pain that kept slicing through him.

He threw the pillow on the ground, dropped the blanket on top of it. Then he braced his back against the door and slid down. Stretching his legs out in front of him, he stared at Sarah's back.

*　*　*

"I'M done."

Gritty-eyed, Quinn looked up as Sarah slipped out of the bathroom. She stared at him, her face a cool, empty mask. Her eyes met his briefly and then picked a point over his shoulder.

Done. They could go.

Make the drive to Chicago, where he would turn her over to her husband and then he'd never see her again. Fuck—his hands flexed, itching to grab her and pull her against him. Cradle her close. Never let go.

Stick to what your heart tells you.

A muscle jerked in his jaw. If he listened to what his heart was telling him, then he would do just that. Never let her go. The part of him that refused to let her go wasn't worried about the damage she'd done to his pride. It wasn't worried about the fact that she was already taken. It wasn't worried about the lies or anything other than the unbearable thought that he had to let her go.

"Are you going to get up so we can leave or just sit there all day?" Sarah asked.

Stick to what your heart tells you. How in the hell could he trust his heart, though?

Time. He needed a little more time. Just a little more to make sense of everything roaring inside him.

"I want breakfast," he said flatly, shoving off the wall. He dropped back into the chair in front of the desk and flipped open the pseudo-leather binder that held the hotel information, blank letterhead, and menus. He wasn't hungry, but it would kill another hour if they ate something before heading out. Maybe he could use some of that time to smooth out a bit of the chaos.

"What do you want?" he asked after he'd skimmed the menu. He watched her in the mirror as she stretched out on the bed and stared at the ceiling.

"Coffee."

Quinn frowned. "Anything to eat?"

"I'm not hungry. Just coffee."

Coffee.

He ran his tongue along his teeth and spun around in the chair, staring at her. "There's a gym here. You want to do your run?"

Pushing up on one elbow, she looked at him as a smile curled her lips—it was a rather satisfied-looking smile. Actually, it was more like a smirk than a real smile, he decided.

"No. I don't want to go for a run." Another one of those odd, indescribable looks flashed through her eyes as she lay back down. "No more. No more running. No more stupid exercising. I'm done."

From the corner of his eye, he saw her hands moving. Fingers flexing, then curling into tight fists.

"You ever going to tell me what's going on?" he asked quietly.

Sarah closed her eyes. "You've already decided you *know* what's going on. Why should I waste my breath? Order your breakfast, Quinn. Order my coffee. Then let's get this show on the road."

Sighing, he turned back to the desk and reached for the menu that didn't have anything on it that he really wanted. He placed the order and then hunkered down over the desk and started trying to unravel some of the knots in his soul.

He wasn't ready to leave yet. Even the thought of turning Sarah over to her husband made his skin crawl.

In his gut, there was a voice screaming *Mistake. Mistake. Mistake.*

"How did you know you could trust him? How did you know you should?"

"There wasn't ever much of a question. Part of me trusted him pretty much from the beginning. Otherwise . . . Look, this is complicated, and very personal, but I never consciously made a decision to trust him. I just did. I just knew I could. I knew I should."

His heart, his gut, they were screaming. Demanding he trust. Demanding he stop what he was doing before he made one huge, motherfucking mistake. In his head, there was scathing laughter, mockery, and voices of self-doubt that told him he'd already *made* one motherfucking mistake by trusting her. Wanting her. Loving her.

Quinn found himself staring at the blank letterhead in the front of the information binder. Without understanding exactly why, he located a pen and pulled a sheet of the letterhead out.

* * *

"IF I've got it timed right, you'll get message number nineteen within the next five minutes," Quinn murmured, flipping the phone closed and looking up at Sarah.

She sat across from him at the diner table and ignored him, much as she'd done all morning, ever since they'd left St. Louis. Quinn laid her cell phone on the chipped Formica tabletop and spun it around.

Her gaze jumped to it, then moved away, just as quickly.

That look again—

Hell, that look confused the hell out of him. He'd seen something similar to it before—anticipation. It reminded him too much of the rush that always hit right before an op back when he'd still been in the army. The rush he got when he located some of the dangerous bastards who'd skipped out on bail.

Excitement. Anticipation. Mixed with fear.

The fear bothered him. No matter how mad he was, he wasn't going to put her in the hands of a man who'd hurt her—of course, she wouldn't tell him a damn thing, either.

She'd managed to go the entire morning without saying a single word to him. The silence hurt. He hadn't expected that. He'd thought the worst of the pain had come when he'd flipped open that file and seen the face of the woman he'd fallen in love with. The *married* woman he'd fallen in love with. He hadn't thought anything could hurt worse than the lies she'd told him.

But her silence did.

She wouldn't talk to him. She didn't offer any sort of explanations, reasons, excuses. He'd been expecting something, he guessed. Tears, maybe, either real or fake. Some sort of story to explain why she'd done what she'd done, why she'd run. An apology. A smile.

Something.

But she gave him nothing.

Quinn, who'd always wanted silence over empty words, would have given anything to have her just talk to him. About anything. About everything.

Hell, she could even keep up the lies she'd been telling him . . .

Be honest, man. How many lies has she actually told you? She lied about her name, and that's pretty much it. You never asked if she was married—

A lie of omission. Still counts as a lie, he told himself. *Still counts.*

The phone chirped out a tune that had become extremely familiar.

Quinn gave the phone a dirty look and then glanced up at Sarah. "So who do you think it is this time?" he asked. "Is it the impatient bastard? Or the other one?"

He didn't bother waiting for an answer. He tapped his fingers on the table and grabbed the phone. "It's gonna be the impatient bastard. The other one's only sent two messages.

"Whaddya know . . . ?" Quinn flipped the phone open and showed her the number on the display. "Impatient bastard. This makes message number nineteen. Must be going for some sort of record here." Sighing, he read the message. "Whoever it is, he wants you to call him. Now."

Sarah gave him a disinterested look. "If the messages are bothering you so much, either let me use the phone or turn it off."

"You want to call him, you tell me who he is and why he keeps calling."

She gave him that same, withering stare. "It's none of your business who it is."

"Then he can just keep calling." Quinn had already tried

calling the number himself, but as soon as he spoke, the call was disconnected.

"Do you plan on returning the phone to me?" she asked.

He slid her a glance. "It's possible you could talk me into it—tell me why you ran away. Tell me what made you do it—the truth—and it's possible I might give you the phone back. Hell, it's possible I might give you your money, get up, and walk away—you can try to lose yourself again."

She stared at him. Her eyes, those warm brown eyes, were cool and mocking. "How very kind of you."

She wasn't going to tell him a damn thing. *Fuck*.

"I don't get it," Quinn said, shaking his head. He was confused as hell, and he didn't like it. He also didn't like how helpless he felt. He didn't like the fact that he'd had a damned hard time looking himself in the eye, and he didn't like all the unknowns in the current situation. Too many of them.

But most of all, he hated the fact that he had already lost her and there wasn't a damn thing he could do about it.

"I don't get it," he said again, his voice quieter.

"You don't get what?" Sarah asked, shooting him a dour look.

"You've spent the past two years hiding. If you wanted to be away from him that desperately, there's got to be a reason . . . all you have to do is tell me *why*. Ask me to let you go."

She blinked and cocked her head. "Would you do it as easy as that?"

"Probably."

"Why?"

Because I love you. Because something made you run and I don't want you running. I don't want you unhappy. I don't want you afraid. He hated the thought of her unhappy. Hated the thought of her being afraid—fear was a fucking *bitch*. Hell, if he wasn't so damned afraid right now, he might be able to tell her all of that.

Tell her . . . and then watch her disappear from his life.

"Because of you," he finally said. He wanted to tell her. Wanted to force the words from his throat, but they wouldn't come. Might have something to do with the fist-sized knot lodged just above his trachea. He swallowed around it and tore his eyes away from her face.

God, that heart-shaped face, those big brown eyes, they were going to haunt him. No matter what happened, for the rest of his life, he was going to see that face every time he closed his eyes to sleep.

He hadn't thought there was anything in the world that could hurt him like he was hurting now. Not even Elena.

"Will you tell me?" he asked, forcing the words out. *Tell me . . . ask me to let you go.* She wouldn't really want to go back to somebody who'd hurt her, would she? She wouldn't want to go back to somebody she hated, would she? So if she was so ready to go back, it meant she didn't hate her husband—meant he hadn't hurt her.

He remembered the flash in her eyes when he'd asked her the first time. She'd told him she'd kill a man who hurt her—he believed her, but it made things that much harder. If she hadn't run because Morgan had hurt her, then why?

Maybe she was playing some bizarre, incomprehensible game, and Quinn was clueless about the rules.

"Shit." He dropped his head into his hands and tried to tell himself the burn in his eyes was anything but tears—that the ache in his chest came from something other than his shattered heart.

"Relax, Quinn."

He lowered his hands and stared at her from under his lashes. "Relax."

She lifted a shoulder and shrugged. "Yeah, relax. You're just an hour shy of getting a nice pile of money. Easy money."

"Easy?" He snorted. "You think this is *easy*?"

She stared at him levelly. "You didn't have to hunt me down.

I haven't tried to get away. I more or less fell into your lap. Easy money."

"Bullshit." He once more focused his attention on the window. A lot easier to stare out over the expressway than look at her. His mind raced. They were an hour south of Chicago. He was running out of time to get her to talk to him, but damned if he knew how to make her do it.

He hadn't bothered calling to check in with Martin, and he had yet to call their client to advise him of their impending arrival. Both were things he needed to do, but he wasn't terribly inclined to talk with Martin, and he definitely wasn't in the mood to get into a discussion with the man married to Sarah.

Plus, he didn't want to clue the man in on anything, not until he had a better idea of what was going on. What had made her run.

He scowled, thought back to just how much money Sarah had been carrying stashed on her body. Close to eight thousand cash. "So where's the rest of the money?" he asked.

She glanced at him and then resumed staring out the window.

Gritting his teeth, Quinn fought the urge to slam his fist into the table. He was sick and tired of being treated like he didn't exist, especially by her.

The waitress appeared at the table, giving them a tired, empty smile. "What can I get for you folks?"

"I just want some ice water," Sarah said, her voice as tired and empty as the waitress's smile.

Scowling, Quinn said, "You didn't eat anything this morning, or last night. Order some food."

Sarah shrugged restlessly.

"Bring us two burgers, fries." Quinn waited until she left before he looked back at Sarah. "You need to eat."

"I'd just as soon have an empty stomach, considering the lovely day you have planned for me."

"I don't want to take you to Chicago," Quinn blurted out. The words echoed between them, and as damning as they were, he couldn't regret speaking them. He didn't *want* to take her to Chicago, to turn her over to somebody else—husband or not. *Quinn* wanted her. All of her, all to himself.

"Of course you do," Sarah said, her voice cool and mocking. "You've got a job to do. All that easy money is waiting for you."

"I don't give a fuck about the money," he snapped. He reached out and caught her hand, tugging on it even as she tried to resist, tried to pull away.

She curled her lip at him. "Yeah. Sure."

"*I don't care about the money*," he snarled. "I care about . . ."

You. The word froze in his throat. It wouldn't come out. "Look, I don't care about the money. I don't want to make you do something you don't want to do. Just give me a reason," he said. "Just tell me why you ran. Just give me the answer to that."

Sarah stared at him balefully. "And you'll what?" she asked bitterly. "Forget you ever saw me?"

Then she snorted and jerked on her hand, tried to pull away from him. Quinn wouldn't let go—couldn't let go. "What's going on, Sarah? This doesn't make sense—if you don't like your husband, divorce him. Why just disappear like that? Why spend your life in hiding if he didn't hurt you?"

It didn't fit—no matter how many times he tried to get the pieces to align in his mind, they didn't fit. *She* didn't fit, not into any of the scenarios he'd constructed in his mind as he tried to explain away what was going on. She wasn't a money-grubber. She wasn't the flighty sort who'd just get bored and disappear—she'd put too much work into disappearing and she'd done a damn good job of doing it.

Hell, if fate hadn't put them on a collision course, would she have been found? He'd spent some time looking deeper into her background over the past two years, using his laptop while she slept in the hotel room and doing a sketchy search. It yielded even sketchier results—for the past two years, it was like Sarah Morgan had fallen off the face of the earth.

He could have gone deeper, but he was having trouble doing so. Part of him suspected he wouldn't like what he'd find if he searched too deep.

There was one plausible scenario, one that would explain her running, even though it left his heart tied into knots and his gut cold with fury. Had Morgan hurt her? Threatened to? Even thinking about it left Quinn feeling sick inside. Sick *and* murderous, but it would explain why she'd run, and it did a hell of a lot better job explaining it away than anything else.

But it didn't fit either. Because the woman he was looking at was a fighter. She had confidence bred down into her bones, the kind of confidence an abused woman couldn't understand.

Nothing *fit* and it was driving him fucking nuts—he wanted this to fit. Needed it to fit, needed to understand *why*.

He stroked his thumb over the inside of her wrist, focused on that, the way his skin looked darker, rougher, compared to hers. "I'm tired of asking you questions, tired of you ignoring me. But I can't *not* say this—if he's hurt you, if he's threatened you, if for some reason you're not safe with him—just say the word. I'll get you away. I won't let him hurt you. Just tell me. Just let me help."

"Offering to protect me now, Quinn?" she asked softly. "First you're all set to sell me off, and now you're offering your protection?"

"If he's hurt you, just say it. If there's a reason you don't want to go back to him, just nod. It won't happen."

Sarah tugged on her hand and this time, he let go. She crossed her arms over her chest and stared at the scarred tabletop. "This has to happen, Quinn. It's time."

Silence stretched out between them, seconds ticking away as he stared at her. *Let me help*—it was a demand that echoed inside him, but even as one part of him insisted Sarah was in danger, that she needed help, another part of him didn't believe it.

Maybe he was so desperate to believe she needed help because it was a way to stay in her life. A way to try holding on to what was slipping farther and farther out of his reach.

The walls threatened to close in around him, and his throat had narrowed down so that it was a chore just to breathe. "I've got to get out of here," he muttered. With a headache pounding behind his eyes and his heart in nasty little knots, he climbed out of the booth and headed for the door.

She watched him go, his shoulders and back rigid and his eyes staring straight ahead. That man was confusing the hell out of her. As he stormed outside, she leaned back against the faded pseudo-leather booth. Tension held his body stiff. He seemed furious. Hell, he *was* furious—she felt like she'd spent the night in the same room with a ticking time bomb.

The anger was easy for her to deal with—even though part of her understood it, his anger didn't make her feel so broken. She'd gotten through the night nursing her own anger, her own sense of betrayal . . . and planning.

Then this morning, something had seemed different. She'd seen something else in his eyes besides the anger. Hurt.

And the hurt was killing her.

Every time he'd offered to help her, it had been like a dagger pierced her heart, and then did a slow, torturous turn. It would have been so much easier if he had just stayed mad. If he acted like she disgusted him. Anything but looking at her like he wanted to play knight in shining armor, if only she'd let him.

But she didn't need a knight. She'd damn well take care of this herself. Even if part of her wanted to tell him the truth, even if part of her wished she could lean on him, she wasn't going to do it. He hadn't trusted her, and she was still rubbed raw over it.

You hurt him, too, though. Maybe you're even.

Grimacing, she shoved her hair back from her face. She hated the lie she'd been living, and the thought that she'd hurt him was rubbing salt into an open wound. She'd take the anger over his hurt any day of the week.

God, why couldn't he have just trusted her enough to ask? Instead of assuming the very worst, right off the bat, why couldn't he have asked what was going on? If he'd just asked, if he hadn't just assumed the worst of her, if he hadn't accused her of ripping off Theresa . . .

If he'd just believed in her, just a little . . .

* * *

This has to happen.

Fuck. Fury and heartache pounded through him. He wanted to scream. He wanted to hit something.

He wanted . . .

"Quinn?"

Sarah. Slowly, he turned around and saw her standing on the busted steps that led to the diner's entrance. The cool mask crumbled and she stared at him with misery in her eyes. Her throat worked as she swallowed and her eyes fell away from his as she descended the crumbling concrete and came to stand in front of him. Small white teeth caught her lower lip. She stared somewhere over his shoulder. "Quinn, I wish there—"

"Don't," he muttered, shaking his head. "Just don't, Sarah."

He didn't want to hear it—didn't want to hear a damn thing she had to say.

No. Not true. There was one thing he needed to hear. He needed her to answer one question for him.

"Why?" he asked hoarsely. "Why in the hell didn't you tell me you were married?"

This was why he didn't let himself want things. Lessons learned back in childhood still had their nasty hooks in him—when he wanted something, it was destroyed. Even something as simple as a book, and Sarah was so much more than that.

He wanted her more than he'd ever wanted anything. He wanted her for always and damn it all to hell and back, he couldn't have her. She wouldn't let him help and no matter what she said, he knew there was more going on than what she was telling him.

She remained silent and still wouldn't look at him. Reaching out, he caught her chin in his hand, forced her to look at him. "Can't you even answer that one simple question, Sarah?"

"I could . . . but it's not a simple question, and there is no simple answer."

"Then how about this one? Can you look me in the eye and tell me, swear that he never hurt you? *Never?*"

She reached up and curled her fingers around his wrist. Squeezing lightly, she tugged his hand away and once he was no longer touching her, she let go of his wrist and stepped back.

"Tell me, damn it," he snarled at her. "Tell me that he never hurt you—but damn you, you'd better tell me the *truth.*"

She smiled at him. It was a bittersweet, sad smile. "James Morgan never laid a hand on me."

He stared at her, into those dark brown eyes that had begun to haunt his dreams. Good dreams . . . for a while. They'd been good dreams. But now those dreams were going to torment him.

Stick to what your heart tells you.

His heart told him there was something wrong here. Majorly wrong. But she wouldn't talk to him, wouldn't explain, wouldn't help him at all. He needed more information, and Sarah was the only one who could give it to him.

And she wouldn't.

She just fucking wouldn't.

I can't do this, he realized. There was no way in hell he could take her to Chicago.

So what in the hell did he do?

But even as the question formed, he knew the answer. He had to walk away. He had to let her go. She would lose herself again, and after he'd straightened up the mess he was getting ready to cause with Gearing, maybe he'd do some nosing around, see if he couldn't figure out for himself why she'd run. Deal with it.

Wasn't much of a plan, but the knot in his gut eased just a little.

Gruffly, he said, "We need to get our stuff." Without bothering to see if she followed him, he headed back into the diner. The waitress appeared in the doorway and he shot her a look. "Sorry . . . something's come up. We can't stay."

He threw a twenty on the table to cover the food they wouldn't eat and then grabbed Sarah's bag. Sarah stood behind him, a frown on her face as she studied him. He caught her elbow and guided her out of the diner, his mind racing.

Back in the car, he turned on the GPS and brought up the menu. He could feel Sarah's eyes on him, but he didn't look at her. He couldn't. He'd been this close to really being happy . . . this close to feeling complete. Every time he looked at her, he remembered just how close he'd been and it hurt. It hurt worse than anything he could remember . . . more than all the shit his mother had done to him. More than losing Elena. More than the distance he too often tried to force between himself and his twin.

It hurt like acid poured on an open wound, and something told him this was one that wouldn't heal with time. It would fester and ache, linger with him long after Sarah disappeared from his life.

Nothing he did was going to change that.

But there were some things he could do that might make things easier for her. That much he could control.

* * *

EYING the counter, she glanced around at the people waiting in line, or sitting in seats scattered here and there. Finally, she turned and looked at Quinn.

She looked at him, but he wasn't looking at her. And he wouldn't, she realized. He stared off past her shoulder, at his feet, anywhere but at her face.

"What are we doing here?" she asked, gesturing to the bus station. An hour had passed since they'd left the diner, but they weren't in Chicago. Instead of continuing on north when they left, Quinn had headed south, and now they were in a bus station in some town she hadn't ever heard of.

"*We* aren't doing anything," he said, shrugging. He reached out and clasped her arm, guiding her away from the counter to one of the semi-enclosed phone booths. It wasn't exactly private, but it was as private as they would get here. "Take this."

Automatically, she glanced down, and when she saw what he held in his hand, she gulped.

It was the money he'd taken from her pocket yesterday.

"What's this for?"

"It's yours," he said. "So take it." Then he reached inside the black backpack he'd grabbed from the car. He pulled out her belt, the one designed to hold money, and gave it to her.

She took it, fumbled with it as she slipped it around her waist, adjusting it so that it lay under the waistband of her jeans. "Why are you giving me this?"

He didn't answer.

"Quinn?"

She stared at his face, trying to see his eyes, but he had a pair of sunglasses on. Frustrated, she lunged for the sunglasses, but he sidestepped out of reach. "Quinn, what's the deal here?"

"No deal, Sarah." He reached up and brushed his fingers over her cheek. "You disappeared once. Do it again."

Then he walked away.

Dumbfounded, she gaped at him, frozen in place. He strode away, his long legs eating up the ground, and it wasn't until he turned a corner and disappeared from her sight that she was able to make herself move.

But she didn't make a beeline for the counter.

She took off running after Quinn. What was he doing? Why was he just walking away?

She caught up with him just outside the bus station, but when she called his name, he didn't respond. Finally, she grabbed ahold of his arm and jerked. "Damn it, would you wait a minute?"

He stood in place, staring straight ahead. When she circled around to look up at him, he didn't once look down at her.

"Why are you doing this? Why are you walking away?"

"Does it matter?" he asked, his voice weary.

"If it didn't matter, I wouldn't have asked," she replied, shoving her hands into her pockets. She was still clutching her money, she realized, the rolled-up bills he'd pressed into her hand. She pushed the money deep into her hip pocket, curling her fingers around it.

"Because I can't take you to Chicago."

Scowling, she shoved her hair back from her face. "I don't see why the hell not—we were only an hour away until you made this little detour."

"Because I *can't*," he snapped. He tore his sunglasses off, glaring down at her.

His eyes weren't blank.

They weren't cold.

They were full of emotions that left her throat tight and her heart racing, although she didn't fully comprehend why. Instinctively, she backed away and just as soon as she did it, she wished she hadn't. "Why can't you?" she asked, lifting her chin. "You didn't seem to have any problem with it a couple of hours ago."

"You don't know a damn thing about what kind of problems I'm having," Quinn snarled. He dipped his head, staring at her eye to eye. Their breath mingled. She could feel the heat coming off him. See the harsh, unsteady rhythm of his breathing as his shoulders rose and fell. "I've got so many *problems* here, I don't even know where to begin."

He spun away from her and lifted his hands. "I just can't do this," he said, his voice low and rough. "I can't take you back to him."

"But that's your job," she pointed out. Damn it, what was she doing? She should be dancing a jig here and instead, she felt a cold knot settling inside her gut. She was so ready for this to be done. So ready for it to be over with, and she'd been this close . . .

"I know what my fucking job is." Quinn shot her a narrow glare over his shoulder. "What are you waiting for? There are three different buses leaving this station in under an hour. Go buy your ticket. Figure out where you're going from here."

Snug in his pocket, her phone chimed, but neither of them paid any attention to it.

"Explain this to me, Quinn, because I'm not comprehending it. Two hours ago, we were heading to Chicago—you were about seventy miles away from getting your hands on a hell of a lot of money and now . . . now what? You're just walking away from it?"

"I don't give a flying fuck about the money. Your husband can shove it up his ass for all I care. I am *not* taking you up there. I don't care how many times you insist that he never hurt you, that you weren't running because he'd abused you. I'm not buying it— you wouldn't disappear just because you didn't like being married to him. You'd file for divorce. So either I'm totally misjudging you or there are things you aren't telling me. Don't take this wrong, but it might be a little easier on me if I believe the latter option."

Dear God, you have no idea just how many things I haven't told you. She swallowed and then dragged her tongue across her dry lips. "So you're doing this . . . just letting me walk away, even though I lied to you? Even though you're so pissed off at me, you can't even look at me?"

"Being pissed off has nothing to do with why I'm not looking at you."

"Then why won't you look at me?" she demanded. She needed him to look at her. She needed to see his face. She needed . . . hell, she couldn't even begin to understand what she needed just then. "Damn it, turn around and look at me."

For a second, she didn't think he would. But finally he did, and when he did, it hurt her like a fist straight to the solar plexus. His eyes . . . was she imagining things, or were they a little damp . . . almost like tears? But he wasn't the kind of guy to cry over things.

Not over *her*.

Shaken to the core, she was unable to do a damn thing except stand there, staring at him while her mind tried to process everything. He dipped his head and brushed his lips over hers. "Goodbye, Sarah," he murmured against her lips and then he pulled back and turned away.

He didn't slow down when she called his name.

When she grabbed his arm, tried once more to make him stop, he just shrugged her away and kept walking. Halfway across the parking lot, she stopped in her tracks and just stared at his back, watching him as he walked away from her.

Watching as he walked out of her life.

EIGHTEEN

IT didn't take her long to figure out what to do once Quinn left her in the middle of the bus station. Stranded her—except he hadn't, not really. She had her money and all she needed to do was figure out where she wanted to go. She could disappear. Nobody but Quinn knew she was here.

Nobody would know if she bought a ticket and slipped away from Chicago once more. She could start running again.

But she was so was damn tired of letting James Morgan control her life like this. He had already controlled peoples' lives for far too long. With that thought burning bright in her mind, she made her way to the ticket counter and requested a bus ticket to Chicago.

"Just one?" the lady behind the counter asked, a bored expression on her face.

Staring at the counter, she answered, "Yes. Just one ticket."

Alone. She was going alone to Chicago.

* * *

AFTER she bought her ticket, she made her way to a phone. She had a call to make.

Actually, she *should* be making two calls. But one of them

would try to talk her out of this, and she wasn't going to waste the time.

She'd made her decision.

Still, that first call had to be made. She needed information. With a bastard like James, information and knowledge were weapons, and she needed to know what she'd have. She couldn't get that info until she made the calls. While she'd rather not do it in such a public place, she didn't have much choice. Quinn still had her phone.

Quinn . . .

She closed her eyes against the onslaught of pain. She'd trusted him, and he'd hurt her.

Look where it had landed her.

She'd trusted him . . . and he'd let her go.

Just walked out of her life. For some reason, that hurt every bit as much as his betrayal. Every bit as much as his lack of faith. He'd walked away. Like she hadn't mattered.

You're not being fair, a quiet, oh-so-reasonable voice whispered inside her mind.

Yeah, he'd walked away.

Hadn't believed in her—but he'd wanted to.

Betrayed her—but she'd betrayed him. Even though she hadn't wanted to, she'd still betrayed him. They hadn't ever had much reason to trust each other.

He'd walked away, leaving her to make her own choice. He hadn't tried to force her to Chicago—that had been the plan and he hadn't been able to do it. Considering the kind of man he was, considering that he'd been doing his job—man, a fucking bounty hunter—she suspected it hadn't been easy for him to just turn his back on his responsibilities. Quinn wasn't the kind of man who took his obligations lightly. She knew that much about him.

Sighing, she leaned against the wall and fed quarters into the phone. Punching in the number from memory, she kept her eyes focused on the crowd of people. In all likelihood, she was safe here.

Only Quinn knew where she was, and he wasn't going to share that information. She knew it as well as she knew her own name.

"It's me."

There was a pause. "Why are you calling from a pay phone?"

"Because I don't have my cell phone anymore."

"That isn't wise. I need to be able to reach you. Especially now."

"Why, because of these 'problems'?"

"The problems, yes." The speaker was cautious. "But there are other concerns—certain issues that are close to being wrapped up. I need to be able to contact you. You need a new phone."

She stuck her tongue out at the phone. "Gee, really?"

"What happened to yours?"

"Long story," she said with a sigh. Once more, she scanned the crowd, unable to relax. "I'm coming back to Chicago."

"I'd expected as much. When?"

"Now."

"*Now?*"

"Is there an echo in here?" she snapped. "Yes, I'm coming back to Chicago. Now."

"Haven't you received the messages I've sent you?"

Frowning, she jerked a shoulder in a restless shrug. "The new ones? No—I haven't had access to the phone." She gave a short, concise explanation, leaving out most of the details. "I knew you were calling, but I couldn't call back. Although I really wish I'd known Morgan had gone to a private investigator. Not that it matters now. Look, I don't have time for chitchat. I just wanted to let you know I'm heading back. You need to be prepared."

"This isn't wise. All I need is a few more days. Give me a few more."

"No." She was tired of waiting. She was tired of putting her life on hold. If everything that mattered to her had to go straight to hell, then damn it, she'd make sure that Morgan had the same problem.

Without waiting for an answer, she hung up the phone. She didn't have time for this. She needed to plan. She needed to see to other details. And she needed a little bit of time to hide in the bathroom and panic.

* * *

DON lowered the phone and smoothed a hand down his tie.

He hadn't been anticipating this, not this early.

He glanced at the watch on his wrist then closed his eyes, blew out a measured breath. "Now what?" he muttered.

"Sir?"

Opening his eyes, he looked up and saw one of the receptionists standing in the doorway. "Yes?"

Although there was puzzlement in her gaze, she gave him a polite smile and said, "I'm sorry, sir. But Ms. Mather is on the line for Mr. Morgan. Should I interrupt him?"

He nodded.

Yes. By all means, let the woman talk to James first. Maybe by the time she was done, he'd have settled his thoughts.

* * *

ALL around her people were moving around, stowing their bags, getting out their laptops or books, chatting. Somewhere in the back, there was a little kid crying and the low sounds of his mother's voice as she tried to calm him.

She tried to tune all of it out.

She needed to think.

Plan.

Push Quinn Rafferty out of her thoughts.

Doubt, fear, and anger waged a war inside her. Doubt—was she doing the right thing? Fear—what she was doing was dangerous. Anger—so much anger—she was pissed off for being afraid, for having doubts, for the circumstances that had put her here.

She couldn't do much about her anger, but she wasn't going to keep dealing with the doubts. She was going to face her fear.

She was this close. This close . . . and if she started running again, she might as well resign herself to never stopping. It was a thought that depressed the hell out of her.

This had to happen. And it was going to happen *now*.

"You have to leave him, Sarah. You have to, or he'll kill you."

"I can't. You . . . you don't realize what kind of man he is."

"Don't I? He's the kind of man who'd beat a woman. That's not exactly a ringing endorsement of his character."

Tears gleamed in Sarah's eyes and she shook her head.

"I can't leave him. I can't."

"Why not?"

Sarah looked away. "I just can't."

"You'd rather let him kill you?"

Sarah's eyes fell away.

"Don't tell me that it won't ever come to that—don't tell me that you aren't scared to death of that happening. You can't honestly tell me that."

"No. You're right. I can't." Her shoulders slumped. "But I still can't leave him."

"Tell me why the hell NOT. Hell, if it's money, I'll front you the money. I've got some in savings and I haven't even touched what Mom left me."

"It's not about money," Sarah whispered miserably.

"Why, Sar? Why can't you leave him?"

Sarah took a deep breath. Then, her voice so soft and faint, she whispered, "Because of you."

"Me?"

Fury blazed inside her, washing away the last vestiges of doubt, clearing the cloud of fear. She was pissed, utterly pissed, and for the first time in years, she could let it fill her. She didn't have to

tamp it down, funnel it away, and store it up. The time to let it out
had come.

* * *

IT was still early in the afternoon, but Quinn hadn't had much
trouble finding a bar. Granted, this one had seen better days. Better nights. The outside of it was every bit as unappealing as the
inside, and the alcohol was so cheap, it was barely drinkable.

He still had her phone.

He sat holding a shot of whiskey and staring at her phone like
he expected it to bite him. The messages had stopped not long
after he'd left Sarah at the bus station.

Guilt ate at him. She needed her phone—he'd seen the look in
her eyes each time she saw her phone, saw the desperation. It wasn't
so much the *phone*, but the link to whoever kept trying to call her.

Whoever it was, the person meant something to Sarah. Somebody from her old life, maybe. Somebody she trusted.

Jealousy settled in right next to the guilt. He hadn't really
meant to keep the phone, but just maintaining had taken everything he had. He hadn't been able to think about anything other
than holding it together. Thirty minutes after he'd left Sarah,
another message had come through and that was when he had
realized he hadn't returned the damn thing.

The phone lay on the counter, next to the folded-up letter that
he had planned to give to her in Chicago. He'd spent hours writing
the damn thing, trying to think up the best way to word every last
line. He opened it, stared at the words without really seeing them.

What good did it do to pour his heart out if he didn't have the
courage to give her the letter?

Blowing out a sigh, he took the letter and folded it back up,
smoothing his finger down the crease and then tucking it back into
his pocket.

Maybe he'd frame it, hang it on the wall, so every day he saw the glaring reminder of why he was better off not getting involved.

Why he was better off not trusting people.

Why he was better off alone.

Fuck, how had this happened? How had he ended up *here*? What in the hell was he doing?

He lifted the glass, stared down at it as though he might find some kind of peace, some answers, *something* down at the bottom, if he looked hard enough. Stared long enough.

An answer came . . . but it wasn't exactly the sort of answer he'd been looking for. Staring into the glass, he saw himself. But not as he was now.

He saw himself as a kid, lurking in the shadows while his mother huddled over a drink, much like he was doing now. *Shit.*

He slammed it down as though the glass had scorched him. "Shit," he muttered, wiping the back of his hand over his lips.

What in the *hell* was he doing? Sitting around. Brooding. Feeling sorry for himself and getting more pissed off by the minute.

He heard the echo of his mother's shrill, whiny voice, every time something had blown up in her face, every time she lost a job, a boyfriend, every time she drank away the money before she could use it to score some dope. *Why?* That plaintive, *whining* tone. That self-pity.

Closing his eyes, he saw Sarah's face.

He'd lost her.

That's all there was to it.

Sitting around and drinking his sorrows away wasn't going to change that—all it would do was nudge him one step farther down a road he didn't want to go.

Slipping off the stool, he stared at the glass. The liquor in it called to him. Beckoned. For a little while, he could numb the pain. Dull it with a wash of heat and forgetfulness.

But it wouldn't last.

The oblivion that came from alcohol never lasted . . . not unless he took the path his mother had taken.

Setting his jaw, he reached into his pocket and pulled out enough money to cover the drink. The he took Sarah's phone, tucked it inside his pocket. He wasn't pitching it. Wasn't tossing it. Just like he wasn't pitching the letter.

Not yet. Not until he didn't need the reminder anymore.

He was going to go back to St. Louis, and somehow, he was going to get on with his life.

* * *

IT was late by the time he got back to the city. Past seven, but he didn't go home. *Unfinished business*—

He needed to talk with Martin, and if he knew anything at all about his boss, the man would still be at the office. A homebody, Martin was not. He'd go home when there was nothing left to occupy him and that was about it.

As Quinn expected, Martin's Lexus was parked in front of the offices and as he climbed out of his rental, Quinn wished he hadn't ever seen that car, wished he'd never seen these offices, wished he'd never met up with Martin—or Theresa, for that matter. That first job had come because Theresa had a friend who had been beaten by her boyfriend and then skipped bail. She'd come to Quinn— why, he didn't know. But she'd come to Quinn and after he located the man and threatened him within an inch of his life, Theresa had mentioned the little fact of a bounty.

That was how Quinn ended up working for Martin.

If none of that had happened, he never would have known about Sarah.

But his heart twisted even thinking about that. To never have known her, would his life have been any better?

Brooding, he stormed into the offices and stopped dead in

his tracks as three of the other employees stood up and started applauding.

Two of them stopped the second they caught sight of the scowl on his face. Juanita kept it up and it wasn't until Martin appeared in the doorway to the main offices that she settled back down in her seat.

"Damn, Quinn. I had a feeling you'd be good at this, but not *that* good," Martin said, whistling between his teeth. He gestured to his office.

"Good at what?" Quinn asked.

Martin closed the door behind him, watching Quinn with a wide, pleased smile.

"What in the hell are you grinning about?" Quinn demanded. Unease snaked through him, turning his gut to ice. His spine was itching again. Through the glass walls of Martin's office, Quinn could feel a dozen pairs of eyes on him—the rest of the staff was staring at him, studying him like they'd never seen him before. It had his skin feeling like it was going to climb right off of his body. He shot a narrow look over his shoulder and most of the people scattered.

Martin snorted. "Shit, never would have thought you'd be modest. You did good, Rafferty. Real good. Hell, no wonder you haven't been answering the damn phone. You put out this kind of results, I don't care if you return calls or not."

"What in the hell are you talking about?" Quinn scowled.

"The job, of course. What the hell else would I be talking about?"

Martin was staring at him now, too. Watching him like he'd lost his mind.

Quinn didn't give a damn.

"What about the job?" he asked in a rough voice.

Martin was quiet. Seconds ticked away. Five. Ten. Twenty. Finally, he answered, "I'm talking about the call I just got—

somebody from our client's offices called and said that you'd found Sarah Morgan and that she would be in Chicago tomorrow morning."

"I never called the client, Martin." The bottom of Quinn's stomach dropped out from under him.

Martin opened his mouth, then closed it, as though he wasn't quite sure how to respond. Finally, in a careful voice, he said, "I'm a little confused, then."

This has to happen, Quinn. The ghost of Sarah's voice rose up to haunt him.

The determination in her eyes.

Martin said something else. Quinn snarled, "Shut up a minute and let me think." He pressed the heel of his hand to his eye socket, tried to think past the roar and rush of blood throbbing in his head.

Martin spoke again. Without bothering to respond, he grabbed Sarah's phone, flipped it open, and brought up the messages.

More of the same.

Where are you?

Call me, damn it. NOW.

Again, no indicator of who the messages were from, other than a phone number.

There were two other messages from a different number. No name . . . just the number.

I need to talk to you. We're getting close.

Come on, girl. Really need to talk to you. Call me.

"Getting close to what?" he muttered.

Sarah's voice echoed inside his head. Over and over.

This has to happen, Quinn.

That odd look in her eyes. That overbright, eager light.

"What in the hell is going on?" he whispered.

"Quinn?"

Looking up, he met Martin's eyes. "You have the file on her?"

"On Sarah Morgan? Yes." He went to his desk and went through some of the files stacked on the corner. He found the right one in just a few seconds and turned it over to Quinn.

It was a lot more substantial than it had been the other day. "Any of this recent?"

"No. There is nothing recent on her," Martin said. There was a world of questions in his voice. "Absolutely nothing. When I got that call from the Renaissance Group, I have to admit, I was shocked as hell. How did you manage to find her?"

Quinn ignored him, flipping through the file.

"You *did* find her, right?" Martin asked.

Quinn shot his boss a narrow look. "Yeah. I found her."

"If you found her, then why are you telling me you never called the client?"

"Because I didn't," he snapped. "I fucking let her go."

Martin opened his mouth, closed it. Opened it again. "Damn it, what in the hell do you mean you let her go?"

"I mean . . . I. Let. Her. Go." He closed the file, clenched it in a fist so tight it made his knuckles ache. "I said it in English, right?"

"Listen, Rafferty, I don't know what the hell is going on here but you'd better explain. I warned you—"

"Shove your warnings up your ass, Gearing," Quinn snarled. "You want to know how I found her so fast? It's because I've been seeing her for close to two fucking months—I'm in love with her and there was no way in *hell* I was putting her in the hands of that bastard."

Violent rage spiraled through him and he could barely contain it. Rage . . . and fear. God, he didn't think he'd been this afraid since . . . since never. He hadn't ever felt this kind of sick, shaking fear.

Sarah was in Chicago.

She'd gone back.

And no matter what she said, he couldn't make himself believe she'd be safe there. His instincts screamed at him. His heart had constricted down to a tight, hard knot, and his chest hurt like a son of a bitch.

She'd gone back.

Still standing behind his desk, Martin looked at Quinn as though he'd sprouted a second head. He blew out a breath and then reached up, pinched the bridge of his nose. "Rafferty, I think this is what we call a clusterfuck."

A muscle ticked in his jaw. He really didn't give a damn what Martin had to say at this point. Once more, he started flipping through the file, searching for answers.

"Look, I had no idea. You should have said something," Martin said, either unaware of Quinn's preoccupation or just not caring.

Quinn curled his lip. "Why? So you could send somebody else after her?"

Martin just stared at him.

Quinn stared right back. It was finally Martin who looked away. "I'm a businessman, Rafferty. You know that. But I wouldn't have put *you* in this kind of position. If you'd told me, I could have had somebody else handle this."

Hell, if he'd trusted Sarah just a little, maybe neither of them would be in their current position.

He turned page after page, skimming all the bits of information about Sarah's life. College. Friends. After she'd gotten married, there was little information—no employment history. A few newspaper articles where she'd accompanied her husband to some sort of function—most of them charity balls or auctions.

His gut twisted as he stared at one of those pictures.

She looked . . . well, beautiful. But there was something about the picture that didn't fit. Her eyes . . . they were dead. Empty. Frowning, he flipped back through the file and found the picture he'd seen just the other day. Her wedding picture.

"Something's not right," he muttered, squeezing his eyes closed.

"What?"

Tuning Martin out, he started rifling through the file once more, pulling out all the pictures he could find. There were more at the back that he hadn't gotten to yet, a few more newspaper articles. Some black and whites. One drifted to the ground, facedown.

Crouching down, he flipped it over.

Just like what had happened a few days earlier, he found himself staring at a picture without really processing just *what* he was seeing. The neurons in his brain fired away but nothing made sense. Nothing connected.

Blood roared in his ears.

His heart slammed against his rib cage with bruising force.

A cold sweat broke out on his spine.

"Quinn?"

A pair of shoes came into his field of vision, but Quinn barely noticed. Numb, he fell back on his ass and continued to stare at the picture.

A hand touched his arm. Dazed, Quinn looked up and watched as Martin knelt down next to him. "Rafferty, are you okay? You're white as a ghost."

He swallowed the knot in his throat and flipped the picture around, showing it to Martin. "Who is this?"

Martin's eyes dropped to the picture. His mouth flattened out in a tight line. "You didn't read a single message I sent you, did you? None of the e-mails?"

No, he hadn't read any of the e-mails. He hadn't seen any reason—why did he need updates when he already knew where to find Sarah? He shook his head and repeated, "Who is this?"

"Why in the hell do I put up with you?" Martin muttered. He grabbed the folder and rifled through it, plucking a sheet from the back and thrusting it at Quinn.

"Her name is Samantha McElyea—Sarah's twin. She disappeared at the same time as her sister. From what I've been able to tell, the police think they disappeared together."

NINETEEN

SAMANTHA McElyea tucked a strand of hair behind her ear and tipped her head back, staring up at the ebony and glass tower that jutted up into the sky. She'd been to the Renaissance Building before, but not often.

James had despised Sam, pretty much on sight. The feeling had been mutual. If she hadn't loved her sister so much, there was no way in hell she would have even attended the wedding. Of course, maybe *not* going to the wedding would have given her sister a much-needed awakening.

No.

It wouldn't have done any good.

Sarah had to make the decision for herself—she had to see for herself. And nothing Sam did would make that happen any sooner.

Sam slid her sunglasses on and tried to release the tension that had turned the muscles in her back into a mess of knots. It had been a good long while since she'd seen James, but she knew she had to be careful around him. He was too good at reading people. He always had been.

It was part of the reason she'd avoided coming here, even the few times Sarah had invited her—always under the guise of some sort of business meeting, something that James's PR people would set up.

As often as she'd been able, she'd tried to convince Sarah to leave. To run away. To get a divorce. Sarah could have absconded with the pool boy and Sam would have been delighted. But Sarah hadn't ever done anything unseemly, not in her life, and she wasn't going to start while she was married to James.

No matter how cruel he'd been, no matter how many times he'd left marks on her, Sarah had remained the picture-perfect, so very polite and proper woman that he'd married.

Sarah had taken being a good girl to the extreme.

Sam had delighted in being the wild one, the one who had probably been responsible for their mom's first gray hairs, the one who'd gotten in trouble at school.

And she'd been the one to recognize, before anybody else, that there was something dangerous about James Morgan. Even their mom hadn't believed it at first. None of Sarah's old friends believed it. They'd thought Sarah was living the fairy tale—some rich older guy had fallen head over heels in love with her and swept her off her feet.

The real-life version had been way different. Morgan had been the rich older guy, all right. But when he'd swept Sarah off her feet, it had been to isolate her—most of Sarah's friends hadn't seen her in years. There had been weeks when Sarah and Sam had gone without even talking on the phone.

Sam had her fears about James, but it wasn't until their mom got sick that she realized maybe there was something to them. Sarah hadn't come to the hospital until three days after their mother had been admitted. Alice McElyea had been in a drugged stupor for those first few days and she hadn't been aware of her oldest daughter's absence. But Sam had. Achingly, painfully aware and she'd left message after message at the Morgan house, each one getting more and more heated, more and more pissed.

The final one had been, *If you don't get your ass down here to see Mom, so help me God, I'm going to come get you and haul you down here myself.* Sam had needed her twin there with her—she'd needed her best friend and she'd been utterly pissed.

Even when Sarah had come into the hospital room, Sam had been biting back her temper. Her twin had arrived that afternoon, full of apologies and explanations—she'd been out of town on a business trip with James and the staff hadn't passed the messages on.

But Sarah hadn't been able to look Sam in the eye while she told her story. And then Sam had glimpsed the bruise when Sarah bent over to kiss their mother's cheek. It had spread over the ivory flesh of Sarah's breast like an ugly stain. If Sam hadn't been standing in just the right place, looking down at just the right time, she never would have seen it. As Sarah had straightened up, the ivory silk shell had fallen back into place and once more the mark had been hidden.

Sarah hadn't confided in her right away.

But Sam didn't understand the meaning of quit and she'd pushed and pushed until finally Sarah broke down. It hadn't been easy, and it hadn't happened overnight. It had taken more than two years, and some threats that even Sarah hadn't been able to live with.

Threats against Sam.

He told me that if I ever left him, he'd kill you. I can't risk it. I am sorry but I can't.

But then James made one huge tactical error. He was so used to controlling people, so used to people jumping when he said jump. He'd made a mistake with Don. Don might be his go-to man when it came to business problems. Don might be one hell of an employee—the kind who never said no, who never blinked when it came to things like tax evasion and fraud. After all, he was a numbers man. If anybody could take dirty numbers and clean them up, make them make sense, it was Don Hessig.

Sam knew all about Don. Unbeknownst to his employer, the general public, hell . . . possibly even his own mother, Don had a double life going.

He was one of the "donors" who helped supply funding for a project of hers.

In a rather karmic twist of fate, James's right-hand man had no tolerance for the bastards who abused women. And Don sure as hell wasn't going to kill somebody for his boss.

Sam could still remember that particular meeting. She'd gotten the call one night when she'd been working late. She'd recognized Don's voice, tried to avoid the conversation because she'd had her hands full.

But Don had been adamant. "We need to talk. Privately."

She'd met up with him, but it wasn't until she arrived at the arranged meeting spot that she realized he'd called Sarah, too.

Sam hadn't understood why . . . not until she saw how Don had watched Sarah. The poor idiot had something for her twin, Sam had realized. And he'd found a way that might get her away from her husband.

It had been a hastily concocted plan, one that Sam still couldn't believe had worked.

James could arrange for somebody to kill Sam, but he'd wanted it to be Don—his trusted assistant could certainly provide an alibi, should either of them need one. Thanks to the fact that Don had been helping James with his little tax evasion problem, James had been utterly convinced that Don wouldn't dare balk at the idea.

Just went to show the man didn't judge people as well as he thought. He might have Don terrified and might be able to make Don break all sorts of laws when it came to white-collar crimes, but Don didn't have it in him to kill.

It had been Don's idea that *both* Sarah and Sam disappear.

"It will throw the cops off. They will investigate when Sarah disappears, but if you both disappear together, it's going to throw

them off." He'd smiled then, giving Sam a rueful glance. "*We keep things quiet, but quite a few of the cops know about the project. If you both go off the grid, they'll assume you did it together. So maybe . . .*"

"*It could help you,*" Sam had guessed—correctly. "*If there is an investigation and the cops come to the decision that we made ourselves disappear, they'll be less likely to look at you.*"

"*Yes. But that's not the only reason.*" He had looked at Sarah, then away. "*It will keep her safe. If you do it this way, both of you will be safe.*"

If Sarah had waited, God only knew what James might have done. Sam had been the reason he held back, because once Sam knew about the abuse, she'd become very persistent in keeping close tabs on her sister. She'd called the police twice—although each time, James made it all go away.

He had wanted her out of the way and had been willing to do whatever was necessary to accomplish it. Once she was gone, she couldn't interfere with him and Sarah anymore.

But if Sarah was gone, too . . . if they *both* disappeared . . .

So that was what they'd done. Sam hadn't liked it. She'd wanted to stay and fight, but Sarah had been terrified. *Finally*, she'd agreed to leave her bastard husband, and there was no way on earth Sam was going to do anything to change her mind. If it took disappearing . . . fine, she'd disappear.

She could make damn sure both she and Sarah all but fell off the face of the earth.

She knew how. She knew the system. All because of her special project—the project that Don had helped bankroll.

Sam had been working that system for years. Instead of going to work at a hospital when she graduated from nursing school, she'd gone to work with the victims of domestic abuse.

Most of her work had been legit.

But there were certain aspects to her career that were less than legal. Not necessarily wrong—helping the abused escape their abusers couldn't ever be wrong.

Still, there were questionable legalities taking place, entire underground networks devoted to helping an abused woman disappear. Once she'd finally convinced Sarah to leave Morgan, Sam had put her sister into that network and to this day, she had no idea where to find her.

She *could* find her, though. And if she could deal with James, she *would*. When it was safe.

After two years, it was time to do just that.

Taking a deep breath, she squared her shoulders and started toward the entrance. The glass walls reflected her image back at her as she strode across the sidewalk. Her hair, that boring, totally blah shade of blondish brown, was pulled back into a ponytail. Her sunglasses were cheap, bought from Walmart a few months earlier. Her clothes were every bit as simple, jeans, a plain white T-shirt, a denim jacket, and a canvas tote that served as a purse.

Once he caught sight of her, James would have a cow.

Of course, he would assume she was Sarah. Seeing his wife dressed so casually would give him a fit of massive proportions. Too bad the bastard didn't have a weak heart.

From the day he'd married Sarah, maintaining appearances had become a huge part of the woman's life. Sarah had never left her home without being impeccably, and acceptably, groomed. T-shirts and jeans were *un*acceptable. Cardigans, trousers, tailored suits, and designer labels—discreetly elegant, of course—replaced Sarah's once casual wardrobe.

Once Sam had clued in on just *how* much James focused on appearances and image and all that other shit, she'd figured out how to work him. She'd used every resource she had at her disposal to make sure he didn't try to force her out of her sister's life—and he'd tried. Up until Mom had gotten sick, he'd been winning, too.

Once she realized what he was, though, once she realized what made him tick, he'd stopped winning. Sam had forced her way back into her sister's life—all it had taken was showing up at a literacy fund-raiser. Thanks to her own job, she had a number of connections and she'd used them to place herself in James's path—and back in her sister's life.

Of course, the twins were close. Of course, they would spend a great deal of time together. The society pages had just loved Sarah. Sam had used that, worked that angle for everything she was worth.

She was prepared to use it again if she had to, and the means to doing so were stowed safely in her tote. She was getting ready to break a promise and it was entirely possible her sister wouldn't ever forgive her.

But Sam was willing to take that risk.

She should have taken it months ago.

Her heart beat a wild tattoo inside her chest, jumping, jittering around like she'd just guzzled a gallon of Monster. Hitching the tote a little higher on her shoulder, she sauntered through the entrance and made her way to the information desk.

I can't believe I'm doing this.

Pasting a polite smile on her face, she smiled at the lady behind the desk. *Hi, can you please tell my bastard-in-law that Sam's here to kick his ass?*

Bravado could be a powerful tool. Desperation, too. As long as she was careful.

Desperate measures. Dangerous measures. Going up against a man with seriously violent tendencies and enough money to make damn near anything he wanted disappear.

Including me.

* * *

IT was the longest night of Quinn's life. He'd stopped by the bus station and to his surprise, one of the women at the counter had remembered selling a ticket to Chicago to a woman she thought might be Sarah—no.

Not Sarah.

Samantha.

The eyes—the eyes were all different. The shy happiness he'd seen on her face in her wedding picture hadn't been burned out of her by a life on the run the way he'd thought. That shy happy bride hadn't been the woman he'd fallen in love with.

He'd fallen in love with her sister. Twin sisters, shit, how had that happened? The picture he'd seen of Samantha, she'd been rounder, softer, all curves where Sarah had been sleek, blonde perfection. Samantha's hair had been black—the raven wing black had made her skin seem paler, her eyes bigger, darker. It actually suited her, but then again, when he saw another picture of her, this time with dark, vibrant red hair, that had suited her, too. Apparently she had changed the color of her hair often—in all of the pictures he'd looked at with her in them, her hair was rarely the same shade more than once or twice.

But the hair wasn't what had clued him in.

It had been Samantha's eyes, those big dark eyes, full of fight. Full of life. Even though physically she looked different in those pictures than she did now, he would have recognized those eyes anywhere.

Quinn didn't know what in the hell was going on, but he knew, as well as he knew his own name, that whatever had inspired Samantha to take off, whatever had inspired her to live a lie, it had to do with her sister.

He also knew that there was very little he wouldn't do to protect his twin and heaven help the person that got in the way.

He suspected all those messages Sam had been getting came from her twin. But there hadn't been a single message since yesterday. The phone was tucked into his pocket, silent. No little tones that signaled an incoming message. Not one single ring.

Sitting on his bike outside the Renaissance Building where James Morgan worked, he waited. He'd been waiting since six a.m., feeding quarter after quarter into the meter and scowling at anybody who slowed down, as though waiting for him to empty out the space where he'd parked his bike.

From the information he'd gotten from Martin, supposedly "Sarah" would arrive at the offices in the morning. Now Quinn just needed for "Sarah" to show up. So he could . . . well, he still hadn't figured out that part.

He'd get to it when the time came.

A few feet ahead of him, a cab slowed down. His heart started to race. Even before she climbed out, he knew it was her. He felt frozen, unable to move as she paid the driver and then turned to stare up at the tower with determination written all over her face.

Determination.

Focus.

Anger.

Icy cold anger.

She hadn't seen him, seemed totally unaware of him, as she started toward the office building. That look on her face, it was one he'd seen before. It was like she was locked on some unseen target and nothing but that target existed for her.

Kind of like he felt just then—only she was his target. For him, nothing else did exist. Nothing else mattered. Kicking a leg over the bike, he headed after her.

Trailing along behind her, he rehearsed words in his head.

None of them worked.

Hell, screw trying to prepare himself to say anything—he'd just go to her and whatever happened, happened.

But he'd let too much distance get between them, and when he pushed through the revolving door, it was just in time to see her step inside an elevator. The doors closed behind her the second she was completely inside.

The last thing he saw was the back of her head.

* * *

FROM the corner of her eye, Sam watched Don Hessig as he led her toward the office.

He'd come down to meet her on the elevator, and it had surprised the hell out of her to see him. As the door slid closed, she'd shot him a look, wanting to ask a million questions.

He should have already gotten out of town. She'd thought that had been the original plan—he'd split and hope James was too keen on self-preservation to come looking for him.

She wanted to know why he was still here. But she didn't ask him—she didn't dare. Not in here. The elevator had cameras and it wouldn't surprise her at all if good old James was watching their every move.

Don wasn't an idiot, though. He wouldn't be here if he didn't have some sort of plan.

But Sam couldn't worry about that right now. All she could think about was the fact that in a few minutes, she'd find out if all of her planning had been worth it.

And if it didn't, she had a backup plan. She actually had several backup plans. Just in case.

A few feet in front of her, Don stopped and pushed open a door. She glanced down at her tote and then started inside. It was a corner office, and the northern windows faced out over the lake. Morgan would have a view from up here, all right.

The ruler of all he surveys. James had always had that kind of mind-set. He liked looking down on the peons. He was doing it even now, standing by the wide expanse of windows and staring out.

Without turning to face them, James said, "Don, thank you. If you don't mind excusing us, I'd like some time alone with my wife."

Don didn't say a word, just left, his feet silent on the carpet.

"Hello, Sarah."

She didn't respond, didn't correct him. Couldn't talk, not yet. Needed a few more seconds to get a damn grip. Behind the shield of her sunglasses, she studied the back of him. His hair was still a dark, near-black shade of brown, although she thought she could glimpse a bit of white coming in along the sides.

"Nothing to say?" he asked, turning around and looking at her.

Even though her gut was cold with fear and nerves, she forced herself to smirk at him as he looked her over, his shark-eyes taking in everything. He had the intimidation thing down pat, she had to give it to him. Her heart raced, her breathing kept trying to speed up on her, and her palms were damp, slick with sweat.

Out of the blue, she found herself thinking about Quinn.

"Tell me the truth, damn it. If he never hurt you, fine—I'll live with the fact that I've been fucking a married woman who just wasn't happy with her husband. But if he hurt you, damn it, you'd better tell me . . . and tell me now."

What would he have said if she'd told him the truth? *I'm not married and James Morgan isn't my husband. He's my sister's husband and up until she ran away from him two years ago, he had made her every day a living hell.*

Would he have believed her?

She just didn't know.

Later on, when her heart wasn't so bruised from his lack of faith in her, later on, when she could think past the rush of adrenaline fogging her brain, it would probably be a little bit of comfort to think of the torment she'd seen in his eyes. Hell, maybe later on, once this was settled, maybe . . . maybe they could try it again.

And maybe she'd sprout wings and fly when she left Chicago behind.

He hadn't trusted her. She hated to admit it, but she hadn't really trusted him much either.

Man, what a mess the two of them were.

Still, she wanted to believe that he had cared for her.

He truly hadn't wanted to bring her here. He'd walked away. She had been the one to buy the ticket to Chicago—she was the sole reason she was here right now. Because she had to see this through.

She might have spent the next few minutes, next few hours, days, years, and decades, thinking about the puzzle of Quinn Rafferty, wondering, wanting to hope, but afraid to do it. Quinn was definitely a more pleasant line of thought, even with the pain, than James.

But then James Morgan had to go and intrude on her thoughts. He'd always been an intrusive bastard.

"Apparently you *don't* have anything to say. Well, my dear, you led me on quite a chase the past two years. Did you enjoy your little game?" he asked. "I certainly hope you had fun."

His voice was cool, but there was no mistaking the anger in it.

Her heart gave one more frantic leap against her rib cage and then abruptly, the fear faded. Adrenaline kicking in, maybe. All she knew was that she could suddenly breathe easier, think easier.

She was even able to manage a cocky smile as she pushed her sunglasses up on her head.

"Oh, I'm just getting started with the fun part, Jimmy."

*   *   *

THE man might as well have placed himself in Fort Knox, Quinn decided, taking in the lobby with a quick, trained eye. The elevator that had taken Samantha away was unmarked, probably went straight to the top and only to the top.

Security cameras were discreetly placed.

The security guards were every bit as discreet, wearing suits instead of uniforms, but they were still easy enough to pick out. Apparently they were good at picking out trouble, too, because they locked in on him as quick as he locked in on them.

He didn't even have a chance to go to the information desk. As they approached him, Quinn resisted the urge to roll his shoulders. He felt like he was getting ready to go into the fight of his life—blindfolded.

"Hello, sir. May we be of service?"

He might be blindfolded, but if there was anything Quinn knew how to do, it was win a fight—the dirtier, the better.

* * *

THE look on his face was priceless.

It was every bit as perfect as Sam had hoped it would be, and God knows she'd spent a whole hell of a lot of time thinking about this moment. Almost two years of planning. Two years of working toward this.

It wasn't carelessness that had her living in cities relatively close to Chicago. It wasn't naiveté that had her choosing the name *Sara*. It wasn't some feminine vanity that had her fighting away the pounds that had crept up on her in school, pounds that had kept her and her sister from looking like mirror images.

It had been for *this*.

She'd known that sooner or later, James would put serious effort into locating his missing wife, and Sam had every intention of being located . . . in lieu of her sister.

James stood behind his desk, staring at her as though his mind wasn't processing what he saw. His face was red, his eyes narrowed down to slits. He didn't wear rage all that well. As he stood there sputtering and glaring at her, she didn't bother hiding her laugh.

Recognition came quickly, almost too quickly for her. Personally, she'd rather drag this out, taunt him until he was all but blind with rage.

But this would work, too.

He'd known who she was the second she took her sunglasses off. There had been times over the past few years when she'd looked in the mirror and done a double take. Oh, the hair was different—but it had always been. The face, though, it was Sarah's.

Speaking on a biological level, the twins were identical and through most of elementary school, only their mom had been able to tell them apart. At least when it came to looks. That had changed in middle school—Sarah had been athletic, popular . . . the golden girl to Sam's goth.

When he stormed out from behind his desk, she spread her feet and lifted her chin. "What's the matter, Jimmy? Not happy to see your beloved sister-in-law? Oh, wait . . . I'm the one you wanted dead. I guess you *aren't* happy to see me."

"Samantha, where is my wife?" he snarled.

He didn't even bother replying to her last two comments, but she hadn't expected he'd just up and confess. Even pissed off, he was too smart for that.

"Sam," she corrected. She hated it when people called her Samantha—only her mother had ever been able to do so without Sam gritting her teeth over it.

"Where is my *wife*?" James demanded again.

His face was florid, a vein throbbing right by his temple. Idly, she wondered if he had any big problems with stress. If he did, and she pushed him to the boiling point, did that make her a bad person? If he dropped dead of a heart attack, that wasn't really her fault . . . right?

Although then her nurse training might kick in—if he dropped from a heart attack, would she maybe feel obligated to do CPR?

Hell. Screw it. She didn't care if it did. Not after what he'd put her through, her sister through. Not after what he'd cost Sam.

Quinn . . .

No. *Don't think about him now. Get through this. There's all sorts of crazy you gotta handle before you can even hope to think about him again. Get through this first.*

Good advice. But man, she sucked at listening to her own advice.

"Damn it, you little cunt, I'm talking to you."

Memory flashed. *"Little cunt, one of these days, I'm going to teach you a lesson."*

She narrowed her eyes. Shifting her stance, she hooked her thumbs in her pockets and spread her legs, glaring at James. "You called me that once—you remember what I told you I'd do if you did it again?"

He sneered at her. "Yes, I remember you threatening me. I'd thought you had at least a modicum of intelligence up until that day. It's never a wise idea to threaten people when you can't possibly hope to win."

"Oh, I've got more than hope." *Hope. Bravado. A whole lot of anger.*

All she had to do was break a promise.

Some promises had to be broken, and sometimes, some promises should never be made. She'd made a few bad ones, and now she was going to remedy that.

"You have to leave him, Sarah. You have to, or he'll kill you."

"I can't, Sam. You . . . you don't realize what kind of man he is."

Sam laughed. "Don't I?" She gently cleaned her sister's lower lip. It still oozed blood and it was three times its normal size. It wasn't the first time Sam had been forced to doctor up a battered woman, but this was the first time she'd been forced to do it with her sister as her patient.

"He's the kind of man who'd beat a woman. That's not exactly a ringing endorsement of his character."

Tears gleamed in Sarah's eyes and she shook her head.

"I can't leave him. I can't."

"Why not?" Damn it, how did we get here? Sarah's husband beating on her, the two twins hiding in a motel room while Sam put rusty nursing skills to work and cleaned up Sarah's busted face.

Sarah looked away. "I just can't."

"You'd rather let him kill you?"

Sarah's eyes fell away, and Sam, sensing the weakness, pounced. "Don't tell me it won't ever come to that—don't tell me that you aren't scared to death of that happening. You can't honestly believe that."

"No. You're right. I can't." Her shoulders slumped and she brushed Sam's hand away, rolled onto her side to stare at the wall. "But I still can't leave him."

"Tell me why the hell NOT. Hell, if it's money, I'll front you the money. I've got some in savings and I haven't even touched what Mom left me."

"It's not about money," Sarah whispered. She glanced back at Sam, misery written on her face.

The two twins didn't look much alike.

They had, at one time. There had been a time when the only way to tell them apart was by the bump on Sam's nose—a bump she'd gotten in fifth grade after getting into a fight with a girl who'd been mean to Sarah.

But in middle school, when puberty hit, it hit Sam a lot harder than Sarah. Both of them developed into a D cup almost overnight, but while both of them were suddenly catching all sorts of male interest, Sam's changing body came with more problems than it'd been worth. Bad periods, days missed due to cramps, she was placed on birth control in eighth grade just to regulate her body. She'd ended up gaining fifteen pounds the year after that

*and in the years since high school, she'd put on another twenty or
thirty.*

*Sarah, captain of the cheerleading squad, had stayed slen-
der. Pretty, blonde, and popular, and Sam had become her exact
opposite—hooking up with the goth crowd. Eventually there came
a time when only their older friends realized they were twins.*

*But as different as they were on the outside, on the inside there
was a bond that nothing could change. Not time. Not distance.
And certainly not Sarah's husband.*

*"Why, Sar?" she whispered, curling up behind her sister and
hugging her close. "Why can't you leave him?"*

*Sarah took a deep breath. Then, her voice so soft and faint, she
whispered, "Because of you."*

"Me?"

*Sam jerked away, staring at her sister in shock. "What do I
have to do with it?"*

"Because he told me that if I ever left him, he'd kill you."

*Sam blinked and then squinted. Rolling off the bed, she
stormed around it and glared down at her sister. "You actually
believe* him?*"*

*"Yes. He'll do it, Sam. I know him. You don't, Sam. You don't
know what he's capable of."*

"You can't stay with him because you think he might *hurt
me," Sam snarled.*

*"I can't leave him because I know he'll do what he says. If I
leave, you're not safe."*

"And if you don't leave, you're not *safe." Sam shoved a hand
through her hair and stomped over to the window. Damn it, Sarah
was supposed to be the smarter twin, grounded and logical. "You
can't worry about me, Sarah. I'm not afraid of that bastard."*

*"You should be. And how can I not worry about you? You're
my sister. You're my best friend."*

Then, three weeks later, their unexpected white knight showed up. Sam had been pounding her head trying to figure out a way to get Sarah to leave him. She'd even played with the idea of kidnapping her own sister.

Then fate had dropped Don into their laps. She'd known Don—for quite a while actually—but that was a fact they'd kept closely hidden from James. Don had his faults . . . a number of them, but deep inside, he was a good man and there was no way he'd kill somebody.

But he'd made them realize they had to do something. Going to the police hadn't seemed the wisest option, because James had people there, people who'd make anything they said against him go away—unless there was proof. Serious, solid proof. Something that took time . . . time they couldn't spare . . . *then*.

Don had been sabotaging his own efforts to "find" Sarah. He'd also been working another end, not that he'd tell her much. He'd only shared a few sketchy details, but it was possible that maybe, just maybe, karma was about to catch up with James—big time.

Maybe that was what had given Don the courage to hang around.

"You might be right about my intelligence," Sam said, forcing her attention back to James, away from the memories. "If I was a smart chick, I never would have let my sister marry you, you fucking weasel."

James's eyes narrowed. It didn't seem possible, but his face was even redder.

This wasn't as excellent as she'd hoped for—it was better. A whole hell of a lot better, almost orgasmic. Her heart was pounding, pounding so hard, she almost didn't feel the pain still tearing through her over Quinn.

"Where is my *wife*?"

Sam shrugged and waved a hand. "I dunno . . . out and about." Then a sly smile curled her lips and she added, "But I really don't think you want to put much more effort into finding her."

"If I didn't want her found, do you honestly think I'd waste precious time and money doing so?" James demanded.

"Money can't be that precious to you—you've got buckets full." She shrugged and cocked her hip, resting a hand on it. "You haven't been able to find her for two years, though. What makes you think you'll be able to find her after all this time?"

"Hardly any of *your* business," he replied, his voice icy.

"Sarah's my sister—anything that affects her is my business."

"She's *my* wife," James bellowed. Then he stopped, closed his eyes.

She could almost see him counting to ten. When he looked at her, he'd managed to conceal some of the rage.

"I want to know about my wife, Samantha. Right now. I want to know where she is." A muscle twitched up by his temple and he was so mad, she wouldn't have been surprised to see him spitting nails. But his voice was almost normal.

"Oh, I bet you do," she drawled, giving him a cheeky grin. "But you're not going to find her by asking me . . . and then there's the fact that I really don't *want* you finding her."

"You think I give a damn what *you* want, you little bitch?"

"You should." She reached into her tote, careful not to disturb the contents as she withdrew an envelope and tossed it to him. "Those are copies. You can keep them."

He didn't go red this time. He went purple. He looked at each picture and then tore it down the middle, letting the pieces fall to his desk.

It was Sarah, more than a dozen pictures, and they all showed different injuries.

"You're going to leave my sister alone. Otherwise, those pictures are going to wind up in the society pages. Can't you just see the headlines? *Behind closed doors, philanthropist and CEO beats his wife.* It will go over really well with some of those who sit on all those charity boards with you, won't it?"

"You actually think you can ruin me?" He stared at her coldly as he let the last picture fall from his fingers.

"Ruin you? No. Ruin your public image? I can certainly take some of your polish off . . . and we both know it." She lifted a shoulder in a shrug and said, "Now those pictures can disappear. I don't give a damn if they do or not, as long as you leave my sister alone."

He stared at her, a calculating look in his eyes. Then he glanced past her shoulder. She didn't bother turning her head. She knew who he was looking at. Don. The man he'd paid to kill her.

She smiled at him and whispered, "You're not going to touch Don about this. You're going to leave him alone."

A cruel smile curled his lips.

Sam returned it. "Those pictures there? If anything happens to me *or* Don, those pictures are going to wind up in the hands of every reporter in the Chicago area. You'll be investigated, Jimmy. And you and I both know that if you get investigated too heavily, the cops will find things you don't want them knowing."

"I don't know what you mean," he said, his lashes flickering, shielding that flash of rage in his eyes.

But Sam knew him. "You can't win this, Jimmy. You touch me, you touch Don, those pictures go public. And if you don't leave my sister alone . . . those pictures won't just go to every reporter in the Chicago area, I'll send them to every fucking reporter I can find."

A muscle jerked in his jaw.

"I hardly plan on remaining married to a woman who's abandoned me," James said.

"No. I bet that would really interfere with your current plans." Sam smiled. "The governor isn't going to be too pleased if you start pursuing his daughter while you're still married, now will he?"

"What does the governor have to do with this?"

Sam laughed. "Jimmy, don't play dumb. I know about you and Alison Mather. She's accompanied you twice to California and you've been seen together at any number of charity functions. Now I could see the occasional chance encounter, but the business trips? If it's not for personal interests, then why? She's hardly business-meeting material, now is she?"

James waved it aside, but she saw the glint in his eye.

"So . . . do we have a deal? Leave Sarah alone . . . and I'll leave you alone. You can file for a divorce on the grounds of abandonment. Yeah, it might sting your pride, but you can do it."

Before he could reply, the phone on his desk beeped.

He ignored it, staring at Sam, undisguised hatred on his face.

"Things would progress more quickly if Sarah came home and dealt with this. I could make sure she received a tidy sum of money and—"

"And the minute you had the chance, you'd teach her a lesson for humiliating you." Sam shook her head. "Sarah isn't coming home. You either file for divorce and agree to leave her be, or the next set of pictures will go to the newspaper. Hell, I think I'll even send them to Alison's daddy."

The phone beeped again.

Giving him a chilly smile, she said, "Do you really think he's going to be interested in letting his daughter marry a man suspected of beating his wife?"

Another beep from the phone. He glared at Sam as he snatched it up. "I'm in the middle of something." He slammed down the phone.

"You have no proof of anything . . . those pictures? Fake. Anybody with a computer can doctor a picture these days. You know what *I* think? Your sister is missing because *you* killed her. In a jealous rage—she was always prettier, more popular . . . and she landed a rich husband while you toiled away in some filthy shelter. You killed her, out of jealousy, and now you think you can come in and blackmail me," James said. He smoothed down his tie, taking an inordinate amount of time to do so. "You can spin whatever stories you wish. Nobody is going to believe anything you say."

Sam snorted. "Damn, you think fast . . . for a snake. But the problem with that? Sarah's not dead."

His eyes gleamed. "But nobody could prove that unless she came home. You think you have me over a barrel here . . . *Samantha*. But you don't. I know people. People who could make your life an utter hell."

"What . . . like you've done?" Curling her lip at him, she held still, watching him as he came out from behind the desk, gliding toward her. Like a shark. His lifeless eyes held her pinned in place, although she could see the promise of violence there. The hate. The need to inflict pain.

Sam lifted her chin as he stopped just a foot away.

"I really did think you were smarter than this," he said, keeping his voice low. "I don't tolerate threats, Samantha. Those who try to threaten me are eliminated."

"You already tried that . . . it didn't work."

James smiled coldly. "I'll handle it myself this time."

"Should I be frightened . . . Jimmy?"

"You should." He dipped his head, putting it so close his mouth almost brushed her ear. "I'm going to bury you, you little bitch."

Oh, that was almost too easy . . .

"Oh, that wouldn't be smart on your part." She grinned at him, hoped it would hide the fear in her gut. Her heart knocked against her ribs. But she didn't back away. Didn't let him see that she was terrified—he would make good on that threat, if he could. If he believed he could get away with it, he would do whatever he felt was necessary. "You see . . . too many people know I'd be here today. The detective agency. Hell, fifty employees saw me coming up here."

"Oh, I wouldn't do it . . . today." He smiled at her. "But it will come. I'm a patient man, Samantha, especially when it comes to things I want. And I want you to wish you were never born."

She gave him Bambi-eyes. "Are you seriously still threatening me? Don't you realize that I'm *this* close to making sure everybody knows you're a fucking wife beater?"

"You don't want to do that, Samantha. You really don't."

"You *are* threatening me. I wonder what the prosecutors would think about this," she said. Her voice trembled, just a bit, before she could steady it. She saw the flicker in his eyes, realized he had seen her fear. Swallowing the knot in her throat, she said in a stronger voice, "You got any idea what they'd say?"

He smirked. "Why? Are you going to threaten me with legal action now? I haven't harmed you."

The door opened, but neither of them looked away from the other.

"No. But it doesn't change the fact that you made the threat and if something happens to me, that won't look very good, will it? Besides . . ."

"If something happens to you, it won't matter how his threats look." A menacing voice promised from the doorway. "He's going to end up an ugly smear on the pavement outside."

Quinn—her knees went a little weak. Her heart skipped and danced in her chest, doing a fast-time version of the jitterbug. Licking her dry lips, she turned and looked at him.

At the same time, James jerked away and did the same. He stared at the man standing in the doorway with fury written all over his face.

With his legs spread wide, thumbs hooked in his pockets, Quinn returned James's intense scrutiny. His lip curled as he raked his gaze over James.

He didn't look her way.

Not once.

"Who are you?" James demanded.

Without responding, Quinn stalked in. There were two men in suits trailing along behind him.

James looked at the suits. "Richard, would you care to explain to me who this is and why he was brought up here?"

"Mr. Morgan, I apologize." One of the suits pushed past Quinn, his face unreadable. There was the faintest flush on his cheeks as he gestured to Quinn. "We tried to call, but you . . . I mean, there was interference. This man insisted he had very important information about your wife. And . . . ah . . . other matters."

James's narrowed his eyes. "Really." He glanced at Sam.

Sam could see the calculation in his eyes, see the wheels starting to spin.

Richard inclined his head. "Yes. As she is already here, I wasn't sure if his information was relevant, but he was rather insistent."

He still hadn't looked at her. Her gut knotted up, forming into a tight, cold ball. Spit pooled in her mouth and she swallowed.

"What sort of information?"

Quinn jerked a shoulder up.

Once more, a muscle started to twitch in James's temple. "What information do you have about my wife?"

"Have your boys leave us alone and we can talk about my information," Quinn said, his voice flat and cold. So cold it sent shivers down Sam's spine.

But in his eyes, she saw heat. The heat of anger. The heat of hunger. Other emotions she couldn't begin to think about. What was he doing here?

"Richard, you and Matthew may go. I'll send word if your services are required," James said, his tone sharp enough to cut.

The room was quiet as the other two men left, and once the doors swung shut behind them, Quinn slid his eyes her way. Finally, he looked at her. For the briefest moment, it was like the past few days hadn't happened. He studied her, from head to toe and then right back on up until once more their gazes connected.

That long, lingering look was an unseen caress, leaving a trail of heat in its wake. Followed by a rush of confusion.

What in the hell was going on?

Why was he here?

"Did he hurt you?"

"No." She angled her chin up and added, "I can take care of myself."

A smirk tugged at his lips. "I know you can, tough girl." He slanted his gaze toward James and said, "Still, if he so much as laid a hand on you, I'm going to feed it to him."

James's lip curled. "I'm not sure who you are, but if you don't have any relevant information for me, you may go. I have a great deal of catching up to do with my . . . wife."

"She's not your wife," Quinn said, shrugging.

So casually said. But the words hit her like a slap, catching her off guard. Her lips parted on a startled gasp before she could stop it. He *knew*. Her voice rusty, she asked, "How did you find out, Quinn?"

James's cold, empty eyes narrowed down. "Quinn?" he echoed. Understanding flashed through those empty eyes. "Quinn . . . as in Quinn Rafferty."

Quinn ignored him. "Doesn't matter right now, does it?" He looked away from her, focusing on James. "So . . . what did I miss?"

"Excuse me?"

Propping a shoulder against a wall, Quinn watched James. "You heard me. What did I miss? Samantha's here on unfinished business and I guess that business is you."

"It's hardly any concern of yours." James frowned.

In an eerie echo of Samantha's comment, Quinn said, "Anything that concerns Samantha concerns me."

"Sam," she corrected. He didn't look her way.

"Hmmm." James once more had his temper under control. "Tell me, Mr. Rafferty, since Samantha has been reluctant to explain what's going on, would you care to enlighten me?"

"Sure. You put out a job request and failed to make a couple of pertinent details clear—namely, your wife has an identical twin. Made it very easy to grab the wrong one. I'm kind of curious how you could leave such an important detail out."

"He thought I was dead," Sam said, giving James a sidelong look. "Not that you'll get that information out of him."

Quinn's eyes narrowed. He said nothing.

"She's always had a wickedly active imagination," James said as he gave Quinn a chilly smile. His gaze was flat, so very cold. "Perhaps you should have done better research, Mr. Rafferty. Seeing as how you failed to collect my wife, I won't be authorizing the reward."

"Actually, you're calling off the reward altogether." He bared his teeth in a mockery of a smile.

Damn, if she thought James had a cold smile, it was nothing like the one on Quinn's face just then. The look on his face was positively arctic.

James didn't look too affected, though. In a bored tone, he said, "Now why would I do that, when I'm so desperate to see her again?"

"You'll do it because if you don't, you won't be very happy." He pulled his phone out.

Sam didn't know what he had in mind, and while she suspected it might involve judicious use of those very capable hands, she wasn't about to let a white knight rain on her parade.

"Quinn, while I appreciate the effort, this is my fight." She bared her teeth at James. "After all, this is *family* business."

"Indeed." James inclined his head and gave Quinn a dismissive look. "That being the case, perhaps you could take your leave, Mr. Rafferty."

"Perhaps you could shove it up your ass, Mr. Morgan." He crossed his arms and leaned back against the wall once more.

For all the world, he looked like a man settling down to watch a cool action flick.

James turned around and stalked to his desk. "You're leaving, Mr. Rafferty."

"No." Quinn shook his head. "I'm not doing that. I'm going to stay right here until this is all over."

"Oh, it's going to be over . . . very soon." She stared into his eyes, wishing she could figure out what was going on inside that head of his. But she couldn't. It was like reading a brick wall. He gave nothing away.

With her heart racing in her chest, she glanced past him and saw Don, still in the lobby area outside James's office. Waiting. Don looked scared to death, sitting in his chair with his fingers gripping the armrests as though that alone would keep him from running.

Don's eyes met hers and he gave a short, jerky nod.

Hot damn.

There was knowledge in his eyes.

A grin curled her lips and she cocked a brow at him. A silent, unspoken question . . . *really?*

The smile he gave her back was shaky, and more than a little strained. Then he nodded and glanced at the clock. When he looked back at her, he mouthed the word *Soon.*

Soon . . . as in seconds, she suspected.

Abruptly, Sam started to laugh. She tried to muffle it, but the harder she tried not to laugh, the harder it was to contain.

"Shut the fuck up, you little bitch," James rasped.

Quinn came off the wall in a smooth, lethal move. Stalking around the desk, he approached James and didn't stop until no more than an inch separated them. "One more insult, James, you'll need a paramedic to scrape you off the floor. And probably a body bag."

Did it make her bloodthirsty that she found Quinn very sexy in that moment?

James smoothed a hand down his tie, a nervous gesture, Sam realized. She scowled. Hell, she hadn't made him nervous. Not even when he saw those pictures. She'd pissed him off, but made him nervous? Not even a little, she suspected.

"I'm entitled to know where to find my wife, Mr. Rafferty."

"Why? So you can teach her a lesson for running away?"

A muscle ticked in James's cheek. "I imagine I know where you've gotten such foolish ideas. Samantha never did like me—I suspect she didn't care for her sister marrying a much older man." He shot a look at Sam. "But I just want my wife back. I miss her."

Quinn smirked. "Yeah. I bet."

Mentally, she huffed. *Fine*. Let Quinn make him all nervous. She shot Don another glance and this time, his gaze slid to the elevator. Man, he hadn't been kidding.

"Jimmy, I think you're about out of time," Sam murmured.

He frowned at her, but any response James might have made was lost when the door opened yet again. Sam turned to look and even before her brain processed what she was seeing, there was a grin curving her lips upward.

James tore his eyes away from Quinn and stared at his newest visitor. A slender blonde stood in the doorway, her hand resting on the doorknob and holding the door open.

James blinked. "Alison, what a pleasant surprise." His voice was sharp enough to cut glass. "But I'm afraid I'm in the middle of an important discussion."

Alison Mather blinked cornflower blue eyes and frowned. "I'm so sorry . . . am I interrupting?"

"Unfortunately, yes." The smile on his face looked brittle. "I wish you'd called."

"Oh." She looked back and forth between James, Quinn, and Sam. Then with a vague gesture toward the lobby area, she said, "Perhaps I could wait . . . ?"

"This could take some time. It might be best if I called—"

"Excuse me, ma'am."

Alison turned. Her shiny, golden blonde hair fell over one shoulder as she studied the people gathered behind her. Three men, one woman. Two of the men were in uniform. The third man was dressed in a wrinkled, rumpled suit, his eyes tired, but sharp.

It was about to get very crowded in James's elegant gray and chrome office.

The woman was dressed in a suit that probably cost more than Sam made in a month. She had the same sharp eyes as the cop, but Sam knew she wasn't one. Natalie Dillard was a lawyer. They'd crossed paths a time or two.

James scowled, his eyes moving past the uniforms, past the woman, to meet the gaze of the man. "If you don't mind, I'm in the middle of an important discussion."

The woman answered. "I'm afraid that discussion is going to have to wait." She glanced behind her and gestured at the cops.

"James Morgan." Tired and Rumpled strode forward. "You're under arrest."

* * *

WHILE she was busy watching the scene play out between Morgan and the cops, Quinn was busy staring at her. He'd listened while the cops read Morgan his rights, mentally filing away the details so he could go through them later. Tax evasion. Corporate espionage.

Sam had something to do with this.

This was why she'd come back. What she'd been counting on.

Hell, he'd shown up to rescue her, but she'd already taken care of it herself.

Most of the crimes he was suspected of were white-collar stuff. Was it enough to lock him up? Quinn didn't know.

He would find out—he'd have to. He needed to make sure Samantha—no, she went by Sam—he had to make sure she was safe. But he'd worry about that later. Right now, he was having a hard time thinking about much of anything other than the fact that she was just a few feet away.

The cops hustled Morgan out, and through the glass walls, Quinn could see a whole slew of people watching with avid interest. The female lawyer lingered as the doors swung shut, stopping by the blonde. Morgan had called her Alison.

"You weren't supposed to be here, Ms. Mather," the lawyer said.

Alison lifted one shoulder in a shrug, the movement smooth and graceful. "Now, Natalie, my presence really makes no difference one way or the other and we both know it."

The lawyer just shook her head and turned away, striding out of the room on ice-pick heels.

"You had something to do with this," Sam said, shaking her head. "I don't know what, but you did."

Alison gave her a friendly, familiar smile and then looked at Don. "Not so much really. Just passed on some information here and there."

"I bet." Sam glanced at Don and saw that he was blushing, staring at his feet with a studious expression. "I wonder where that information came from. Hell, Don, you could have clued me in you were *this* close."

"I did try," he said, smoothing his tie down. "But when you finally called, you were off the phone in under thirty seconds."

"I had a bus to catch," she said, evasively. With a restless shrug, she looked away from Don, found her gaze drawn to Quinn, but she didn't look *at* him. Not yet.

Quinn scowled and crossed his arms over his chest. He wasn't going any damn where. Not just yet.

Dragging her attention back to Alison, she hooked her thumbs in her pockets and asked, "So is the case against him solid?"

"I don't know. That's a little out of my league, and trust me, Natalie isn't going to be overly enthusiastic about sharing details. Dad might have some luck, but that just depends on if Natalie is in a cooperative mood or not." Alison frowned, flicking an invisible piece of lint from her sleeve.

"He's in trouble, though, right?"

Alison smiled. It was a wide, delighted smile, one that lit up her entire face. "Oh, yes." She slid Quinn a look and then focused a bright smile on Don. "You know, Don, I think you owe me lunch, after all of this."

Another steamroller, Sam knew, watching as Alison politely dragged Don out of the office. The door closed behind them and finally, she was alone with Quinn.

Well, not entirely alone. They were being watched. Gathered out in the lobby area were a good fifteen people, and most of them weren't even bothering to hide their interest—including Don and Alison.

Sam ignored them, turning to study him. She went to slide her sunglasses down over her eyes and Quinn strode across the room, snatched them away. He wasn't about to have this conversation with her hiding from him. Not in any way.

"You've got a bad habit of taking my belongings, Quinn." She scowled at him.

He tossed the sunglasses in the direction of Morgan's desk, not looking away from her face. Damn it, how could he have made the mistake he'd made? The face might technically *look* the same, but there was a strength in Sam's that the woman in the wedding picture hadn't had. Strength. Pride. Determination . . . everything that made her Sam.

Everything that made her the woman he'd fallen so hard for.

He swallowed the knot in his throat and forced the apology out. "I'm sorry."

"Oh, really?" She cocked her head and rocked back on her heels as she studied him. "What exactly are you sorry for?"

"For what I did. For what I was going to do. For not trusting you." He wanted to touch her, so bad. Wanted to brush that hair back from her face, look into those amazing eyes. Hold her against him. He didn't, though. He needed to get this done, and if he touched her, she was likely to belt him one. And if by some slim chance she didn't lay into him, he didn't know if he'd get the apology out because he was likely to be all over her—glass walls or not. "I don't trust people. I don't like trusting people. But that's my problem—not yours—and you shouldn't have to deal with my problems."

"Did you want to trust me?"

"What in the hell do you think?" he snapped. That cool, disconnected tone of hers was really starting to piss him off.

She shrugged and turned away from him to restlessly pace the carpeted floor. "Frankly, Quinn, I don't know what to think." She sighed and pushed a hand through her hair. She paced as far as she could and pivoted, started back up the floor.

She didn't look at him—stared straight ahead, but Quinn suspected she wasn't looking at anything outside the expanse of windows. She was seeing things within her own mind. Whatever she was thinking about left her face looking grim, resigned.

Quinn found himself remembering the way she always paced before she'd go on one of her runs, bracing herself. *Mental pep talks—*

"What was the deal with the running?" he asked.

Sam jerked her shoulder in a shrug. "Sarah and I are twins—technically, we're identical, but we haven't looked much alike since eighth grade. Sarah was the golden girl, cheerleader, ran track.

When we hit puberty . . ." Her voice trailed off and she blushed. Spinning around to face him, she stared at a point over his shoulder. "I ended up having some issues and had to go on the pill, put on weight."

She paused but Quinn didn't need her to fill in any more blanks. He'd already suspected it. "You were doing it so you could pass yourself off as your sister. Why?"

"Isn't it obvious?" she asked, her voice dry. "I had to face him, Quinn. I had to. I had to try to make him stop, try to make him let my sister go."

"He abused her."

"On a regular basis. Not at first, and he was good at hiding it, and Sarah was so ashamed. He was very good at isolating her—I should have known—"

"How?" Quinn's heart clenched. That shattered, angry look on her face was going to haunt him. Just one more ghost to keep him company late at night. "You're not a mind reader."

She scowled. "You don't have sisters, do you?"

"No. But I've got a brother." He rubbed the heel of his hand over the ache in his chest as he started to pace. Unaware of Sarah's intense gaze, he continued, "There's been a time or two when he's had things going on in his life—bad things. Things I felt like I should have been able to stop, or at least control. Times when he's had problems going on and he kept quiet about them. I know what it's like to feel like there's something you can do to make things better, but it isn't always possible. Besides, in the long run, you did help her, right?"

"Not enough," she said, her voice cold and hard.

"Why not? You got her away, right? This taking off thing, was it her idea or yours?"

Sam just stared at him.

He wanted to make it better for her . . . and he knew he

couldn't. "She's safe. She's alive. She's away from him. That's going to have to be enough for you."

Those eyes of his were somber, intense. Sam tore her gaze away from him and braced against the pain in her heart, a pain that slowly, insidiously crept through her body. Looking at him, she ached to touch him. She couldn't. There was too much going on inside her head, too many thoughts to process, too many emotions to understand.

She needed to get away from him, get herself under control. But she had a question first. Looking at him over her shoulder, she asked, "How did you find out?"

Thick lashes lowered, shielding his gaze from her. A dull, ruddy flush crept up his neck, until it had stained his cheeks. "I saw your picture."

Sam stared at him, confused. "You saw a picture?" she parroted back.

"Yeah. And I figured out there were things going on that I didn't know jack about. I just knew that the woman I saw in that picture wasn't the same woman I saw in the wedding picture."

"I can only imagine what picture you saw that clued you in there." Sam smirked and stroked a hand down her hip. "Let me guess . . . in the picture, I was a little bit rounder, maybe a little bit dumpy. My hair was anything but blonde or brown—"

She stopped in midsentence as he crossed the carpet to stand in front of her. He wasn't avoiding her eyes now. No, he was staring at her with eyes that glittered and burned. He caught her chin in his hand, angled her head back. "It was your eyes," he said gruffly, pressing his thumb to her lips. "You have the eyes of a fighter and your sister doesn't. I should have seen it right away."

Now Sam was the one blushing. The heat of him scorched her. All along her front, she could feel the warmth of his body, reaching out to hers, warming everything that had gone cold and tight the minute she realized why he'd tracked her down at the train station in St. Louis. She wanted to melt against him, feel his arms come around her and then she wanted to cry.

She didn't know if the mess with James Morgan was over. She didn't know if her sister could come home. She didn't know if Sarah would ever be safe. But for the first time, it seemed like maybe she could get her life back. Hell, maybe her sister could even find a life.

But Sam didn't know where to go from here.

Too much emotion, too many fears, all trapped inside her, struggling to break free with tears. But she couldn't give in. Not with him. Too much had happened between them, and she didn't know if they could get back to where they had been.

Or if he even wanted to.

The thought of that chilled her.

She pulled free of his grasp, letting her hair fall down to shield her face. Calling on the stubbornness that had gotten her through the past two years, she composed her features and when she looked at Quinn, she had locked down. "I'm not much of a fighter, Quinn."

Edging around him, she started across the carpet but then stopped. There was still a whole hell of a lot of people out in the lobby, staring in through the glass walls with avid interest. Don was out there, playing the peacekeeper and from what she could tell, he was running interference, too, trying to keep some of the others from barging into the office.

She really wasn't in the mood for an audience.

"If you're not a fighter, then why did you come here to face him?"

"Because of my sister," Sam snapped, turning around and glaring at him.

"Because she wouldn't stand up to him?"

"She *couldn't*. She was terrified of him. The one time she tried to leave him, he came after her and threatened—" She snapped her mouth shut. The ice in Quinn's eyes was sharp, blade-sharp.

"Threatened what?"

Glaring at him, she said, "Why does any of this matter?"

He ignored the question, his eyes narrowing down on her face. "You. He threatened you. That's why she finally left him."

Sam crossed her arms over her chest and averted her gaze.

"She left him because she wanted to protect you," Quinn murmured. "And you came back here to face him. To protect her. To fight for her because she was too afraid of him hurting you."

"I don't need protecting, Quinn. And I came back because I was sick and tired of letting him run our lives." Swallowing the knot in her throat, she added, "I'm more than capable of taking care of myself."

"I noticed." She looked so pissed off. So angry. And somehow, vulnerable. Quinn hated seeing that broken, confused look in her eyes. Hated knowing she was still worrying, still scared.

He shoved his hands in his pants pockets. It was that, or reach for her. Haul her close. Maybe go to his knees and tell her he was sorry—so fucking sorry. Sorry and desperate—he needed her. With him. Always.

Pride kept him from begging, though. Pride and uncertainty. He felt something for her.

Something—*shit, man, you really are a coward. You're in love with her. Deal with it.*

What if she didn't feel anything?

What if . . . *stop. No what ifs, not right now.*

"I'm sorry. I don't know if I can say it enough times to make you believe me, but I am sorry. You are a fighter," he said, quietly. "I should have remembered that."

Sam glanced at him. "You know something, Quinn? If we get right down to it, neither of us really knows the other."

"Bullshit." He scowled at her.

Once more, that cool, composed mask settled over her features and she cocked a brow at him. "We *don't* know each other. You know as much about me as I know about you. Hell, less. You only know what I've *let* you know. And now, if you don't mind, I've got a million things I need to take care of."

It's the truth, Sam insisted. She started for the door and as her heart cried out in agony, she tried to bury the pain under a layer of ice. She had a life and she wanted to get back to it. It was way past time.

"I know you well enough," Quinn said from behind her.

She ignored him and reached out for the doorknob. Some of the people had finally drifted out of the lobby, but she wasn't going to be able to slip away unnoticed. That was pretty obvious.

Quinn came up behind her, silent. He reached up and braced a hand over the door, keeping her from opening it. Sam refused to look at him, refused to turn around. "I know what I need to know," he said gruffly.

He touched her. Sam jumped as he brushed his fingers over her hip. Her heart skipped a few dozen beats, it seemed, and then settled down into a rapid-fire tango, beating madly against her rib cage. But he didn't linger. All he did was push something into her pocket and then his hand fell away. Automatically, she reached down and patted her pocket, felt the familiar outline of her phone.

He brushed his lips over her cheek and murmured, "I know I fell in love with you . . . and I know I fucked things up. I'm sorry."

Then he let go of the door.

Sam stood there, numb and frozen. Her mouth opened. "You can't love me," she said, her voice rusty.

"Not your call, Sam."

She tried to force herself to talk, but she couldn't get a damn thing out. Her throat was frozen. She couldn't manage even a whisper as he gently nudged her out of the way and then slipped outside.

Frozen, she stood there and watched as he cut through the tangle of bodies and made for the elevator. Frozen, she stood there as he climbed on. Just before the doors closed, he turned and looked at her.

That look in his eyes—naked and bruised.

Hurt.

Broken.

TWENTY

"**D**EAD?" Quinn repeated, staring at the TV in his hotel room without really seeing it.

"Yes." It was Alison Mather on the other line. "He was found this morning by a member of his house staff. There's nothing official yet, but from what I've heard, he put a bullet in his head. Since his crimes were all white-collar, he made bail."

She paused then sighed. "The cops had a solid case against him. There was no way he'd go to prison, arrogant prick—should have known he'd try this."

"Look at it this way . . . he saved the taxpayers some money."

"Hmmm. True. Dad's rather pleased with that part, I'll say."

Since he hadn't gotten the name of the lawyer who had been there when James Morgan was arrested, Quinn had tracked down Alison Mather's number, kept in contact with her.

It had been a week since he'd walked away from Sam, but he hadn't left Chicago. He hadn't been able to, not until he knew she'd be safe. Morgan had been released on bond—Quinn hoped he would try to disappear, because he wanted to get his hands on the bastard who had put Sam through such hell.

Hadn't happened, though, and now Quinn knew why. The

man had a serious, solid case against him and even if he didn't do jail time for some of the more serious white-collar crimes, he'd be a long time in recovering, if it ever happened. A number of his employees had bailed on him, and several of the board members were also looking at charges.

James Morgan was an arrogant bastard—Quinn had known that the moment he saw the man. If he couldn't live his life the way he wanted, he'd just end it.

"Does Sam know?" he asked.

"Yes. I spoke with her a little while ago."

"And her sister . . . ?"

"Sam said she'd let Sarah know. I wouldn't know how to reach her—Sam did a damn good job of putting her under."

In the past week, Quinn had done everything he could to learn as much about Samantha McElyea as possible. She and Alison had actually known each other in college, and from what Quinn had been able to put together, they had done a number of charity-type things together over the years.

Sam was a nurse, a fact that didn't surprise him. He'd suspected she had some sort of medical background the day he'd gotten that black eye. She worked with battered women and children at a shelter, and although nobody had really confirmed it, he suspected she was also responsible for helping abused women disappear.

Women like her sister.

It wasn't any wonder that she'd managed to stay hidden for two years. She knew all the tricks.

"Are things with Sam going to be okay?"

"There are some issues, but I know some people." Alison didn't pretend ignorance. Disappearing came with consequences. Things like losing a home, possessions. She'd spent those two years getting paid under the table, which meant she could be looking at trouble with the IRS. "We'll get things worked out."

"Thanks."

"Sam's a friend of mine. No need to say thanks." She hesitated and then asked, "Are you going to try to talk to her?"

It was the first time she'd asked, although Quinn wasn't surprised. Since he'd been calling her every day to check on things about Morgan, it wasn't like the woman could ignore the obvious. "There's no reason to," he said.

No reason. He'd told Sam he'd fallen in love with her, and her only response had been, *You can't love me*.

When he'd walked away, she hadn't stopped him. Hadn't so much as said his name. And she hadn't tried to call him, either.

Definitely no reason to try talking to her again.

Shoving a hand through his hair, he scanned the small hotel room where he'd been living for the past week. It was time to go home.

Morgan couldn't hurt Sam now.

Her sister could come home.

No reason for him to talk to her . . . and no reason for him to stay.

* * *

"HE checked out?"

The woman behind the counter couldn't have looked more bored. She sat with her feet propped up and a book in hand. So far, she hadn't taken her nose out of that book to look at Sam even once.

"When did he check out?" Maybe he was still in Chicago—

"Yesterday." She said it without even looking away from the book.

Waited too long . . . Gritting her teeth, Sam barely managed to keep from grabbing the book and hurling it across the room. "You're sure it was yesterday?"

"Positive."

Sam left without another word, feeling oddly deflated. Up until she'd met Alison for coffee yesterday evening, Sam hadn't even realized he was still here. He hadn't left her—

But she'd waited too long. If she hadn't spent the night replaying things through in her mind, if she'd just listened to her gut, she might have . . .

"Might have what?" she muttered as she made her way to her car. Well, not *hers*—her car had been repossessed. Fortunately her house hadn't—she'd paid the house off with money she'd gotten after Mom died. She was borrowing one of Alison's cars.

"You keep doing me favors, I might as well sign over my first-born to you," Sam had told her yesterday while they drank coffee and ate yummy cheesecake at a little café close to the Sears Tower. *"Hell, after what you've done the past few years, watching James and all, I probably already owe you my first-born. And a kidney."*

"My kidneys are good, thanks. As to the first-born, you might want to run that by the potential dad first." Then Alison had grinned at her. *"I'm curious who that might be . . . maybe Mr. Hot and Sexy that you still haven't talked about?"*

Hot and sexy . . . yeah, that was Quinn. Hot and sexy and so much more. She couldn't even begin to describe the complicated mess of Quinn Rafferty. And now she didn't even have a chance to try and talk to him.

He was gone.

"So you're just going to let him leave?"

Sam slumped against the car door, staring at the hotel without really seeing it. It was on the outskirts of Chicago, in a less-than-nice neighborhood. Not exactly the kind of place where she'd been nervous to go, but definitely not the sort of neighborhood where she'd feel safe walking alone at night.

He'd left.

But she could go after him.

"I know I fell in love with you . . . and I know I fucked things up. I'm sorry."

"You can't love me."

"Not your call, Sam."

Call—she could call him.

She started to reach for her phone, but then she stopped. No. She wasn't going to try and have this conversation on the phone. She wanted to see him. Had to. Which meant she'd have to leave Chicago. She'd spent the past two years desperate to come home, come home and never leave again.

But if she was going to see Quinn, she'd have to do just that.

TWENTY-ONE

Two weeks.

It had been two weeks since Quinn had left Chicago.

Three weeks since she'd seen him—almost a month. It had been the longest month of her life.

It almost seemed like another lifetime, but at the same time, her memories of him still remained so vivid. And the dreams . . . man, those dreams were going to lay her low.

Sam smoothed a hand down her hair, staring into the mirror. It was black, midnight black and cut to chin length, framing her pale face. The cut made her eyes appear larger, and the dark color made her skin seem even paler.

But she found herself wondering what Quinn would think. Found herself wondering if she should have left it alone.

But . . . well, it hadn't been *her*. *This* was her. And she'd missed it—missed looking in the mirror and seeing deep red hair . . . or black shot through with thick streaks of blue. Missed her poet blouses, her long skirts, black leather boots that went up over her knees and clung like a second skin. Missed half a dozen earrings in one ear and only one in the other. She'd missed her jewelry, her clothes, her makeup . . . her life.

She'd missed being herself.

Although she wasn't so sure Quinn would like her like this. And she missed him so bad it was an ache in her chest.

"Stop stalling," she muttered. Flipping up the visor, she turned off the ignition and climbed out of the car, staring up at Theresa's old house.

She didn't go to the front door. Instead, she headed toward the path alongside of the house, the one that would lead to his door.

He was still living there.

Sam had called Theresa back when she'd made the decision to come down and see him. She hadn't called him, even though she'd longed to hear his voice. The things she had to say to him, she needed to say in person.

She wasn't going to take the coward's way out and—

Shit.

Her heart bumped against her rib cage as she spotted a familiar head of hair. Golden blond, shot through with rich shades of brown, paler shades of gold. Wide shoulders, straining against the seams of a polo shirt.

Quinn—

And he had another woman in his arms.

Fury punched through her.

The echo of his voice rang through her ears—"*I know I fell in love with you . . .*"

"You son of a bitch!"

He looked up just in time to see Sam's fist flying at his face.

His head jerked back at the impact.

The woman yelped, startled.

But Sam was too busy staring into stunned gray eyes to pay the woman any attention.

Gray eyes—like Quinn's . . . but not.

"Oh, shit," she whispered, looking him over from head to toe.

The hair was the right color, but cut wrong. Quinn's hair

fell nearly to his shoulders. Body was right, but the clothes were wrong—she'd never seen Quinn in anything but faded jeans and equally faded T-shirts. The face was right—the eyes were wrong.

All wrong.

No fucking way.

Swallowing, she fell back a step and stared at a complete stranger. "Uh . . . I'm sorry, I thought you were . . ."

The man grinned, despite the blood on his mouth. The woman at his side glared at Sam. She was shorter than Sam by maybe two inches, and reed slender, the kind of slender that probably defined the phrase *a stiff breeze could blow her over.* But Sam suspected it would take more than a stiff breeze. A lot more.

"What the hell is your problem?"

Sam licked her lips and tried to find her voice. Her hand was starting to hurt, the knuckles throbbing. "I'm sorry. I thought he was . . . uh . . . well . . ."

The man's lips curled as he reached up, probing the area with his fingertips. He wiped the blood away and said, "You've got one hell of a right hook."

God, just let the ground open up and swallow me. Please. She swallowed and tore her eyes away from the man in front of her, although looking at the woman at his side didn't help much. She was eying Sam with an awful lot of curiosity and slowly, the light of anger in her eyes bled away to amusement. "You're looking for Quinn, aren't you?"

Sam blushed and shifted from one foot to the other, then started to turn around. "Yeah. But I'll talk to him later—"

"Oh, no, you won't." The woman placed her diminutive frame in front of Sam.

Sam decided she had a good twenty pounds on the other woman, easy. Two inches, twenty pounds, and she'd bet she had a longer reach, too. Although she was still trying to figure out how to remove her foot from her mouth with the man who was obviously Quinn's brother, she sure as hell wasn't letting some short, skinny woman keep her from Quinn. Narrowing her eyes, she said, "I beg your pardon?"

It was the tone she always used when she wanted to freeze somebody in their tracks. Wasn't always effective, but for the most part, it did the job.

All the woman did was smile. "I'm Devon. Quinn's sister-in-law. The man behind you is Luke—Quinn's twin, although I guess you sort of noticed that part."

Luke. He came around to stand by Devon's side, putting his arm around her shoulders. Devon leaned into him, a gesture that looked so automatic, so natural. Envy welled within Sam's heart, and she had to swallow around the knot that had once more taken up residence in her throat.

"What did you want to talk to Quinn about?" Devon asked.

"It's personal," Sam replied.

Luke was playing with his wife's hair, Sam noticed. He had one long curl that he kept twining around his finger. Devon didn't seem to even notice, too busy staring at Sam with blatant curiosity.

"Is he down in his apartment?" she asked. She was hoping Devon would say *No.*

All of a sudden, she wasn't quite ready to face him.

Well, she hadn't been ready, period. But now she felt even less ready.

She was terrified.

"He had to work today," Luke said before Devon could answer. He glanced at his watch and then smiled at Sam. "We were actually heading out—going to meet him for dinner at some pizza place a few blocks away—Imo's, I think."

"I'm sorry. I guess I should have called." Her heart sank. No, she wasn't ready. But she was quite desperate to see him. Needed to see him, like she needed to breathe. She hoped none of her disappointment showed on her face. Forcing a smile, she nodded at them and said, "I'll just talk with him later."

"Why not now?" Devon cocked her head. Her hair, dark reddish brown, fell over one shoulder. A breeze kicked up, blowing one wild curl across her face. She brushed it back absently and gave Sam an understanding smile. "He called not long ago, said he'd meet us at the pizza place at five."

"I don't want to interrupt."

Devon glanced up at Luke. Luke's mouth curled into a smile, one that was so like Quinn's it made her heart ache. "You won't be. I'm not much in the mood for pizza, now that I think about it."

Sam's heart did that crazy little dance in her chest and then settled down to something resembling normal. "Are you sure?"

"Trust me." Luke grinned. "My brother hasn't exactly been in the best of moods lately. If I have to choose between dinner alone with my wife or having him growl at me, I'm choosing the dinner with my wife."

* * *

THE place was packed. Especially for a Wednesday. Quinn had to fight to get a table and if he hadn't already told his brother he'd be there, he wouldn't have messed with it. Sitting at a small table that would seat two easily, three not so easily, he shot his watch another look.

Five twenty.

If Luke and Devon didn't show in the next ten minutes, Quinn was leaving.

He wasn't that hungry. Hell, he wasn't really hungry at all, but Devon had mentioned it would be nice to have a meal together before they left in the morning, and he had a hard time telling her no.

Sighing, he slumped down in the chair. He was tired, tired

down to his bones. Ever since he'd gotten back from Chicago, he'd been sleeping even less than normal, working twice as much as normal, and getting by on caffeine, peanut butter sandwiches, and not much else.

"We still waiting?"

Quinn glanced up at the waitress stopped by his table. She had a harried look in her eyes, and judging by the crowd gathered at the door, he figured she wasn't too happy to have him taking up a table and just *sitting*.

His instinctive response was *tough shit*. But he kept the thought to himself and glanced at the menu on the wall over the cash register. "I'll go ahead and take some wings and a coke."

She nodded and headed off. Alone in the chaos again, Quinn rested his chin against his chest and let his tired thoughts drift. Voices rose and fell around him, laughter, the strident cry of an unhappy baby. He tuned it all out.

Distantly, he heard the staccato sound of heels striking the tile floor.

The skin on the back of his neck prickled as those heels came to a halt, stopping by his chair. From under his lashes, he stared at the booted feet just a foot away from his chair. The boots were black, judging by the tips that peeked out from under the long skirt. The skirt was black and close-fitting, clinging to long legs, round hips.

Blood started to roar in his ears as he forced his gaze higher.

Dark, velvety brown eyes met his. The floor seemed to drop out from under him and a hundred different sentences formed in his mind, then every last one of them got stuck in his throat as he tried to make himself speak.

Tried to make himself say something, instead of staring at Samantha McElyea like a fucking moron.

"Hello, Quinn."

He couldn't say a damn thing.

Her lashes flickered but nothing showed on her face as she gestured to one of the empty seats at the postage stamp–sized table. "Is it okay if I sit down?"

He could nod, he discovered. At least he could move. That was a good sign, right?

Sam settled in the seat across from his. She licked her lips, and Quinn found himself staring at her mouth, entranced. He wanted to do the exact same thing, trace his tongue over the path hers had taken, gather up her taste, feed on it. Then he wanted to pull her close and do it again. And again. But not just on her mouth. All over.

"I hope you don't mind me showing up like this."

He shook his head.

A brow winged up. She was wearing makeup, gold and green on her eyes that shimmered and glittered. Lipstick—dark, wine red lipstick—he wanted to see if it kissed off easy.

The blood in his veins heated, and inside the confines of his jeans, his cock started to ache. *Down, boy.*

"Cat got your tongue tonight?" she asked, leaning back in the seat. She pushed a lock of hair back from her face, tucking it behind one ear. The hair was different, too, inky black and cut to chin length. She had six silver hoops in one ear. The other ear had just one earring, a silver cross. He wanted to nibble on that earlobe, he decided.

Sam sighed and Quinn swallowed as he once more looked into her eyes. "You going to even say two words to me?" she asked quietly.

He wanted to say those two words. Wanted to say a lot more. But he couldn't quite manage it. He didn't know what he wanted to say, or how to say it, or anything.

"Fine." Sam's shoulders went stiff and she sat up poker-straight in the chair. "I'll just get this done and leave you to your lonesome.

"I'm sorry," she bit off. "Yeah, you didn't trust me, but I didn't really trust you, either. So maybe we're even."

Even? Frowning, he finally managed to get a couple of words out. "Were we keeping score?"

"He speaks . . ." Her smile was hard and cold.

Shoving back from the table, she said, "No, we weren't keeping score. I just wanted to tell you I'm sorry."

She stood. Quinn tried to get his muscles to unlock. He needed to reach out and grab her. She was getting ready to walk away—

Her lashes fell over her eyes and her shoulders rose and fell, an uneven breath escaping her. Then she looked back at him.

There was a look in her eyes—fleeting, then hidden behind that cool mask. Her wine-slicked mouth curled up in a bitter smile and she said, "You have a nice life, Quinn."

She was halfway to the door before he could make his body move.

She was on the deck, heading toward the ramp before he cleared the door.

But as she started to go down the steps, he caught up with her. "Wait."

She stopped and glared up at him, her eyes flashing.

Quinn didn't care. Using his body, he herded her back up against the railing and then put his arms on either side of her, caging her in.

"Wait for what?" she demanded. "Wait so you can sit there and just glare at me all night? I thought . . . I mean . . . hell. This *isn't* easy, you know. I don't know how to deal with this. I'm scared. I'm nervous. When I'm scared or nervous, I get . . ."

"Mean?" he offered, cocking a brow.

Her mouth twitched in a smile. "I was going to go with 'bitchy.'" Then she sighed and looked away. "Neither one of us trusted the other, we both screwed up. You said your apologies and now I've said mine. I had to at least do that."

"So that's all you came for?"

Her shoulders moved in a restless shrug. "I don't know. I really don't know . . . maybe I thought . . . I dunno." She rubbed at the back of her neck. "I just don't know. Look, I'm done. We've said what we needed to say, so I'm going to go."

"What if I haven't said what I needed to say?"

She just stared at him. Her mouth, that soft, sexy mouth, firmed into a flat, unyielding line, and unable to resist, he dipped his head and rubbed his lips against hers. She held herself still, rigid, for the longest moment and then she sighed, her body softening against his, her mouth yielding to his.

But he didn't deepen the kiss. Instead he lifted his head and stared down at her. "Seriously, Sam . . . why are you here? If you just wanted to say sorry, you could have sent a Hallmark card."

She reached up and pressed her hands against his chest. Although it felt like he was cutting off an arm, he moved back and watched as she started to pace the deck. The heels of her boots made dull little clicking sounds with every step.

"Would you believe I'm not really sure?"

A group of people came out the doors and both of them remained silent until they had the deck to themselves. "You drive three hundred miles but you don't know why?"

"I wanted to see you. Does that make more sense?" She jerked a shoulder in a restless shrug.

"Why?" When he'd walked away in Chicago, she hadn't seemed to care all that much. She didn't once tell him not to go, didn't once call his name. In the month since they'd last seen each other, she hadn't once tried to call. The first week, he hadn't slept much more than an hour or so a night, hoping the phone would ring. But it never did.

She slid him a glance from under her lashes. "You heard about Morgan."

"Yeah. That doesn't answer my question, though."

Sam made a face at him. "Give me a few minutes. Morgan's gone. Since he never filed for divorce, Sarah gets everything." Then she snorted. "Of course, there are some lawsuits in the works—Sarah will be okay, but she's probably going to have to sell his business—stocks or whatever, maybe the house. But she came home . . . and she's safe."

"Good. But that's still not an answer."

"She's safe . . . whether I'm there or not. Whether I'm a phone call away or not, she's safe. She can get back to her life." Sam shifted from one foot to the other and caught her lower lip between her teeth. "She can get back to her life . . . and so can I."

She didn't stay anything else, just stared at Quinn.

Brows dropping low over his eyes, Quinn studied her face. She was trying to tell him something—he thought. He was pretty sure. But what if he was wrong? His heart jumped and banged around inside his chest, and he found himself remembering the day they'd gone to the mall. *Pitter-pat*—that was what she'd said he was doing to her heart.

His heart was about to leap right out of him. But still, he was afraid to hope.

Coward—

He reached up and was pleasantly surprised to see that his hand wasn't shaking. At least not yet. Cupping her cheek in his palm, he rubbed his thumb over her lower lip. "So if you can get back to your life, why are you here?" he asked, his voice gruff, but steady enough. "You left your life behind in Chicago."

"Part of it," she said. She caught the tip of his thumb in her mouth and bit down gently. His cock jerked painfully inside the confines of his jeans. Then she turned her face into his hand and sighed, leaning into his touch. The ache in his dick was suddenly nothing compared to the sweet, painful clenching of his heart.

"Sam?"

Her voice husky, she said, "Yeah, I left my life in Chicago, but I think I left something more important here . . ." The words trailed off and a ragged sigh escaped her. She nudged him aside and started to pace. The narrow deck kept her from going too far. Five steps this way and then five steps back. "Quinn, I've been living a lie for so long, half of me has forgotten who I really am, and I never showed you *me*."

She pushed a hand through her short dark hair, tugging on it. The inky, silken strands fell through her fingers to settle back into place.

Quinn frowned. "I didn't fall in love with your hair."

"It's not the *hair*," she said, scowling at him. She flicked the silver rings that marched in a neat little row in her left ear. Her right ear had only one, a silver cross that was close to two inches long. "It's not about my *hair*. It's about me. You fell in love with an illusion, a fake. Hell, what are you going to do if I go and put thirty pounds back on?"

Why in the hell did that suddenly ease his shattered nerves? He didn't know. But it did. When she came close enough, he reached out and caught her arm, hauling her against him. Wrapping an arm around her waist, he slid his free hand into her hair and tugged her head back, forcing her face up to meet his.

He might be a little less nervous, but still, forcing the words from his throat wasn't easy. "You care about me, right?"

"Care about you?" she echoed. "Hello, I'm standing here, aren't I?"

A grin tugged at his lips. Lowering his head, he pressed his brow to hers and whispered, "The first day I looked into your eyes, I knew I was in trouble. I saw you—even though you tried to hide from the world, you never really hid yourself, Sam. And that's who I fell in love with."

"And if I go and put thirty pounds on? Fifty?" she demanded. But her voice was shaking. Something gleamed in her eyes.

"What if all my hair falls out?" He grinned down at her.

She reached up and pushed her fingers through his hair. Pursing her lips, she said, "Does baldness run in the family?"

"Nah."

She smiled at him, but it was strained around the edges. "That's not much of an answer for me, Quinn."

He knew she wasn't talking about his hair, though.

He didn't know what to say, didn't know how to make this any easier. There were words in his mind, but they danced around in a jumble, not a single clear thought in his head. Taking a slow breath, he said, "There's only been one woman who ever really mattered much to me—but I couldn't ever tell her that I loved her. Because I just didn't know. But I know how I feel about you, Sam. It doesn't have a damn thing to do with anything but you." He cupped her face in his hand, forced her reluctant gaze back to his. "Just you, Sam. I didn't fall in love with an illusion. I fell in love with the woman, and there's a hell of a lot more to you than the way you dress, what you do with your hair, and whether or not you're a size eight."

Her eyes glittered, a pink flush creeping up her cheeks. "I'm a size ten," she told him.

"Ten. Eight. Who gives a shit? They're just numbers." He had to kiss her. Had to. Quick and hard, and then he lifted his head and studied her face. "So what's going on here, Sam?"

"That's what I'm trying to figure out." She kissed him back, soft and light butterfly kisses that did an awful lot of damage to his self-control. Along his jaw, up to his ear. She kissed him there and then whispered, "We really don't know each other, Quinn. We know we're attracted to each other—"

Tightening the arm around her waist, he rocked his hips against hers. "Attracted—yeah. But it's a hell of a lot more than that, and you know it. You feel it, too. You can't tell me you don't."

"You're right. I can't. But is it enough?" Rising up on her toes, she rubbed her cheek against his and then eased back. "What if the things we want in life are totally different?"

Quinn toyed with her hair and said, "And what if they're not? What if we figure out a life that we want together?"

"What if I tell you I want to live in Chicago?"

He shrugged. "Doesn't matter to me. One city is pretty much like any other as far as I'm concerned."

"Okay—what if I want to move to the country?"

"Are you trying to make this difficult?" He kissed her, slanting his mouth over hers and giving in to just a little of the hunger ripping through him. "I lived on a ranch in Wyoming for seven years, out in the middle of nowhere. I still go back there every now and then—it's where my dad is. It's where home is. The country, the city, I don't care. Not if I can have you with me."

A smile curled her lips. "Really? You're serious?"

"I wouldn't say it if I wasn't serious," Quinn whispered. He wrapped both arms around her, tucking her close and tight against him. That ache in his heart—it was spreading, rolling through his body in hot, pulsing waves.

Hope—Quinn wasn't much for hoping. Hope was even worse than trust. It was too damned dangerous. But he couldn't stop it. Not this time. Not now.

"One more question." She studied him solemnly.

He waited.

"What if I say I want kids?"

The ground threatened to drop out from under him. Reflexively, he clutched her closer, staring down into her face while his heart jumped into his throat. "Ahh . . . kids?"

Sam shrugged, the movement disjointed, lacking her normal grace. "Yeah. I don't mean right now, but . . . well, I've kinda always thought I'd want kids."

Kids—the thought terrified him. Images flashed through his mind, nights when he spent hours hiding in a closet while his mother drank herself into oblivion or screwed her way into scoring some drugs. The times she'd hit him—the times when he'd wondered if he wouldn't be better off dead.

A hand touched his face. "Where did you go?"

Quinn swallowed and made himself look into her eyes.

"See what I mean?" Sam said gently. "You say you love me, but something like that . . . I don't know if I want to hook up with a guy who doesn't like kids."

Quinn caught her hand. "Doesn't have anything to do with not liking kids." Hell, he didn't know if he liked them or not. He'd gone out of his way to never spend time around kids. Even when he'd been one himself, he'd steered clear. "It's . . . shit, Sam. I've got a whole hell of a lot of bad shit inside me."

"No." She shook her head, staring at him somberly. "You don't. I'd say you've gone through some bad shit—I can tell that just by looking in your eyes. But all it did was make you into who you are."

She leaned against him, working her arms around his waist. "I really kind of like who you are."

Closing his eyes, he tried to breathe past the knot threatening to choke him. "Is this something we could kind of work up to?"

Sam laughed. "Well, I've got to be honest . . . it was kind of a test."

"A test?" He lifted his head and gaped at her.

She looked at him from under her lashes. "Yeah. I'm being difficult, I guess. I get like that when I'm worried, too. Mean. Difficult. Maybe I'm just trying to chase you off."

"You don't make a lot of sense sometimes, Sam. First you show up here, then you tell me you're trying to chase me off."

She made a face at him. "I frequently don't make sense." Then she grimaced. "Okay, I'm being a bitch. Look, I'm just . . . nervous."

Rubbing a thumb over her jaw, he asked, "So does that mean the kid thing was just a test?"

"Well, not exactly." She grinned at him. "I was kind of curious how you'd handle that. I said the words *kids* and you didn't take off running screaming in the other direction."

No—it had been close, but not for the reasons she probably thought.

"Does that mean you don't want kids?"

Sam shrugged. "No. It means that I might want them." She gave another one of those restless shrugs and added, "Maybe I'm just trying to muddy the waters. I don't know. I told you I'm nervous."

"Yeah. Maybe now you can tell me *why* you're so nervous."

She caught her lower lip between her teeth and then rested her hands on his chest, smoothing his shirt down. "Maybe because I'm getting ready to tell this guy that I love him—and if it doesn't work out, I think it just might break me."

"What?" he croaked.

Sam pressed her lips to his and smiled. "Let's go back to your place, Quinn."

* * *

It was less than ten minutes from Imo's to the apartment, but ten minutes could drag on endlessly.

Especially when he was alone on his bike, while Sam followed along behind in a snazzy little red BMW convertible. "Not mine," she'd told him. "But I can't leave it here—Alison would kill me."

By the time Sam had squeezed the little car into the garage next to Theresa's car, Quinn was a mess. A complete mess. He needed to get his hands on her. Needed her to come right out and say it, say the words he needed to hear.

Kicking a leg over his bike, he strode into the garage, meeting her as she climbed out. She looked at him, her dark eyes so warm and soft, her lips curling in a smile. "Quinn—"

Crowding her against the car, he crushed his mouth to hers. "Say it," he rasped against her lips as he came up for air. "If you really feel it, damn it, then tell me."

Sam gazed at him solemnly.

Quinn boosted her up and planted her butt on the trunk of the car, leaning down until they were nose to nose. "Sam . . ."

She reached up and traced his lips with her finger, a smile curling her lips. "I love you."

For a second, Quinn thought his legs were going to give out from underneath him. Bracing his hands on the trunk of the car, he buried his face in her neck and blew out a harsh, shaking breath.

Sam combed her fingers through his hair, cupping the back of his head and cradling him close. Quietly, she murmured, "I don't know how this happened—I kept telling myself to stay away from you. I think some part of me was afraid this would happen and that was why I needed to stay away."

"You still afraid?"

"Oh, I'm terrified." She laughed, the sound a little wild. "What about you?"

"Terrified." He laid a hand on her calf, gathering up the material of her skirt. "But I think I know something that might make me feel better."

Sam reached down and caught his wrist as she looked over his shoulder. "The garage door is open. The lights are on. Anybody could—"

He reached out blindly. Straining, he managed to reach the button to close the garage door. It came down with a creak and groan. Then he hit the light switch, plunging the garage into darkness. "Lights out, door down," he muttered. "Now lift your hips."

He shoved the black cloth to her waist and eased back, staring down at her. Moonlight filtered in through the small, high windows, just enough for him to see that the black boots she wore reached up over her knees, clinging to her legs.

"Fuck," he whispered, tracing the tips of his fingers over the top edge of one boot. Then he slanted a look up at her. "Sam . . . I love the boots."

Her laugh caught in her throat as he traced his fingers higher and higher. "So glad to hear that."

He brushed his fingers over the lace that covered her heat, hissing out a breath as he felt the moisture there. "You're already wet."

She fell back, bracing her hands on the truck. "Touch me," she demanded, spreading her thighs. "Please."

She didn't have to ask twice. He stroked her through the lace, seeking out the hard bud of her clit and teasing it until she was rocking to meet his touch. "More," she pleaded. She reached down, caught the edge of the lace, tugged it to the side, baring the slick, heated folds.

Quinn pushed two fingers inside and twisted them. "More like that?"

Sam whimpered. Bringing her legs up, she curled one around his hips and tugged him closer. "No . . . not enough. Make love to me, Quinn. Please."

She must not have trusted him to listen, though, because she sat up and went to work on his jeans. Quinn rested his hands on her thighs, staring down at her pale fingers busily freeing the button, then dragging the zipper down. He groaned at the kiss of cool air on his flesh, and then almost immediately, started to swear. "Damn it, I don't have anything with me."

Sam smiled at him and reached for her purse. She pulled out a rubber and then tossed the bag back down. It slipped off the trunk. Change, a pair of sunglasses, more condoms, and her cell phone fell out, but neither of them noticed. "I believe in the power of positive thinking."

"Good way to think," he muttered, grabbing the rubber and tearing it open. His fingers shook. Hell, *he* shook. All over. If he had ever been this nervous, this desperate to touch a woman, he couldn't remember it. He rolled the slick rubber down over his cock and then tugged Sam close. He pulled her panties off, swearing as his normally nimble fingers fumbled with the lace. "Wrap your legs around me," he ordered as he leaned into her.

When he pushed inside, they both groaned. Seeking out her mouth, he kissed her as he sank deeper and deeper inside. Through the condom, he could feel the hot silk of her pussy, gripping and squeezing him, drawing him in. "Not enough," he rasped, leaning back and grabbing the hem of her white shirt, shoving it up over her breasts. The soft, pale curves strained against ivory silk. He shoved the cups down, forcing her breasts higher. With a growl, he dipped his head and licked one nipple, then sucked it into his mouth.

Sam cried out and reached up, fisting a hand in his hair. She arched against him, her movements frantic, desperate . . . an echo of everything tangling inside of him.

She tasted so good, soft and female, vanilla and spice. He nipped her nipple, using his teeth and grinning against her flesh as she shivered and held him closer. "I love you," he muttered, straightening up and staring down into her face.

A smile, hot, sweet, and female, curled her lips. "I love you. Now stop talking . . . it's been way too long."

She kissed him and he gave himself up to it, let himself fall into her. Let himself get lost in her. With greedy, hungry hands, fevered kisses, and demanding strokes, they pushed each other higher. Hot little whimpers, dazed cries that she muffled against his lips—Quinn gritted his teeth and tried to fight it. But it was like fighting the tide—impossible.

"Too fast," he muttered as she clenched down around him.

But he was already coming. And so was she, flying apart in his arms and whimpering out his name as she shattered around him.

* * *

DEVON craned her neck as she followed Luke out onto the deck. "Hey, I thought I heard his bike."

Luke glanced at the garage but then looked back at his wife, tangling a hand in her hair. "You're too interested in my brother lately," he teased.

"Nah. I don't need a sexy brooder—I like my sexy doctor much more." She rose onto her toes and pressed her lips to the corner of his mouth.

The light in the garage went out and she watched, waiting for Quinn to emerge, but he didn't. "Hell," she muttered. "Maybe it didn't go well?"

Luke frowned. "No . . ." He squinted his eyes, searching inside for that indefinable bond he had with his brother. Over the past month, there had been a sadness, a grief that was unlike anything he'd ever felt from his brother. It was gone now—that pain.

But Devon was already crossing the deck, jogging down the steps. She'd gotten very protective of his twin lately, something that made him adore her even more. Quinn wasn't the easiest person to like, but Devon loved him, just the way he was.

"Damn it, Dev, wait," he said, jogging to catch up with her. For such a petite woman, she moved like a rocket when she wanted to.

Halfway down the walkway, his rocket stopped. As he drew even with her, she glanced at him, her lips curling into a grin. Before he could ask why, he heard something—

It was hard to tell in the dim light, but he could see the faint blush creeping up over her cheeks. "Ahhh . . . maybe we should go back in."

He slung an arm over her shoulders. "Good idea." Both of them were smiling as they headed back into the house and up the stairs to the little apartment Quinn's landlady had let them use while they were in town.

As he shut the door behind him, Devon turned to look at him. He didn't even have to say anything—she knew. Devon came to him and slipped her arms around him. Against his chest, she whispered, "He's going to be fine, Luke."

"I know that . . . I just . . . fine isn't enough. I want him happy."

"Something tells me that woman won't rest until he's just that, baby."

An ache, one that Luke had carried around for far too long, slowly began to fade. "Yeah. I think you got that one right."

* * *

HOURS later, Sam lay curled against Quinn, stroking his hand. She was tired, but she couldn't sleep. Being this happy was a high she could get used to, way too easily.

"You're thinking too loud," Quinn murmured against her shoulder.

She craned her head around and kissed his chin. "Sorry. Can't help it." Turning in his arms, she cuddled into his chest. "Did I tell you I met your brother?"

A grin tugged at his lips. "Really?"

"Yeah." She smirked at him and said, "Gee, a twin. Fancy that."

He shrugged one shoulder and brushed her hair back from her face. "Maybe one of those things we really need to know about each other, huh?"

"Maybe. Of course, if I'd known *earlier*, I might not have punched him."

He blinked, staring at her with a rather adorable, confused look on his lean face. "Punched him?"

"Yeah. He was kissing his wife. I thought it was you. So I hit him."

Seconds ticked away as he stared at her and then abruptly, he started to laugh. "You hit my brother because you thought it was me, kissing some other woman?"

She sniffed. "You don't have to sound so happy about it."

"Why the hell not?" he asked.

He didn't sound *happy*, she decided. He sounded utterly delighted. She tried to glare at him, but it fell flat. Something popped into her mind and she pushed up on her elbow, smiling down at him innocently. "You know, it's a good thing I had those rubbers with me."

He slid a hand down her hip and said, "Damn good idea."

"Yeah." She watched him from under her lashes and added, "Especially now that I think about Luke and all."

His brows dropped low over his eyes. "What in the hell does Luke have to do with me wearing a rubber?"

"Well . . . think about it. You're a twin. I'm a twin . . ."

Quinn went white. "Oh, shit."

Giggling, she pushed him onto his back and climbed astride him. "Oh, the look on your face . . ." Then she dipped her head and rubbed her lips against his. "Hey, don't look so panicked, baby. We've got time to think about that. Plenty of time."

He swallowed. "How much time?" he asked.

"The rest of our lives, if we need it," she whispered.

"Hmmmm." He slipped his arms around her and pulled her close. "That might be enough time. Maybe."